About the Author

Peter Knyte was born and grew up in North Staffordshire, England, where more by chance than design he first stumbled across the works of J.R.R. Tolkien, Arthur Ransome of Swallows & Amazons fame, David's Gemmell and Eddings through their Legend and Belgariad series, and met Jonathan Livingstone Seagull through the eponymously named title by Richard Bach.

North Staffordshire and the Staffordshire Moorlands are also where Peter developed his love of walking and the countryside.

After leaving Staffordshire, Peter moved to Middlesbrough, Birmingham, London and Leeds during which time he grew to love Neil Gaiman's Sandman comics, Asimov's Foundation series, Rider Haggards tales of She Who Must be Obeyed and King Solomon's Mines.

Peter still lives in Leeds, West Yorkshire, where he continues to enjoy walking and the countryside, as well as gardening, motorcycling, rock climbing, snowboarding and cooking.

The Ashes of Time is his sixth novel and the third and final part in his Flames of Time Trilogy.

For more information about Peter and the stories he is writing or reading please visit:

www.knytewrytng.com

Other titles by Peter Knyte
The Flames of Time
The Embers of Time

Through Glass Darkly
By a Blue and Crimson Light

The Ghosts of Winter

Forthcoming titles by Peter Knyte
A Shadow on the Sky (Glass Darkly series)
Death & the Creator – short story

THE ASHES OF TIME

PETER KNYTE

DEDICATION

For H. Rider Haggard, Alexander Dumas, Jules Verne, Bram Stoker, Nikolai Tolstoy, A.A. Milne, Jonathan Swift, Mary Shelley, John Buchan, John Wyndham and Anthony Hope for the years of entertainment and inspiration.

ACKNOWLEDGMENTS

With special thanks to John and Tasha Williamson, Lisa Bath, Philip Hall and Shirley M. Addy for the invaluable feedback and proofreading of this title, which has improved it in countless ways.

I hope I can return the favour sometime.

DISCLAIMER

This book is entirely a work of fiction, and while it plays fast and loose with the names of historic figures, places and events, no part of this book should be viewed or understood to be factual, or attempting to be factual in any way. This story is set on other worlds of imagination, which at best may bear a superficial similarity to our own, and in all probability, will be wholly different and bear no resemblance to any actual people, personalities, locations, circumstances or events whatsoever.

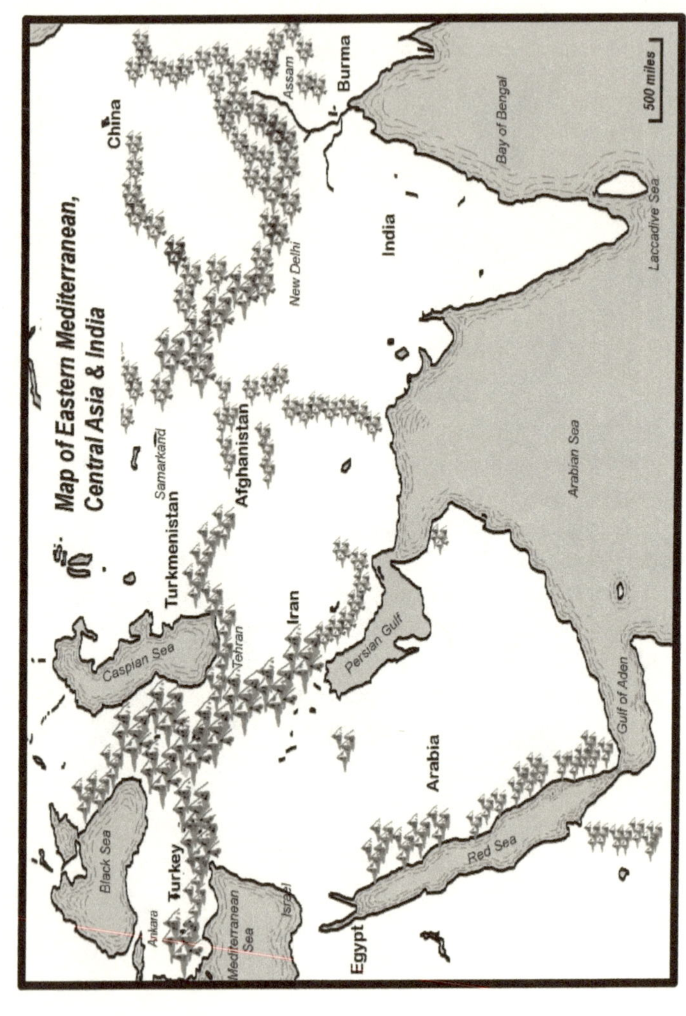

Map 1 – Turkey, Central Asia and India

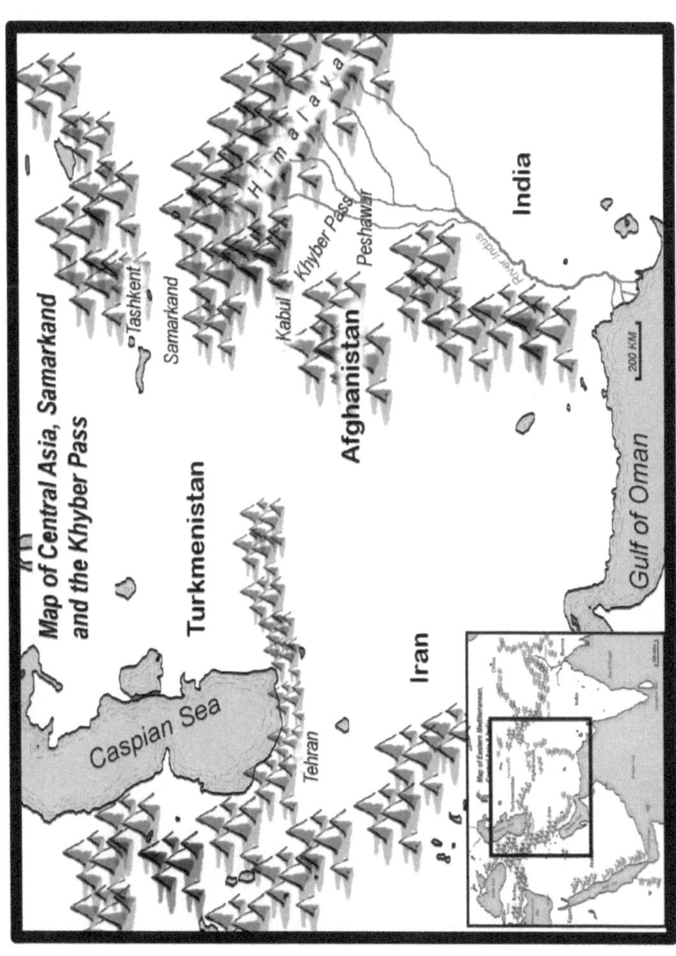

Map 2 – Map of Central Asia, Samarkand and Khyber Pass

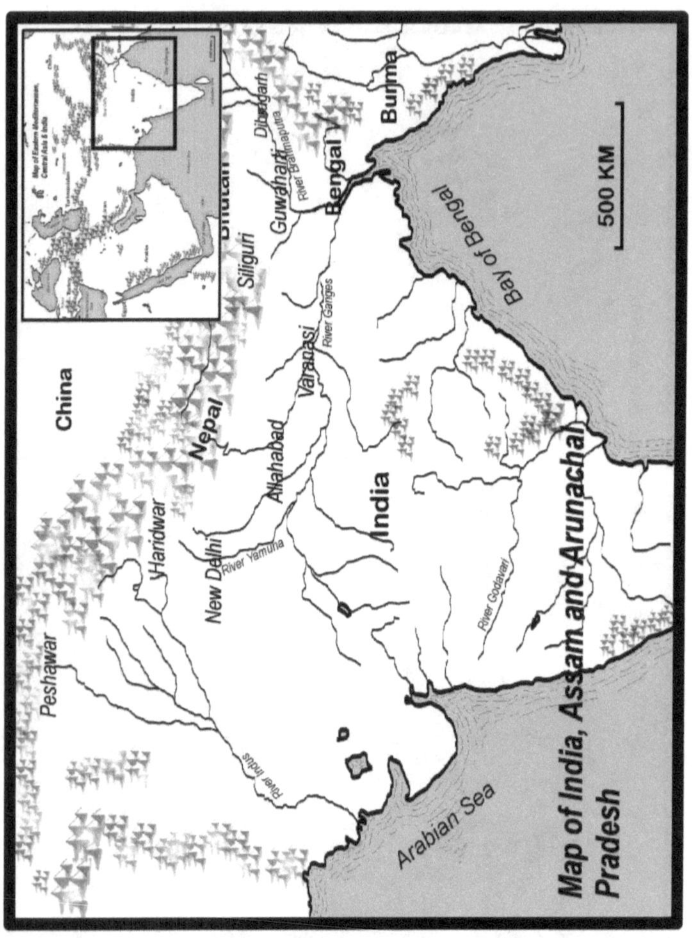

Map 3 – India, Assam & Arunachal Pradesh

LANDS OF THE DJINN

S AMARKAND IS A GHOSTLY SILHOUETTE on the horizon, partly comprised of heat haze and partly imagination. It is a pale grey-blue outline of a city below the gold and orange clouds of evening, which almost reach the tops of the fading minarets and shimmering domes.

Between the clouds and the city are the even fainter shapes of the Tien Shan, the mountains of heaven, and one of several possible routes that we must follow beyond the city before us.

We are close to the city, perhaps an hour's walk, so the great snaking caravan of people, wagons and animals which stretch out behind us will reach their final destination in the central market by mid evening.

Samarkand is finally in sight though, and in celebration some of the merchants begin to give thanks and prayers for the safe completion of yet another journey.

Moments later I hear the first high-pitched sounds of the Zurna, the traditional clarinet-like instruments played by folk musicians and snake-charmers in this part of the world, spreading the news of our arrival down the length of the caravan.

Despite the sun having set, it is still warm, and the festivities of the caravan quickens as we approach the city, growing louder and more insistent each time the road turns to reveal the city a little closer, before dying down as we weave back through the orchards and woodland which line the road and obscure our view.

Adding to the sights and sounds of the caravan, and filling the warm autumnal air with their gentle fragrance are the ripening peaches on the trees all about us.

Why are we walking this long route to this most ancient of cities? The question is so familiar to me. It seems almost the only thing I have thought about for each day of our incredible journey.

These last six months have been the hardest of my life, but with the hardships have come rewards and a strange sense of fulfilment. Each day we have walked, not ridden, twenty miles or more. Hard miles with heavy packs over often rough terrain. Days that were tiring beyond belief to begin with, but which are now just our normal routine. So much so that rest days with no walking seem unnatural, even uncomfortable.

There have been times in my life when I have wished for nothing more than to get away from the boundaries of civilisation and out into the wild, but now, having sampled a wilder form of life than I even knew existed, the idea of craving more of it brings a brief smile to my heavily tanned face.

For nearly a year we stayed in Ankara, licking our wounds at the Anubis Hotel owned by the ever present and benevolent Osman, one of Androus's many cousins.

It is another home away from home, like Nyrobi, Jerusalem and Corinth, where I felt instantly more comfortable than I ever did at my house back in Shropshire.

After reaching Ankara, we take some time to mourn the loss of Stephanos, and to digest the events of the previous weeks, but before long the need to stop looking backward arises, so we hire another couple of rooms in the hotel where we can study and research the route ahead.

The research is familiar work for us now, and it provides an excellent distraction from the grief we each feel over the loss of our friend in Nice, so before long we are making good progress again.

Our skill and understanding when working with the cryptic directions found on the tablets has also developed considerably over the last year, since our first amateurish attempts at deciphering the lapis lazuli tablets, and then transposing their directions onto our maps.

Both Marlow and Harry have become much more conversant in reading Sumerian cuneiform, but more importantly, we have all become much more experienced at matching the directions which the tablets contain, to the world as it is today.

It is this experience, a few months later, that persuades us to commit to the long and gruelling overland walk.

The problems are familiar to us. So much time has passed since the directions were written that not only the names of places have changed, but also the very landscape itself.

Eventually it is Androus who calls us all together to break the stalemate.

'As you all know,' he explains, after we have struggled with the finished translations of the tablet text for several months. 'Between them, the different sets of tablets contain several possible routes to the first great temple of Ziusudra, which is clearly located somewhere in Asia.

'Unfortunately, the lowland routes through Iraq and Iran have changed so much over time they will be almost impossible to trace.'

'More so than the routes through the mountain passes and the high country?' Peter asks, sceptically.

'Yes, I'm afraid so,' replied Androus. 'You see, the arid landscape which we are now all familiar with, after our trip to Uruk, was once a fertile and green place. But that fertility was man-made, created by harnessing the annual flood waters from the Tigris and Euphrates. In much the same way that the Nile was later managed, by constructing canals and smaller waterways to take the flood water further into the dry land of the open plains, creating a huge amount of cultivated land.'

'And, the directions we have, date from when this irrigation was at its height?' Peter asks.

'Ah, no. If that were the case, we might still stand a chance,' Androus, replies. 'The directions on the tablets date to the time before the waters of these two great rivers were first tamed by the extensive irrigation of the landscape. Irrigations which have subsequently been abandoned and allowed to fill in, changing the landscape significantly for a second time.'

'Of course,' nodded Jean, 'And while we might recognise the landscape after one such manipulation of the topography, the chances of doing so after a second such change is much lower.'

'Precisely,' continued Androus. 'What hope can we have of finding some of the places mentioned like Meluhha or Meyan, Anan or Markush when we know the geographic features surrounding them might have been changed by subsequent cultivation and then drought. Even such places as Agade, the ancestral home of the Akkadians, has still to be discovered for the same reasons, and that was lost far more recently than the features we seek.'

'But the mountains you don't think will have changed as much?' asked Marlow, simply.

'In truth, I do not know,' Androus admitted. 'Rock slides and avalanches could well have transformed large sections of the route described through the mountains, but when these routes were established, they were made in stone, and the environmental factors like sand and dust, which can completely cover and hide all trace of a lowland settlement within just a few dozen years, are much slower to take effect in the mountains, often leaving historic sites completely unobscured for centuries.

'In addition, the directions we have for the routes through the mountains are more numerous, but also a little more cryptic, and to my reading will only be intelligible to us by following the route on foot.'

'The mountains of Turkey alone would take us weeks of walking to cover,' observed Harry, with dismay.

'Yes,' conceded Androus.

'But you think it would be enough to set us on the right track,' Harry asked, more hopefully.

'Of that I am not certain,' confirmed Androus, holding up his hands at seeing Harry's alarmed expression.

'One of the biggest problems we have with the directions are the features which *aren't* described. Geographic features which for us give essential indications of distance and direction.

'In this case, as you are all aware, no mention in the directions is made of the Caspian Sea, that huge body of water to the east of Turkey.

'Now in reality this is to be expected,' he explained, placing a large map of the region on top of the other paperwork which covered a nearby table.

'You see, while it may appear unavoidable on a large-scale map, the walking routes through that area all focus on the valleys and low mountain passes, from which the Caspian Sea is not visible, due to the high mountains which surround much of its western edge and all of the sea to the south.'

'So, just how much of this route do you think we'll need to cover on foot?' Jean asked.

'In truth, my friends, I do not know.

'If the directions take us to the north of the Caspian then we will need to stop and begin our research again, as the directions will be taking us across the Russian Steppes, of which we have only very poor maps and information.

'If, on the other hand the directions take us south of the Caspian, then we will almost certainly need to find our way along the old silk and spice routes to the east, south and north, and match the directions we have to the many ancient settlements that cover that area from Herat, Farah and Kandahar to the south, to Mashad, Merv, Bukhara, Samarkand and even Tashkent to the north, and Kabul and the Khyber Pass in the east.

'Until we positively identify one of these places from the directions, the route will not be clear.'

Of the long walk through Turkey to the south of the Caspian Sea, the directions seem to indicate we should begin travelling in the spring, so we make our preparations and leave Ankara at the end of March.

Over the next three months Androus's suspicion that the path will have changed less, proves to be correct, and while the walking is quite hard at times, we quickly get a feel for the route, and just as importantly, develop a sense for when we should continue following the path, and when we should be looking for the next feature described on the tablets.

We are also fortunate to be walking through a mild and dry spring. So while the route still physically toughens us up, by the time we approach Tehran we have seen very little of the snow and ice that could still blanket the mountains at this time of year.

In contrast, the second part of our journey with the trade caravan eastward and then north, up the other side of the Caspian Sea, goes less well.

The route this way seems easy to follow as we wind our way eastward, skirting the curving mountain range which surrounds the bottom edge of the Caspian Sea on our way to Mashhad, but of sprawling Mashhad itself there is no mention in the tablets, nor any mention of the features from the surrounding territory.

After leaving Mashhad we encounter a series of sand storms. Small by the standards of this part of the world, but severe enough for us, in our western travel clothes, to be painfully uncomfortable for several days, until one of the merchants travelling with the caravan takes pity on us, and offers us some of the all engulfing Bedouin robes and turbans that almost everyone else in the caravan is wearing.

As the sand storms cease we walk out of them transformed. We had entered wearing our usual light-weight travelling attire of sturdy boots, canvas trousers and cotton shirts, beneath heavier waxed jackets and wide brimmed hats. Now these things have been exchanged for the looser fitting sarong trousers, thobe and cloak-like overcoats, which we have learned to wear in several different ways along with the turbans, depending upon the conditions, and whether protection is needed from the sun, sand or wind.

During our time in Ankara we had all become fluent in Turkish, as it not only made every aspect of life easier, from buying new research materials, clothing and food, but also because it made us less conspicuous.

As a bonus, when we leave Turkey and begin travelling along the great silk roads, we discover a variation of the Turkish we all speak is used interchangeably with the local dialects along the route.

This in its countless local variations is known simply as Turkic, and is spoken by all.

Consequently, now as we approach Samarkand in our new clothing, hardened and tanned by the incessant walking, and speaking to the merchants in the Turkic language of the spice routes, we are no longer recognisable as westerners.

The leader of the caravan, a hard, but fair Afghan known only as Paylin or Master Paylin, explains to us that upon entering the city the caravan will wind its way through the streets before taking up residence in the merchants quarter amongst the local warehouses, shops and bazaars, where there will be much feasting and celebration of our safe arrival, and which he would like us to enjoy as his guests.

It would be impolite, if not impossible for us to decline such a gracious offer, so as the lamps and fires are lit across the merchants quarter, we find ourselves following along amongst the noise and hubbub of it all, stopping eventually beside one of the big auction platforms that will used over the next few days, as the caravan merchants sell the goods they had brought with them, and then buy new merchandise to take back to Tehran.

A tea seller stops to provide us all with hot mint tea in small glass cups, courtesy of Master Paylin.

Beneath the folds of our carefully wound turbans I see my friends smiling at one another in the lamplight, as we point out acrobats and jugglers, greet fellow members of the caravan, or receive the polite salutations from the local people, everyone is content to simply enjoy life for the moment.

Selene is one of us now, more relaxed and at one with herself than I have ever seen her, and for a moment she even looks like she is going to dance with Jean, as the spiralling notes of the clarinet like Zurna once again begin to fill the night air.

After finishing our tea and returning the glasses I feel in the mood to investigate the sights and sounds of this most ancient city, and am just about to take my leave of my friends, when the hair on the back of my neck prickles, and I become aware of a faint, half-heard sound mingling with notes of the Zuma.

The sound is unmistakable. It is the sound of the distant drums from back in Africa, once again floating in on the night air. That writhing serpentine sound which so effortlessly curls around the corners of my mind, reminding me once again of the shamanic ceremony and the strange insight filled dreams which followed.

Before I can even begin to doubt what I am hearing I see recognition dawning on my friends faces, even Selene and Androus appear to hear the strange whispering rhythm.

FIRE

WE CONTINUED TO LOOK AT ONE another for a minute or two. Those of us who'd heard the sound before knowing what must surely happen next.

'Is there something odd about the music… Something behind it?' Selene asks, looking at the rest of us as we simply stood there allowing the drums to wind their way around our minds.

'There's something familiar,' she added, with a frown. 'And yet the rhythm is one I don't remember hearing before.'

'It sounds like it's coming from many miles away,' Androus declared, half lost in thought. 'Rather than here in the market.'

'This is what we've described to you before,' Harry explained, patiently. 'The same rhythm and sound of the distant drums which called us to the shamanic ritual with Nelion back in Africa three years ago.'

'The same drums that you claim to have also heard in Corinth?' Selene asked, uncertainly. 'But how can that be?'

'There is much we still do not understand about this journey we are on,' Marlow added, simply.

'But…' she began, still frowning, before thinking better of it.

'The sound is beginning to feel a little… intoxicating, n'est ce pas?' Jean asked, with a flush in his tanned features.

I was starting to feel it also, as the rhythm entwined itself with my mind. It had been so long since I'd last experienced the drums, even in my dreams, that I wasn't sure I trusted myself to withstand their influence for long.

'Perhaps we should find someplace where we won't be disturbed,' I suggested, thinking of a hotel or even one of the tents we'd used on the long journey with the caravan.

'The sound now seems to be coming from those low cliffs to the north of the city,' Peter observed. 'Perhaps we should head over in that direction.'

'Yes, that is where the old fort was located during the time of Alexander the great, when… when the city was known as… Maracanda.' Androus offered, rather confusedly.

Somehow, we wound our way through the unfamiliar city streets which were thronged with people who had turned out to celebrate the arrival of the caravan.

Following the call of the drums as they continued to fade in and out of the night air, though they became more pronounced as we moved away from the merchant's quarter where the main celebration was taking place.

Eventually we drew near to the pale cliffs which bounded the north of the city. These were quite low, perhaps only seventy feet for the most part, but they were almost vertical, with deep channels cut into the dun coloured stone by the past action of rainfall.

Still the drums sounded, pulling us onwards through an old residential area, until we found a steep, but manageable slope, cutting across the cliff face, which looked like it climbed all the way to the top.

We somehow navigated our way through the labyrinth of ramshackle houses until we found a slender footpath, badly overgrown with tall grasses and wild plants, in a narrow gap between the high walls of two old buildings.

Making our way down the path, single file to the rock face, we found crude steps cut into the cliff, creating the slope we'd seen from the road.

The stonework here was old, with the steps, such as they were, so badly worn in places that in the twilight they almost seemed natural. But the ascent was an easy one, and within minutes we found ourselves standing atop the cliffs looking down on the sparkling lights of the city below.

To our backs, the area on top of the cliffs was a gently undulating landscape of pale stone and scrubby, half stunted trees. A way over on the far side of this area we could see the glow of a camp fire, which appeared to be burning against the ruined remains of an old stone wall.

Again, the drums seemed to drift closer on the night air pulling us on toward the fire.

Unsure of what we'd find, we spread out into a long line as we approached, until we found ourselves standing against the ruined remains of what had once been a substantial wall, wondering who it was that had set the fire only to leave it now completely unattended.

As we stepped into the circle of firelight, I noticed that what I'd taken for the natural ruggedness of the ground, was actually quite regular in places, geometrically regular in fact. So much so that it reminded me of the ruins we visited on our way to Great Zimbabwe back in Southern Rhodesia.

I realised then, that the ruins atop these cliffs were far too extensive to be a simple fort, the city of Samarkand itself must have surely stood up here at some point in history, perhaps even all those years ago at the time that the directions on our lapis lazuli tablets were written.

With this idea in my mind, I quickly started to make sense of the worn and rounded features, to pick out the buildings and streets of the settlement.

The wall which the fire illuminated was located above a spacious hollow in the ground that was deep enough to keep us out of the gentle breeze which blew across the top of the cliffs, allowing the fire to burn clean and bright.

Around the fire some food and drink had been laid out along with several bedroll carpets and a scattering of cushions, but of their owner there was no sign.

Still the drums continued to sound, their incessant serpentine rhythm building as it twisted around our minds like the smoke from the fire, and then as we continued to look about us, three figures appeared from around the corner of another low wall.

They approached, each heavily swathed in flowing robes, each carrying a tall staff to walk with.

Like the three shaman, Batian, Lenana and Nelion who we had met beneath the singing stones in Kenya, these three figures seemed lean with age, though they walked with long strides and then stood with confident postures, leaning only lightly on their staffs.

They were dressed much as we were, in long flowing robes and turbans, but while similar I didn't recognise any of the individual garments that comprised the whole, as everything they wore seemed to be literally cut from the same dun coloured cloth, that was almost identical in hue and tone to the stone which surrounded us, giving the odd impression in the firelight of these figures being extensions of the cliffs on which they stood.

They all kept their eyes on the ground as they entered the circle of firelight and stopped between the fire and the ruined wall, casting impossibly tall shadows onto its surface as they did so.

Now they finally raised their eyes and looked at us. The central figure amongst them using a slender hand to untuck the cloth which covered her face, revealing she was female, closely followed by her two companions, both of whom were also women.

They were all tall, with confident postures that reminded me more than a little of Selene's former colleagues in the Icarii. But while that organisation seemed to favour young women for their agents, there was something about these three individuals which gave an impression of age.

From what little I could see of the hair which escaped from their head dresses, they were all dark haired rather than grey, nor were their complexions noticeably lined with age. Which together, would normally have given the impression of youth, but at the same time, there wasnothing soft in the complexions of these women, which made them seem older, but in a way which made it impossible to guess their age.

All three women could easily have passed for members of the local Afghan or Tajik community, though there was something about the face of their leader, the woman who had uncovered her face first, which separated her from her companions and suggested an almost Spanish or southern French ancestry.

They all wore a self-possessed confidence with ease, without seeming condescending or aloof, but the woman in the centre was so motionless in her posture she was almost like a statue.

When she addressed us, it was in the Turkic tongue of the silk and spice roads, though an oddly unaccented version of it. Her voice was clear and her speech precise.

'You have travelled far,' she began. 'Please rest and refresh yourselves before we talk.'

'You have been expecting us then?' Peter asked, simply.

The woman nodded, 'There are many that watch those that embark upon the path, both to aid those who seek, and to protect that which is sought.'

'You are aware then of those that have tried to stop us from… walking this path?' Jean asked, emulating the way this woman was talking to us, just as he had done back in Kenya.'

Again, the leader of the three women simply nodded by way of response, before she and her two companions gathered their robes about them and sat down where they had been standing.

After we had done the same, sitting down on the other side of the fire, the temptation of the prepared food and drink was simply too much, so after thanking our hosts for what they had provided, we ate and drank.

One of the very noticeable effects of walking the huge distances we had covered over the past several months, in addition to us all becoming leaner and deeply tanned, was that we had grown accustomed to eating as frequently as we were able, just to have the energy to sustain ourselves.

The sound of the drums had whispered away to almost nothing as the women arrived, but now as we each ate our fill and turned our attention back to our hosts, their soft heartbeat became noticeable once more.

The lead woman then spoke.

'I am Undaria,' she began, 'And these are my sisters in the breath, Anahita and Mitra.'

This was followed by first the woman at her left-hand nodding as she was introduced, and then the woman on her right.

'There are many dangers behind you and many yet which lie ahead,' she continued.

'There are also those who would stop you from following this path,' added in Anahita. 'Those who will bring death to the path you walk, and who would happily see you and what you seek destroyed.'

'And are you able to see whether those who bring death will succeed in stopping us?' Jean asked, still emulating their manner of speech.

'We are not,' responded Mitra. 'Even the spirits of this place may not know such things.'

'Then why have you sent the drums to summon us?' Asked Marlow, looking directly at Undaria.

His turn of phrase seemed to amuse her for a moment, and she smiled faintly as she returned his gaze.

'The drums are not sent, Mr Marlow,' She finally responded, startling us by referring to him by name. 'To some they sound continually, while to others they can only be perceived in time of need.

'Your people have not walked this path for many generations,' Anahita continued, rather sternly. 'In large measure because they choose not to hear the sound of the drums.'

'Please forgive our ignorance,' Jean interjected. 'There is much we have still to learn.'

'You must travel the path as all before you have done, in your own way.' Undaria replied. 'But remember, it winds its way through both the waking world and that of the dream. In neither realm can you follow it all the way to what you seek.'

As soon as Undaria said this, it all became so obvious.

After the first ceremony beneath the Singing Stones, Marlow had dreamed of the route we must follow and had used his memory of that dream to guide us to the buried temple near to Great Zimbabwe.

And again, when we had re-created the ceremony beneath the escarpment in Corinth, only then was it that Harry had realised where Nelion's tablets were hidden.

Yet after stealing the tablets back from the Icarii in Rome, and then experiencing the brutal murder of Stephanos we had somehow forgotten how these dreams had helped us.

The murmur of the drums began to increase again now, and as I watched the three women, I saw Mitra retrieve a wide but shallow bowl from within her robes, while Anahita produced a flask of some liquid to pour into the bowl, closely followed by Undaria sprinkling some powders she had produced from a leather pouch that had been concealed within the folds of her garments.

It was all just as Nelion, Batian and Lenana had done beneath the Singing Stones.

But I'd forgotten that neither Selene nor Androus had witnessed the first ceremony, and now as the women prepared their potion ahead of passing it to us, I saw them both looking enquiringly at the rest of us.

'It is the same ceremony as the one we experienced in Kenya,' I explained. 'This substance they prepare will cause you to dream in a way which you have never experienced before.'

'But it is safe to consume?' asked Androus, looking more curious than afraid.

'It can be very… revealing,' I offered, after a moment's hesitation. 'Sometimes a little more so than we might like.'

THE DREAMING RETURNS

THE HIGH MOUNTAINS marking the end of the earth rear up like a monumental wave to my side. So massively far above me I can barely bring myself to turn and look at them for fear that the sight alone will be enough to crush me.

To the west, the towering wave of stone dips steadily south before curving away to the north at its far end, while to the east the mighty peaks approach and then recede from the fertile plain which lies beneath them, along with the twisted and silvery forms of numerous great rivers.

Time flows over this landscape like the rivers which flow through it, and now, as I move slowly along the mountain range to the east, I see the ghostly images of forests receding to be replaced by farmland. All the while the rivers continue to flow, slowly cutting their way through the fertile plains.

The great wave of stone seems to spasm for a second, and then the great rivers writhe in protest below, suddenly changing their courses, some growing, others shrinking to nothing.

Finally, I notice the cities and settlements which hug the banks of these life-bringing water sources, and they too dance along the suddenly skittish riverbanks. Some swell to stay near the receding waters, while others are brutally bisected by the passive waters suddenly squirming and intolerant. Some settlements fade back into the landscape at these changes, closely followed by new villages and towns forming a short distance away.

For an age I seem to watch the ever-changing scene, looking first eastward then back to the west. Eventually I realise the silent form of my father is with me, watching, waiting. We travel without words this time, content to walk beside these shining rivers as they snake their way through endless plains. Only the mountains to the north remain largely unchanged, though the sky flickers from dark to light above them and the snow creeps steadily down their sides and then back up again as the days and seasons pass, the dark rock below never seems to alter.

When I wake the following morning, still atop those low cliffs above Samarkand, the image of the route we must follow remains like a ghost within my mind.

The fire still smoulders, but all three of the female shamen are gone.

There is a small pile of gathered wood near to the fire, and as the first person awake I unravel myself from the layers of fabric wrapped around me, and then crouching, coax the embers back into flame, to warm my companions, before leaving them to look around the clifftops and out over the sleeping city beyond.

I feel as though I have slept deeply and well, much like the quiet city I see below me from the cliff tops.

The music and festivities no doubt continued long into the night, but are over now, and not a soul seems to wander the streets below. Though the morning air does bring the tantalising aroma of fresh bread with it on the breeze, and after scanning the neighbourhood below I spot the tell-tale sign of a bakery, its already smoking chimney unique amongst its neighbours.

I return half an hour later with fresh flat-breads and dates, courtesy of the bakery and their one other customer at that time of the morning.

Jean is awake and sat near the fire tending a small pot of coffee, which he seems to have found somewhere among the provisions left by the women.

As I approach he motions me over to one side of the group, away from the fire to where we can talk without disturbing the sleepers.

'Good morning, George,' he murmurs as he sits down beside me on an anonymous mound of low earth, before handing me a small cup of the strong coffee he has just made.

Together we enjoy our makeshift breakfast as the hazy light of dawn slowly gives way to the warmer glow of morning.

'And how did you dream, my friend?' he eventually asks.

'Long and well,' I reply, before going on to explain the strange visions I received of the route ahead and how it had changed over time.

'I'm sure I saw the passage of many hundreds, perhaps thousands of years,' I said, reflecting upon the evening's dreams. 'I can't remember exactly what I asked my father to show me, but he certainly didn't skimp on the detail!'

'And you, Jean, do you mind me asking what you dreamed of?' I asked, after realising how self-absorbed I had been.

He hesitated for a moment before replying, but then with a slightly sad smile he continued.

'Ah yes,' he began, turning his gaze to the horizon. 'I dreamed of my young son again, still in his uniform, just as he had been when he died in the great war.'

Kicking myself for the clumsy way I'd intruded upon what was obviously a private experience, I tried to stop him and explain that he didn't need to go on.

'No, it is good to talk of these things,' he replied.

'I don't think I ever told you, but he was called George also, like yourself, and was only a little older than you are now. As I have before, I tried to find out a little more about the nature of his existence now, but as is right, he bade me wait until my own time before knowing such things.

'We walked from the fire here, down into the city below to enjoy the revelries of the caravan and city folk, and then he showed me the fire with those glistening spirit forms gathered around, just as I think you described seeing them, during your vision at the Singing Stones.'

I confirmed he was correct, and asked if he saw Marlow or any of the others there.

'Ms Autieri was there with an older woman who I did not recognise, both watching as Robert once again stepped forward into that blazing fire at the centre of the circle.

'Like him she didn't seem to feel the heat quite as keenly as those spirits which surrounded the fire, and as they stepped back, I saw her raise a hand against the light before stepping forward as though to get a better view.'

'The heat was a little too much, so George, my son, took us away, far to the east along the Himalaya where another shaman or priest appeared to be waiting for us on a small island in a river.'

I'd had no idea that Jean had once had a son, or that he'd ever had a family of any kind, and as he told me the tale of how he'd once again been guided through one of these strange dreams, I couldn't help but wonder if he'd seen his son during that very first dream back in Kenya as well.

Obviously, I knew only too well what it was like to be greeted in these dreams by a deceased loved one, but I was also well aware that my relationship with my father had been a distant one, and if anything, it had been improved significantly by the dream journeys we'd subsequently engaged in together.

How it must have felt to be greeted by one of your own children in such a dream, I couldn't begin to imagine, let alone by a child killed in war.

There was a part of me that wanted to ask about the rest of the family, but I felt like I'd already trespassed too far into what must be some very personal memories.

As Jean finished describing the rest of his dream, he continued to look away into the distance, his gaze anchored on the horizon.

'I would dearly like to tell his mother that I have dreamt of our son,' he explained, unprovoked. 'To perhaps suggest a walk through the woods that surround her house in the Fontainebleu forest, and while surrounded by the green, explain to her about the Singing Stones and the strange dreams we have all had, and how in mine our brave son George had once again appeared to me.

'It was her house we stayed at in Fontainebleu?' I asked, unable to believe the obvious.

'Oui, it had once been our family retreat away from Paris, but after George's death, neither of us had the will to use the place, and when we finally separated, my wife, Marion, requested the house, which I was happy to concede.'

'She is still kind enough to allow me its use from time to time,' he continued. 'And it was good to be there with the rest of you, and create some new memories in the place, albeit brief ones.'

We talked for some time after our cups of coffee had long been finished, and just as we started to discern movement from the others around the fire, a strange thought occurred to me, which I carelessly voiced before really thinking it through.

'I find it curious how these shamen keep talking about "our" people, from the developed countries of the west, and how we have become separated from the dreaming world which seems so integral to their existence.' I began, as we stood up and started to make our way back to the fire. 'I wonder if they think we will help "our" people to remember how to enter the dreaming again, once we've finally found what we're looking for at the first great temple of course?'

It was such a casual thought, but it brought Jean up short, and for a second he simply stood and stared at me with an unreadable expression.

'The idea of actually sharing one of these dreams

with Marion, of leading her to a place where she could see and talk with our son again…' he said, almost breathless. 'That is something I think she would like a great deal, my friend, something I too would like a great deal.'

'George, once again you surprise me with your thoughts,' he continued, walking forward again. 'I had heard the words of these shamen about our western world being out of touch with this strange dreaming side of our natures, but despite the strange relevance of those dreams I had never once considered that this quest of ours might also allow us to introduce others to the experience, to share this dreaming with the wider population.

'I cannot begin to imagine the impact it would have on the world as we know it. The sorrows it could help to alleviate, the fears it could calm.'

Fortunately, Jean had been so preoccupied with the idea which my comments had triggered, he didn't notice my own shock at what he was saying.

It was certainly something I would need to talk about with him again, but as we approached the group I could see that Marlow was now up and tending to the fire, closely followed by Harry, Selene, Androus and Peter, who were at various stages of gathering their wits.

As Marlow made some coffee for everyone, it was clear that we had all dreamed long and deep, but it was Androus and Selene that I was paying particular attention to, as I knew neither of them had encountered these strange dreams before.

Selene had wrapped the veil of her turban back around her face so that barely a sliver was left open for her eyes, while Androus was sitting very still and looked a little bit pale.

Now was clearly not the time to ask either of them about their experiences, and fortunately when Jean and I reappeared, Marlow took the opportunity to raise the altogether more practical topic of where we should head next.

'I appreciate the experience we all shared last night may take some time to properly digest,' he began, addressing his comments toward Androus and Selene. 'But these experiences have previously given us insights into where we should be heading next, insights that can't always be clearly explained.

'It seemed to me as though our route forward lay to the south of the Himalaya, but my own dreams roved over many topics, lacking the detail I would like.'

'The route I saw was to the south also,' Harry added, very matter-of-factly. 'Though I saw ancient sites and peoples in this area, of which the field of archaeology as yet knows nothing. From here it seemed the route moved first to an ancient settlement near to modern day Kabul, then on to Peshawar, Lahore and Delhi.'

I nodded my agreement.

'I saw the route going via a city near to modern day Delhi,' I explained. 'On the banks of the Yamuna river, though at the time it seemed to flow further to the north than it does today.

'But I didn't see much of the route to Delhi,' I added, feeling as though I were probably not helping so much now. 'Though it did seem closer to the start of the journey than the end, which to me seemed still a very great distance off to the east.'

Marlow and Jean both nodded their agreement at this, without having anything more to add.

I'm not sure why, but we all seemed to turn toward Androus, perhaps because we'd depended on him so much while translating the directions contained on the lapis lazuli tablets.

It took him a moment to realise we were looking at him expectantly, before he pulled his thoughts together.

'I still feel a little confused about the dreams I had last night,' he began rather hesitantly, unlike his usual professorial manner. 'But it was clear to me that our path does indeed lie to the south of the mountains, and right the way across India, perhaps even beyond Assam into that wild and little explored region that falls between the boundaries of Bhutan, China and Burma.'

'Will we need to continue making our way there on foot?' Peter asked, neutrally. Though I was sure he, like the rest of us, did not relish the idea of walking the distances it would take to cross India.

'No, I… um… No,' Androus began, struggling to find his usual focus. 'Now that we know roughly which direction the route takes, we should be able to match the directions on the tablets to the key locations along the way.'

Nobody said anything about Androus's confusion, but while we packed up our few things and prepared to move on, Harry indicated he'd have a word with him to find out if he was alright, and that it might be worthwhile someone else doing the same for Selene, which Marlow offered to do.

THROUGH THE NIGHT

CENTRAL ASIA WAS EVIDENTLY one of those places where the old empires of Britain and Russia had come into direct contact with one another, and consequently direct competition, through the medium of their state run infrastructures, and in particular the railways.

Samarkand was a case in point, the central railway station was not only colossal, it had an opulence and style that wouldn't have been out of place in Moscow itself.

We'd returned to the caravan, while it was still quite early, with the aim of retrieving our baggage and making our final farewells to the merchants that we had been travelling with, and with whom we'd developed a great camaraderie.

While we picked up our luggage and other

belongings, which it had been so expensive for us to transport, many of the individuals we had hoped to say farewell to were still nowhere to be seen, as they slept off the previous night's festivities.

We didn't want to leave Samarkand without saying goodbye and giving thanks to everyone who had helped us, so we decided to stay for another day, but to use the time well, by preparing for the next leg of our journey overland to New Delhi, nearly two thousand miles, much of which we hoped to complete via train.

We needed a base of operations, so decided to check into the hotel next to the main railway station in Samarkand, the Konstantin, a huge marble and sandstone edifice built in the imperial baroque style, matched only by the adjoining railway station which had been built at the same time and in the same style.

The doorman clearly had his doubts as we approached, bristling quite noticeably until Harry greeted him with a hearty 'Good Morning', while waving him toward the cart carrying our belongings, as Jean settled up with the driver.

I couldn't help but smile at the idea of us, as Europeans turning up to a grand old Russian hotel in full Bedouin garb, complete with dust and grit. Surely if there was still anyone involved in the 'great game' of international espionage, as it used to be known, then messages would even now be flying in all directions.

We checked in using the fake identities that Selene had helped us to create while we were in Ankara, and then I was presented with a hotel room of my own, with an enormous bed, and luxury of luxuries, an adjoining bathroom, complete with full-sized enamel bath.

The prospect of a proper bath was just too much for me, and as though in a trance I saw my own hand stretch out to turn on the abundant hot water, and then add a handful of the complimentary bath salts.

Steam swirled around me in moments, filling the

bathroom with warmth and the mineral fragrance of the salts, before I'd even divested myself of the Bedouin robes and stepped into a soft white hotel dressing gown.

An hour and a half later I emerged from the bathroom as someone once again recognisable as the person who had set off from Ankara. Not only had I the benefit of a good soak, wash and shave, but my Bedouin robes had also been carefully folded and rolled into a single portable package that I would take with me in my luggage, while I dressed myself in the loose flannel shirt and soft calico jacket and trousers that I normally wore when walking or travelling.

I was still thinner and more muscular than when I'd set off all those months ago. How much so I hadn't realised until I'd seen myself without a shirt in the bathroom mirror while having a shave. But I felt healthy for it, and a few weeks of travelling by train across India would no doubt do a great deal to soften me up again.

With my transformation complete I went down to the hotel bar to meet up with the others and perhaps catch up on the newspapers.

Jean and Selene were the only ones already there, so I joined them around a long table in one corner of the room.

'You look a little more like your old self, mon ami,' Jean said by way of a greeting. 'Ms Autieri and I have just returned from the railway station next door with the departure times for the trains heading eastward.'

They had both also freshened up and put on their western clothing, though Selene now also wore a light headscarf over her long hair, in consideration for the local customs, which included most women covering their heads in one way or another.

'Yes, I feel better for a good long soak in a decent bath, I must say,' I replied, taking a seat at the low table beside them.

'In fact, I think I could get quite accustomed to the

comfort, if we don't need to move on for a day or two?' I asked, speculatively.

'It doesn't look promising I'm afraid,' Selene replied, with an indulgent smile. 'It's the route through the Khyber Pass that's likely to cause us the greatest problems.

'From the timetables,' she continued, producing a small notebook from her coat which she consulted. 'It looks like the British-Indian trains arrive in good time to join up with the Russian trains heading west or north into Uzbekistan, Afghanistan or Tajikistan. But the trains coming from those places, as we will be doing, arrive in Torkham just a fraction too late for passengers to catch the British-Indian train through the Khyber Pass.

'Our best hope is the overnight train which leaves tonight at ten o'clock and arrives at the border crossing in Torkham just one hour before departing for Jamrud.'

'That doesn't seem like much time to move from one train with all our bags and then board another train after buying our passage.' I commented.

'And passing through the border controls,' Jean added.

'The trains run every other day during the week,' Selene continued, 'So if we miss our connection, we'll be stranded for nearly two days beneath the gaze of the bored border officials. Which of course could lead to problems if they were to start telegramming for information about a curious group of individuals who appear to be coming from the Russian controlled territories into India.'

'You don't think our new identities would stand up to such scrutiny?' I asked, knowing the answer.

'The papers we all carry are completely authentic, Mr Whitaker.' She patiently explained. 'So, I would anticipate no problems on that front. The difficulty would come if anyone attempts to cross check any of our names and addresses with the local officials where we claim to be resident, or with the banks we hold accounts with, the lack of corresponding tax records and so on.'

'Ah yes, of course,' I replied. 'And if they were to see through that thin outer veneer of identity, and find it lacking, then they would of course detain us while they looked deeper.'

It was doubly irritating that these problems would be caused by the British authorities that controlled the Khyber Pass, who would have absolutely no problem at all in verifying at least mine and Peter's real credentials, if we were only in a position where we could risk travelling under our real names.

During the course of the day we booked our passage from Samarkand to Kabul, and then from Kabul to Torkham the garrison town at the northern end of the Khyber Pass.

We also walked back over to the caravan to make our farewells to the people with whom we'd shared our lives for the previous three months, and then before we knew it, we were following our things as they were bundled out of the Konstantin Hotel and around the corner into the train station proper by the hotel's porters, onto the sleeper carriages that would carry us through the night.

I was sharing one of the double cabins with Jean, while Peter bunked up with Marlow, Harry with Androus, and Selene had a single birth cabin to herself.

Each cabin was comfortably appointed with soft seating that had already been transformed into our beds, then laid with pristine linen sheets, subtly monogramed with the letters of the pre-soviet era Trans Caspian Railway.

The rooms also contained a couple of slender wardrobes complete with elegantly inlaid mahogany drawers, for those guests travelling a little further than we were, and of course there was a discreet push button bell on either side of the cabin within reach of each bunk by which a steward could be summoned.

We'd boarded the train about half past eight in the evening in order to get settled in and comfortable before setting off, but of course as a consequence of the train steward's care and consideration we were not only settled, but had retired to the elegantly lit bar by the time the train finally pulled away from Samarkand station at ten o'clock, and out into the deepening autumn twilight beyond.

We weren't due to arrive in Kabul, nearly nine hundred miles distant from Samarkand, until just after eleven o'clock in the morning, when the train would stop to refuel and allow passengers to board or alight before steaming on to Torkham a further hundred and fifty miles and just over two and half hours travel from there. According to the timetable this would see us arrive at thirty-five minutes past three o'clock, local time.

Meanwhile the Khyber Pass Express, operated by the British Raj would pull into a completely different railway station just over half a mile away on the other side of Torkham at approximately half past two, and was due to depart at four thirty.

This gave us approximately fifty-five minutes to disembark from our Trans-Caspian train, make our way through a busy station to the exit, find a couple of cabs to get us across Torkham to the British-run train station, pay for our tickets, pass through the border checks and board the train with our luggage.

Naturally, it wasn't unknown for long distance trains in this part of the world to run a little late. Operating over such vast distances and through such wild terrain meant there were many things that could delay a train.

'Of course, it is equally likely for a train such as this one to arrive early,' Jean explained, over his brandy, with a knowing glint in his eye.

'How on earth are you going to persuade the train driver to bring us in early?' Harry asked, in unnecessarily hushed tones.

There were a dozen or so other passengers in the bar where we were talking, a young couple who looked as though they might be on their honeymoon, a solitary business-man enjoying his evening paper, a small group of

Russian military men, and two young nurses, who appeared to be travelling in the company of their matron.

But even with our own group and the waiting staff, the carriage was still barely a third full, so everyone had naturally spaced themselves out, with the exception of the soldiers who had installed themselves a little nearer to the nurses than was strictly necessary.

'My dear Harrison, we're going to give the drivers of this train the opportunity to demonstrate the excellence of their superior Russian engineering,' Jean replied, with an outrageously innocent look upon his face.

THREADING THE NEEDLE

I HAD LONG AGO come to the conclusion that Selene was one of the most capable people I had ever met.

Perhaps it was her training as an Icarii agent from a young age, or just her natural intellect and insight which resulted in her never seeming to get flustered or concerned, even when faced with the bizarre and dangerous situations which we had of late found ourselves in.

The flip-side of her demeanour though, was that she often appeared thoughtful and reserved when she allowed herself to relax, neither happy nor unhappy, but perpetually observant.

Even after a year of working together in Ankara and six months of travelling to Samarkand, she still seemed guarded and cautious with us, often preferring to refer to us formally rather than by our forenames.

There was however, one small gap in her armour, through which the real Selene Autieri occasionally became visible, and I noticed that real Selene again now, as Jean outlined his idea for speeding up the train in order to ensure it arrived on time, or better yet early.

I recognised the exasperation in the gentle smile which now genuinely illuminated her face, as once again she encountered our unconventional, yet often very effective way of doing things.

I think she was aware of her 'tell' as the card players amongst us would call it, so she attempted to hide her amusement by looking away from Jean, shaking her head almost imperceptibly as she did so.

We'd travelled through the night in our sleeper compartments before meeting again in the dining carriage for breakfast, a few hours before we were due to arrive in Kabul.

'And you really believe you can goad the honest staff of this excellent steam train into a race against the clock?' Peter was asking, quietly but incredulously of Jean.

'Ah no, mon ami, for this ruse to be successful we must rely upon a certain level of national pride. Suggesting to the staff of this locomotive that while it is a wonderous work of engineering, it is perhaps a little slower and less efficient than the counterparts of our own countries, especially those of the United States and the British Empire, perhaps even the Union Express trains of South Africa as well, as the papers belonging to George indicate he is a native of that country.'

'Of course,' Peter retorted. 'But as you are currently identified as a certain M'sieur Perrault of Brussels in Belgium, you must be excused this bragging because the trains of your own country are…'

'Slower but incredibly punctual!' Jean emphasised.

Something in Peter's expression must have registered with Jean as still not understanding the reason for this peculiar emphasis.

'I must confess I did not anticipate any of you having such difficulty in understanding the nature of this deception,' he confessed, before going on to outline the plan once more, this time in the simplest language he could muster.

'Over the next few hours our plan is a simple one,' he began. 'We will attract the attention of a train steward or the conductor while we are still on the approach to Kabul, pretending to be simply interested in the performance of our locomotive.

'This is merely to bait the hook so to speak,' he continued, patiently. 'There is no point in encouraging the train staff to speed up the train before we reach Kabul, as any time gained will be lost anyway when the train stops to refuel and exchange passengers.

'No, our aim is for the train staff to take our bait while the train sits "in" Kabul,'

'And by telling them that the trains in Belgium are slow but punctual will be our bait?' Harry asked, looking confused.

'No, Harrison, that is very much not correct, please concentrate,' Jean replied, looking at the rest of us for help.

'I believe the comment about the trains in Belgium is reverse psychology,' Selene added, still smiling gently as she attempted to assist.

'If for example, you, Harry, were to make a casual comment to the conductor of the train about how slow the train seemed to be travelling, in contrast to the trains of your own United States, then it would be natural for the conductor to feel the sting of your comments only lightly, because it is natural for you as an American to think your trains are quicker and better, because they are the trains of your own homeland.

'But, if your comment is then followed by an observation from Jean, as a resident of Belgium, not claiming that the trains of his country are also faster than this train of the Trans Caspian Railway, but quite the opposite, claiming that it is the same as the slow but punctual trains of Belgium, then now the conductor will feel the sting of Harry's earlier words all over again, and feel them all the more strongly because a second guest of the train with no obvious bias has observed the same. As such these comments cannot be dismissed as bragging, because they are offered in a tone of commiseration or defence of slower trains!'

'Yes, precisely, Ms Autieri,' Jean practically gushed. 'Thank you.'

'Oh, oh I see now,' Harry conceded, with a barely perceptible glint of amusement in his eye, indicating he had perhaps been stringing Jean along. 'Why didn't you just say that, Jean?'

'Harrison!' Jean began, on the verge of being offended, until he spotted the half-hidden smiles from around the group. 'You really are quite impossible sometimes!'

Over the next couple of hours, we identified which member of the train's staff would be our target, double checked a few figures against our maps and train timetables, and made our move.

With the breakfast service out of the way, and the dining car needing to be cleaned and prepared for lunch, we made our way back to the lounge, where Harry made the first move.

We were sat where we had been before, toward the rear of the bar area with coffees and teas, with still a couple of hours steady travel to go before we were due to arrive in Kabul.

Harry was poring over his train timetable as the conductor himself entered the cabin doing his usual rounds, and seeing Harry bent over a timetable, approached to see if he could be of help.

He was a tall and noble looking fellow, probably in his mid-thirties, and wearing an immaculate uniform of the trainline in a deep blue wool. liberally decorated with perfectly polished brass buttons and gold braid, over a formal starched shirt and perfectly tied black bowtie.

'Is there something I may be of assistance with, sir?' he asks Harry.

'Well, actually yes there is,' Harry replies, all sweetness and light. 'We're travelling through into north-west India, via the Khyber Pass railway, and I was wondering if there's any chance of this train arriving into Torkham early, as there's only fifty-five minutes for us to make the transfer?'

'We may arrive five or perhaps ten minutes early, if we have a clear run, but it is unlikely we will arrive any earlier than this,' the conductor explains reasonably.

'Ah yes, I suspected as much,' Harry concedes, magnanimously. 'I'm far too accustomed to the fast trains of my own country. I keep forgetting that not everywhere else is so fortunate.'

'But M'sieur the distance involved is not a short one...' our well-dressed target begins to protest.

'Yes, of course,' Harry cuts in, good naturedly. 'What is it? A hundred and fifty miles or so in two and a half hours?'

'Precisely, M'sieur,' the unsuspecting conductor confirms with a smile, clearly still not realising his peril. 'We will average a speed of sixty miles per hour for the duration of the journey.'

'And is that considered a good speed for your Soviet trains?' Harry asks, still the picture of innocence, before ploughing on to deliver his coup-de-grâce.

'You know in America, I was on a train from Chicago to Milwaukee a few years ago, and the train reached a speed of one hundred and four miles per hour as we travelled along the shore of Lake Michigan, a ninety-mile journey in one hour and four minutes.'

'Ah! You Americans and English, you are obsessed with the speed at which your locomotives and automobiles can travel,' Jean interrupted from the table I was sat at with him, on the other side of the central walkway, just as the conductor's posture stiffened in response to Harry's comment.

'What is wrong with taking a little extra time to

reach your destination, just as the locomotives in my own country do?'

'It is not that the train cannot travel any faster, Messieurs,' the conductor replied, addressing them both, and in the process rising to the challenge, 'We travel at an average of sixty miles per hour because it is considered the most comfortable for our passengers.'

'Oh, that's just what you were saying, Archie,' Selene breaks in, using a convincing Manhattan accent, and addressing Harry by the fake name he was travelling under. 'You said these Russian trains couldn't go any faster without shaking themselves to pieces.'

'Madame, I assure you this train is capable of much greater speeds without any pieces being shaken off it,' the conductor adds, clearly feeling he has to defend the reputation of the trainline and the very train on which we are riding.

'Well, that's easy to say, Sir,' replies Harry, but I don't see how you can be so confident unless your train has previously travelled this route and arrived much earlier than it was scheduled.

For a moment, it seems as though we have reached an impasse in our heated little discussion, but of course Jean had prepared us for this very eventuality.

'Gentlemen, let us not get carried away,' he begins, as though to calm the situation. 'Unless you are about to suggest a wager, there is no practical way for us to settle this matter, and we must just resign ourselves to spending a day or two in Torkham.'

'A wager you say,' replies Harry, as though the idea hasn't occurred to him before. 'Well, I would certainly be prepared to put my money where my mouth is.'

'Messieurs, Madame, please, I am but a humble employee of the people's railway…' the conductor protests, thinking Harry was suggesting a personal bet with him.

'Well, I for one, think this excellent train is more than capable of reaching say eighty miles per hour,' added

Marlow, from beside me, before suggesting a wager that couldn't have been far off the conductors annual salary

'I'll take that wager,' Harry agrees, if the train company will accept the challenge.

'Messieurs, really I cannot…' protests the honest conductor, before Marlow, as planned, ups the stakes.

'No, of course not, it's unfair of us to even ask, just because we'd like to catch the next train in Torkham.

'But… what if we were to make the wager worthwhile for you and your crew also,' he continues, as though thinking through the problem.

'Suppose… suppose, if I win the wager and the train can reach an average speed of eighty miles per hour between Kabul and Torkham, then I will donate half my winnings to you and the crew of your train, to do with as you will.'

'M'sieur, that is a very kind offer,' the conductor responds, after hesitating for a moment to think over the proposal. 'But I…'

'Yes, I like it,' Harry interrupts. 'And if I win, then I'll donate half my winnings to the crew of the Khyber Pass train that we will be travelling on next, from Torkham!'

Well, that did the trick, with a ramrod straight back and just the hint of a smile on his face, the conductor informs us he will first need to consult with the engine driver, but promises he shall return to us before we reach Kabul with an answer.

RACING INTO SUMMER

THE AUTUMNAL TWILIGHT of Samarkand seems an impossible distance behind us as we approach Kabul.

In the previous three months we have travelled just

over one thousand miles on foot, walking through the entirety of June, July and August to arrive in early September. And yet, in the past twelve hours we have covered a comparable distance on the Star of the Orient, as it steams the last few miles into Kabul.

Of the conductor we have seen nothing more, but as we round the spur of a mountain and see a large city in the distance, he steps back into the saloon carriage where we have once again been sat enjoying the views of the rugged landscape.

'Gentlemen, Lady,' he begins, with an air of confidence that I can't help but interpret positively. 'I have now consulted with the driver of this train and his senior engineer, and I am pleased to inform you that on behalf of the Trans Caspian Railway, we accept your wager.

'The precise distance from the railway station in Kabul to its counterpart in Torkham is one hundred and forty-four miles, which the Star of the Orient will attempt to cover in one hour and forty-eight minutes or less, in order to achieve an average speed of eighty miles per hour or more.

'This will reduce the normal arrival time by forty-seven minutes, which is considerably faster than this stretch of the route has ever been traversed before.

'Would this be acceptable proof for you of the excellence of our Soviet trains?'

To his credit, Harry had played his part perfectly, and now after standing up he responded graciously.

'Sir, if your train can manage to maintain so high a speed over so long a distance, I assure you I will have great pleasure in informing everyone I meet of the excellence of the Trans Caspian Railway, and in particular the jewel in its crown, the Star of the Orient.'

With that he offered his hand to the conductor and the wager was accepted.

The idea of the wager might have had it's genesis in the

Machiavellian mind of Jean, as a way to increase our chances of catching the next train through the Khyber Pass without first having to spend a couple of days stuck in the garrison town of Torkham, but seeing Harry and the conductor shake hands sent an unexpected shiver through my body.

We were going to be involved in a real-life race against the clock through the mountains and foothills of Afghanistan, on a powerful steam train of the Trans Caspian Railway. And not only that, but we were going to have front row seats to the entire venture through the panoramic windows of the saloon car.

I looked around the table at my friends and saw that they felt it too. This was one of those moments you only normally get to read about in the newspapers, when by chance or whim the stars align to create a moment in history.

Word of the speed attempt had evidently travelled ahead of us by the time we pulled into Kabul station, and the platform as we pulled-in was already full of well-wishers, press and railway men, including a small orchestra which the authorities had somehow managed to gather together at short notice.

None of us could resist the temptation to go down onto the platform to witness the spectacle.

Several times the press men and women tried to interview one or another of us to find out how we felt about taking part in the speed trial, but with nothing particularly notable to add we were soon left alone.

In the meantime, the powerful looking steam engine was quickly detached from the carriages, along with its tender, to be refuelled, greased, polished and topped up with water ahead of the trip ahead.

The stop-over in Kabul was almost two whole hours, but it passed in what felt like the blink of an eye, and before we knew it, the now shining locomotive engine was being slowly reversed along the platform and re-connected with the main body of the train, including the sleeper carriages and saloon car.

Finally, as the minute hand ticked down toward our departure time, a small number of officials, presumably from the railway company, gathered on an impromptu stage which had been set up on the platform alongside the engine.

From our vantage point in the crowd, I could see the conductor was with them along with the young soldiers who had earlier been trying so hard to impress the nurses travelling in the saloon car.

After an introduction the conductor was finally allowed to step forward and speak.

'Ladies and gentlemen,' he began. 'As the conductor of this train, the Star of the Orient, I thank you for your support and encouragement in this venture.

'It is, as I am sure you will all appreciate, not possible for such a challenge to be even attempted without the contribution of many citizens of the United Soviet Socialist Republics, from the engineers and craftsmen who constructed the Star of the Orient and laid the tracks upon which it runs, to the signallers, stewards, furnace men and the driver who controls the train, all must work together, pulling their weight for this attempt to be successful.

'And today I am pleased to say that the attempt to reach the station at Torkham in just one hour and forty-eight minutes will also receive the support of the brave men of the 17th Mountain Cavalry Division, who have kindly offered to support Chief Tabakov and his men in driving the train, by shovelling our good Ukrainian coal into the engine.'

'You know, George,' Jean commented quietly from just beside me, as he lit his pipe. 'I think this idea of Harrison's is getting a little out of control.'

It was all I could do not to laugh out loud at this feeble attempt to transfer the blame to Harry for the song and dance we now found ourselves involved in.

But realising this was just Jean's way of having a

joke at his own expense, I decided instead to simply join in the fun.

'Oh, I don't know, Jean,' I offered, equally dead pan. 'What could possibly go wrong?'

A small cloud of smoke and ash puffed from his pipe, followed by some furious re-tamping of the bowl, as we both wandered back to the saloon car, chuckling to ourselves as we did.

Once the great pomp and ceremony of the speeches were completed and all those coming aboard had done so, and those staying on the platform had stayed where they were, the band struck up the tune of the Soviet national anthem, and then suddenly the crowd were counting down the last ten seconds to our departure, followed by the platform on which they stood, starting to slide past the saloon windows where we had once again taken our seats.

The anticipation of the journey ahead had filled the train with a sort of static energy that only continued to grow as the Star of the Orient gathered speed at an impressive rate.

Within three minutes, we had reached the train's normal travelling speed.

It was around this time that the conductor entered the saloon car again, amid a gentle round of applause from many of the other passengers, who he now turned to address.

'Ladies and gentlemen, first of all, thank you for joining us on this our first attempt at setting a new speed record between Kabul Central and Torkham West railway stations, a distance of one hundred and forty-four miles.

'If all goes to plan, and I am confident that it will, then our target is for the engine at the front of this train to pass the clock tower at the western edge of the train station at Torkham no later than forty-eight minutes past two pm, a whole forty-seven minutes earlier than scheduled.

'However, in order to give you a better idea of our

progress, the engine driver and his senior engineer have agreed to provide me with updates via a special telephone line, which is being installed even as I speak.'

With this he directed our attention down the corridor toward a small team of men, who were busy unwinding a spool of telephone cabling, which they unravelled as they moved down the carriage to the bar, where a solid looking telephone was attached, before the men retreated, tucking the trailing cable beneath the main carpet runner which ran down the length of the carriage.

A minute later, and as though on cue, the phone on the bar rang, before being picked up by the conductor, who listened intently for a moment or two, before acknowledging his understanding and then covering the mouth-piece of the phone with his other hand.

'Ladies and gentlemen, the engine driver has informed me that the train has now reached her normal travelling speed of sixty miles per hour, the boiler pressure is still building and the track ahead is clear and level, so further acceleration should occur quickly.'

Two minutes later and the phone rang again, after which the conductor informed the carriage that we had now reached seventy miles per hour.

A few minutes more and we reached eighty miles per hour, with still no sign of the train slowing down.

It was amazing the difference that twenty miles an hour made at that speed. At sixty miles an hour the countryside seemed to pass by the window much more quickly than a motor car, but it was still somehow relaxing to watch. At eighty miles an hour the scenery seemed to blur, and with that sensation my pulse began to increase also.

Of course, to reach an average speed of eighty miles per hour the train would have to go a little bit faster for the majority of the journey, to make up for the start and end when the train was either speeding up or braking to reduce speed before entering the station at Torkham.

The countryside really seemed to be zipping past now, as the telephone on the bar rang once again.

'Ladies and gentlemen,' the conductor announced, still the picture of calm and equanimity.

'I am pleased to inform you that The Star of the Orient has now reached ninety miles per hour, her new best speed.'

'Ah yes,' Jean observed, with a slightly resigned expression on his face, as he looked past us to the countryside beyond. 'The Russian mind-set has always been a little... uncompromising. I remember some of the Tsarist soldiers I met...'

'When you say uncompromising,' Harry broke in, unceremoniously. 'Are you suggesting they might not be content to hit the eighty mile per hour average speed, which they said they would?'

'Well, I must admit that talk of the American train which reached one hundred and four miles per hour, on the route along Lake Michigan...'

'Yes, what about it?' Harry replied.

'Well, for a certain type of proud Russian,' Jean replied, looking out at the blur of grassland beyond the window. 'That kind of talk can be taken very literally as a challenge...'

'To beat one hundred and four miles per hour?' Harry asked breathlessly.

'Oui,' Jean replied, slipping into French involuntarily, as the train started to sway slightly from side to side.

'I think I might order a drink or two,' Peter observed, calling the waiter over to our table, just as the phone rang once more.

'Ladies and gentlemen,' the conductor began, an unmistakable fervour now gleaming visibly behind his eyes. 'I have the greatest pleasure in announcing we have now reached one hundred miles per hour.

'Unfortunately, he continued there is now a steady

uphill gradient ahead, which will prevent us from increasing our speed any further for the moment.'

'Oh, thank goodness for that,' whispered Peter, just as the waiter arrived.

'Two bottles of your finest champagne,' Jean suggested, before Peter could order anything stronger.

'Perhaps if we demonstrate the correct level of celebration, our conductor will consider his bet won, and that there is nothing to prove on the downhill stretch.

'You are thinking the conductor and the driver may use the other side of this incline to increase the train's speed even further?' Androus now asked very quietly, from the next table.

'Well, that and the fact that Kabul is one thousand meters, one kilometre higher in altitude than Torkham.' Selene added, just as the champagne arrived.

'So, in addition to any altitude which we're now gaining, we also need to lose a whole kilometre in height before we reach Torkham?' Harry asked, drinking his first glass of champagne a little quicker than would normally be considered polite.

Any hopes we had that the gleaming eyed conductor was going to be satisfied with the speed of one hundred miles per hour which the Star had already reached, were quickly abandoned, after Harry attempted to offer him a glass of champagne by way of celebrating the great achievement of his locomotive and staff.

'It is a kind offer,' conceded the elegant maniac in the conductor's uniform. 'But both myself and the driver are convinced that we can set a new record this day, the like of which even your great American trains will not be able to match.'

'Ah, really rising to the challenge eh,' Harry replied, with a slightly forced smile on his face. 'Well, you'll forgive us if we continue to toast the incredible speed you've already achieved.'

And with that he returned to us, looking a little pale.

'He's going to run us off the rails in order to try and beat a speed record that I may have invented,' he explained in a very strained and quiet voice.

'You weren't actually on that train which you mentioned?' Peter asked, in an equally strained voice.

'No, not as such,' Harry conceded. 'But I did read a fairly lengthy newspaper article about it at the time, and I'm sure it was either one hundred and four, or one hundred and fourteen miles per hour which they reached.'

'Well thank goodness you went with the lower number when you were ad-libbing with the conductor,' Jean added. 'I cannot imagine what speed he would be aiming for if you had claimed to be on a train that had reached one hundred and fourteen miles per hour.'

'But this was all your idea!' Harry replied, looking even more exasperated than he had before.

'More importantly,' Jean evaded, after taking a sip of his champagne. 'It is now well past luncheon, and all this excitement has given me quite an appetite.'

I couldn't help but chuckle out loud at Jean's irrepressible optimism and indestructible appetite, which released what little tension had been building between Harry and him.

'They do have some very nice cakes,' Harry conceded, with a smile and nod of his head that said, if he was going to meet his doom today, it was going to be with a fork full of gateaux in his hand.

It was as we were placing our order with the steward for several rounds of sandwiches, tea, coffee and a good selection of scones and cakes that the phone on the bar once again rang, closely followed by the conductor announcing we would shortly be reaching the top of our climb, after which we would again begin our acceleration.

We still had an hour left of the journey when we finished our climb, if the train managed to average eighty miles per hour, which it now seemed likely to exceed quite easily.

At fifty miles an hour our tea and coffee arrived with the sandwiches we'd ordered, and like condemned men we fell upon them with gusto, something I couldn't help but notice elicited another one of those quiet little smiles from Selene, before she too picked up a sandwich to join us.

Somewhere just before we reached eighty miles per hour, we finished our sandwiches, and requested refills to our gently quivering tea and coffee pots.

Just as we reached one hundred miles per hour the steward returned with the cakes we'd selected, along with some small pieces of linen which he politely inserted beneath the lids of the tea and coffee pots, which had been audibly rattling.

And as the conductor announced the train reaching one hundred and ten miles per hour our fresh tea and coffee appeared, along with fresh cups and saucers, all of which were now brought to the table with small cotton doilies between the cup and saucer to absorb the not insignificant shaking of the train as it flew over the tracks.

We reached the bottom of the descent a few minutes later, after which the conductor announced that the train was now travelling at one hundred and seventeen miles per hour, which would see us arrive in Torkham at approximately half past two o'clock, representing an average speed of ninety-six miles per hour.

How the entire thing didn't derail amongst all the shaking and swaying, I will never know, but somehow, we luncheoned our way through the worst of it, much to the incredulous glances of some of the other passengers, many of whom looked like they were truly sorry to be aboard such a lunatic locomotive.

At Torkham of course the station fell into absolute pandemonium when the train came charging into sight a whole hour before its scheduled arrival time, with another brass band striking up a welcoming tune, confetti being thrown and paper finish lines being broken, all while the press, the public and the railway officials vied to be at the front of the platform to welcome their record-breaking train.

Anticipating not only his victory, but also the nature of the welcome which his train was likely to receive, our conductor accepted his winnings graciously, before personally escorted us off the train with our baggage, which had already been unloaded, and with a genuine hope and invitation that we would return and visit his train again, he passed us into the hands of one of his colleagues from Torkham station, who guided us through a discreet freight exit, to where a couple of railway trucks were waiting to carry us with our things through the town and over to the Torkham East station, where we could board the British Indian Khyber Pass train.

Somehow, by arriving so early, we managed to avoid the main rush for the train, so were able to buy our tickets, pass the border checks, and board the train in just an hour, leaving us sat in the saloon carriage, wanting nothing more than to sit quietly for a few minutes while our nerves and our wits returned.

PESHAWAR

TRAVELLING INTO INDIA via the Khyber Pass was blessedly slow and uneventful. So much so that Selene, Androus, Harry and Peter all nodded off for a short while along the three-hour journey, during which we travelled through the infamous but unremarkable valley into the sub-continent.

Before falling asleep Androus and Harry tried their level best to make something of the rugged, hilly landscape which was reputed to be much valued in ancient Bactria, and the self-same route by which countless invaders, including Alexander, had entered southern Asia through the mountains. The same route used centuries earlier by those anonymous mounted nomads who had brought the Sanskrit language and early Vedic culture to the area.

From the train though, there was very little to see that wasn't part of the railway or the British army.

Unlike the trip into Torkham, this route through the pass involved a great many stops at local stations along the way, where everything from soldiers, food stuffs, animals and local tribesman all exchanged places on the carriages to either side of us.

As we headed south-east through the Khyber Pass, the weather became noticeably warmer and more summery than the cooler, autumnal weather so evident in Samarkand. It wasn't difficult to imagine winter still coming to claim this rocky north-western corner of the sub-continent, but it didn't feel imminent any more.

As we descended from the rugged terrain of the gorge to the open and more gently undulating landscape of north-west India, the train swaying this way and that on the tracks, I found myself slipping into a strange day-dream state, in which I imagined the land around the train overlaid with the strange views from dream I'd had atop the cliffs in Samarkand.

With my half-lidded eyes staring out of the carriage window I 'knew' this route. It was like a childhood memory made real again. I recognised feature after feature amongst the otherwise barren landscape leading into Peshawar. I saw the tall robust walls of old forts and fortifications in what were now merely rounded mounds of earth, and the ghostly outlines of villages and small towns beside the winding streams and rivers, where today no hint remained of their former existence.

Without realising, I must have started to drum my fingers on the table in front of me, unconsciously recalling the rhythm of the distant drums as I gazed and dreamed.

The sound I was making must have attracted the attention of Marlow who was sat in the aisle seat opposite, but if he spoke to me at that point, I didn't hear him. It was only when he too started to drum upon the table with his fingers that my awareness gradually returned and I became aware of his voice.

He spoke to me quietly, as though still talking to a sleeper.

'What are you looking at, George,' he asked, simply. 'What are you seeing?'

'I'm not sure,' I replied truthfully. 'This place has had many names, Purusapura, Vaekareta, Peshawar. I see them all, like ghostly layers one above the other, though the course of the rivers was different and the places in which people live have shifted.'

'And can you see the route we must follow from here,' he asked, calm and quiet to my day-dreaming mind.

'Yes, yes, we just follow the mountains toward the rising sun.'

'How far must we follow the mountains?' he pressed.

'It is farther than I can see from here,' I answered. 'Perhaps as far as the mountains themselves extend.'

I was straining my vision to see as far as I could, but the distances seemed so huge. So much further than we'd already travelled, an impossible distance to look across even in a dream.

In that moment though, we were disturbed by the conductor making his rounds to advise all passengers that we would shortly be arriving at our final destination, Peshawar.

The change of tone jolted me out of my dream with a small shock, just as Marlow was about to say something more.

'I'm sorry, Rob, I think I must've nodded off,' I apologised, feeling a little confused. 'Were you saying something else?'

He indicated it wasn't important, and together we roused the others, all of whom were still soundly asleep in the gently swaying carriage.

Peshawar was a city of contradictions. According to Androus and Harry it was considered by many to be the Paris of the Pathans, and the jewel of ancient Bactria, the first major city at the southern end of the Khyber Pass and consequently an unavoidable stop on the main trading route with Kabul, Samarkand and beyond.

It was this location, a major junction of trade between central Asia and the Indian sub-continent that also made Peshawar a melting pot of cultures and peoples.

After a full day of enforced idleness aboard trains, we were all missing the exertion of our usual routine, and consequently we were feeling the irritable lethargy that now followed such unaccustomed inertia.

As we left the elegant new railway station, I was only distantly aware of the new city which surrounded us, with the countless different races and cultures all rubbing along together, with what seemed a hundred different styles of fez, cap and turban to be seen in as many yards.

We were being bustled through the crowded streets with our luggage in two big horse drawn carts, of much the same design as those used by the British army, and were heading for a hotel which had been recommended to us by the train conductor.

It was apparently an old Moghul Palace which had been bought by the former rulers of India, the British East India Company, but was now owned by the Raj who had converted it into a hotel for the huge number of western guests passing through the city.

This was my first taste of India, but even with the novelty of my surroundings, I could feel my attention drifting and fading.

It was just too much for me to absorb in my lethargic state. Instead of being fascinated by the sights which no doubt abounded around me, I just started to find it all overwhelming.

I'd felt like this before though when I'd first visited Jerusalem and met Androus, so knew I just needed some time and space to allow my mind to adjust. Speeded perhaps by a cup of mint tea, that perennial revitaliser of the senses. If I could find one.

Although only a few minutes ride from the station, it was well into the evening by the time we reached the hotel. the train not having arrived in Peshawar until almost eight o'clock.

The hotel staff were prepared for such late arrivals, and even without reservations they dealt with us quickly and efficiently, getting us checked in and escorted up to our rooms with the minimum of fuss.

As the valet was dropping off my various bags and cases, I must have looked as weary as I felt, for with a gentle smile he asked if I would like some fresh lemonade sending up to my room, to help me recuperate from my journey.

As soon as he mentioned it, I knew that was exactly what my weary brain needed, and with a level of gratitude I felt barely able to express, I accepted his offer.

A few minutes later, after one of the elegant sari wearing hotel maids arrived with a pitcher of the chilled beverage, I poured myself a large glass, and simply sat down in the nearest chair to drink it.

Like the fabled elixir of life, the lemonade worked its magic, and within just a few minutes my mind cleared and my curiosity started to return.

I'd been given a suite of rooms containing a spacious bed chamber connected to a slightly smaller sitting room, both of which had wide balconies concealed by elaborately carved sandalwood screens that looked out over the main street in front of the hotel. On the other side of which was a small city park filled with mature trees.

Eager to see more of the city, I took a second glass of the lemonade out onto the balcony, just to watch the world go by for a while before going back in and changing for dinner.

We hadn't planned our journey any further than Peshawar yet, as we still needed to match as many of the directions contained in the tablets with the cities and towns of northern India.

I made my way down to the hotel bar, now marvelling at the wonderful carvings in the red stone from which the former Moghul palace had been constructed, as well as the gentle fragrance of spices and exotic flowers that filled the air.

It felt good to have a new base of operations, from which we could plan our next steps and begin to explore this strange new land, so much so, that I was seriously tempted to suggest we stay in Peshawar for at least a couple of days so we could all get out and stretch our legs a little bit.

I needn't have worried, for when I reached the bar, I found both Jean and Marlow talking to the concierge about the practicality of going out for a long walk that evening. In response, while polite, the man made it clear that Peshawar, after dark, was not a place for foreign visitors to walk around without guards to provide protection.

Over dinner, once all the others had joined us, we agreed that going forward, we should break our journey down into shorter sections, and if we were to travel by train, we should use the overnight sleepers to make better use of our time. In this way we could hopefully arrive refreshed in the mornings, and then have a full day ahead in our new destination to stretch our legs and continue our search.

From Peshawar our next stop would be New Delhi, where we hoped to sort out any licenses or permissions we might need for the journey ahead.

In the meantime, at Selene's urging, we agreed to do a thorough trawl of the newspapers from the past several months in order to look for any mention of Thea, Miriam and the mercenaries that we'd helped to deliver into the hands of the police in Tunis.

We'd monitored the newspapers while we were in

Ankara for any further indication of how the police and prosecution were preparing their cases against both those they already had in custody, and those shady individuals who the mercenaries had identified as having hired them. However, once we'd started the long walk to Samarkand, it wasn't often possible to find recent newspapers, so after a while we'd stopped trying.

'It is possible that nothing more has yet occurred,' Selene explained. 'But the quieter the news reports become, the more we should worry, because it is only once things quieten down that the Icarii will begin to come out of their hiding places, at which point they will surely concentrate on finding us.'

We'd been relying upon Selene's advice about travelling under the false names we'd set up in Ankara, just to make it more difficult for the Icarii to find our trail when they started to hunt us again, but we'd also definitely started to relax some of the less convenient measures we had earlier taken, like not travelling as a single large group, and staying in out of the way hotels. Let alone getting involved in high profile public events like an attempt to set a new speed record aboard the Star of the Orient.

The following day I headed out to the city library with Selene to take a look through the newspapers for the past several months, while Androus and Harry once again reviewed the directions translated from the tablets. This would leave Peter and Marlow to go in search of some more maps, and Jean to return to the city railway station to research the trains heading onward along the line of the Himalaya, to Rawalpindi, Lahore, Amritsar and New Delhi, and if need be further south via Jaipur and Agra.

Despite the length of time we'd now spent together, I still found Selene's company a little awkward at times. I hadn't noticed it so much while we'd been walking with the caravan to Samarkand, where the silence between us seemed natural, but here in Peshawar amongst the general hubbub and tumult of the streets I felt like talking.

The streets of Peshawar could be considered broad boulevards, much like their counterparts in Paris or Tunis, had it not been for the thronging mass of people which walked or gathered along both sides of almost every road.

Merchants, musicians, even story-tellers had their own quarter, but everywhere the pavements and roadsides were festooned with the sloping canvas awnings of a thousand and one tradesmen, providing shade from the hot sun, or shelter from the dust and more rarely the rain, with goods of one sort or another stacked high beneath them, along with an eager salesman crouched and ready to pounce on unsuspecting passers-by.

In equal measure, the gaps between merchants were filled with beggars, who would immediately encircle anyone who wasn't part of their own number in the hope of receiving even the smallest act of charity.

The hotel had changed a small amount of currency for me that morning into rupees until I could visit one of the banks to change a larger amount. Though dollars and sterling were accepted for more expensive purchases, these were inappropriately large sums to use for everyday items like a cup of tea or a newspaper.

After taking a couple of wrong turns and literally paying the price to extricate ourselves from the attentions of several small groups of child beggars, I noticed a slightly wistful look on Selene's face as she watched the small horde of boys and girls as they retreated, complete with the handful of small coins they'd extorted from us.

'You look at them with fondness,' I observed, deliberately leaving the statement as open for her to respond as possible.

'They remind me of my own childhood in Florence,' she replied, after a momentary hesitation, but still smiling slightly.

'My mother struggled to keep a roof over our heads after my father left,' she continued, as we retraced our steps, in the direction in which we hoped the library was located.

'As a consequence, I was allowed to run wild for a time, with my own little crowd of similarly dissolute urchins.'

'I had no idea,' I blurted in surprise. 'How did you…?'

'How did I go from being an impoverished urchin on the streets of Florence to become a trained killer for a secret organisation?' She replied, completing my sentence for me, a flash of the cold stone returning to her gaze momentarily, before softening once more.

'My mother died, killed trying to intervene in a struggle between one of our neighbours and his wife. We'd been fortunate to be given one of the new low rent rooms at the top of an apartment block where she worked as a cleaner for the wealthier Trenino households nearby.

'There was a struggle at the top of some stairs, a fall, and a few days later she passed away without ever regaining consciousness.

'They moved me away to an orphanage, but I didn't stay. Instead I took to the streets full time, stealing what I needed to keep body and soul together. Sleeping in abandoned outbuildings or unused boats.

'It was hard at times, but my fingers were quick and nimble, and as long as I kept my hair brushed and my clothes looking presentable, I could pass amongst the crowds of nice wealthy people without attracting attention… or so I thought.'

'The Icarii noticed you?'

'Sabine of Florence noticed me picking her pocket as she was leaving the opera,' Selene corrected, before continuing.

'I'd stolen her favourite cigarette case from her pocket, but she allowed me to think I hadn't been noticed.

'Over the next few weeks she studied me carefully. Buying back the cigarette case from the pawn broker I'd sold it to. Then one night as I returned to the abandoned room I'd been hiding in, in the upstairs of a derelict old house, she was waiting inside for me.'

We'd found the library by now, in a quieter part of the city, and had stopped beneath the canopy of a large cypress tree, in a little park on the other side of the road.

'She was already a mother superior in the Order at this point, on the verge of becoming a Reverend Mother, but she still took the time to educate and train me herself before formally bringing me into the Order as her protégé.'

'How old were you at this point?' I asked, unable to believe how wrong I'd been in my assumptions about her background.

'I was thirteen. Young by comparison with many of the recruits, but not as young as some.'

'So, the Order and Sabine has been your family for almost your entire life,' I sympathised. 'I cannot imagine how hard it must have been for you to step away from them.'

'It was difficult,' she conceded. 'But the Order had been losing its way for some time, even back in Sabine's time. Perhaps if she'd had longer as the Reverend Mother Prime, she could have brought it back onto the right path, but that wasn't to be.'

I didn't want to ask whether Selene's mentor had died of natural causes or whether the Order had disposed of her in much the same way it had nearly disposed of Selene, but after doing all she was doing to help us reach our goal, I felt it was important she understand that we too now considered her a part of our family.

'You know,' I began. 'Before you joined us, our little group enjoyed a surprising amount of success against a very powerful and very secret organisation.

'Terrible bunch of people that tried to stop us from finding this lost temple full of ancient secrets.' I continued, trying not to smile at my own joke.

'Oh really!' she replied, playing along as we crossed the road toward the library. 'And yet you managed to overcome them?'

'We did,' I continued. 'You see as capable as they

were, and the main trio that tried to hunt us down were definitely above average.'

'Above average, how magnanimous of you,' she interrupted, with an arched eyebrow and a broad smile on her face.'

'Oh yes,' I continued, unflustered. 'You see as above average as they were, they were just no match for the inherent foolishness of which we are all masters!'

She could contain herself no longer in the face of my silliness, so broke out into a hearty laugh, which it took her several seconds to recover from.

'Oh, George, if only you knew the trouble you all caused with your inherent foolishness,' she replied, a little more of her earnest nature returning. 'Agostine and Miriam would never admit it, but I don't think the Order has ever underestimated anyone as badly as we did with your group.'

'Perhaps,' I conceded, with a shrug. 'But in my considerable experience, most people struggle to believe just how foolish we can be individually, let alone as a group!

She chuckled again at my continued silliness, shaking her head as she struggled to find a repost. But now, having lightened the mood appropriately I felt it was time to make the point I had wanted to make from the start.

'In fact, when all this business with hidden temples is over,' I continued, lowering my voice as we entered the hushed entrance hall to the library. 'When we've discovered the secret to everlasting life, I wouldn't be at all surprised if as a group, we didn't all volunteer to help you guide your former colleagues and family in the Icarii back onto the right path.'

She stopped abruptly beside me and placed her hand on my arm so she could look me squarely in the face, clearly a little shocked that I should make such an offer.

'It's very kind of you to say that, George,' she began, all trace of humour now vanished from her face. 'But I don't think you appreciate just how dangerous that task will be.'

'Selene,' I replied, earnestly. 'I don't think you've quite grasped how foolish we can be, especially in the defence of our own family, of which, I assure you, you are now a part.'

My comments seemed to surprise and move her, but rather than replying she turned her face away, and made some comment about dispensing with the foolishness for the moment in order to get on with the job at hand.

TRAPPED

IT DIDN'T TAKE US LONG to find the information we were dreading in the library. Miriam had escaped the prison she had been transferred to in Nice, while Thea and the mercenaries, who were being held at separate locations had been murdered.

The original scandal had died down while we were in Ankara, with only the occasional news article still being published, and even those being increasingly dry and repetitive, outlining the progress being made in compiling the vast amount of information found in the mercenaries' files, rather than any new information about when the trials would start. As a consequence, even the articles that were still being printed started to appear further back inside the newspapers rather than on their front pages.

We'd been making notes on the case as we progressed through the back issues, and I was just beginning to think the entire matter was going to be keeping the Icarii in hiding for months if not years, when suddenly Selene found the first article about Miriam's escape from three months earlier, printed at the time we'd been passing through Tehran.

As if Miriam's escape wasn't bad enough, the subsequent issues revealed that the mercenaries had also been killed in a fire at the separate prison where they were being held. The story flashed across the front pages, reinforcing the evidence for a wider conspiracy and affront to justice.

Soon details emerged that Thea had been shot through the bars of her cell by Miriam, using a gun she had taken from one of the guards she had killed earlier in her escape, before doubling back into the prison, killing three more prison officers in cold blood, and eventually making good her escape.

As for the fire, which appeared to have broken out at the other end of Nice at the same time that Miriam was escaping, that was clearly carried out by another group of operatives who had a similar disregard for human life.

'Miriam has always been a problem,' Selene commented, as she read the same newspaper articles I had been reading. 'I knew she didn't have the right temperament for the work we were doing, she was always too cruel, too happy to consider options that should only ever have been a last resort.

'I should've stopped her while I had the chance, but that fool Agostine never understood where it would all inevitably lead us. And now Thea is dead at Miriam's hands.'

'This wouldn't be how the Order would normally deal with its problems then?' I found myself asking, hoping to hear something that made them sound a little more human.

'No, no,' Selene replied, wearily. 'Justice can only ever prevail in the presence of truth and honesty, and the Order are past masters of manipulating both of those things to get what it wants.

'Even as Miriam was escaping there would be agents and operatives of the Icarii steadily undermining the ability of the police to do their job. Tampering with evidence, bribing real witnesses or creating false witnesses, blackmailing key officials, compromising the personal lives of journalists and judges.

'Never enough for the manipulations to be obvious, but enough to delay, damage or impede the case for the prosecution, until eventually nobody would remember or care anymore, and those held in prison could be quietly released back into obscurity.'

'Even with a scandal the size of this one?' I asked, incredulous.

'Oh yes, in fact the bigger and more complex the case, the easier it is to delay or derail. Even without external interference a case such as this could take six months or a year to reach its first court hearing.

'So, no, what Miriam has done in killing poor Thea is something even the Order would not normally consider, not the order I swore to serve anyway.'

We continued to check through the papers right up until the most recent issues held by the library, but while the outrage once more frothed and boiled over amongst the civilised nations of Europe, with a manhunt that never stood a chance and nobody left in custody to prosecute, it all started to die down surprisingly quickly.

Selene and I continued to chat, but by early afternoon we had finished at the library and needed to take the dark news we'd uncovered back to the others.

When we returned to the hotel, it was to discover that everyone else had made it back before us, and were now preparing to board another train later on that day to New Delhi.

They'd been waiting for us to return and had ordered a late lunch to be served in Jean's rooms, where we could again talk freely.

'Well, the good news is that we are all booked on the overnight train from here in Peshawar to New Delhi,' Jean explained. 'It departs at fifteen minutes to seven this evening and arrives in Delhi at half past ten in the morning, after stopping at many of the smaller stations along the way.

'The bad news, if we want to continue our trip

across northern India along the line of the mountains, is that several of the provinces are currently operating under a heightened state of security, requiring special permissions and passes to enter, on account of some anti-British sentiment which is being stirred up there at the moment.'

'Special permissions and passes sounds rather… official,' Peter observed. 'If anyone questions our identities while we're trying to get access to an area where someone has been agitating the locals, it won't take long for us to be highlighted as credible suspects!'

'Precisely,' Jean replied. 'With British nationals among our number we should be able to get the passes we're after, but we are going to need a reason to be going into those territories, and identities that will stand up to a face to face scrutiny.'

'You mean, we're going to have to apply for these passes in person, while we're in New Delhi?' Harry asked.

'Time to fall back on our real identities then?' Peter suggested, looking around the room.

'That could be a problem,' I explained.

Between us, Selene and I outlined what we'd discovered about Miriam's escape, Thea's murder and the fire at the prison where the mercenaries were being held, before letting everyone absorb what that could mean for us.

'We have to assume they will be hunting us,' Jean began, ever the first person to work through the implications. 'And while they probably won't have much luck in tracing us through Turkey, they might well have transcriptions of the directions on the tablets and enough understanding to figure out we will be heading east.

'We certainly understood as much from Androus's early work,' Selene explained. 'Though at that time we had no idea whether you might end up being directed above the mountains and through the Karakorum desert, through India, or along the coast to Indochina, Malaysia, Singapore or even China and Japan.'

'And if you were to guess what your former

colleagues would have done with a three-month head-start?' Marlow asked, looking concerned.

'That's the question,' Selene replied, thinking hard.

'The order has assets in India and China, but not in large numbers,' she began. 'Similarly, there will be agents located in Japan and Singapore, but it's unlikely there will be anyone in the smaller countries or islands, as in many of these countries neither the Church of Rome nor the Orthodox church have a well-established or influential presence to support local operations.'

'That makes it sound like the net will be spread quite far and wide again?' Harry asked.

'Yes, to an extent,' she conceded. 'Most of the ports and airfields will probably have been penetrated by the local or regional crime organisations, at the very least people who will be prepared to sell information about the comings and goings of foreigners for a price.'

'And our stroll across Turkey and the caravan route to Samarkand?' Jean pushed.

'Very unlikely,' Selene conceded. 'Turkey, Iran and Afghanistan are quite openly hostile to the Christian churches, so they won't waste their time trying to find us in any of those locations.'

'What about New Delhi itself?' Jean pressed her further.

'New Delhi, as the administrative capital of India will have numerous agents and Icarii sympathisers present,' Selene replied, without hesitation. 'I know we use India with its liberal culture and values as a rich source of information on the officials that work here.'

'That sounds a lot like capturing the indiscretions of these individuals while in India to use against them in later life back in Britain.

'Then I'm afraid it sounds exactly as it is,' replied Selene, unapologetically.

'So, we cannot move forward to New Delhi without the risk of being seen while we're there, and we cannot circumvent New Delhi without then having to avoid the authorities for the rest of our journey through India, which could yet be a considerable distance,' Jean concluded, looking around the room at each of us, to make sure he'd understood and summarised everything perfectly.

'If that is the case,' he continued. 'Then we have only one option available to us. We must go to New Delhi, we must be seen, but we must not be recognised.'

'You are thinking of the travelling robes we used on the way to Samarkand?' Peter asked.

'No, no, we can't use those again,' interjected Marlow, rather quickly and a little too forcefully.

'Robert, they are by far the best option for us if we wish to travel as a group without appearing to be who we are.' Jean replied, clearly not understanding his hesitation.

'It is something I would ask you all to trust me on,' Marlow replied.

He offered no further explanation, so we had no choice but to honour his request, knowing he wouldn't make it lightly.

'As you wish,' Jean, continued, nodding as he did so. 'That leaves us with the same options we had in Tunis. We'll have to disguise the make-up of our group by checking into different hotels in ones and twos, and if we have to stay in New Delhi for more than a day then we'll gradually converge on the same hotel, checking in on different days so we can't be recognised from the paper trail.'

'What names will we use though?' I asked. 'If we use our real names it won't matter where we stay, we'll be recognised immediately. If we use our alternate identities it will look odd to the authorities should they come looking for us.'

'Well, we cannot use our real names,' Jean agreed. 'So, we will have to use the alternatives we're currently travelling under and hope we can get the paperwork sorted out using face to face contact when we get there.'

We all nodded our agreement.

'Which brings us to why we need to travel into the northern states,' Harry reminded us. 'The only thing I can think of is the wildlife. I seem to recall reading about a game reserve at the foot of the Himalaya somewhere.'

'Yes, that might work,' Peter agreed. 'I think I read something similar a few years ago. Didn't the Viceroy or his wife set it up.'

'It was the former Viceroy,' Jean added. 'Lord Curzon I believe. Perhaps we can check before we travel to Delhi, or before we approach the authorities there. Not to mention figuring out where the reserve is before committing to that as our story.'

'Any other options?' Jean asked.

'There is also Luke of course,' I added, unsure how everyone would feel about imposing on his friendship again in this way. 'He will have been working for his humanitarian mission now for several months.'

'Yes, that is a very good idea,' conceded Jean. 'And perhaps we may actually be able to help out briefly at his mission on the way, though as I recall he was working further to the east.'

We spent another few minutes discussing the preparations we could make and then returned to our rooms to pack, before heading out to the nearby city bazaars in order to buy our disguises, in much the same way we had in Tunis. Then we were once again boarding a train, though this time we all felt that when we reached out destination, we would surely risk stepping into a trap.

IN PLAIN SIGHT

AT SOME POINT IN THE NIGHT, and unknown to us we'd crossed an invisible boundary into a very different part of India.

Gone were the steep sided gorges and the tumbling streams of white water that twisted their way down from the high country, and in their place the land was now full of vivid greens from an abundance of vegetation, interspaced by broad and lazy waterways that seemed almost still, more like long winding lakes or pools than rivers.

Everywhere farmers were busy planting rice, lentils and other crops in the shallow waters and the moist looking earth, while well-fed animals waded up to their knees or middles as they were moved from place to place.

With this abundance of water came insects and birds in their thousands, swarming, flocking and wading with the people and larger animals, apparently oblivious to the increased humidity and heat that also now permeated the shady interior of the train carriages.

As planned, when we stopped at the central station in New Delhi, we immediately scattered in different directions to attract as little attention as possible.

The contrast between Peshawar and New Delhi could not have been more extreme. Peshawar was a working city crowded to bursting with merchants and traders, story-tellers and performers, pick-pockets and conmen. New Delhi by comparison felt empty, as though it were still under construction. There were plenty of people around, but the city had an air of newness and space that I don't think I'd encountered in any other capital that I'd visited.

The buildings were grand and clearly also very recently erected, and everywhere there were parks and gardens with immaculate lawns and flower borders across which brightly coloured peacocks called to one another.

Before alighting from the train on my first day in New Delhi I once again placed a small stone in my shoe and produced a walking cane to go with it, before checking into a boarding house not far from the station, where I pretended to be a slightly unkempt mining engineer who hadn't shaved recently, looking for work with the British Raj or anyone else that would pay.

The morning after I shaved all but my upper lip and chin, leaving me with the beginnings of a goatee, and then on the second day moved out of my boarding house and into a hotel after rendezvousing with Peter. Now, we both pretended to be freshly arrived in the city on a scouting mission as land surveyors, working for an interested third party.

The others were doing something similar, with the exception of Androus and Selene, who had reprised their father and daughter act from Tunis and checked straight into one of the finest hotels in the city, the Imperial, where the rest of us would gradually join them over the next few days.

We were playing it cool as far as applying for our permits was concerned, spending some time gauging the lay of the land, identifying why the permits were currently required, which areas they were used for and which government office was responsible for issuing them, while at the same time trying to identify any Icarii agents or sympathisers that might lie in our path. There was only one Roman Catholic church in New Delhi, and according to Selene, while it had been built by the Franciscans, if the Icarii had agents in the city, then the cathedral was where they would meet their controllers, without the Franciscan order being any the wiser.

The drawback with using the different hotels to hide our presence in the city, was that it also hampered our communication. So while we all had different tasks to complete, none of us had any idea how any of the others were getting on until we started to form back into pairs and small groups prior to checking into the Imperial.

In my case, I had met up with Peter, who had been looking for maps and information about the journey ahead.

'Well, you remember that game reserve that Harry mentioned?' He explained while regarding me over the wire rimmed spectacles which he now routinely wore as part of his disguise. 'It looks just about perfect for our needs.

'It's the Kaziranga game reserve, created by Lord Curzon at the turn of the century to please his wife, and located in the north east region of India, near to Assam. This area is normally very strictly controlled because of the tea plantations, which are barely tolerated by the countless hill tribes in that area. They only remain amenable because the number of Europeans in the area is restricted.'

'So, does that mean we can get a permit or we can't?' I asked, unsure where it left us.

'It actually means visiting the game reserve is probably one of the very few, if not the only area we're likely to get a permit to visit.'

'That is good news,' I replied. 'Now if Luke's mission were only over in that region as well, we could really apply with confidence?'

'Well, it is,' Peter confirmed with a smile. 'I ran into a couple of British Geographical Society members in one of the shops where I was looking for a map, and they understood Luke's directions perfectly. The mission he's working for is right on the border or Sikkim and Bhutan, again, pretty far over into the north eastern territories and on the way to Assam and the Kaziranga game reserve.'

'That gives us two bites at the cherry then,' I replied, thinking about the visions I'd had in Samarkand. 'If only I could've seen further across India, just so we knew roughly how much further our destination was.'

'It would certainly be helpful from my perspective,' Peter added. 'I'm trying to find some decent maps of Bangladesh, Nagaland and Arunachal Pradesh at the moment, just on the off chance we end up going that far, but we're talking some pretty serious frontier country up there. If it weren't for the fact that China has voiced a claim to that same territory, I don't think anyone would have gone anywhere near it, let alone mapped it.'

'You never know,' I offered. 'When we meet up with Androus tomorrow at the Imperial, perhaps he'll have made a breakthrough with the directions on the tablets.'

'I hope so, George, I really do,' Peter replied. 'But we shouldn't expect miracles from him. We've all seen how sketchy the details on those tablets are.'

We talked a little more as we finished our dinner in the hotel, the topic of conversation shifting gradually, but returning again and again to the strange dreams we'd all had, which had led us to where we were. I couldn't be certain, but there was something about the way that Peter kept bringing the subject back to these dreams that made me wonder if there wasn't something more specific he wanted to talk about.

Eventually, as we retired to the hotel lounge with a glass of brandy each and our pipes, I decided to just ask the question.

'I know the dreams we have after listening to those strangely distant drums can be very personal for some of us, Peter,' I began, cautiously. 'But while you've mentioned a few details from your dreams, I don't think I've ever sat down with you before, to talk about how you find them.'

'Ah, yes, I've always found it a little bit… awkward to really… to discuss the details,' he began, struggling far more than I'd anticipated.

He wasn't changing the subject though, so I decided to push him a little more.

'Is it the guide you see when you're in the dream?' I asked, remembering the heart-rending account that Jean had given, about being guided by his own dead son. 'Perhaps a relative you didn't know had died, or an old friend?'

'No, no, it's not… she's not… not a person at all,' he finally said, his entire posture relaxing noticeably as he spoke.

But his answer left me surprised and a little bit confused.

'I don't understand,' I said, as I tried to follow what he was saying. 'Everyone else I've spoken to, with the exception of Marlow, who just steps straight into that blazing fire each time, we're all guided by someone we know. There's nobody else there.'

'There are the spirits around that circle of fire, the elementary forces which shaped the world as we know it,' Peter explained, now completely relaxed, as his eyes seemed to focus on the memory. 'The earth, the rocks and mountains, the moors and grasslands, forests, lakes, clouds and the ever-running springs and rivers.

'I can't explain how it happened,' he continued after a moment. 'I think I saw Rob being led off by the lion spirit, and I just started to follow them. There were other figures around, and they might have included someone waiting to guide me, I'm not sure.

'Anyway, I saw the circle of spirits that surrounded the fire, and approached as Rob was talking to them, but as I drew closer one of the glittering silvery forms seemed to look away from Rob and straight at me instead.

'The moment I saw her, I knew she was the most beautiful woman I had ever seen in my life, and I fell in love.'

I completely forgot about my brandy and my pipe, and just sat stunned by what Peter was saying to me.

'You've fallen in love with one of the spirits from the dream place?' I half heard myself saying.

'Yes,' he replied, simply. 'She is the spirit of streams and rivers, of flowing waters, deep and shallow.'

'So, when you dream...'

'We spend the time together, she has many names of course, but to me she is Danu.

'When we meet, she shows and explains her world, and I show and talk about ours. She talks about the shaping and movement of the waters, its colour and sound and the many creatures that worship it as their home. And I talk of the engineering I have done, the things I have built, the strengths of materials and structures...'

I didn't know quite what to say, so took a sip of my brandy, to see if he would continue.

'Occasionally, I sense her presence when I'm near to a quiet river or stream away from other people. I even talk to her when I'm there, and I know she hears what I say.'

'And the future? Your future together?' I asked, uncertain where this conversation was going.

'That is more difficult,' Peter acknowledged. 'It is possible, as the shaman in Samarkand said, for us to learn how to hear the drums, which are sounding constantly, but only occasionally heard. But Danu has explained to me that this comes at a cost, for a person cannot spend more time in the dream without being absent from the real world, and for her the same is true in reverse. She can with effort come to our world, just as we can go to the dream.'

'Then what will you do?' I asked openly, sympathising with the situation that Peter now found himself in.

'I will continue as I have been,' he answered with a wry smile. 'If I can learn how to hear the drums more clearly then I will dream more frequently, and hope to find a better answer in time.'

This seemed like a reasonably positive note on which to leave things, and already I could tell that Peter was feeling better because he'd been able to finally tell someone about the strange double life he'd been living in the dream, an existence I found almost impossible to imagine. But then, I now felt closer to my father than I ever had in life, purely because of the time we'd spent together in the dreamlands.

PRETENCE

THE FOLLOWING DAY Peter and I checked out of the hotel we'd been staying in, and moved over to the altogether more luxurious surroundings of the Imperial hotel, where everyone else should already have checked in, albeit in smaller groups and using fake identities.

We'd checked in around mid-afternoon, so it might appear as though we'd just arrived in New Delhi on the train, and then retired to the hotel lounge for a coffee before heading out for the afternoon.

This was the designated meeting place we'd agreed on with the rest of the group, so that one of the others could come to find out what room numbers we'd been given.

It was the simplest trick in the world in a hotel like the Imperial, where all the hotel guests needed to do to pay for anything was to tell the barman, waiter or concierge their room number for any charges to be added to their tab.

As planned, Jean was already in the hotel lounge, reading one of the newspapers at a small table next to the bar, half fringed by some potted palm trees.

As Peter and I entered he continued reading, completely ignoring us, just as we ignored him. Then as we ordered our drinks from the bar, we each told the barman which room numbers to charge them to, which Jean would also have clearly heard and made a mental note of.

With the necessary information now delivered, it was just a question of Peter and I popping out for a while, and when we returned there would hopefully be an innocuous slip of paper with further instructions beneath each of our doors.

We'd both already accomplished as much of our allocated tasks as we were able, Peter having identified the locations of the game reserve and Luke's humanitarian mission, while I'd been tasked with finding some cars or trucks for hire, which I'd struggled with.

I could find one thoroughly worn out old truck for sale, which had clearly been used for ferrying coal into the city, and a couple of equally tired old saloon cars, which were available on a chauffeured basis only and which we'd have to specify our final destination upon booking.

The only other options I'd come up with were some riding horses and a horse and cart, which were much more widely available to buy from several places in the city, at quite reasonable rates.

With Peter's information about the game reserve and the humanitarian mission being located another thousand miles away, and the farthest corners of Nagaland and Arunachal Pradesh stretching a further nine hundred miles beyond that, at least I knew there was no point looking to hire vehicles anymore. If we were aiming to go that far, then horses would clearly be the much better option, though now, as I thought about it, I began to wonder whether pack animals rather than a cart might not be even better still.

There were a couple of stables located on the same side of the city a little over a mile away from the Imperial, near to a polo club and one of the big new parks that had clearly been modelled on London's own Hyde Park. But while comparatively close to the hotel, the weather seemed to be going from hot to hotter, which made any kind of exertion a damp affair.

Despite the heat, Peter still agreed to join me, as I went out to enquire about pack animals.

I managed to flag down a horse drawn taxi cab, to take us out to the stables and then wait outside while we went in to discuss the availability of the animals we'd need to go with the horses.

The stable owner was an ancient Sikh gentleman, who couldn't have been more knowledgeable about his animals, so within an hour we'd not only discussed how many animals would be required, but also the harnesses, feed and other associated equipment likely to be required.

I was tempted to shake hands on a deal there and then, but not having spoken to the rest of the group in several days made me hesitate, so I left him with the name I was travelling under and where I was staying at the Imperial, so he could contact me in the event of a problem developing or someone else wanting to purchase his stock.

With a good transport option lined up, we hopped back in the waiting taxi-cab and headed back to the hotel in the hope that there would now be a message waiting for us.

As expected, on opening my hotel room door, I discovered a small sealed envelope from Jean, addressed to me under the false identity I was using. Inside, was a short but cryptic message, informing me that enclosed were the thirty-three dollars which had been borrowed the previous night, with thanks.

Almost as an afterthought, there was a tiny post-script, informing me that the writer of the letter would see me in the lounge bar at half past five o'clock.

It was a simple cypher that we'd agreed on beforehand, where the number of dollars represented the room number, and the time proposed for meeting in the bar, was actually the time I should make my way to room thirty three.

Peter, who had been given a room on the next floor up from me, would no doubt have a very similar letter, with a suggested meeting time of a few minutes earlier or later so we weren't both turning up together.

There was a little over an hour before the time on my note, so I had time to freshen up after my short trip into the heat and humidity of the New Delhi streets, so I drew myself a quick bath and pressed the bell for room service while it filled.

The fresh lemonade I'd ordered was brought to my room while I was in the bath, which allowed me the greatest imaginable luxury on such a warm day, of climbing out of the cool water a few minutes later, getting quickly dried off, and then sitting behind the sandalwood screen which partitioned off the balcony in my dressing gown, with a tall glass of cold lemonade while the gentle afternoon breeze evaporated the last of the moisture from my skin.

By the time I needed to be heading out to suite thirty-three I felt completely refreshed and ready to hear how everyone else had faired with their respective tasks.

Suite thirty-three was easy enough to find, and when I

knocked Androus opened the door immediately to allow me in before anyone might see me.

Everyone was there with the exception of Peter, who turned up as anticipated ten minutes later with a handful of rolled up maps, on the dot of when his note had asked him to arrive.

A few minutes later and we settled down to the business of catching everyone up.

We were meeting in the suite of rooms which Androus and Selene had checked into as father and daughter, which comprised two adjoining suites with a larger reception room connecting them. This came with a large dining table at one end, a circle of armchairs around a coffee table at the other, and a piano of all things in the centre, separating them.

Niceties aside though, there was space for us all to sit around the dining table.

Jean started us off, with an altogether more serious note than I would have liked.

'Thank you all for coming,' he began. 'And for taking the precaution of being discreet in your arrival. We have, unfortunately already identified a likely Icarii agent working in the hotel as a valet, so we cannot be too cautious.

'There is much to discuss I suspect, and we must keep our meeting to as short a time as possible in order to avoid suspicion. Peter, George, may we start with you?'

While I was eager to hear how they'd all gotten on, it made more sense for the rest of the group to hear from us first, as they were all probably aware of what one another had discovered.

Peter whisked through the details he'd uncovered about both the location of the Kaziranga game reserve, and the humanitarian mission where Luke was working, before explaining that irrespective of the unrest taking place in the territories immediately to the north and north-east of New Delhi, we would need separate permits if we wanted access to Assam, Nagaland and Arunachal Pradesh, to the far north-east of India.

I noticed several members of the group nodding their understanding of what Peter was saying, with slightly resigned expressions on their faces.

I knew what Peter had said hadn't been what they'd all wanted to hear. However, there was no point sugar coating what we'd discovered, so when it came to my turn, I simply laid out the position when it came to hiring or buying vehicles, and then gave them the alternative that I had managed to find, in the form of the riding horses and associated pack animals, the equipment we'd need to buy to go with these animals, and a quick outline of the provisions we'd need to take with us for a week's journey.

'Well, we still have the option of taking the train if we wish,' Jean added, by way of another option. 'But we have travelled as far as we can, based on the visions we all had in Samarkand.

'And as I understand it from your last update, Androus,' he said, deferentially, indicating our modest epigraphist. 'The directions from the tablets are not compatible with skipping any further ahead.'

'No, alas not,' Androus confirmed. 'As it is, I am guessing as to how far forward into the directions we may have moved. The only details I have that may be relevant are a reference to the cattle rearing Newar people living in the mountains to the north of the river which we must follow, and the flatness of the landscape in this section of the directions.

'In combination, I am conjecturing these are references to the Nepali people, with their long-held traditions of rearing cattle in the high alpine pastures of the mountains in the summer, and the Gangetic plain to the south, which has been the breadbasket of India for centuries.

'If that's correct then the major rivers which the tablets describe can only be the Ganges and the Yamuna, and the settlements it describes would be the modern-day cities of Agra, Bareilly, Lucknow, Kanpur, Allahabad, Gorakhpur and Varanasi.'

'You sound far more confident in your interpretation of the directions, old friend,' Harry observed. 'Than you have since we travelled through the southern Caspian mountains.'

'In truth, Harrison, I am.' Androus replied. 'There is not another place within five hundred miles that fits these directions.

'The only question that remains to be answered for me is scale.'

'You think we need to travel on foot again for a while?' Jean asked.

'Yes,' came Androus' simple reply.

'Either that or by horseback,' he added, nodding his head in my direction.

'And our course?' Marlow asked.

'There is only one route in this part of the world,' Androus answered smiling, and with a noticeable twinkle in his eyes. 'And that is the great Ganges river, which passes through some of the most sacred and ancient cities in the world.'

'Perhaps a boat would suit us better?' Harry asked, looking around the table.

'I have only seen very small boats on this bit of the river around New Delhi,' I added. 'And from what I can see the water is so slow moving that we would need some method of propulsion for it to be as fast as riding.'

'I would agree,' Peter added, unfurling one of his larger scale maps for us to look at. 'From what I can see, the rivers through this plain drop only one or two hundred feet over the next thousand miles, which means the water will be almost stagnant.

'Having said that the Ganges is a much bigger river, and certainly by the time it reaches Allahabad, it might be big enough to have a more discernible current.'

'Well that gives us a direction and means of

transport,' I summarised. 'But what have you been able to find out about the permits we would need to travel through these northern territories to wherever the Ganges may lead us?'

'Jean and I have been looking into the matter.' Marlow explained.

'It looks like there have been a few incidents of what the Raj are calling 'civil disobedience' across the Gangetic Plain and down into the Kaimur Hills to the south. The suspicion is that this is being stirred up by the Chinese following both the provincial elections and the separation of Burma, which happened last year and which were viewed as highly significant for the future of British rule in India.'

'Why would China wish to interfere with the government of India though,' Peter asked, sceptically.

'Well as chance would have it, the answer may also be relevant to us, depending on where we travel to from here,' Marlow added, looking over at Jean.

'Indeed so,' Jean added. 'By chance I ran into one of my fellow countrymen when I checked into the hotel, who has been working as a journalist here for several years.

'He informed me that the Chinese were not only considered to have designs upon the Tibetan plateau, they also openly challenged India's claim to the far north east territory of Himachal Pradesh.

'The speculation in the halls of the British Raj is that China's agents are attempting to stir up discontent in the region in preparation for an attempt at seizing one of these territories or the other.'

'What does that mean for us though,' I asked. 'It would be clear to anyone that we have no sympathies with China or anyone attempting to stir things up.'

'No, perhaps not,' conceded Marlow. 'But the Commissioner's Office here in New Delhi are taking a very simple stance when it comes to permits, and that is to vet everyone to make sure of two things. Firstly, that they're not agents of the Chinese government, and secondly, that our presence could not be used by said agents to help stir up resentment or ill feeling toward the government of India.'

'Well, I don't see how our presence could be used to stir things up?' I half suggested and half asked.

'For what it's worth. From the research we did on all of you in the Icarii, there was nothing we could find that could be used as leverage,' Selene offered. 'Granted we weren't looking for anything specific in relation to India or China. But none of you appear to have held any particularly contentious posts, or to come from famous families.'

'And obviously your identity and associated recent history, Selene, would only be as contentious as you wanted it to be?' Peter added.

'Naturally,' she replied, with a gentle smile.

'So, it will probably be just a formality,' Jean suggested. 'But we do not know for sure.

'Either way, Robert and I have an appointment at the Regional Commissioner's Office tomorrow morning to present our paperwork and be interviewed about our intentions.'

We spent a few more minutes talking through what our stated reasons for wanting to travel through the northern provinces would be, agreeing that we would claim our main aim was to visit Luke at the Mission he was working at in Sikkim, followed if allowed by a hunting trip to the famous game reserve at Kaziranga.

Marlow and Jean would be the ones visiting the government offices the following morning to apply for the permits on behalf of the entire group, while the rest of us waited for them to return.

OPPORTUNITY

TODAY WAS THE POINT OF NO RETURN. In applying for permits to travel through northern India, we were not only alerting the government to our existence, we were also telling them where we were headed. So, if they then refused to grant us the permission we needed, we were stuck.

Nobody could stop us from sneaking into the northern territories if we put our minds to it, but wherever we went we'd have to avoid the authorities. Using our false identities and probably travelling in pairs or threes to make it more difficult to identify us, which would severely complicate the already complex logistics. Hence, a lot was riding on Marlow and Jean making a good impression.

Their meeting with the regional commissioner was scheduled for mid-afternoon, leaving a lot of free time for the rest of us to kill, but the weather was once again hot and humid, so my usual habit of going for a long walk looked less than appealing, until I remembered the large park which had been created on the other side of the stables I'd visited the day before.

It wouldn't be the same as getting out into the wilderness, but the park would be big enough to get in a few hours riding, and if I took my Bedouin robes with me which I'd walked to Samarkand in, I'd be a lot more comfortable in the heat, while the large turban would completely protect me against sunstroke.

I told Peter what I was thinking of doing, to see if he'd like to join me, but understandably, he wanted to stick to the cool of the hotel and do some work with his maps.

So, with my robes rolled into a small bundle, a bottle of beer, an orange and some tasty looking little savoury pastries which the hotel had managed to put together for me, I limped out of the hotel with that awkward little stone in one of my boots and a walking cane in hand, which I used to hail a horse drawn taxi to take me over to the stables.

Even with the breeze from the nimble little buggy as it sped through the wide-open streets, I was still painfully aware of the heat and sun beating down upon me.

A few minutes later we arrived at the stables, where I paid the driver and asked him to come and pick me up around three o'clock, before heading into the office attached to the stables to arrange the hire of a decent riding horse, with the elderly Sikh owner I'd met the day before.

As I walked through into the large courtyard surrounded by the stables, I traded 'Good afternoon' greetings with a couple of men who looked like they were in the process of buying new polo ponies, before I disappeared into the owner's office.

He was more than happy for me to exercise one of his horses for him, and took me through to have a look at a couple of mares that he informed me would enjoy a gallop through the adjoining park, should I wish to let them have their heads. This I admitted was exactly what I was after.

After agreeing a price, I decided to play it safe, rather than risk offending anyone, so explained to him that I was hoping to get changed into my loose-fitting robes and turban, if such a thing wouldn't be likely to cause offence with the local people.

'Ah, Sahib,' he replied, with an indulgent smile on his face. 'To see you British dressed so sensibly in such heat would bring nothing but relief to the eyes of those who see you.'

With that he pointed me to a room where I could get changed and leave my western clothes while I went out for a ride. He even offered to assist me with the tying of my turban, should I need it, before I informed him that I could manage.

Getting changed out of my normal clothes and back into the loose fitting and lightweight robes that we'd travelled to Samarkand in was a relief. I instantly felt cooler, even with the turban wrapped around my head, desert fashion, so that I could form the loose ends into a veil to protect my face.

The proprietor clearly approved of my proficiency in wrapping my turban as he met me with the mare I had selected in the courtyard. He immediately recognised I'd learned to wear it somewhere near the Caspian sea, because he spoke to me using the Turkic language so common along the old silk roads, to ask where in the region I had acquired my skill.

I couldn't help but smile at his insight, and replying in the same language, I explained about the long walk with the trade caravan to Samarkand, and how the merchants had eventually taken pity on me in the summer heat, by first equipping me with the robes, and then teaching me how to use them.

We talked cordially for a few minutes about the journey, and how he had also visited that part of the world when he was younger. But eventually, he waived me back to the horse to go and enjoy my ride.

Stashing my bottle of beer and other provisions in one of the saddle-bags, I mounted the grey mare I'd selected and rode off in the direction of the park, nodding at the slightly surprised looking polo players on my way out of the courtyard, just before securing my veil in place against the sun.

The stable proprietor had provided me with an excellent animal, and no sooner were we in the wide-open terrain of the park than it nosed into a canter, and when I didn't attempt to check its speed, jumped into a gallop. Suddenly the warm air was rushing past so quickly it sent a shiver down my spine and set the loose robes fluttering wildly around me.

For a solid hour with the pale mare beneath me I was content to gallop and canter around the park, under the low branches of some mature trees, splashing along the water-course of a shallow stream, around the odd rocky outcropping, or between the more densely planted trunks of some young trees. I was even tempted into jumping some fallen branches, which though only a foot high, got my heart racing more than I was expecting.

There were few other people out and about in the park, most just walking their own horses, or sitting in the back of open carriages, so I was able to give everyone a nice wide birth as I raced this way and that like some demented dervish.

Eventually, we both needed a rest, so after giving the mare a few minutes to drink her fill, I picked a shady spot nearby with some convenient boulders amongst the long grass for me to sit on, and cracked open my picnic while the horse nibbled at the grass.

After a good rest, I remounted the grey before returning at a steady trot back to the stables.

Once back in the courtyard I handed the animal over to one of the grooms, who had a pail of fresh water standing ready for the still thirsty creature, and went back to the changing room to get back into my regular western clothes.

A few minutes later I returned, back in my western clothes, and was just about to step back into the proprietor's office, when one of the polo players who were still looking at horses, a slightly older man in immaculately tailored clothes, came over to talk to me.

'Excuse me,' he said, politely. 'I couldn't help but notice the extraordinary outfit you wore to go out for your ride.'

'Ah, yes I suppose it is a bit unusual,' I conceded. 'But I can assure you it's a far more comfortable way of dressing on such a hot day.'

'Yes, I'm sure your right,' he agreed, amicably. 'But

it had never occurred to me to even try it out until I saw you after you got changed.

'I couldn't help but notice you speak one of the local languages as well?'

'A little,' I conceded, wondering where this conversation might be going. 'It's actually a version of the Turkic language spoken on the old trade routes throughout central Asia. Though it seems to have quite a lot in common with Hindi, enough for me to get by anyway.'

'You don't say,' he replied, looking a little wistfully at me. 'I don't suppose you'd be looking for some work while you're in New Delhi by any chance?'

'Thank you, but no,' I replied, before informing the curious fellow that I wasn't intending to stay in the city for long, as I was hoping to head east across the Gangetic plain toward Sikkim and Assam.'

'Some friends of mine are just trying to sort out the necessary permits, before we leave.' I explained, hoping that would be an end to his questions.

'You don't say,' he replied, with a broad smile on his face as he did so.

'These friends of yours, they're applying for their permits through the regional commissioner's office I assume.'

'That's right,' I replied, wondering why this fellow should be smiling so.

'Well, you know those permits normally take several days to process, what with the number of people applying and all, but I might be able to help you out, speed it up a bit.'

'Oh!' I said, even more confused than ever. 'That would be very kind of you?'

'Jenkins is the name,' he replied, still grinning at me like a man who'd heard a really good joke. 'I'm the regional commissioner for New Delhi and the northern provinces.'

With that it all fell into place. Why he'd come over to talk to me, why he was interested in my use of Turkic and why he suddenly started grinning at me when I informed him I wasn't looking for work while I was in New Delhi, because I was hoping to travel west into the northern provinces where all the trouble had been recently reported.

Feeling rather disconcerted I shook hands with the regional commissioner, gave him my real name without thinking, and agreed to pop by his office for lunch the following day, with the friends of mine that had gone to sort out the permits.

We talked for a few moments more, just to exchange details, before he went back to his polo ponies and I went out to my waiting cab, kicking myself for my slow wits as I did so.

CONSEQUENCES

I COULDN'T STOP REPLAYING my encounter with the regional commissioner in my mind as I returned to the hotel.

If only I'd been content to go riding in my ordinary clothes, while I might not have been quite as comfortable, once that splendid horse came up to a gallop I would still have been cool enough, and my fedora would've helped to keep the sun off.

I'd been a fool to give away so much information about our plans so easily. But what was done, was done, and I couldn't undo my mistake, all I could do was hope we could salvage the situation somehow.

Perhaps he just wanted someone to travel through the northern territories, on the lookout for the suspected Chinese agents, or whoever was stirring up local sentiment, and he thought my Bedouin robes and command of the Turkic language would be a good disguise.

When the next note appeared under my hotel door,

it was all I could do not to snatch the door open in the hopes that it might have been Jean so I could ask his advice. Instead I simply opened the note, which indicated the time of our meeting was only an hour away.

There was nothing else for it, so I rang for some more lemonade to be delivered to my room, and then once again drew a cool bath.

I still hadn't resolved the situation in my own mind by the time we were all gathered in Androus and Selene's suite again, but I had decided to just come clean with what had happened so we could use the limited time available to figure out what to do before we went to see Jenkins for lunch.

Jean had just finished telling us that the meeting had gone well at the commissioner's offices, but just as Jenkins had indicated, the processing time for our permits, should they be granted, would be around two weeks.

'Now our application contains our real names, and the details of where we should like to travel,' Jean explained. 'Which means it will only take one Icarii sympathiser within the ranks of the commissioners offices, of which there are surely several hundred people…'

'And our goose will be well and truly cooked,' Harry added.

'Two weeks is also more than enough time for the Icarii to get here, or use their influence to make life difficult for us,' Selene added, clearly concerned at our options.

'Well as chance would have it, I may have put my foot in it, and in the process provided us with another option.' I confessed, after taking a deep breath.

'That is a very intriguing statement, Mon Ami,' Jean declared, clearly surprised. 'Why don't you start at the beginning?'

I didn't attempt to excuse or explain what I'd done. I just started at the beginning and finished with my conversation with Jenkins, when he'd asked me to join him for lunch, telling it exactly as it had happened, and trying not to leave anything out.

'And I presume you have been kicking yourself, George, for the casual way in which you explained our plans to a complete stranger,' Jean began. 'Who now turns out to be none other than the regional commissioner himself.'

'Yes, of course,' I replied. 'I presumed he was just some local club type after a colourful story to share over dinner somewhere, so I didn't think.'

I didn't even dare look at Selene after all the training she'd given us while we were in Turkey.

'I realise now, this could so easily have been an Icarii agent or hired mercenary, who was just goading me into talking, just as Selene has explained countless times, and I walked straight into it.'

'Well, on this occasion at least, your indiscretion may have served us well.'

At the same time, I could see Marlow was distracted by his own thoughts, and I couldn't help but wonder if it was related to the idea of us travelling in our Bedouin robes again.

'I know it's probably stating the obvious,' I began. 'But it occurred to me after speaking to him, that Jenkins may want to meet us because he's looking for people he can trust to send into the northern territories, to identify whoever is stirring up local ill-feeling. And after seeing my robes he's thinking we might be able to do it without scaring the guilty parties off.

'I also recall you weren't keen on the idea of using our robes again, Rob?' I asked, hoping he would finally explain why.

'Yes, George, you're right, if we could have avoided it, I would much prefer we not use these robes again while we're in India,' he continued. 'What I've not told you though, is that the reason for this is the dream I had back in Corinth, when we deliberately tried to re-create the shamanic ceremony.'

'I remember you being unusually difficult to rouse

the following morning,' I replied, trying to remember the details. 'And when we did finally rouse you, you cried out for… Selene.'

'Yes,' he said, nodding slowly as he did so. 'It's been preoccupying me ever since. It's also why I haven't been able to offer any guidance on our journey from my own dreams.

'In that second dreaming experience we had outside Corinth,' he began, with some hesitation. 'I was determined to control and remember more of what I saw.

'The lion-spirit guided me back to the circle of figures, urging me to be more cautious this time. To consider approaching the flames more slowly, and perhaps to just touch that burning inferno with my outstretched fingertips. But of course, I did not listen, and walked straight into the heart of the fire once again. The agony of which, all but overwhelming me once again.

'Knowing I wouldn't have long, I tried desperately to focus my thoughts on finding the tablets, so that we could find the first great temple, but in the agony of the fire my focus slipped, and before I knew it I was seeing this journey across India, and I could see that Selene was with us, but then, I saw us being attacked by Selene's former colleagues, including Miriam, and other members of what we later came to know as the Order of Icarus.

'That first time that I saw the attack, it was all I could do to remember that it took place in some kind of run-down warehouse area.'

'And Mademoiselle Autieri is injured in this place?' Jean asked diplomatically.

'She is,' Marlow confirmed, sombrely. 'As are you Harry, and you Androus. Though your wounds are superficial. But Selene, I'm afraid your wound appeared much more serious, though not immediately fatal.

'I've dreamed of that moment several times since,' he continued. 'When the drums seem to have come to me in my sleep, but I could never make out any more detail until we reached Samarkand.

'Finally, I listened to the lion-spirit and was able to control what I saw a little more. And only then did I manage to pick out that we were wearing the same travelling robes we wore on the way to Samarkand, and that the warehousing seemed to be near to a river and in the mountains somewhere.'

'This is troubling news indeed, Robert,' Jean added, gravely. 'And your vision of these attacks have been the same each time, in all other details?'

'That I cannot be sure of,' Marlow replied, concentrating. 'It is only in the first dream that I saw Androus being grazed on his arm by a bullet. Since that first time, it's almost as though we recognise the scene and begin to react before Miriam and her accomplices spring their trap.'

'That is very curious indeed,' replied Jean, now thinking hard himself.

'If that is the case, then it suggests the future is still mutable and subject to change,' he explained. 'So perhaps we can avoid this ambush all together now that you have told us about it.'

Marlow still appeared concerned about the prospect of taking a step closer to the vision in which he'd seen Selene get seriously hurt, but we had little choice but to go and meet with Jenkins if we wanted to avoid being stuck in New Delhi for two whole weeks while our permits were processed.

We discussed the matter for another half hour or so, but everyone was in agreement about what Jenkins was likely to want from us.

'The difficulty, of course is that he could ask us anything,' Jean conceded, thoughtfully. 'Why were we walking with a merchant caravan from Tehran to Samarkand? Why do we want to travel through the northern provinces, rather than just hop on another train? The questions are endless.'

'Perhaps,' Selene agreed. 'But remember what I've always told you about a good deception.

'Keep it simple, and as close to the truth as possible!'

'You have a suggestion in mind, Ms Autieri,' Jean asked, a twinkle of curiosity in his eyes.

'Gentlemen, you know one another from Africa, where you spent your time travelling and hunting. What would be so very unusual about you continuing to do the same across central Asia, and now down through India and across the Gangetic plain. The area is after all rich in sites sacred to both Hindus and Buddhists, and if I am not mistaken, there are several other game rich hunting areas along the watery margin that exists at the base of the mountains.

'Your insight is as always inspired,' replied Jean, an even more devilish twinkle now filling his eyes.

'Of course, there is perhaps another way in which we might hope to avoid some of the more difficult questions,' he continued, clearly entertained at his own idea. 'A strategy which I believe you demonstrated perfectly when we were questioned by the police in Nice!'

'Jean, I love you as a brother,' Marlow observed, with a generous smile on his face. 'But even I am unsettled by how much you enjoy your own jokes before you've shared them!'

'Ah, Robert, one day I am hopeful you will all see and enjoy the world as much as I do.'

'Good lord,' Harry observed with mock alarm. 'Can you imagine!'

'Thank you, Harrison,' Jean continued, without losing a beat.

'But to return to our interview with Mr Jenkins.

'We have all guessed why it is he wishes to meet with us. He has a problem that he thinks we may be able to help him with.

'Now, as far as he is concerned, we are simple

sportsmen and tourists. We wish to go one way because we have heard that the northern provinces and in particular the Kaziranga game reserve are worthy of a visit, but if we are delayed, or worse our permissions are declined, what would such men do?

'Yes, of course!' Peter added. 'If we were just interested in the game, then we'd move on to the next area, Burma or Ceylon perhaps?'

'Precisely,' Jean conceded, smiling. 'So, if this Jenkins wants to put us to work. Would we allow him to dictate the terms, or would we perhaps try to strike a mutually beneficial deal?'

'A deal? What kind of thing have you got in mind?' Marlow asked.

'Well, to begin,' Jean explained, a large smile on his face as he counted off our demands on the fingers of one hand. 'It would be a nice gesture I think for Mr Jenkins to provide our horses and provisions.'

'Of course,' Harry added, shaking his head in wonder.

'Secondly, we will want our permits to be ready within two days, or we will simply move on.'

'Thirdly, our permits will last for at least twelve months, so that we can take our time, if the hunting proves any good.

'Fourth and final, we will want a bounty payable on any good intelligence we pass back to the commissioner's office.'

'Are you sure you wouldn't like poor Mr Jenkins to provide us with ammunition for our rifles while he's at it?' Harry asked, facetiously.

'Harrison, really!' Jean replied, now rolling his eyes in mock disbelief. 'Our ammunition would obviously be included in the provisions that comes with the horses.'

I couldn't help but chuckle slightly at the sheer daring which Jean exhibited.

'And you think we should just stroll in with this list

and demand the lot?' Marlow also asked, an incredulous smile on his face.

'Robert, honestly you should know better. If we wish our ruse to work, we must be daring.'

Like a whirlwind, Jean had once again persuaded us to follow his lead, and the following morning I left the hotel once more with my Bedouin robes under my arm, on the way to a local bath house, where I met Marlow and Jean to get changed into our travelling clothes, before then striding through the broad and quiet streets like a three-man invasion force on the way to the commissioner's offices on Connaught Place.

To say that we caused a stir as we entered the offices and presented ourselves to his staff, would be an understatement, but whether it was confusion or amusement they felt, they hid it well, and soon we were sat in the shade of a big mulberry tree in the private gardens at the back of the commissioner's offices, drinking tea and coffee while several plates of fresh sandwiches were brought out to us.

Jenkins, unlike his staff, was royally entertained by our get-up, but despite his smiles and compliments, this mild mannered polo enthusiast that I'd met at the stables was otherwise completely unfazed as he talked to us.

Jean of course attempted to exploit the situation by delivering what we hoped would be our distracting first salvo.

'Commissioner Jenkins,' he began, 'I appreciate that the situation you wish to discuss with us may seem a little delicate in nature. So perhaps we may summarise our own thinking and assumptions in order to speed things up?'

'Of course, M'sieur De Gris, if you feel that would be of help to us, then please summarise away,' Jenkins replied, helping himself to another cucumber sandwich from a plate overflowing with them.

Between the three of us we outlined our suspicions

that he wanted us to work for him in an 'undercover' capacity in order to root-out any Chinese backed dissenters or trouble makers in the northern provinces, and how in our Bedouin robes, while we couldn't hope to pass as members of the native Indian community, we could at least pass for non-Europeans.

'Excellent,' Jenkins commented, finishing off another sandwich and picking up his teacup. 'You're aware of the pressures which the government is currently operating under, and where you might come in. 'Now, suppose you tell me what you think you're worth.'

He was too confident by far, and clearly had much more experience than us in conducting this kind of negotiation. But, we'd prepared, so we gave him the list of what we wanted, the horses and equipment, the year-long permits and cash rewards for each piece of useful intelligence that we provided.

'Hmm, that's a reasonable list of demands,' Jenkins observed, sipping his tea and leaving us to stew for a moment. 'But, you know, you can tell a great deal about someone from what they want. You've got to be able to see through the trickery and slight-of-hand that's used to distract your attention, but if you can do that, then surprising things can be learned.

'Now,' he continued, holding up his hand as Jean attempted to interrupt him. 'Let's see if I read your list of demands accurately.

'We can start with the monetary compensation,' he began, selecting a nice-looking fruit scone, which he carefully cut in half while continuing to talk to us. 'This is so obviously an irrelevance for you, I really think you could have tried harder to come up with something more credible. Perhaps something like the services of an expert guide. That would have been much more realistic. But for a group of people staying at the most expensive hotel in the city and who shop for horses and mules without bartering with the stable owner, money is clearly not a consideration.

'Likewise, the horses and provisions, this is just more of the same, especially after I checked with Mr Suri the stable owner after you left, and discovered from him that your only real concern was getting the animals and equipment you needed.

'This leaves us with the permit,' he said, looking up at each of us over his cake, knowing full well he had us dead to rights.

'If you'd gone for two months, maybe three, that would be pretty much standard, and would have suggested you're not all that bothered about where you head as long as you don't have to rush. But twelve months, oh my goodness, that tells me you want to go there desperately, and for you to be contemplating staying for that length of time! Well, you must be after something very valuable to be prepared to spend a whole year looking for it, especially through the insect filled, humid and monsoon struck months as well as the milder, fresher good months.

'Yes, that's your weakness right there,' he continued, finally taking a bite of his scone.

'You also failed to consider the problem from my side, and what kind of assurances I might want that you're actually going to do any work for me once you leave New Delhi, and not just use the permits and equipment I provide to pursue your own intriguing ends.'

'And yet, M'sieur, you do not seem unduly surprised at the lack of dexterity in our negotiations with you,' Jean observed. 'Does this mean you have an offer you still wish to make?'

'Naturally, M'sieur De Gris, naturally,' Jenkins replied, pleasantly. 'And while I'm tempted to ask you about the true nature of your visit, and why you require such a long permit for the northern territories, I will content myself with your reassurance that you will do nothing to interfere with or harm the Crown's interests here in India.'

He paused for a moment while we all gave him our assurances on this matter, and then clearly satisfied, he continued.

'Good. Now, as I see it you are all observant and capable people, so if you want a twelve-month permit, you'll have to earn it. I will give you the horses, pack animals and provisions. I will also find a learned local guide for you, who will be instructed to take you to wherever you wish, provided it is within the northern territories, and who will also feedback to me every once in a while, about your progress.

'This man will share what intelligence we have with you, as well as advising you on any local travel arrangements that may assist, or sensibilities that you should take into account.

'In return, as you provide my officials with useful intelligence about the nature of any insurgents or individuals you think may be acting as foreign agents, I will reward you with extensions to your travel permits. Each solid lead you provide me with will earn you an extra month on your permits.' he said, holding up his hand again as we all started to protest at the amount of intelligence we were being asked to provide about people who would, by their very nature, be trying their best to avoid detection.

'However, when you provide me with six solid leads or useful pieces of intelligence then I will extend the remaining duration on your permits to twelve months.

'Finally, I will provide you with a letter of introduction, should you encounter any resistance from my own officials, as well as the necessary credentials for you to command the use of local police or army units, purely in the apprehension of identified trouble makers.

'Does that seem like a reasonable compromise, gentlemen?'

'Yes M'sieur,' Jean replied, thoughtfully. 'And you will be able to make these arrangements quite quickly?'

'Indeed I shall,' Jenkins replied, sitting back to regard us fully over his cup of tea. 'The necessary paperwork and credentials will be delivered to your hotel under the false name that Mr Whittaker here is checked in under. The guide, horses and provisions will be ready tomorrow morning at the stables.

'One final thing gentlemen, while the guide who will be accompanying you will be instructed to send word of your progress and movements, I would like you to send me more detailed weekly updates, as and when you are able, explaining where you are heading, how long you will be staying and what, if any leads you are following.'

Jenkins had us, and we knew it, so after exchanging a quick glance between us, we indicated his proposal was acceptable, but just as I thought we were finished, Marlow added one final comment.

'While I'm sure you have your speculations about the true purpose for our visit to India,' Marlow began, fixing Jenkins with that impossibly calm gaze of his. 'Especially as I'm sure you have already identified the academic background which some of our party share. For the moment we are striving to keep our presence in India as quiet as possible, something which may not sit well with an administration and bureaucracy the size and complexity of your commission.'

'That you were trying to keep a low profile and that your party includes two eminently qualified archaeologists, did pique my interest,' Jenkins admitted, drumming his fingers quietly upon the arm of his chair while he considered. 'I could arrange for your permits to be drawn up under the names you are checked into the Imperial Hotel with, instead of the real names you appear to have originally submitted your request under…

'I can also keep the nature of this arrangement confined to my senior staff, rather than having it processed as normal by their various departments.

'However, Gentlemen, if you give me any cause to suspect you are not acting within the confines of the law, or the best interests of His Majesty's government, I will not hesitate to involve any and every resource available to me to find out what it is you are engaged in.'

This was more than reasonable from Jenkins, and as we finished our lunch with him, we thanked him and stressed how much we appreciated his trust and support.

SOURCE OF THE GANGES

I T SEEMS LIKE NO TIME at all between when we are having lunch with Jenkins in his garden and when we are riding north along the road to Haridwar, passing the spectacular Red Fort of the Moghul emperors in old Delhi, and through the city's crowded streets.

My eyes were hungry to see more of the old city, but there just wasn't enough time to take in the detail, as we moved steadily through the streets, passing countless covered bazaars full of precious metals, fabrics and spices.

Far too quickly we had made our way through the centre and were heading out through the suburbs into the verdant landscape of the Ganges plain, with its hazy far off horizon, upon which no sign of the mighty Himalaya could yet be seen.

There was a simple beauty to that landscape, with its apparently never-ending fields of bright green crops, interspersed only occasionally by a solitary shade tree or small copse of bamboo.

It was easy to imagine how great spiritual enlightenment could come to anyone prepared to sit beneath one of those trees and contemplate the hazy line where the earth met the sky. In that moment and in that place, I think I could have happily found myself one such shady spot to watch the world go by for a month or two, it was so mesmerising in its beauty.

The reality though, was that this journey north was taking us a hundred miles and at least a week out of our way, into the foothills of the Himalaya, rather than eastward along the route of the lower Ganges.

Haridwar is located at the point where the mountains meet the plain, and is the start of the sacred river Ganges. It is because of this position and other legends that surround it that this city is considered one of the seven most sacred pilgrimage sites, visited by thousands of Hindu pilgrims every month from all over the sub-continent, but especially those from the north.

This was Jenkins best guess as to where the agents of the Chinese government may be operating. Blending in with pilgrims on their way to and from these sacred sites, all the while slowly sowing the seeds of discontent amongst men and women who then return like disease carriers to their homes, carrying the now sprouting lies and half-truths that have been cultivated in their minds, to bear a much later crop of civil disobedience and social unrest.

For us however, this trip to Haridwar means heading in exactly the wrong direction. We want to be travelling eastward down the meandering path of the great Ganges river, not northwards, upstream and back into the mountains.

'I must confess, Harrison,' I can hear Androus comment, from just ahead of me as we make our way toward the town of Baraut, one day's ride from Delhi.

'Despite the inconvenience of this detour, I'm quite looking forward to seeing Haridwar, a place of which I've read so much during the past year.'

'I remember you mentioning somewhere to the north of old Delhi,' Harry replied, before continuing on in a quieter voice. 'Weren't you considering it as a potential location for the lost temple at one point?'

'Yes, that's right. I thought it quite a promising option to begin with,' Androus replied, amiably. 'But after reading several accounts of the different pilgrimages which the devout make to this part of the Himalaya, and cross referencing the details with the directions described on the tablets, I realised the job was impossible to do at a distance. If we stood any chance at all we'd have to come here in person.'

'Ah, gentlemen,' broke in Abhra our newly appointed guide. 'If you are interested in the sacred sites of the Ganga, then surely there is no better place for you to begin your journey than in ancient Haridwar, or Gangadawara as it was once known.'

'You are familiar with the history of Haridwar?' Androus asks, instantly seduced by our guides infectious cheerfulness and good humour.

'Am I familiar with the history of Haridwar, Sahib Chuk,' our guide replies with mock disbelief, picking up on Harry's nickname for Androus. 'What kind of a guide would I be if I could not tell you all you wish to know of Haridwar, one of India's most sacred cities.'

I had to admit I was beginning to like our government appointed guide, Abhra Balakrishnan. Not that I didn't have my reservations to begin with, after meeting him at the stables where his primary concern appeared to be the provisions we would be taking with us, to make sure we weren't 'skimping on any of the essentials'.

He was, in many ways the very picture of a well-dressed urban Indian modernist, wearing the smart Indian style shirt and waistcoat made so popular by the current nationalist leader Jawaharlal Nehru. Though in contrast to the slender Nehru, Abhra could only be described as well-fed.

Having said that, while larger in the waistcoat than many of his countrymen, Abhra was also exhaustingly optimistic in both his outlook and general helpfulness, provided that his duties did not require anything more tiring than sitting on a horse, and even that, he only agreed to because we weren't taking a cart or other vehicle with us.

For the rest of us, sitting astride a horse was better than being cooped up inside a railway carriage or an elegant hotel, but we were still very much in the habit of walking for numerous hours a day, and the enforced leisure and heat of the previous week had led most of the group to express their heartfelt relief at getting on our way again.

As Abhra began to expound upon the many historic temples that surrounded Haridwar to Androus and Harry, I suddenly felt as though I'd had enough of plodding along on my grey mare, the same energetic animal I'd ridden around the park in New Delhi.

I either wanted to let the animal have its head for a while and enjoy a good gallop, or I wanted to get off and at least stretch my legs while we travelled at such a slow pace. But we were still far too close to the old city, and as a consequence were stuck in a seemingly never-ending line of slow-moving carts and pedestrians, as local farmers and merchants brought goods to and from the markets. Any notion I might have of just going around them was also quashed by the rich green crops of wheat and barley, lentils and rice that stretched for as far as the eye could see, and right up to the road edge in most places.

I could've wound my way in an out of the various travellers on the road if I'd had to, but instead I decided to pull up my horse and dismount, so that I could walk for a while.

'That, George, is an excellent idea,' Jean observed from beside me, as he too dismounted his horse.

With the carts, wagons, overladen bicycles and barrows that were travelling in the opposite direction we could only travel two abreast along the road, so Jean was able to walk along beside me, leading his large chestnut coloured mare with a white flash on its forehead.

Ahead of us, Peter and Selene were at the front of our little column, followed by Marlow and Abhra, then Androus and Harry, and finally myself and Jean, with several of the riding horses also leading a pack horse with our baggage strapped to it.

It instantly felt better to be walking, though upon hearing us stop and dismount, Abhra looked around and seemed genuinely troubled at the idea that we might want to walk in preference to sitting our horses.

'Sahibs, it is still many miles before we reach the town of Baraut, the next stop on our journey,' he advised, before shrugging his shoulders when we indicated we would still prefer to walk.

Over the next hour, the slow pace and continual heat was enough for the others, barring the increasingly alarmed Abhra, to dismount from their horses and begin walking. Consequently, when we finally came within sight of Baraut a few hours later, it was with a blend of concern and embarrassment that our guide pleaded with us to re-mount our horses and enter the town like 'respectable people'.

'Gentlemen, lady, please consider remounting your horses and riding into the town before we get any closer. For all of you to walk beside such fine animals on such a warm day will make you seem like madmen, and it will be much more difficult for us to find accommodation in a good hotel.'

It was still a near thing, but in our robes, we would already attract a good deal of attention, so reluctantly we succumbed to Abhra's pleadings and remounted our horses.

Over the next two days we fell into a similar routine of riding or walking our way north through the flatlands of the Ganges plain. On the second day the ghostly outline of the impossibly grand Himalayan mountains came into view, and then with each passing mile the great peaks became more distinct.

The other travellers on the road gradually changed also as we moved north, and instead of just farmers and merchants we started to see more and more pilgrims, often walking barefoot over the rough road surface, or bearing some other mark of their devotion and sacrifice. Many wore the simple clothes of a pilgrim, and carried only a begging bowl, which Abhra explained to us would be their only source of food during the several weeks of their pilgrimage.

This was an extraordinary hardship for an individual to impose upon themselves, especially those who travelled from the far south like Kerala or Ceylon.

'Those pilgrims intent upon the greatest demonstration of devotion will travel far beyond Haridwar,' Abhra explained one evening over a meal of pureed lentils and boiled rice. 'Up into the mountains they will go in order to visit the true source of the Ganges, the point where the waters of the sacred river first descended to this earth through the dreadlocked hair of Lord Shiva.'

'Where will these pilgrims stay overnight?' Peter asked, in response.

'That will depend greatly upon their means,' our guide explained, wistfully. 'For those with the financial means, there are many hotels and guest houses along the route where they may recover from the exertions of the road. For the majority though, they will depend upon the shelter offered by the temples along the route, or the charity of the villagers and townspeople who may offer space in their own homes. Those who do not have the strength to travel so far, will simply stop and rest where they can beside the road.'

'Then perhaps, if we wish to succeed in our mission, we too should stay in the places where the pilgrims shelter?' Peter asked, looking at the rest of us for our thoughts.

'Sahib, you are making a cruel joke at your poor servant Abhra's expense?' our guide replied, clearly disturbed at the idea of not staying in a comfortable hotel each night.

'I assure you no joke was intended,' Peter explained, sympathetically. 'Unless you think the people stirring up the sentiment amongst the pilgrims are likely to also be staying in the hotels along the route?'

Clearly that was not something which our erstwhile guide considered very likely, for he made no attempt to persuade us that such a thing was at all plausible. Instead he countered with the more reasonable point that we could hardly go begging for places in villagers homes each evening while riding valuable horses laden with our possessions.

'Unless, gentlemen and lady, you wish to abandon your possessions and travel as poor pilgrims,' he explained, with just a touch of desperation in his eyes at the idea. 'Then it is only the hotels and temples that would seem fitting for you to be staying in.'

It was a fair point. For while we'd arranged with the Commissioner to leave our non-essential possessions back in New Delhi, from where we could request their transfer as and when we needed anything, we still carried a huge wealth of equipment with us by comparison with many of the pilgrims, including our guns and ammunition, changes of clothes, several days' supply of food for us and the animals, books, ledgers, camping equipment and of course the balance of gold and other currencies which we'd taken from the mercenaries that had tried to kill us in Tunis.

The temples though sounded like they might be a good compromise. Reluctantly, perhaps realising he was talking himself out of a comfortable bed for the night, Abhra explained how it was common for wealthier pilgrims to travel from temple to temple, where, as part of their own devotions they would make offerings of food and money not only for their own shelter and accommodation, but also toward the food and shelter which the temples provided to the poor pilgrims free of charge.

'Even the poorest temple will offer those sheltering within their grounds some kind of meal in the evening,' he explained. 'Much of it donated by either the local people or those pilgrims passing through who can afford to offer more.'

This seemed like a good option and so over the next few days, whenever we found ourselves within the vicinity of a reasonable sized temple, we would choose that as our camp for the night, making offerings of a few rupees or bags of rice or lentils in exchange for being allowed to shelter within the grounds.

We had to be careful at these times, especially during the communal meals provided by the temple to try and keep our real identity as Europeans hidden from the other pilgrims.

Abhra was a huge help in these circumstances, as he was able to explain away our strange attire and manners to the other pilgrims without any of us having to try and explain ourselves using the Turkic we'd picked up as we'd travelled along the silk route.

This probably would have been enough for us to be accepted no matter where we travelled on the Gangetic plain, but Abhra, ever resourceful came up with a better cover story after another couple of days.

'Gentlemen, lady,' he began, presenting a small lidded iron pot to us after we'd finished setting up our camp in the grounds of the temple we were staying at.

'May I present you with the remains of your dear friend Manush Hari Chowdary, a former companion to you all in your trading and business ventures across Persia.

'I have to say, while I'm saddened to hear of dear… Manush's passing, I'm struggling to understand why we would be carrying his earthly remains in an old cooking pot?' Peter asked, obviously a little perplexed, like the rest of us about our guides intentions.

'Ah ha!' exclaimed Abhra, in true theatrical fashion. 'But what if I were to explain to you that Manush was a devout Hindu, like myself, and that amongst the devout the River Ganges is most literally believed to be a divine incarnation of the mother goddess, and consequently anyone who bathes in her waters either during their life, or like poor Manush, after his passing, will be blessed by the Goddess and perhaps allowed to escape the great cycle of Samsara.'

'Do I understand you correctly?' Jean asked, with the flicker of a smile passing over his lips. 'That if a Hindu, such as yourself, Abhra, were to die in a foreign land, but his or her ashes were to be returned to the Ganges, then even in death they will receive a blessing which may free them from the cycle of reincarnation?'

'Precisely, Sahib Jean,' Abhra beamed. 'But not just anywhere on the Ganga will convey this blessing for the dead, only at the most holy city of Varanasi, where Lord Shiva is known to have spilled several drops of sacred nectar may the ashes of the dead receive such a blessing, and only the most steadfast of friends would agree to bear the remains of their colleague across the wide lands of India so that he may receive such a blessing.'

'But we are not travelling to Varanasi,' Androus observed.

'This is true,' Abhra conceded, with a slight shrug. 'But who is to say that our non-existent friend Manush did not ask you to bear his remains to each of the most sacred sites on the Ganges from Haridwar to Kanpur, Allahabad and Varanasi?'

'And this would seem credible to any of the pilgrims we may encounter?' Jean asked.

'Not only credible, but for non-Hindus to go to so much trouble, it would seem noble and praiseworthy almost beyond measure.' Abhra conceded.

It was such a small detail, but the more I thought about it the more I realised it rounded out our cover story. Up until now we'd been pinning our hopes on just not looking or sounding like Europeans and in particular not like agents of the government. But this idea of Abhra's, while simple, made sense of our presence in a way which would allow us to pass, if not without notice, at least without suspicion to each of the sacred cities along the Ganges river, culminating in Varanasi. By that time we would hopefully have provided Jenkins with enough information for him to grant us the extended permits that would allow us to travel across north India.

HIMALAYA

B Y THE TIME WE LEAVE SHAMLI, the ghostly outline of the Himalaya could be seen on all but the haziest of days, growing stronger and more distinct with every mile we headed north.

We were on the road again, walking and riding, doing what we all enjoyed most, simply travelling through foreign lands.

Gradually our new routine formed.

We would set off in the early morning without breakfast, leading our horses as we walked for the most part, with even Abhra walking with us for a significant section of the day. We would then find somewhere shaded to stop and rest around midday, when we would eat our first meal and take a couple of hours to relax and talk, planning the route ahead so that we would arrive at a sizeable town or city well before sunset, thus avoiding the hottest part of the day, which was exhausting for both us and our animals.

Along the way Abhra would always maintain a steady stream of conversation, explaining more about the Hindu faith and the ancient legends which the pilgrims around us would already be so well versed in, as well as explaining about the different types of holy men and teachers that we would be likely to encounter around the temples and along the roads, and in particular when we arrived at the holy sites where Jenkins suspected the seeds of discontent were being sown.

This included a bewildering range of Yogis and Swamis, Sadhus, Sanyasi, Pandit, Pujari and Purohits, many of whom would in turn belong to one of several sects or further subdivisions.

In return, and to give even the inexhaustible Abhra

a break, we would, at his request, explain a little about our travels and some of the ancient sites we had visited along the way, from Jerusalem and Corinth, to the Singing Stones in Kenya and Great Zimbabwe. We also explained about our journey with the trade caravan to Samarkand and how we'd all come to adopt the Bedouin style of robes as a protection against the great sandstorms, as well as the daytime heat and night-time cold, which were so common in the trans Caspian region.

He listened with rapt attention at these tales of far-off lands and peoples, asking countless questions about their manners and dress, their food and faiths and habits.

During the evenings, on arriving at the town where we would stay for the night, we would buy supplies and establish our camp, generally in the vicinity of the temple, but a little apart from anyone else, so as not to cause offence or make it obvious when we were speaking in English.

Temples and shrines were everywhere in India. Walls were painted with religious depictions, and often the presence of a local holy site or shrine would be noticeable more on account of the offerings that had been left beside it or the worshippers gathered around it in the process of making their devotions.

Wherever we camped, we would always make a point of waiting patiently in line to pay our respects at the temple, by making an offering of rice, onions, lentils or flour. In exchange asking only their blessings in our broken Turkic or the few Hindu phrases which Abhra was teaching us.

These encounters gave us an excellent opportunity to observe both the pilgrims and the holy men that we were being educated about, so that gradually we started to develop a familiarity with the habits and behaviour of the holy men and pilgrims that were making their way to Haridwar.

With our offerings given and blessings received it was then time for us to settle down for the evening, to look after the animals and make our camp as comfortable and vermin free as possible for the evening.

This was also the time when Abhra could sow the details of our back-story among any of the pilgrims who showed any interest in us.

For our part, we used this time to quietly discuss our observations of the day, our plans or progress, as well as to eat our main meal of the day, frequently provided by the temple, or cooked over a low fire where we were camping.

We still weren't used to the food, and now that we were walking for fifteen or twenty miles a day again, it was an added pressure we could've done without, but thankfully, the ruse which Abhra had invented for us allowed us some leeway, and he used this to find us some cooked meat whenever he could, but even with this extra food, we all still felt hungry most of the time.

The practicalities aside, the closer we drew to Haridwar, the more distracting and fascinating the stream of pilgrims heading the same way became.

What had been a handful of figures as we'd left Delhi, had now become thousands of people as we began the final day of travel to the sacred city.

Despite the fact that I recognised them as pilgrims on a conscious level of my mind, subconsciously, the sheer volume of people making their way north along the roads made me think there must be some other reason for so many people to be travelling in the same direction as us. But when I asked, Abhra simply shook his head with the gentlest of smiles before addressing us all.

'Lady and gentlemen,' he began, from horseback, while the rest of us continued to walk.

'This year is a very special year in the Hindu calendar, only one year in twelve does the great Kumbh Mela take place, so a great many people and a great many holy men and women will travel here to celebrate it. Perhaps even as many people as live in the great city of London will travel here to Haridwar over the next few weeks.'

We all nodded our understanding at these words, but I still couldn't help but think our guide was a little naïve in comparing the number of people that might be turning up to this religious festival with the millions that lived in London.

'It will be very crowded,' he continued. 'Very difficult to find somewhere good for us to make our camp and stable our animals.

'It will also be very easy for you to get lost amongst the many people and the many streets and gathering places, so even if we must travel slower than the trees grow, we must stay together and not become separated.'

By mid-afternoon the constant line of pilgrims which surrounded us was periodically slowing our pace to a halt, before once again moving forward at a shuffle. The sheer mass of humanity seemed to have suddenly built up to the point where people were everywhere on the road and beside it.

It was already an extraordinary sight to witness, thousands of pilgrims filling every square foot of road and verge as we shuffled toward the city. Then without warning, at a bend in the road around one of those huge solitary shade trees we suddenly catch sight of the Ganges and the antique city of Haridwar a mile or so ahead.

There were low foothills to either side of the city, but the countryside immediately below this sacred place is so flat that the vast volume of water in the Ganges cascades over a final set of falls and then splits into a dozen separate channels, almost like the river has formed a delta across the plain, or thinks it has reached the sea, rather than still being nearly two thousand miles away from it.

But its beauty and the majesty of the scene was enough to catch my breath.

I just couldn't believe what my eyes were showing me, for everywhere in and around the city there was a strange shifting quality, almost like a heat haze was rising in the foreground, or the light was reflecting off the rippling river in an odd way.

After what feels like an age, my mind finally grasps the scale and context of what my eyes are seeing, and with a shock I realise the place is literally covered in people, like bees swarming over a hive. There are tens of thousands of people here. They are thronging along streets, crowding upon balconies and rooftops and even massing in huge numbers down to the river's edge and onto the islands between the river tributaries.

'Incroyable!' I hear Jean quietly comment from beside me, as he too gets to see the view of the city that we're heading towards.

'Just as I begin to think I am developing an understanding of the people and culture of this strange land,' he explains, falling back into the Turkic language which we have all been using. 'I witness something which makes me realise I have not even developed the understanding of a child.'

We travel on for another two hours, eventually crossing the mighty river and winding our excruciatingly slow way through the streets until we reach the outskirts of the sacred city, before stopping outside the offices of what Abhra informs us is a merchant's guild property, with which his family is connected.

'The guild does very little business in Haridwar, but they maintain these offices and grounds for the convenience of its members,' he explains.

'And you think they will have sufficient space left during the festival to accommodate us?' Peter asks, rather hopefully.

'No, no, Sahib MacHandru,' our guide replies patiently, while we picket our horses in a line outside. 'The accommodation within the guild building is quite limited and must be arranged many months, if not years in advance, but the grounds contain a sizeable fruit orchard and stables within which we should be able to keep our horses, but where we should also find space to make a camp.

We wait patiently while Abhra goes into the guild hall to make the necessary arrangements, and we are rewarded a few minutes later with the news that several of the rooms are surprisingly still free for our use, as a large party that were due to arrive from Bombay several days ago have failed to show up, and as our guide had apparently sent a telegram requesting accommodation before we left New Delhi, the rooms are now ours.

It takes us almost as long to carry our belongings into the building and up the stairs to the apartment where our rooms are located as it would have taken us to set up our camp. But at least when we return later on, we will be able to remove our disguises and talk to one another in English if we wish.

For the moment though, we need to see to our animals and source both wood and fresh provisions, all of which, Abhra assures us should still be readily available despite the colossal numbers of people visiting the city.

We also need to find our bearings in the city, so that we can safely find our way back to the guild hall, but also to enable us to accurately report the location of any useful intelligence we might happen upon.

To help us in this, Abhra begins by drawing a rough map of the city and the location of the various outlying temples and shrines. Next, he marks the location of the guild-hall and then the different places where pilgrims can make their way down to bathe in the waters of the Ganges.

Large steps called Ghats have been constructed in most places to facilitate this bathing. These are often the most crowded areas he informs us, and probably the least likely of the places where we will find either fake or real holy men. Many of these he informs us will be found in a heavily tented area where the majority of the holy men, but especially the Sadhus will be found, those who renounce all worldly belongings and often walk around without even clothing, just ashes to cover their skin.

We each make a copy of the map which Abhra has drawn, most of us taking copious notes to go with it, and then it's time to head out, in pairs, into this strangest of strange lands.

THE PITCHER FESTIVAL

I FELT I SHOULD BE ACCLIMATISING to India by now, and the relentless barrage of the new and strange. But Haridwar was so far beyond my ability to comprehend that in mere minutes I was feeling overwhelmed by the constant assault upon my senses.

I'd joined Marlow to complete our tasks and then begin our exploration of the city, but even he seemed ill at ease in this place, and more than once I notice him involuntarily recoil from something, before clenching his fists to get a grip on himself.

In fact, watching Marlow, and seeing those little indications of his discomfort helps to take my mind off my own problems.

Then I realise, it's the crowds of people that Marlow is recoiling at. This man, who feels so at ease in the wilderness, does not like to be surrounded by such a huge mass of humanity. He is forcing himself to get on with our errands, but he is having to exert his will to do so.

Unbidden the description that Agostine had given of Marlow's early life comes flooding into my mind.

'…he was raised in west Africa by his adoptive parents who were working there as missionaries, and he'd come close to going completely native in his teens, spending days at first and then weeks away from home in the jungle, as much a wild creature as a civilised

human being, before being sent back to England to bring him back in line.'

As much a wild creature as a civilised human being… the phrase echoes around my mind.

A wild creature, suddenly dropped into the centre of Haridwar during one of the largest festivals in India and surrounded by hundreds of thousands of pilgrims, was bound to be uncomfortable, just as Marlow now appeared to be.

He was beginning to attract unnecessary attention, constantly pulling at his robes and fidgeting with his hands as he scanned the crowds. I had to get him away from the street to somewhere a little quieter, if it existed, or I wasn't sure what he'd do.

As we crossed a narrow side-street, I noticed a splash of greenery down the road, and on impulse I pulled at Marlow's sleeve and indicated we should go that way.

There were still dozens of people around as we made our way toward the verdant green at the end of the street, where we found a small shrine to Hanuman the monkey god. It was well tended and cared for by someone, who also watered a young fig tree that had grown up and bushed out around it.

It was an oasis of calm by comparison with the main thoroughfare, and as we entered, a chai seller appeared and sold us two cups of strong sweet tea, poured from a large polished copper urn strapped to his back.

'You looked like you needed to get away from the crush,' I commented to Marlow as he finished his tea.

'Yes,' he replied, as he waved down the salesman for another cup.

'I've never liked crowds,' he continued. 'But the sheer number of people here is beyond anything I've ever experienced. Everywhere you look there are so many pressing in around me, I feel like I can barely breathe.'

'I was feeling very much the same,' I admitted,

sipping at my own second cup of tea. 'Perhaps we could try the crowds again for a short distance until we find another refuge and some more tea?'

Marlow didn't seem enthusiastic about the prospect of returning to the busy main road, but at least he seemed himself again, as we made our way back into the crush.

It was still a while until the sun would be setting, but it was that time of day when everyone begins to think of their evening meal, so as we made our way over the next hour, the oppressive density of the crowds lessened until we could walk and talk side by side, rather than having to follow one another in single file.

I slowly started to build a picture of the street plan in my mind as we walked, and while I still checked the hand-drawn map I had from time to time, I no longer really needed it.

Marlow also seemed to relax once the crowds lessened, so much so that on the way back to the merchants guild, with the supplies we'd agreed to pick up, we both felt confident enough to start taking shortcuts through the smaller streets, and even stopped off to try out our fledgling Hindi on a couple of the street vendors who were selling some divinely spiced and delicious treats. These were exactly what we need to boost our food intake, and they tasted so nice it would have been rude of us not to take some back with us.

We were the last ones to return to the hall, and Abhra, perhaps anticipating how difficult we would all find our first experience of the city, had already prepared a small feast of rice and duck with fragrant spices, which he informed us was a popular Tibetan dish.

All that was needed to finish it was a handful of the fresh coriander that we'd returned with, and some butter which one of the other groups had brought back.

As Marlow and I dropped off the rest of the provisions I looked around the room and discovered everyone, with the possible exception of Jean and Selene, appeared to be absolutely exhausted.

'I cannot believe anyone could get accustomed to being surrounded by so many people,' Androus commented, from the low bed he was sitting on the edge of. 'Even moving a short way down a street was exhausting.'

'Ah yes, Sahib Chuk,' Abhra responded. 'And yet I assure you that within two, perhaps three days at the most, you will be so accustomed to moving through the streets you will barely notice the multitude of people that you currently feel are pressing in around you.'

'You'll forgive me if I remain sceptical of that particular claim,' Peter commented, from the other side of the room and one of the other low beds.

'It is only natural that you should Sahib,' Abhra replied with a patient smile, as he continued to tend the food he was preparing. 'But I have travelled to this and other festivals with foreigners like yourselves on many occasions, all of whom were convinced, like you, that only those of us born and raised in the great lands of India could possibly feel relaxed in the presence of so many people, and yet, lady, sahibs, I assure you, within a few days they have all learned that Abhra was indeed most correct.'

'I would like to believe you,' offered Selene. 'Though I would feel more comfortable if my understanding of Hindi were better.'

'Yes, this too is true,' Abhra conceded. 'This is why I have been attempting to teach you a little of my language on our way here. Though it does take some time to develop an ear even for this most perfect of languages, especially with all the different dialects you will hear across the many areas of India.

'But,' he continued, after looking out of the window at the now golden sunlight. 'Our meal is ready to be eaten, and we must be quick if we are to witness the aarti devotions.'

Realising we were not familiar with this particular part of the festival, Abhra went on to explain the aarti ceremony while he served the food. Describing how it was a daily occurrence, during which the pilgrims would again gather by the river, but this time it was to sing and play music while they offered flame and light to the gods, as a sign of their humility.

He went on to explain, that this was one of the more relaxed activities practiced both during the festival and at other times, which he urged us to attend every evening if we wanted to 'acclimatise' to our surroundings as quickly as possible.

We were all hungry after our busy day, but at Abhra's urging we ate only a light meal before heading out again to witness this evening ritual of flame and light, with the intention of eating again, later when we returned.

The streets were busy as we made our way through the town, but now there were pilgrims carrying ornately decorated lanterns or lamps, bundles of brightly coloured flowers or loose petals, which combined gave the movement of the crowds an altogether more relaxed and festive atmosphere.

The trip to the river was only a short distance, but with the slowly undulating crowds that would slow to a complete stop once in a while, it took us a little longer to get to the shore, where thousands of people had already congregated.

At Abhra's urging we made our way along the waterfront until we found an area with a low pier that provided us with a good view of the Ganges.

The last slice of the sun's disk lay on the horizon as we settled into our position, allowing Marlow to indulge his usual evening custom, and then as the fiery disk settled behind the horizon, and the light turned slowly from gold to copper and then deep red, then the lanterns we had seen people carrying were brought forward, toward the water's edge and lit, illuminating the river in a scintillating array of flame and light.

The scene had a natural beauty, enhanced by the

singing and chanting of the pilgrims around us, and I felt myself relax. Content to listen to the soft music and watch the bejewelled water as it flowed past, but eventually my eyes lifted of their own accord to look around at the other sections on the river, both above and below us, as well as on the opposite bank.

Everywhere, relaxed and smiling people were doing the same as us. A few were clapping their hands in time with the music, while others simply talked, watched or made their prayers.

Amongst the crowds there were jugglers and dancers responding to the music, whirling and spinning smaller lamps around themselves, while other pilgrims came forward to the water's edge with flowers in shallow dishes in which candles and incense burned.

They placed these tiny candlelit bowls gently into the water as they offered their prayers, before finally letting the current carry them away from the bank and into the river proper.

These makeshift boats were rocked and splashed by the currents in the river, with some being sunk or extinguished. But most of them seemed to survive, gradually building in number until the entire river was alight with golden light.

I didn't know how long the tiny lamps would continue to burn, but as the glowing stream of lights found their way to the calmer waters below Haridwar, where the river split into numerous broad channels, the stream of tiny lights slowly divided, with groups of the fragile little boats floating along the new river channels, almost like a second heaven of stars against the dark waters.

It was a beautiful and humbling sight to watch those offerings make their fragile way down the river.

'These tiny flames are a beautiful metaphor for this most unique of faiths,' Jean commented quietly in English from beside me. 'The individual embarks upon life alone, like these tiny floating lamps as they are released from the shore, then becomes one with the universe and part of something bigger when they reach the centre of the river…'

'Only to return to individuality when the river splits,' I replied, continuing his metaphor. 'Like being reincarnated.'

'Precisely,' Jean breathed, clearly moved by the experience.

We watched those drifting flames for about two hours before winding our way back to the guild hall in silence.

I couldn't yet pretend to understand this strange country and the faiths which seemed so closely woven into the fabric of everyday society, but like my experience with the supposedly more primitive peoples of east Africa, I found myself once again wondering if it were not our sophisticated western cultures that were the primitive ones, because we'd lost touch with something simpler and honest in our natures, something almost elemental that we in the west rarely appreciated.

INTRODUCTIONS

THE FOLLOWING MORNING, we began our mission for Jenkins in earnest. We'd spent nearly a week getting to Haridwar, which had given us some precious time to acclimatise to our new surroundings, learn a little of the Hindi language and, perhaps more importantly than anything, to build our understanding of the different types of holy men and their roles within the Hindu faith.

When we added these things to our disguises and back story, we hoped it would be enough to enable us to spot the charlatans posing as holy men, that we'd been sent to find.

'Remember, Lady, Gentlemen,' Abhra reminded us

before we left the guild hall. 'The Hindu faith contains many contradictions, because there are many routes to enlightenment, some of which will only be relevant to a few, others relevant to the many. But perhaps unique to all is the respect for the journey we must all make, perhaps through many lives, before we will eventually escape the cycle of samsara.

'For this reason, it is unthinkable to us that anyone should claim to be a holy man or woman capable of helping others on their journey, when they are not and cannot.

'Some may perhaps think they have made more progress than they have, while others will have made more progress than they realise. Both of these and a thousand other permutations you will encounter today and in the days that follow.

'More guidance than this I cannot give, for like my fellow Hindus I am blind in this matter. But all the same I wish you luck in your venture, or perhaps I should say, good hunting.'

We split into groups, as we had the previous day, with Marlow and I agreeing to be the ones who would present our warrant from Commissioner Jenkins to the local city official, in the form of one Captain Butterworth, who Jenkins informed us, was the local captain of police and a good man, who had been based in Haridwar for nearly twenty years. During that time he had mastered several of the local languages and also married a local woman.

In many ways he sounded like a much better candidate than any of us to go spying on the local holy men, which we'd suggested to Jenkins at the time, only to receive a genuine chuckle in response, along with the rather enigmatic explanation that 'Any Chinese agent worth their salt would see Butterworth coming from a mile away, disguised or not!'

With this thought still in my mind, we made our way to the police station where Butterworth was based.

We had no appointment, so we hoped that if we called in early, we might catch him before his daily duties took him elsewhere.

The police station was easy enough to find, and like much of Haridwar was built in the Moghul style with a high arched entrance and battlement style walls constructed out of the local pinkish sandstone.

Unsure what kind of reception we might receive in our Bedouin robes, we strolled in and presented ourselves at the tall, leather fronted reception desk, much to the surprise of the desk sergeant, who eyed us suspiciously, as we joined the small queue of other people waiting to be seen.

There were quite a few police officers and clerical staff coming and going through doorways and corridors leading off the reception, as well as several locals and pilgrims waiting patiently in a waiting room to one side.

One after another the sergeant, who had the square shoulders and erect posture of a former military man listened to what those in the queue in front of us had to say, clearly understanding English when he was addressed in it, as well as the Hindi or Urdu which most people seemed to speak in the north of India.

Most of the time he nodded his head as he took some notes on a form, and gave them a number before dispatching them to the waiting room while he handed the completed form to one of his colleagues on the desk next to him.

This seemed like the standard routine for those in the queue, with the exception of one elderly looking gentlemen, who evidently had something more serious to report, and for whom the sergeant immediately summoned one of his staff, who then took the individual through one of the side doors instead.

Finally, it was our turn to step forward, at which we bowed and presented our written warrant, without saying a word.

Silently the sergeant unfolded the document from the regional commissioner, and with a barely perceptible stiffening of his already ramrod straight posture, he read what it contained.

Without saying a word to us, the sergeant asked one of his subordinates to take over from him, and then motioned for us to follow as he stepped round the corner of his high interview desk to personally escort us further into the police station, revealing that he was wearing a highland kilt in the process.

Quickly and quietly the tartan wearing sergeant led us through a door, into what appeared to be a mail room where several people were busy sorting letters and parcels, then through another door and down a long corridor flanked on both sides by offices.

As we passed the last of these, the sergeant quietly turned to us and informed us that we could dispense with our disguises if we wished as we wouldn't be likely to run into any locals or pilgrims from this point onward.

'Thank you,' Marlow replied, untucking his veil to reveal his face, complete with week old beard and moustache.

'You're clearly expecting us,' he continued. 'Have you received the letter from Commissioner Jenkins already.

'Yes, surr!' the sergeant replied with what sounded like a Glasgow accent, and casting a glance back at each of us, now that he could see our faces. 'It arrived two days past, so we've been watchin' furr ya ever since, though o' course we had no ken what we might be lookin' furr.

'Ya arrived yester eve?'

We confirmed we had, before explaining where we were staying.

He continued to lead us through a maze of corridors, presumably on the way to see Captain Butterworth.

'Ye gentle-men may be wantin' to cover yurr faces agin now,' he explained, just before leading us up some stairs into a high-ceilinged reception area outside the captain's office. 'The commander is often visited by local dignitry's and holy gentle-men during the festivities.'

After indicating some seats where we should wait, the sergeant spoke to the clerk who was manning the reception, who in turn stepped inside the office for a few moments before inviting us all to go in and see the captain.

Captain Butterworth, it had to be said, would indeed be a hard man to miss. He must had stood at least six feet six inches tall in his stocking feet, barrel-chested with a huge handlebar moustache and an eye-patch over his left eye.

As if that weren't enough, he also walked with a cane and a pronounced limp, which didn't seem to stop him covering the large room in just a few giant strides before grasping our hands in a firm handshake, and waving us over to some padded leather chairs around a low coffee table.

'Will you join me for a cup of tea?' he asked simply by way of introduction.

'You too, Studgeon,' he said, addressing the sergeant.

'Thank ya, surr!' the sergeant replied, before sitting in the comfortable chair without allowing his spine to relax an inch.

Butterworth then rang a small bell on the table and ordered some tea, before finally settling down to talk to us.

'You can relax for the moment gentlemen,' he informed us. 'Walker, my aide de camp will bring the tea, so you can dispense with your disguises if you wish.'

Thanking him, we removed our veils, but kept our turbans tied, as these took several minutes to both remove and replace, which meant a quick change was not possible.

The tea arrived and we turned our attention to the problem at hand.

After introducing ourselves and accepting some already much needed tea, Butterworth began by complimenting us on our disguises.

'Gentlemen, I have to say that you look every inch the part of the Turkic traders, and very definitely not the Englishmen you are. If you stay in Haridwar long enough I would like nothing better than to hear the tale of how you came by such convincing disguises.

'But for now, the job at hand, is I fear going to be more than difficult enough for you.

'After suggesting that the festivals may be the mechanism that our enemies are using to spread discontent in the North, my men and I have been doing our best to try and identify any individuals who may be posing as holy men in order to win an audience.

'The difficulty, as I'm sure you can imagine, with the majority of the police force here in Haridwar having been recruited from men with a military background, is that all their training and work to date has been to help them stand out and command the respect of the civil populace.

'When it comes to blending in with the visiting pilgrims, we are therefore at a huge disadvantage.

'Your party, on the other hand, may be the perfect alternative, for whilst you will never be mistaken for a native Hindustani, in your desert robes and speaking your Turkic language, you will also never be suspected of being agents of the British empire.

Thinking it would help to break the ice between us, I thanked this giant of a man sat opposite to us, using the very Turkic language which he had just alluded to.

'Ah, bravo, bravo Mr Whitaker!' the captain replied. 'And all of your party speaks this language as fluently?'

'We do indeed,' I replied. 'Though we're all beginning to pick up a little Hindi as well, we're a long way from being able to eavesdrop on what the locals are saying.'

'That is as Jenkins had informed me,' Butterworth conceded.

'If ya cannae speak the local lingo, gentle-men,' Sergeant Studgeon commented. 'Then how will ya be hopin' to spot a fake guru talkin' lies about the Crown?'

Butterworth couldn't help but chuckle at his sergeant's bluntness, but thankfully he had an altogether more pragmatic mind.

'The way I see it,' he began. 'Your job gentlemen, is to spot the fakes and charlatans, or anyone for that matter who seems odd or out of the ordinary, and then to let us know, so that we can investigate further.

'My men, including Studgeon here, will be able to get the truth of the matter, without offending the local sensibilities or adding fuel to the fire which these enemy agents are trying to kindle.

'The only question as far as I'm concerned,' Butterworth continued. 'Is how we get you into those places where you're most likely to come across any fraudsters that may be operating?

'Well, in that respect we've started to work up a back-story, that might help us,' Marlow explained, pouring himself another cup of tea.

'On the way here, our guide, Abhra suggested that we pretend to be returning the ashes of a former business colleague and friend to the Ganges following his death in Turkey, and in accordance with his final wishes.'

'I see,' Butterworth replied, nodding.

'But being non-Hindus your group would naturally wish to seek the counsel of an appropriate religious leader about how you might best respect your friends wishes.'

'Lord alone kens how long ya could spend trying te get these Stani's te agree on that!' Stugeon butted in.

'Yes, yes, precisely,' Butterworth agreed, smiling as he twisted one side of his fearsome moustache.

'You could start with the obvious places,' he continued, thinking out loud. 'The tent village of the sadhus' and other holy men, the temples and shrines.

'That should give you a good grounding in what the legitimate priests and holy types are like, and then we could feed you a list of other locations where pilgrims have been known to gather to seek informal blessings and advice.

'What do you think, sergeant?'

'Ay, surr, the men could gie ye a good lang list o' such places.'

'Well, if you could arrange to give us that list of target sites first thing in the morning, we could check them and report back via the same messenger the next day,' Marlow suggested.

'Excellent,' Butterworth replied. 'And if you spot any strong candidates that we might need to act upon more urgently, you can always get a message to the station house.'

We discussed a few final details based on some of the covert training which Selene had given us over the previous eighteen months, agreeing some code words we could use in messages or over the phone to make it more difficult for anyone to understand what we were talking about, in the event of our communication going astray or being overheard.

After our discussion, I could see that while he saw the sense in what we'd suggested, our knowledge of these techniques had made the commander of police suspicious about who we were, and just as importantly, where we might have received the training we'd so obviously had.

'I appreciate it may all seem a bit on the arcane side, making such preparations,' I spontaneously added. 'But one of our group is a former military man, like yourselves, and over the years he's gradually gotten us all trained to follow his lead.'

'Ah, of course,' Butterworth replied, appearing a little less suspicious. 'Perhaps if you're here for long enough we could have a chat about what kind of thing you gentlemen like to occupy your time with that necessitates such precautions.'

We waffled on for a few minutes more, assuring the captain and his sergeant we'd like nothing better than to talk to them about the journey which had brought us to India, before we were finally able to take our leave, knowing full well that we'd made both Jenkins and now Butterworth suspicious about who we were and what we were up to.

HOLY OF HOLIES

AFTER LEAVING THE POLICE STATION, Marlow and I followed Butterworth's recommendation and headed over to what Studgeon referred to as the 'Guru Headquarters', where the majority of the festival's holy men and women chose to pitch their camp while they were visiting Haridwar from their respective ashrams and remote mountain retreats.

I was fairly sure it wasn't going to be anything like a boy scout camp, but whatever I had been expecting, it certainly wasn't the crowded several-acre site located just outside the city, which looked like it had been constructed by some kind of mediaeval architect with a passion for canvas.

Unsure of how to proceed, we started by walking around the edges of the site, on a crowded path perhaps ten feet wide, and onto which a network of interconnecting side-streets and canvas-lined alleyways emerged. Some of these were barely wide enough for two people to pass abreast, while others were wide enough for street vendors to ply their trade.

Along these wider streets the front men for the different gurus and sects gathered like market traders to entice the undecided in one direction or another. The majority of these yelling and waving street hawkers still wore the distinct orange cloth that marked them out as disciples of a particular Guru or sect, but they could just as easily have made a living at any of the fish markets the world over.

There was never one such salesman in operation at any given place, so within moments of one pitch finishing another would start, offering healing or blessings more powerful or effective than their predecessor.

Fortunately, dressed as we were in our robes, many of these street hawkers had no idea how to address us, so they tried every combination of Hindi and English, as well as Arabic or Farsi. I even detected some French at one point.

We, in turn, replied using the language of the silk roads, and when that went unrecognised we pretended to speak a few words of broken English, enough to explain that we sought advice about how to get the remains of our friend blessed.

It took a minute or two for us to make our meaning clear, and then with a rush, one of the young salesmen grabbed Marlow by the sleeve of his robe and led us to the tent enclosure of his master Yogi Nandh.

Deep into the Guru city he led us, with dun coloured canvas walls on every side of us as far as we could see, past one entrance after another, until finally we were ushered through an opening in the canvas wall into a carpeted and scented foyer. Here the young huckster leading us uttered some incomprehensible words to a middle aged man with an impressive beard, who was sat on the floor beside a flap opening into a second chamber.

Despite the crowded paths and walkways outside, the interior of this Guru's tented abode was surprisingly light and airy. The canvas roof appeared to have been raised around several tall wooden poles that were held upright not by being sunk into the ground, but rather by an intricate network of guy- ropes and knots.

'One moment please, gentlemen,' the man said to us in English before clapping his hands to summon someone else.

Seconds later a shaven headed young man appeared through the flap, and after kneeling in front of the man in reception, he was given some instructions in Hindi before disappearing back inside.

After issuing his instructions to his shaven headed

colleague the seated figure then turned to us and motioned for us to sit, which we gladly did.

'What do you think,' Marlow asked me in Turkic.

'Difficult to say,' I replied.

'If we're lucky they'll be trying to find someone who can speak with us in our own language.' I continued, looking him in the eye as I said the latter, at which he simply nodded his head.

A couple of minutes later, our question was answered, when another young man entered through the same entrance onto the street that we had used.

He was dressed like the others in orange cloth, but he had an almost Afghani look about him rather than a northern Indian.

After bowing to the man at the door, he sat down on the carpet in front of us, before addressing us in a slightly broken form of Turkic.

'I am told you are speakers of the Turkic tongue?' he began.

'We are,' Marlow responded, fluently. 'We have travelled from the west with the ashes of a former comrade who died on his way back to his homeland here in India.

'However, before he died, when he knew he could not complete the journey, he begged of us that we would bring his remains to the side of this great river where even after death he could be washed clean of his sins.'

'I understand,' our translator confirmed, before going on to ask which sect of Hinduism our friend had belonged.

'That there is more than one sect within your faith is something we have only recently discovered,' I responded.

Nodding his understanding, the translator, asked a few more questions, before turning back to the older man who had been sat next to the flap to relay what we had spoken.

Together they conversed for a minute or two,

before the translator turned back to us.

'That you are prepared to accept this burden for your friend brings you much honour in our faith,' he began. 'But this problem is something we must put before our master, to seek his insight.

'Will you wait here while we do so?'

We thanked the translator for his words, and then indicated we would be happy to wait, while they consulted their Yogi.

It didn't take long for the translator to return, but in the meantime, I took the opportunity to better study the layout of this tented entrance hall, and the orange clad man who sat beside the doorway that led further into the tent building.

The place really was completely unremarkable, the walls were plain uncoloured cloth, the tent poles were simple polished wood as was the simple incense burner at the back of the room. The carpet in fact was the only decorative feature, for while it was fairly thin, it had been woven with an abstract geometric pattern in a variety of earthy colours from yellow through to a dull red.

Having exhausted everything of interest about the room, my attention next fell on the bearded gentlemen who sat beside the inner door. And again, there was little of interest in his appearance or garb, but he sat there perfectly still, with his eyes three quarters closed, almost as though in some deep form of meditation or on the brink of sleep.

His breathing was silent and so shallow I couldn't see his chest moving in the slightest. He was almost like a statue in his stillness.

Fascinated by this man's stillness, I simply sat and watched him for a few minutes until the Turkic speaking translator reappeared.

Effortlessly the man who had been meditating by the door returned to a normal animated human being, so that his colleague could explain to him what the Guru had said, just before he turned to us and repeated the same in his broken Turkic.

'Guru Nandh has heard your request for guidance and has offered the following advice,' he explained, before turning back to the other man to explain what he was about to convey again in Hindi.

'If you are willing to carry your friends remains a little further, the Guru suggests you should seek a blessing for his remains at each of the shrines on the Ganges from Haridwar down to Varanasi, at which point you may deliver your friends remains into the arms of mother Ganga in the knowledge that he will surely be released from the wheel of Samsara.

'If you are willing to accept this additional burden, then our master will bless your friend's ashes personally and each of you who help to carry him upon this final journey.'

We thanked the disciple of the guru who had translated for us before confirming we would do as he had instructed, to see our friend blessed at each of the shrines along the river.

The sun was long past its zenith and the afternoon nearly over as we took our leave of Guru Nandh's enclosure. As we left I couldn't help but wonder whether what we were doing in accepting this holy man's blessing wasn't taking our cover story a step too far.

Yes, we needed to maintain our cover story if we wanted to succeed in the task which Jenkins had set us, and yes, that task would hopefully help to reduce the spread of civil unrest in the region, which could otherwise threaten the lives of thousands of innocent people. But at the same time, we were lying to a holy man and taking advantage of his trust.

'You look as though you're having second thoughts,' Marlow observed in Turkic, as we returned through the centre of Haridwar after leaving the tented enclosures occupied by the holy men.

'I don't like the dishonesty we're being forced into,' I replied, looking at him for the first time since we'd received the Guru's advice.

'No, me neither,' he conceded. 'Though I can't think of any other way to proceed.'

'Nor I,' I admitted.

'What we need,' he explained, with what may have been a smile beneath the cloth that covered his face. 'Is to put the problem to someone wiser than ourselves…'

'A philosopher perhaps?' I suggested, picking up on where Marlow was leading.

'Precisely,' Marlow replied. 'A lover of wisdom… a student of the human condition…'

'Someone who could see through the complexities of the situation and provide a solution for us with the minimum of fuss and linguistic trickery.'

'Well, that rules Jean our then,' Marlow finally replied, with a laugh. Much to the shock and bemusement of several people that we were passing.

I couldn't help but laugh also when Marlow then proceeded to do his own, rather convincing impression of our friend, albeit translated into the Turkic language.

'Ah my friends, is the problem not simplicity itself,' he parodied, including the amused glint in his eye. 'In fact, in Gascony we have a saying. You cannot make an omelette without first feeding the chickens!'

We continued to make fun of our friend as we travelled through the town, stopping off on the way to enjoy a few minutes sat in a shady corner with some food and chai tea from the street vendors, the hot sweet liquid quashing my thirst and refreshing my wits after the heat of the day.

An hour later, and we finally emerged from the slow-moving streets back at the guild hall, and I was ready for some shade, some rest and something refreshing to drink.

Peter had arrived ahead of us with Jean and Selene, and was just putting the finishing touches to a large pitcher of home-made lemonade as we walked in through the door.

Despite having stopped for refreshments only an

hour or so earlier, I found I was parched again as Peter handed me a glass, and I practically downed the contents in one.

While we'd been visiting the police station and then the 'Guru Headquarters', Jean, Peter and Selene had visited the northern most part of the city where several ashrams provided lodgings for some of the wealthier pilgrims in exchange for money.

Abhra had suggested checking these places as they also frequently accommodated some of the solitary holy men who might eschew the more crowded and competitive 'Guru Headquarters'.

While only a mile from where we were staying, the overflowing streets made the journey there and back into a day-long exercise, which had been exhausting.

They hadn't managed to visit all the ashrams in that part of the city, but from the sound of it, the experience had still given them all more confidence in their ability to identify genuine holy men.

For our part we explained about the meeting with Studgeon and Butterworth, before going on to explain the advice we'd received from Guru Nandh.

'Why that is excellent, is it not mes amies?' Jean began. 'Not only does this suggestion from the Guru help us to deepen and strengthen our cover story, it also necessitates us travelling back down the Ganges to the other holy cities, just as Commissioner Jenkins had suggested.'

'You're quite right old friend,' Marlow responded. 'But the question we find ourselves struggling with, is whether it would be fair of us to accept Guru Nandh's blessing, for what is in effect a cooking pot full of wood ash?'

'Ah yes, of course,' Jean replied. 'The deception of an honest person is no small thing to consider.

'But may I first ask what line your thinking has taken on your walk back from visiting this Guru Nandh?'

'Well,' I began, rather tentatively. 'We could take

the view that we are not followers of the Hindu faith, and therefore any offence we might create is an irrelevance.'

'Pah!' Jean replied, clearly unconvinced by my first attempt.

'George, if I honestly thought that was a serious option, I would be sorely disappointed in my own ability to represent a good influence in your life. Please proceed.'

Accepting this reproach with good grace, I did as I was instructed.

'The best argument we have been able to come up with is that we are acting for the greater good, and in essence if we were able to take the Guru into our confidence then there is a good chance that he would understand and forgive our deception.'

'That is certainly better,' Jean conceded. 'But should we not first understand the harm which we do to the Guru and the followers of the Hindu faith that would likely ensue, if we were to follow this course of action?'

'Well,' I hesitated, trying to think through the question as I was answering it. 'The harm would be minimal, I suppose. The Guru might be offended or feel his judgement had been impugned, that his trust had been betrayed.'

'Ah, this is a very good game, Sahib Jean,' Abhra broke in, clearly much amused at what I had considered a serious point upon which he too might well be offended.

'M'sieur Balakrishnan, you think my young friend is mistaken.' Jean offered, clearly happy to engage a wider audience in my trial.

'Oh yes, Sahib,' Abhra continued, shaking his head from side to side in traditional Indian style to indicate the affirmative.

'The Hindu faith is not so fragile and easily broken as you are thinking, and nor are our great Gurus so easy to offend.'

'Because they have already reached a stage of enlightenment above that at which such small things are considered important?'

'Yes, yes, Sahib,' Abhra confirmed, clearly delighted at Jean's insight.

'The wisdom and blessings of the Guru are freely given, in the hope that they will help you upon your own journey,' he explained, patiently. 'If you wish to seek a blessing for a cooking pot full of wood ashes from a holy man, then your path to enlightenment may be a slightly longer one, or for you this may well be the shortest path, who can say.'

'This was my understanding also,' Jean confirmed.

'You are most wise, Sahib Jean.' Abhra replied, bowing slightly to the Frenchman. 'For if there is any harm done in such a circumstance, then it is surely upon yourself that you have inflicted it.'

I understood what our guide was saying in that moment, and felt the truth of it resonate within me. Yes, there were almost certainly actions that would be equally harmful to others, but this idea of the principle harm associated with committing a sin, being against yourself, while new to me, simply made so much sense.

With this new realisation fresh and bright within my mind, I stopped for another moment to consider how I now felt about lying to the Guru.

In the light of this new understanding I realised that Abhra and Jean were both correct. We would be harming the Guru in no way whatsoever, and motivated as we were, not out of selfish benefit, but rather for the greater good, I thought it likely we were also causing no harm to ourselves either.

'You look more content, now that you've had time to consider the situation properly,' Jean commented, as I sat down with another glass of Peter's lemonade.

THE SACRED HEARTH

THE FOLLOWING DAY we returned as a group to the Guru's canvas abode in the tented village of the holy men.

We had brought the cooking pot full of ash that we'd picked up on Abhra's advice. But now, as we entered not only the reception room, but also his inner sanctum, where we found the silver haired guru sat cross-legged, atop a low wooden platform at one end of a long mud brick hearth, in which glowed the orange embers of a low fire.

We'd brought rupees, rice and lentils as gifts, just as we'd done at the temples and shrines we'd stayed at along the way to Haridwar.

On entering the main chamber, one of his devotees whispered in his ear about the purpose of our visit, taking a moment or two to point out the clumsy pot in which we carried what was supposed to be our friends ashes.

The same devotee who had translated for us was also present, and after the Guru had accepted our gifts and listened to why we were there, he closed his eyes for a moment, before turning to address us via his translator.

He began by thanking us for the service we were doing for our dead Hindu friend, before going on to offer us his blessing.

'You have agreed to take the remains of your friend to seek blessings at all the shrines between Haridwar and Varanasi, a significant but worthwhile journey,' he explained.

'To aid you on this endeavour I will send a letter with you containing my blessing and my hope that others of the faith will assist you on your way.

'I will also give you these tokens of the service

which you do for your friend.' At this, he gestured toward one of his aides, who stepped forward with a second devotee carrying what looked like a number of slender orange sashes.

I wasn't quite sure what we were supposed to do in response here, but I was stood directly in front of the man with the sashes, so I stepped forward, and then at the urging of the translator I knelt down on one knee.

At this, the guru's acolyte took a sash from the man holding them and fastened it carefully but firmly around my turban at a forty-five-degree angle, before then attaching a small metal pendant in the centre of the sash just over my forehead.

Once this was done the translator bid me to move back to my friends, before the same process was repeated on each of them.

The Guru then motioned for us to one at a time approach the low platform on which he sat. After kneeling down beside him, he extended his arm and placed his fingertips on the pendant fixed to the sash, before chanting a small prayer, which the translator did not explain.

After he had repeated this for each of us, we were motioned back to the other end of the sacred hearth, opposite the guru.

Now, after a simple nod from the guru, one of his followers came forward from the side of the room with a small sandalwood casket, covered with exquisite carvings of the Hindu gods in their legendary settings.

The acolyte who had produced the box then opened it up to reveal a plain wooden interior and polished wooden spoon. Then with a bow to his guru and another bow to us, he motioned toward the pot in which we carried the ashes of our supposed friend.

After we handed these over the same man opened up the pot, and with a gentle chant that was picked up by the other acolytes and the guru, he carefully spooned the ashes from the pot into the sandalwood casket.

The reverence and consideration which the guru and his acolytes showed to performing this simple task was quite humbling, and despite our conversation from the previous day, I once again felt a little uncomfortable about this pretence of a dead friend's ashes.

I kept my feelings to myself though, and simply averted my gaze while the holy men completed their task, then sealed the box with a large wax seal.

The ceremony continued on for another half hour, when the ashes were returned to our care, now contained within the handsome sandalwood casket. After which, more prayers were chanted, incense was burned and we expressed our thanks for all that had been done for us.

It was a humbling experience to go through this ceremony, and to realise just how caring and considerate these people were being to someone they didn't know, but who happened to share their faith.

How different our goals were in coming to this country, and searching for the first great temple of Ziusudra, and what was possibly one of the sources of the legendary fountain of youth. It seemed so shallow somehow, so lacking in the philosophical enlightenment that flourished in this country.

Not for the first time did I feel the spectre of doubt enter my mind, followed by the question I had so frequently wrestled with, of whether we were doing the right thing.

Even though it was still early in the day, we decided to make our way back to the guild hall, so we could discuss what to do next.

Winding our way through the streets, I couldn't be sure, but it seemed like the pilgrims responded differently now that we wore the orange head sashes of the guru around our turbans.

I didn't know what the sashes represented, and not for the first time found myself wishing my knowledge of the Hindu faith and culture were greater, but at least we had Abhra waiting for us back at the apartment, so I could put the question to him before too much longer.

'The experience with this guru is again making you re-evaluate your life, is it not mon ami?' Jean asked, bringing my attention back to our walk through the streets.

I nodded by way of a response, to indicate that it had.

'That is a good thing, and as it should be,' he replied, in that all too familiar and all too infuriating way, that typified my Gascon friend.

'You think it a good thing that I am again plagued by doubts?' I asked, with as much good humour as I could muster.

'But of course,' he replied, with an equally infuriating shrug. 'Was it not Socrates who told us that, an unexamined life is not worth living.

'Only by making our decisions and then sticking to them doggedly, without being open to changing our minds, can we fail in life.'

'Is there no part of you, Jean, that would be happy to settle for a compromise once in a while?' I asked resignedly, and without thinking about what I was saying.

'No part of you that doesn't just yearn for a simpler life again, where you know which way is up.'

It had probably sounded more pointed than I'd wanted, but it had summed up how I was feeling, and while perhaps a little unfair, for the moment I didn't mind putting the question to him as I had.

'Ah, George, how can you even ask such a question?' Jean responded, a little bluntly too.

'There are times when I sit and wonder whether it would have been so very terrible to be spending my life in Paris, entertaining my friends who come to visit, discussing art and philosophy with the great thinkers and conversationalists of the south bank, holidaying in Fontainebleu or Annecy in the summer, followed by a little skiing in the Alps during the winter.

'These things would make for a good life, would

they not?' he asked.

'And yet you seem to leave them behind with very little difficulty,' I observed.

'Perhaps so,' he replied thoughtfully. 'And yet the best friends I have in the world, are those people gathered around me now, on this impossible and unthinkable adventure across the strange lands of India.

'The same was true of my time in the army.'

'What? You're suggesting you enjoy your home in Paris more, because you spend time away from it?' I asked, not quite sure of the point he was making.

'No, my friend,' he replied, patiently. 'When you have a family, your home becomes your castle, as you English are so fond of saying, and you devote your time and energy to providing for your family by working hard, by keeping your home clean and safe and comfortable for your children to grow up in.

'When you are alone, your home becomes something different. It becomes your retreat, your place of rest and renewal.

'But if you have no family to strive and work for, then you must find something else to consume your energies, to stretch your muscles, your wits and your will. Without this challenge you have no need of your rest or renewal, and then because this is all that your home can provide, you find yourself lost with no purpose either at home or away from it.'

I nodded again, knowing what he was saying was true.

'Of course,' Jean continued, unexpectedly. 'There have been times on this particular journey when I would've happily popped back to Paris for a few days all the same!'

I couldn't help but smile beneath my veil, as he said this.

'The Star of the Orient springs to mind,' he added, without me having to remind him. 'There were many times on that particular train journey when I wished I was back at my home!'

The thought of it made me laugh aloud, much to the surprise of the pilgrims in front of us, who then did their best to give us a wide berth.

TO CATCH A THIEF

AFTER BRINGING THE SANDALWOOD BOX BACK to the guild hall, we found one of Butterworth's men loitering in an alleyway nearby. He'd been sent with a written message suggesting we investigate a couple of locations on the outskirts of Haridwar, out near one of the bigger shrines.

Apparently, a couple of constables had seen the tail end of a group as it was dispersing, which might have been coincidental, or they may have been dispersing because of a tip off that police officers were close at hand.

It was as good a lead as anything else we had, so we informed Butterworth's man that we would be checking it out that afternoon, and should be able to report back in the evening.

In the meantime, I was eager to question Abhra about the meaning of the blessings and golden-orange sashes that we all now wore around our turbans.

As always, he was happy to share his knowledge with us.

'Ah. Gentlemen, Lady, you do indeed look very much the religious pilgrims now,' he began, almost chastising himself for not thinking of this extra wardrobe flourish himself. 'It is such an obvious touch, it really should have occurred to me before now.'

'Are these orange coloured sashes used commonly to denote a religious following or mission in Hinduism?' I couldn't help but ask, convinced it must mean something specific.

'Ah, Sahib, the sash around your head is the saffron cloth of the holy man,' he replied, all patience and smiles. 'In the Hindu faith this colour it symbolises the sacred fire which burns away our impurities, and it is only ever worn by holy men who have renounced the world in their quest for enlightenment.

'For the guru to adorn your turbans with this saffron cloth is highly unusual, but to any Hindu it will instantly inform them that you are on a religious quest and have renounced the world until that quest is complete.'

'Thank you, Abhra,' I replied, earnestly. 'I think I understand the blessing we received a little better now.'

'Indeed so, Sahib,' he acknowledged, with a slight bow of his head. 'Guru Nandh has perhaps perceived the truth of your reason for being here in India, and has provided you with his blessing to help you on your journey.'

'Yes,' I replied awkwardly, knowing that Abhra was probably referring to the mission we were on for Jenkins, rather than our goal in coming to India in the first place.

'And when you say that the wearing of this saffron coloured cloth indicates that we have renounced the world, at least until our quest is over?' Jean asked.

'Ah, Sahib Jean,' Abhra replied, knowingly. 'For foreigners such as yourselves there is no knowing what it is that you have renounced. It is perhaps that you will not eat meat or drink alcohol while on your pilgrimage, which are two of the things which we native born Hindus forswear. Alternatively, it may be that you have promised not to conduct your business until your quest is completed.'

'Then there is no behaviour which could potentially give us away as not being real pilgrims?' Jean asked, just to double check.

'No, Sahib, you may live and act as you will, provided you show no outward disrespect for the gods or the symbols of Hinduism.' Abhra confirmed.

There were a few more questions from the rest of

the group, which Abhra answered with good humoured patience, and then after a quick lunch we were ready to face the heat of the day again, and to continue our search for the impostor holy men who Jenkins and Butterworth believed had been operating in the area.

It made no sense for us all to follow up on the intelligence which Butterworth's man had delivered about the Bilkeshwar temple, so Jean and Selene agreed to go and investigate the place, while the rest of us split up to visit some of the other holy sites.

Harry and Androus were naturally curious about the more antique sites, so they volunteered to visit the Mata Mansa temple to the north, which was a little further out of Haridwar and perched atop a sheer red-stone cliff face.

It would involve a long climb up the mountainside in the heat, but it was reputed to be one of the three most ancient sites in and around the city, so they were already speculating on whether there would be evidence of purely above ground structures, or whether there might also be some troglodytic antecedents.

That left Marlow, Peter, Abhra and myself free to visit the other shrines, ashrams and holy sites which Abhra had previously identified.

Many of these were small and didn't merit a special trip by themselves, so Marlow and I volunteered to do a sweep of several of these on the eastern side of the city, taking in several as we walked out, and several more on the way back.

Peter volunteered to do the same with Abhra on the western side of the river.

It was only after Marlow and I had been walking through the city streets for an hour or so, following the crude hand-drawn map provided by Abhra that I realised how comfortable we'd both become in winding our way through the crowded thoroughfares.

The saffron sashes that we each wore around our turban's may have contributed to this increased ease of movement, but in large measure I felt it was because we were adjusting to the different rhythms of the city.

We'd stopped a handful of times as we made our way through the centre of Haridwar, observing the incredible feats of abstinence and self-mortification which different holy men had achieved, as well as taking the odd break to shelter from the heat and drink some much needed tea or lemonade.

It had been a while since we'd last stopped for a drink, and I could feel the heat getting to me again, as we were stood watching a holy man meditating beside one of the many Vishnu shrines.

It was the first tell-tale sign of dehydration, which we were both more than familiar with now, and knew could easily be countered if we took a break to find something to drink.

In the meantime, the holy man's helpers continued to chant and play their instruments while we watched him meditate.

As the moments passed with my concentration wandering, I slowly became aware of an all too familiar beat within the music, the unmistakable sound of those distant drums.

Like a gunshot the holy man's eyes snapped open and fixed upon Marlow who was stood beside me, looking toward the holy man, but even from the side I could see that Marlow had slipped into some kind of trance, and was now completely oblivious to his surroundings.

The drums continued to build as we stood there, and like an uncoiling serpent the Sadhu, slowly unwound himself from the yogic posture in which he'd been sat. Rising from the ground in a slow, almost predatory fashion, his eyes fixed on Marlow the entire time, never wavering to another member of the crowd.

The holy-man's helpers had immediately noticed their master was no longer meditating, but after casting a few uncertain glances between themselves they continued to play.

I felt the drums still coiling around my mind, twisting and turning their way into my consciousness.

My thoughts began to follow the twisting rhythm of the drums also, and I felt my mind slipping into that other state that immediately preceded the dreaming.

With an electric shock the holy-man's eyes snapped over to look at me also, and it was this alone that pulled me back.

Slowly, and with an effort I thought beyond me, I forced my attention to return to the present, until I could concentrate on where we were again.

Somehow, I found the strength to reach out and grasp Marlow's arm, which instantly broke his trance.

The holy man was speaking now, looking from one of us to the other, and becoming slightly agitated when he realised his words meant nothing to us.

As we backed away from the increasingly agitated holy man, and the hundreds of people who now openly stood and stared at us, I could sense that he was asking us a question, demanding to know something, but more than that my primitive grasp of Hindi couldn't discern. As soon as we were safely away from the throng I paused to make a few notes about the words or sounds I thought I had heard.

Marlow, was quiet while I did this, and from what little I could see of his face, he seemed unfocused still, as though his wits hadn't yet fully returned.

We needed shade and something to drink, and we found both a few minutes later under a wide canvas canopy stretched from a stall on the edge of a market. There were no tables or chairs, just a patch of ground that had been swept clear, but squatting there in the cool shade, with a drink in hand felt like paradise.

A few minutes later, I began to feel the benefit of the cool spiced yoghurt drink, or lassi as the locals called it.

The same was evidently true of Marlow, who had ordered the same, and now as I watched him empty his glass, it seemed his eyes came back into full focus.

'Do you remember what happened?' I asked, hoping he'd have some idea.

'My memories are vague,' he replied. 'One minute I was just listening to the chanting, and wondering how long we could reasonably be expected to watch somebody just sitting there.

'The next I knew, I could feel my mind drifting back to the shamanic ceremony we witnessed beneath the Singing Stones, back in Kenya, with the drums sounding all around us.

'Then I was in the dream place again and walking towards the fire surrounded by those strange figures, but as I grew close to the blistering heat, I was distracted by images I could see within the flames.'

'Do you mean the vision where we get ambushed by the Icarii?' I asked.

'No, I think this was Ziusudra, the builder of the temple we found in Africa, and the very place we're trying to find. I'm sure he was here in Haridwar, though the place looked completely different.

'He came here?' I asked, incredulous.

'Yes, and I think he may have had something to do with the origins and myths that surround this place.

'When I saw him, I'm sure it was on the journey he made after leaving his first great temple, on his way to Africa in the company of a young Brahmin, and he was carrying several things with him, from the first temple.'

'You mean tablets or scrolls of some sort?'

'I think one of them may have been a text he was adding to as he travelled. Another appeared to be a vessel full of water or some other liquid, but I can't be sure.'

'That would be an incredible coincidence,' I replied. 'The festival taking place in Haridwar all around us is called the Kumbh Mela, the 'Pitcher festival', which celebrates an occasion when the Hindu gods spilled a few drops of the nectar of immortality into the river here.'

'The same thought was just going through my mind,' Marlow added.

'Can you remember what this figure was doing, when you saw him?' I asked.

'The details are a little vague,' he reiterated. 'But to me, it looked a lot like he was taking samples from the various streams and watercourses that fed into the river running through Haridwar.'

'And you're sure it was here that you were seeing?'

'Yes, the town was nothing like it is now, but the mountains and the way the river spreads out into several channels once it drops over that final set of falls was unmistakable.'

'What about the holy man? Could you understand what he was saying just now, or catch any of his meaning?'

'Only the odd word as we were leaving,' he admitted. 'Something like "Sarvetand ra hey" which sounded like a warning. Then something like "Aap yar tra karay" of which I only recognise the first word of as "you".'

This was pretty much all that I'd recalled as well, but I took a moment to add Marlow's recollections to my own in my pocket book, including another word which he thought he'd heard, "sandkeer" or "sankeer".

Hopefully, Abhra would be able to make some sense of it for us, without us having to explain about the drums and the real nature of our trip to India.

It also put us in the awkward position of having to find a way of updating the others about what had happened, without making our guide suspicious.

Once again feeling better after a drink and some shade, Marlow and I headed back through the town, stopping off to visit another couple of the smaller shrines on the way, while discussing how we could best bring the others up to speed with the visions Marlow had experienced.

Androus and Harry were obviously the first who needed to know. If Ziusudra had visited Haridwar, like

Marlow had seen in his vision, then there was a possibility that there was some mention of it on the tablets which Androus had translated. Or, if what Marlow had seen was somehow related to the myths surrounding the origins of the Kumbh Mela, which was celebrated at several other sites along the Ganges, then we may well have stumbled upon a much-needed corroboration for our planned route going forward.

'It would make a lot of sense,' Marlow speculated in Turkic, as we made our way through the crowded streets after visiting the last shrine on our list, on our way back to the merchant's guild.

'Harry and Androus have mentioned several times that the entire Gangetic plain was covered in thick forest and grassland before it was brought into cultivation, and that as a consequence, the easiest and probably safest means of travel would have been by boat.'

'Yes, and if there is some link between the water and the locations of Ziusudra's temples, then what better way of travelling than along one of the largest rivers in the world?'

'That alone would be an important clue,' Marlow replied. 'Haven't all the sites where we've found tablets been located near to running water? Even the sea cave that we found in the gulf of Corinth had a small trickle of a spring running out of the rock at the back. The same on Mount Erciyes in Turkey, where we found only the shattered cover-stone for the tablets. Wasn't there a little pool with a stream running into it?'

'Yes, that's right,' I confirmed, as I recalled each of the sites we'd visited. The Gilgamesh tablets were buried under the city gate, but the city itself was positioned right next to the ancient course of the River Euphrates.

'Ah, but what about the Singing Stones,' I asked. 'Where Nelion had hidden his set of tablets? There was definitely no source of water there.'

'Yes, yes, you're right. I remember Harry having a

good look around on our first visit there to find the source of the drums, and he'd have mentioned a stream if he'd found one.'

'Although…' I added, about to contradict my own point. 'Didn't we walk up a large gully with a dried-up stream bed at its bottom.'

'We did indeed,' Marlow replied. 'And while it was certainly dry on the surface, it's always possible the water might still be running below ground.

'It could still be a coincidence though,' he conceded. 'But I'm sure it was Ziusudra I saw, or at least the same person that was gazing back at me through the flames on that first occasion when I dreamed at the Singing Stones.'

While it was all speculation, we agreed it was still worth mentioning to Androus and Harry, once we managed to talk to them without Abhra being present.

SHEEPS CLOTHING

WHEN WE GOT BACK TO OUR APARTMENT we discovered we weren't the only ones who'd had an exciting afternoon, as Jean and Selene had spotted our first suspicious character posing as a holy man.

They'd been checking some of the shrines on the opposite side of the river to where Marlow and I had been working, when Selene had spotted a young street urchin who'd evidently been posted as a lookout for somebody.

'It's a world away from the city streets of Europe,' she explained. 'But that young boy would have fitted in on the back streets of London, Paris or Madrid just as well as any native-born urchin.'

'But how did he differ from any other child living in the city?' Harry asked innocently.

'It's the watchfulness that gives street people away

more than anything,' Selene explained patiently. 'People with a home to go to never need to develop that level of alertness. But those living on the streets have to be on the lookout for everything and everyone, from the police and other street dwellers, to the punters that they may have duped previously, charitable and criminals. Those who want to help, those who want to take advantage, and those dangerous individuals that are just interested in people that won't be missed.'

I couldn't help but remember the conversation I'd had with Selene in New Delhi, when she'd told me about her own early life living homeless and alone on the streets of Florence, surviving on her wits and her ability to steal valuable items from the wealthy.

This was surely how she had recognised the young boy acting as a lookout. Such a job was probably one of the easiest ways of earning a crust. Who knew, perhaps Selene had even done this kind of work herself before she was adopted by the Icarii.

'Having spotted one such lookout,' Jean added, smoothly. 'It was just a matter of time before we spotted the other street children who were doing the same. Each of them relishing a chapati full of rice and vegetables, or some other morsel clearly given to them as a down-payment for their services.

'With the lookouts identified,' he continued. 'It was a matter of simple trigonometry to identify which of the holy men they were working for.'

'That is excellent news,' chipped in Harry. 'Did you report the impostor to Butterworth's man yet?'

'Not yet,' Selene replied. 'We can inform them tonight. But more importantly, if there are other charlatans working in the city who are employing the vagabond children in the same way, then this is our opportunity to catch them all.'

'This is indeed excellent news, Memsahib,' Abhra suggested. 'Your work for Sahib Jenkins will very soon be completed.'

'Perhaps, perhaps,' conceded Jean, thoughtfully. 'But how exactly Butterworth and his men will want to proceed is the big question. It will not take much to alert these children and send their employers scurrying away to resurface somewhere else when the attention has died down.'

This was obviously big news, and if it paid off, we might even get the travel permits which Jenkins had promised early.

We had another half-hour before we were expecting Butterworth's man to show up at the usual meeting place, so we didn't have long to decide on how much to tell him.

'There is of course a case to be made on both sides,' Jean agreed, starting the discussion. 'If we don't tell Butterworth what we've discovered then it will appear we have made little progress, and in the event of these charlatans noticing our interest in them and disappearing or lying low for a while, we could be left with nothing.

'On the other hand,' he continued. 'If we share what we know, then we may get some credit, but Butterworth may choose to act and in doing so, ruin our chances of finding any other fake holy men operating in the area.'

'But if he does choose to act and gets a good result?' Peter asked.

'A good point, mon ami,' Jean conceded. 'Our work here would be complete and Jenkins may reward us with the travel permits we require.'

It was difficult to know which option would be best, so after a few minutes more discussion we decided to share what Selene and Jean had discovered, in the hope of getting our travel permits extended by at least another week or two.

This left Marlow and I with the problem of how we could tell everyone about the vision Marlow had received without tipping off Abhra in the process.

We'd invented some code phrases way back when we'd first discovered Luke's betrayal, which were intended to alert the others to the fact we had something to share, and while we hadn't used them in a long time, both Marlow and I felt sure the others would still remember them.

Most of the code phrases wouldn't really work while we were in our current disguises in India, as it involved several items of kit that we just weren't using at the moment. We could hardly ask 'if anyone had a spare razor-blade' or mention 'that a button had come off a garment' when we were all growing beards at the moment and had been wearing buttonless Bedouin clothing for the last couple of weeks.

We did have one code phrase about our tobacco drying out, and while none of us could smoke our pipes while in disguise, Abhra had confirmed that our apartment was private enough for us not to have to worry about it.

With the decision about what to tell Butterworth made, I took my pipe out of my pocket along with my pouch of tobacco and proceeded to use the code phrase while filling my pipe.

It was subtle, like a small electric current had been passed around the room, which neither Abhra or Selene seemed to notice, but which everyone else picked up on instantly.

Jean created the opportunity for the rest of us to talk.

'Well, it's just about time to go and meet with Butterworth's man,' he said, casually. 'I'll pop out to brief him and pick up some fresh tobacco for you George while I'm out.

'If there's somewhere nearby of course, Abhra?'

'There is indeed, Sahib Jean,' Abhra confirmed, 'Though you may find it easier to get what you want, if I were to accompany you?'

'Excellent idea,' Jean agreed, and with that he

wrapped himself in his robes and left with Abhra.

As soon as we heard them go into the street Peter turned to us and said.

'We might not have long, George.'

Without further ado, we quickly described our encounter with the holy man, and the vision which Marlow had seen.

'It was you then?' Peter asked. 'Both Selene and I were sure we heard the sound of the drums in the air, this afternoon.

'Yes,' I confirmed. 'It was only very subtle even for us, despite nearly dragging us both in.'

'More importantly,' Harry broke in. 'You're sure this figure you saw was Ziusudra?'

'I am,' Marlow replied, earnestly. 'I've seen his face on two occasions before this. The first time during the vision or dream I had at the singing stones. The second time while we were in Corinth.

'Both times I've seen flashes of him at his temple in Africa, and then longer glimpses of his face looking straight into the flames, as though he were attempting to look forward in time to those who would follow the clues he'd left behind.

'This was definitely the same man,' he concluded.

'Remarkable,' Androus replied.

'One of the legends from early Hinduism comes from a legend known as the Sumudra Mathan, in which the gods churn an ocean of milk to produce the nectar of immortality, Amrita.

'But this nectar of immortality is carried by a deity known as… now what was his name? Dhan… Dhanvantari I think, a being who is often referred to as the physician of the gods and the founder of Ayurvedic medicine.'

'That is a most intriguing coincidence,' Harry chipped in, filling his pipe.

'Robert sees this Ziusudra carrying what could be the secret of his immortality with him as he passes through

Haridwar, maybe even on his journey to find a place to build his second great temple, and in ancient Hindu cosmology the god of medicine also supposedly carried the secret of immortality with him in the form of this substance, Amrita, the nectar of immortality, on his travels to Haridwar, Prayaga, modern day Allahabad, and Varanasi, all cities on the Ganges.'

'It is a very speculative line of enquiry,' Androus commented, while clearly more than a little distracted by the thought. 'As soon as I can find a good source of information about this Dhanvantari I will attempt to cross reference any further mention of his travels with the directions mentioned on the tablets.'

This all sounded very promising, and while we were talking about it, I almost forgot about the notes I'd taken of what the holy man had said to us both. Luckily Selene had been paying attention to our account of what had happened earlier on, so she reminded us that we'd mentioned the holy man talking to us and asked us what he'd said.

It wouldn't be as straight forward as asking Abhra, but I extracted my pocketbook from my robes and read out the different snippets of what the holy man had said.

'Well that part is clearly a warning of some sort,' Peter added, as soon as I read out the first bit that sounded something like Sarvetand rah hey!

'Yes, we figured as much from the tone,' Marlow confirmed.

'Well,' Harry added, thoughtfully. 'That word at the end that you mentioned… 'sandkeera', by chance it featured on several of the footpath signs that Androus and I followed today, describing the slender little paths that wound their way along the cliff edges to the temple at the top.'

'So, you think it relates to a cliff edge or drop?' I asked, trying to understand the warning which the holy man was giving.

'No,' Androus corrected. 'I think that word was more likely to be describing the path as narrow or single file.

Wouldn't you agree Harrison?'

'Absolutely,' Harry agreed, without hesitation. 'There was one point lower down the mountain where the path wound its way through a boulder-filled ravine, nowhere near the cliff edge, and with the benefit of hindsight I'm sure the signs were trying to tell us that the path was too narrow to travel with a cart or even large backpacks.'

'Well that gives us either end of what he was saying,' Selene summarised. 'So, it sounds like the holy man was telling you to "Beware" of something or other, because it is too "Narrow" or "Slender". Does that sound right?'

'Androus, I know you've been compiling a list of Hindu words and phrases to help with our search,' I added. 'Do you happen to have any words written down for Path or Way?

'Yes, I believe I do,' he added, rifling through the various notebooks he carried.

'Yes, here we are,' he confirmed after flipping through the pages of the relevant notebook.

'The words I have for Road or Path in Hindi are - Sadak, maarg, pat or nishaan?'

'Hmmm, they don't sound familiar,' I had to reply, disappointed. 'But I could have missed it.'

'What about words for Follow or Pursue?' Selene asked, picking up on my train of thought.

'I don't think I have anything for Pursue,' Androus replied, reading several pages to make sure. 'But I do have a few options listed for Follow, including – Meeri, Karay, Karna.'

'That's it,' I confirmed. 'The middle phrase was "Aap yar tra karay". The last word of which must mean Follow.'

'Then it must have been a warning about the path we're following,' Marlow suggested. 'Beware, the path you follow is a narrow one, or words to that effect.'

It was only as Marlow pieced the holy man's

warning back together that the strangeness of that encounter really struck me.

Without knowing us in any way, or a word being said, when Marlow began to slip into the trance-like state caused by the distant drums, the holy man had not only detected it and recognised it as something to do with us, but he'd somehow known we were on a mission.

I saw the same thoughts passing across the faces of everyone else in the room, but none of us could make sense of it.

THE GANGES

I WAS BEGINNING TO FEEL at home in our apartment in Haridwar. After informing Butterworth's man of how the local street children were being used to keep a lookout for at least one impostor, Butterworth must have decided it was better to have a bird in the hand than two in the bush, because the following day, he sent his police officers out, to lay a trap for the charlatan.

Unfortunately, the method they used was all too predictable, namely to approach from every side as quickly as possible, through the busy streets of Haridwar.

When they'd informed us of this plan, both Jean and Marlow had voiced their concerns about the wisdom of such an approach, and had suggested that we might help by infiltrating the scene first, by taking our sandalwood box of ashes to the holy man to receive his blessing. Butterworth and Studgeon would hear none of it though, convinced that their men could manage without us, and reluctant to allow us to break our cover unless it was absolutely necessary.

Needless to say, the small army of constables was spotted by the local urchins before they got anywhere near their target, and the charlatan was long gone by the time the police reached where he'd been preaching.

To his credit, while he was fuming at the debacle, Butterworth made no attempt to blame us for the failure, and instead telephoned Jenkins while we were there to explain that the undertaking had not succeeded, but that the responsibility for its failure was his alone and that we had in fact raised concerns about the plan, even offering to help out with the capture by infiltrating the scene.

Jenkins received the news rather philosophically, and without hesitation agreed to extend our travel permits by a whole month if we would agree to make our way down the Ganges to the next holy city of Allahabad, where our new papers would be waiting for us at the police headquarters.

It was a disappointment not to have succeeded in apprehending one of the fake holy men, but at least we would be taking a significant step back in the right direction by heading to Allahabad.

The downside, was that Allahabad was nearly four times the distance that we'd travelled from New Delhi to Haridwar, so it was going to take us another three or four weeks to get there if we travelled as we had before.

Abhra tried to offer us some suggestions that might save us some time and effort, including selling the horses and travelling overland by train. But this was just too quick, and would leave us with at least three weeks to kill before there was any realistic chance of the fake holy men turning up there.

River boats were also out of the question at this point, as no suitable boat would be available on the river until much further down its course.

The only real alternative to walking, as we had done for most of the journey to Haridwar, was to ride for a good section of each day. This would give both ourselves and the horses some exercise in the process.

With no other credible choice available to us, it was just a question of making the best use of the time. As a consequence we continued our study of Hindi and the Hindu mythology as we journeyed along, effortlessly steering Abhra into telling us all he could of the origin myths of Dhanvantari, and the creation of the Amrita, the nectar of immortality, along the way.

We also took the time to visit several of the larger holy shrines that were close to our route along the Ganges. At each one presenting the sandalwood box which Guru Nandh had given us to carry our friend's ashes in, as well as the letter from him asking other holy men along the way to also give their blessings to our mission.

Over the succeeding three weeks as we travelled toward Allahabad, we collected over a dozen additional seals or signets to that piece of paper, and just as many golden ribbons or ceremonial cords added to the box.

There were some who even offered us additional saffron sashes for our turbans, which we continued to wear.

Like many of the pilgrims, we tried to follow the river as much as possible, though it was a considerably longer route than going via Moradabad, Bareilly and Sharjahanpur.

One of the advantages of following the river, was that along the way just north of Gangeswari we travelled through an area of natural wilderness, where, Abhra informed us, Tigers were still known to have roamed wild as recently as ten years previously.

The contrast with the cultivated farmland that bordered so much of the rest of the river couldn't have been more extreme. Here in this small pocket of wild 'terai', the trees grew in great abundance with a thick tangle of underbrush pierced only sporadically by shafts of light from the ever-brilliant sun. It was easy to imagine just how well this environment would have suited those now vanished tigers with their striped camouflage, which would have blended in amongst those occasional shafts of light to perfection.

When the road we followed left the trees and the

natural habitat of the tiger, it entered the wild grasslands and marshes where elephants roamed, with the lush green and brown stems of the tall grasses reaching over our heads, even while we were on horseback.

This area of wilderness, no more than five miles long, was considered to be a dangerous route to take by the local villages unless they were travelling in groups. We were advised to keep to our horses with plenty of space between riders while travelling through it, just in case we should come into contact with any of the area's wild inhabitants and needed to evade them.

In former times, when most of the Ganges plain would have been this kind of wilderness, full of big cats, elephant and rhino, I could imagine how similar it would have been to those wild areas of Africa that I loved so.

'You miss it don't you,' Selene asked, riding alongside me.

'Am I so obvious?' I replied, as my attention returned to the road ahead.

We were riding two abreast along the cart track, with each pair of riders six horse lengths apart from the next.

'If you were looking at the trees and grasses around us and were thinking about the life you had back in Kenya, then, yes.'

'Yes, you are correct first time,' I admitted, looking over at her. She was riding, like the rest of us, without a veil, her face bared to the sun for once, enjoying the fresh air and the languid breeze which occasionally stirred the surrounding grasses.

'The light is a little different here,' I continued. 'And the earth smells different to Kenya, but it's close enough to stir fond memories.'

'Does it perhaps give you second thoughts about whether you're doing the right thing?' she asked openly, for the first time in the whole journey.

'In truth, Selene, I've already had second, third, and

more thoughts about what we're doing, and I'm still far from certain that it's the right choice for any of us.'

'Then why do you persist?' she asked. 'You could easily fade back into your life in Africa until my organisation has forgotten all about you. You could perhaps even settle down there if you wanted.'

'Well, if I could settle anywhere it would be in Africa,' I conceded, wondering if she was finally going to try and persuade me to abandon our mission.

'But it's… complicated,' I continued, struggling to figure out where to start.

Somehow without realising it, I slipped into the story of my early life and how I'd felt constantly in the wrong place, in a home with a profoundly unhappy and inward facing parent, a day pupil at a boarding school, forever leaving my friends behind, and finally the owner of my father's house, where I'd never really felt at home or welcome.

'I'm not saying I'll never settle down,' I eventually concluded, just as we were leaving the wilderness and returning to open farmland. 'But travelling with these people, including yourself, has been the closest thing to a real home, to a family, that I've ever known. So, for the moment, where they go, I go too.'

I was tempted to ask her something about her time amongst the Icarii, but as we rode out into the farmland there was no longer any need for us to ride quite so far apart, so we regrouped to where we could all hear one another again.

A week later and we arrived in Allahabad. Our disguises by now had become completely normal, and I couldn't remember when I'd last been clean shaven and not gotten up in the morning to don a turban and loose-fitting desert robes, rather than trousers and a shirt.

More importantly our command of Hindi had improved considerably, aided by its relation to Turkic which we already spoke, so much so that we were all now capable of basic conversation, reading and writing.

To help us improve we'd adopted the practice of speaking to one another in Hindi for most of the day, until when we made camp for the evening. We then reverted to English if we weren't likely to be overheard, or Turkic if we were.

As was the case with understanding any culture, the language was the key, so as our Hindi improved, so too did our grasp of the Hindu faith, mythology and wider Indian culture.

Unfortunately, we'd timed our arrival in Allahabad poorly, after being misdirected by a Brahmin we'd asked along the way for directions.

As a consequence, we arrived in the gloom just after sunset, and took a wrong turn on our approach to the city. This led us along the riverbank and then via three or four small ferries from one river island to another, before finally landing us in one of the least glamorous, commercial areas of the city.

By the time we spotted our mistake, it was far too late to turn back, forcing us to navigate our way through an extensive area of grubby docklands, with dozens of dead end roads, and countless crates and other rubbish obscuring or blocking the way.

Our horses, had also had enough after a long day's travel in the ever-present heat, and were increasingly reluctant to be led by us as we made our way toward the city centre, where we hoped to find shelter for the night.

It was then, as we were at our lowest ebb, our horses dragging behind us, that I suddenly heard Marlow up ahead, shout for us all to take cover in English.

I was walking beside Abhra at the time toward the back of our column, who just looked completely stupefied by Marlow's alarm, and continued to stand there holding his horse.

Without thinking, I dropped the reigns for my own

animal and barrelled into our unsuspecting guide, half pushing and half falling with him behind a large wooden crate, while simultaneously struggling to free my pistol from its sheath beneath my robes.

Our sudden movements had frightened the horses, and despite their tiredness, they were twisting and stamping on the ground, one or two half-rearing in their alarm.

'Robert! What is going on?' I heard Jean call from just in front of me, as I continued to scan the gloomy shapes of the dock all around us, with my pistol out in front of me.

'Robert!' I heard Jean call again, after not receiving a response.

'False alarm,' Marlow finally answered, before stepping out from behind the pile of lumber he'd taken cover behind.

I hadn't realised that I'd been holding Abhra down on the ground with my off hand, while I searched for trouble with my gun, but now as we realised there was no danger, I put my gun away and helped him back to his feet, for the first time aware that my heart was thumping in my chest louder than a drum.

Abhra was clearly more than a little confused by what had just happened, but our priority was to calm the horses, which were still responding to the tension in the air.

We pulled them together in an open area just ahead of where Marlow had taken cover, and gave them the last of the water we were carrying, before Marlow explained what had happened.

'It was my dream,' he explained quietly while Abhra was out of earshot. 'The ambush that I mentioned to you before. I saw it happen in a place very much like this, just after dark, but I was mistaken. This is clearly not the place or not the time.'

'Well, it is better to be safe than sorry,' Jean responded, just as Abhra joined us, having finally calmed his horse.

'Robert was just telling us he thought he saw

bandits or robbers moving amongst the shadows,' Jean explained.

'But there was nothing?' Abhra asked.

'A couple of dogs, looking for food, nothing more,' Marlow replied.

'All the same we should make our way out of this area with all haste,' Abhra explained. 'It is unlikely that robbers would attack such a large group, but there is little point in running the risk.'

We didn't need telling twice, and a few minutes later, we found our way out of the dock area and onto one of the main thoroughfares leading toward the city centre. Along the way Abhra managed to obtain directions to a stable yard large enough to take care of all our horses, and some lodgings, where we could hire rooms.

A crescent moon was high in the sky and the stars were clearly visible before the animals and our lodgings were taken care of, leaving us just needing to find something to eat.

Here the street vendors came to our rescue, and after just a few minutes of looking, we returned to our lodgings with a veritable feast for our evening meal, followed by some much needed sleep.

ALLAHABAD

ALLAHABAD AND HARIDWAR could hardly have been more different. Both were large and comprised a medley of highly decorative Moghul and British Empire architecture mixed with plainer, functional buildings.

But where Haridwar was a city squeezed in between the slopes of the Himalayan foothills, with building after building seeming to clamber higher and higher up the hillsides in a desire for more space, Allahabad was constructed on the never ending flat of the Ganges plain.

Where Haridwar was constrained and appeared piled up on itself, Allahabad seemed to sprawl, with on impossibly long road leading on to another and another.

Only later did we learn this was because the city encompassed not only both sides of the Ganges, but also the land beyond where the Yamuna river, sister to the Ganges, joined from the south.

Perhaps it was because of this junction of the rivers that the city had spread so much, or perhaps it was the flatness of the surrounding plains, but whatever the reason Allahabad had grown to cover a huge area.

Abhra was of course familiar with the city, and the morning after our arrival, he did as he had done on our first day in Haridwar, and drew us a rough map with the rivers, roads and temples marked on it, as well as the police headquarters and some of the hotels.

Our first order of the day was to call in at the police headquarters and introduce ourselves to the local police commander. With luck we might also get to pick up our new travel permits, which should have arrived by now.

I would go with Marlow and Peter to the police headquarters, while Harry and Androus would visit an Ajurvedic library on the eastern outskirts of the city, where they were hoping to find out a little more about the legends of Dhanvantari as the god of medicine.

Selene had quietly let us know that she wanted to have a look around by herself to see if she could spot any sign of Icarii operatives being present in the city, so Jean asked Abhra to help him in researching the transport options from Allahabad down to Varanasi and then on to Calcutta, which in Androus' considered view was our most likely destination on the Ganges.

Mindful of how the fake holy men had operated in Haridwar, we were hoping to wrap things up in Allahabad within a couple of days, before heading on down to Varanasi to pick up on the directions contained on the tablets again.

As with all of the ancient directions which Androus had translated, there was no guarantee we'd correctly identified Varanasi, but it was one of the better candidates apparently.

Our increased understanding of Hindi and our growing familiarity with the way in which these large Indian towns and cities worked, made acclimatising to Allahabad relatively straight-forward, and by mid-morning Marlow, Peter and I had made the trip from the far north-eastern corner of the modern city, across the central peninsula of land that existed between the waters of the Ganges and the Yamuna to the civic district.

According to Abhra, Allahabad was considered one of the most sacred sites in India primarily because of this geographic location between these two holy rivers.

'Gentlemen and Lady,' he explained. 'The location of this city between the two great rivers of the Ganges and Yamuna is considered to be very sacred, but Allahabad is also reputed to be the place where the now extinct River Sarasvati also met the Ganges and the Yamuna. In fact, the former name of this great city "Prayag" means the place where the rivers join, or more literally, the place between where they join. This old name for Allahabad is thought to refer to the land between the two rivers that still exist, which was once an island surrounded by sacred rivers on all sides.

'It is because of this heavenly location that Brahma chose this site to perform his first sacrifice after creating the world.'

Unknown to Abhra, this meeting place of the three sacred rivers was also very similar to one of the locations described on the tablets, which had mentioned a trading town located on an island at the confluence of the three great rivers, and where the banks of the rivers had also been completely cleared of trees for five hundred steps in every direction to provide pasture for the town's domesticated animals and safety from the wild creatures of the forest.

There was no mistaking the meeting place of the two remaining rivers, but the encroaching forest described on the tablets was now a distant memory, with only the odd tree or fruit orchard providing a break from the miles of cultivated fields which stretched as far as the eye could see.

The police station was located between the two rivers, in a prosperous section of the city amongst a group of other civic buildings, including the courts, government offices, banks, lawyer's offices and the central post office for the district.

The building was more like a bank or office building than the miniature fort which the headquarters in Haridwar had been, but as we entered through a broad archway that led through to a shaded central courtyard, the feel of the place was immediately recognisable.

There was the tall reception desk with the long line of people waiting to be seen, while clerks and police officers passed through numerous side doors and corridors.

I'd scanned the place as we entered, but was paying more attention to the architecture of the building, when Peter subtly nudged my elbow to get my attention, and then indicated I should look along the queue toward the reception desk.

Behind the desk, dealing with the person at the front of the queue was Studgeon, or someone who could only have been his twin.

Unsure what to make of the sergeant's presence, I looked back at Peter and Marlow with a question, but both responded wordlessly to indicate they didn't know what to make of it either.

With no idea what was going on, we could only wait our turn, then just as we had in Haridwar, we presented Jenkin's letter to the completely deadpan Studgeon, who accepted it, pretended to read for a minute and then, after asking one of his colleagues to take his place, he walked us down one of the corridors into the backrooms of the station.

'Nice to see ye made it, gentle-men,' he said without any further preamble. 'Myself an' the captain were beginnin' ta wonder whether you'd taken a wrong turn somewhere.'

Sensing we'd have to go into the details again for the captain of police here in Allahabad, we tried to turn the question around and find out why he'd followed us from Haridwar.

'I'm thinkin' it's probably best if I leave that fur the captain te explain,' he replied, leading us through a small ante-room containing a separate reception desk, manned by a corporal.

'At ease, corporal,' Studgeon commanded, as the man shot to attention. 'Please see if the captain has a few minutes fur us?'

The corporal promptly disappeared through the office door behind him, re-appearing a moment later to wave us through.

There, just rising from behind a big desk at the end of the room was the towering figure of Butterworth, who, entertained by our evident surprise, indicated we should take a seat at the highly polished table to one side of his office.

'Some tea and sandwiches as soon as you can.' Butterworth ordered of his corporal, who simply saluted before leaving the room.

'Gentlemen, how nice to see you again,' the captain began, shaking our hands before taking a seat at the table opposite to us.

'I realise you must be wondering why Studgeon and I have travelled down here to meet you when we made no mention of it while you were still in Haridwar,' he said. 'Well, it's a simple matter of Commissioner Jenkins not wanting the same mistake to be made again here as happened in Haridwar.

'And what better way to ensure it doesn't, while simultaneously teaching me the lesson I needed to learn, than sending me down here to swap places with Captain Arbuthnot for a few weeks.'

While it was a surprise to see Butterworth and Studgeon again, I knew they'd genuinely regretted how things had turned out in Haridwar, and had made no attempt to blame us for it, so I had no qualms about working with them again, and after glancing at Marlow and Peter I could tell they were of the same opinion. If anything this made our job here in Allahabad a little bit easier.

The pleasantries out of the way, we quickly described our journey from Haridwar and where we were staying, so that Studgeon could arrange somewhere for one of his men to rendezvous with us each evening in order to give us any intelligence the local constabulary had gathered, while simultaneously giving us an opportunity to feedback on anything we'd found.

The tea and sandwiches arrived as Butterworth and Studgeon were describing what they'd discovered so far.

Apparently, they'd both been in the city for a little over a week, having travelled by train to get here. Since arriving they'd acquainted themselves with the men under their command, explaining the commissioner's suspicion to them that agents of a foreign power were thought to be operating in the area in the guise of visiting holy men.

They'd also communicated to the men that these fake holy men were thought to be employing the local street children as their lookouts.

'We know many o' these young bairns are tricked into working under the hand of some petty crook, so once we grab these fake guru's we'll pick up some of the bairns as well, and from them work our way back to their masters.'

'The question is, gentlemen,' Captain Butterworth continued. 'How are we to proceed when we do once again identify where these charlatans are preaching their lies to the public?'

It was a good question, and one which we'd spent several days discussing on the journey down to Allahabad.

Fortunately, we'd come up with what we felt would be a good idea.

'The children are the key to the operation,' Marlow explained. 'We'll never be able to disguise enough of your men well enough to sneak them past these street children, all of whom can spot a police officer from a mile away.'

'But we can't arrest any of these children without at least some of the others noticing,' Butterworth protested.

'Very true,' Marlow conceded, unperturbed. 'But supposing we merely incapacitated them, or better yet gave them the tools to incapacitate themselves?'

'You want te poison these wee bairns?' Studgeon asked, slightly incredulously.

'Not at all,' Marlow replied with a smile. 'What we're suggesting is merely a walk through the target area with a basket full of sweets and pastries to offer as a sacrifice to one of the nearby temples.

'Each pastry will include a mild sedative, just enough to put a child asleep.'

'… And any street urchin worth his or her salt will relieve you of any "spare" pastries as you walk past, whether they're supposed to be on lookout or not!' Butterworth guessed, with a dry chuckle.

'Precisely,' Peter confirmed, taking over the explanation from Marlow.

'All we need to do is stroll past each of the lookouts, giving them the chance to steal some of the pastries as we pass, after which it will only be a matter of time before they fall asleep and your men can walk right up to the charlatans without anyone being the wiser.'

'Simple yet elegant,' Butterworth commented, nodding to himself as he pondered the idea. 'We can have one of the police surgeons put the sedative together and the pastries can be had from anywhere.'

We talked through a few more details, finishing both the sandwiches and the tea as we did so, before Butterworth went on to point out on a map of the city some of the more popular spaces where the various factions of holy men tended to congregate.

This included another tent village populated mostly by the Sadhus again, as well as some smaller areas near to particular shrines.

'The main event takes place in another two weeks of course, when all the holy men in the city will form a procession through the city to the tip of the peninsula where the two rivers meet.'

'Aye, and they walk all the way there with not a stitch of clothing on, as casual as you might walk down the Princes Road in Edinburgh.'

'Well, hopefully we'll have routed out the fakes for you long before then,' Peter added.

The two policemen had taken the trouble to mark the different sites they were talking about on a large-scale map, so they could point them out as we talked about them.

Finally, we got to current intelligence which the two men had ordered their beat-officers to collect, just as they had in Haridwar. Any holy men pitching up in unusual places, or sites where crowds had gathered without a speaker or holy man being present.

These locations they also marked on the map in a red ink. In total there must have been nearly a hundred red crosses on it by the time they were finished, most of which would doubtless turn out to be nothing. If we were lucky, the locations that our charlatans were preaching from would also be on there, just waiting for us to find them.

The briefing provided by Butterworth and Studgeon had taken a while and contained a great deal of detail, so much so, that I'd completely forgotten about our new travel permit.

Fortunately, Butterworth needed no reminding, and now as we prepared to leave, he produced it from a dossier of other documents on his desk without us even having to ask.

'You still wouldn't care to share your reasons for

wanting this permit I take it?' he asked, after he handed it to Marlow.

'Perhaps on our way back,' Marlow replied, gently.

'I look forward to it,' Butterworth responded, as we said our goodbyes and left.

FIRE AND WATER

WE WERE STALKING OUR PREY. The map provided by Butterworth and Studgeon contained a wealth of locations for us to check, so over the next few days we split up into pairs and started to work our way around the dozens of locations marked in red ink, discounting all those that didn't seem to have a perimeter of watchful street urchins surrounding them.

And just like that, we started to spot them. They were often enthralling individuals, and all too plausible, plying exaggerated or false information to anyone who would listen, sometimes more than a hundred people at a time. Hindu myth and scripture artfully woven in with criticism of the local Mohammedan or Christian population.

At other times we heard them speak more directly, often of the terrible deeds committed by the British, and the dark days under the brutal and dispassionate gaze of the East India Company. Closely followed by the allegory of India's benevolent neighbour to the east, the Chinese, who had evicted these same British tyrants from their shores and now lived rich and fulfilling lives by comparison.

The propaganda was by turns subtle and then crude, and in response some of those in the audience simply turned and walked away when the speaker began to talk of things other than the faith. But for every person that walked away, there were more that stayed.

We listened to the lies and half-truths without

comment, and baited out traps as we went, taking sweet pastries which hadn't yet been doctored with the sedative, as offerings to the different holy men we spotted, carrying them in long lidless baskets, so that the nimble fingers of street children could easily dart over the lip to liberate a handful of the tasty morsels.

There was always plenty left in the baskets we carried to donate to both the genuine holy men and the fakes that we passed, and if making such offerings was a little unusual, after the first day it was no doubt attributed to our foreign ways and lack of understanding.

After three days we'd visited all the sites which Butterworth and Studgeon had marked on the map, as well as another dozen locations which had been passed to us since.

Along the way we had identified six different fake holy men operating in the city, aided by local street urchins posted as lookouts.

Butterworth and Studgeon were eager to move in on the fakes we'd identified before they had a chance to once more vanish, but they had learned their lesson, so didn't even try to pressure us into moving before we were ready.

At the end of the third day though, we'd identified no additional charlatans, which we took as an indication that we'd found all the fake holy men operating in the city.

It was time to make our move.

We notified the constable sent by Studgeon later on that evening that we were ready to make our move, knowing he would report back promptly, and the plan we'd agreed upon would begin to swing into action.

But while the police would be busy behind the scenes, arranging the manpower they'd need to swoop on the fake holy men, we had little to do. The baskets of pastries and snack foods would be collected in the morning, as we had done on the previous three days. This time we would discreetly apply the sedative which the police surgeon had provided, and then we would visit the locations where the charlatans were working, three sites at a time, giving the youngsters who had become used to our presence, the opportunity to once more relieve us of the treats we carried, before moving on to the next three sites.

After that it would all happen very quickly, and within half an hour we would know whether our plan had worked.

In the meantime, we had time to kill, so after having a bite to eat at our lodgings, I decided to venture out to watch the aarti fire sacrifice down by the river again.

Most of the others had already decided to stay in, and relax with a pipe or two without having to wear their turbans and disguises, but Peter offered to join me, as did Marlow, who would doubtless be following his usual routine of watching the setting sun.

I don't know why the fire ritual had captured my imagination so, but there was something about the way the countless numbers of devotees placed their tiny floating boats into the water, containing nothing more than a single little candle made of butter-fat, surrounded by brightly coloured petals, that I found entrancing.

I'd watched the ceremony several times in Haridwar, and a few times on a much smaller scale on the way to Allahabad, but I'd never yet made an offering myself, despite the fact that there were always people selling the flowers, candles and boats in the vicinity.

'I think I'd like to take part in the fire ceremony this evening,' I said to Peter and Marlow as we made our way to one of the long Ghats where people bathed in the river waters during the day.

'I'll join you,' Peter replied. 'I don't think I understand its purpose properly, but it's a spectacular sight when all those tiny flickering lights start to congregate further down the river.'

'You'll forgive me if I follow my own routine?' Marlow asked, knowing we would understand what he meant.

I'd fallen out of my habit of paying close attention to Marlow since we'd been in India, but we all knew that when he ventured out in the evening, it was invariably to find some solitary spot in which to watch the sun go down once again.

While we had been in Haridwar I remember thinking it would be impossible for any more people to be gathered together in one place, but I was sure there were more people here in Allahabad. Granted this was a bigger city, sprawling as it did across the rivers. Rivers which themselves appeared almost lake-like in their extent, because their pace was so slow, allowing the Ganges alone to spread to five times the width of the fast-moving version of itself in Haridwar.

We walked down to the water's edge, passing many groups of people talking and singing, dancing or playing instruments, until we happened upon one of the vendors selling the component parts of the little flower filled boats with butterfat candles at their centre. I didn't yet have the language to answer the questions the vendor was asking me, but eventually after much pointing and gesturing I managed to buy everything I needed to make a dozen boats, half of which I gave to Peter, Marlow having already left us.

We carried our votive offering down to the water's edge, where one of the other pilgrims offered me a light from a long slender stick that he was carrying, and then one by one I laid my half dozen flickering and flower filled boats into the placid water, where they glided, ever so slowly in a ragged line away from the shore.

I had no prayers or thoughts to send with these flame-filled little boats, but even so, I found this simple offering to the river a calming gesture.

After watching my flame filled boats for a few minutes until they joined the countless other offerings drifting out into the river, I stepped back from the water to allow Peter to do the same with his.

We'd chosen the shoreline of the Yamuna, a few hundred yards away from where it joined the Ganges. As a result, while there were still thousands of people congregating at the shore, there was more room, and the pilgrims gave one another plenty of space to make their offerings and offer a prayer before moving forward to make their own.

Peter had waited patiently behind me while I gave my own offerings, and now as I stepped back he moved forward to release his.

One by one he lit the stubby little candles in the centre of the six little boats I'd given him, and then gently placed them on the surface of the water next to him.

A few seconds later all six boats were in the water and had formed a ragged line as they started to drift away from the shore, but then, ever so slowly they seemed to drift back toward Peter a little, who was kneeling down beside the water's edge, with just his right hand resting effortlessly on the water's surface. Not submerged, just barely in contact with the calm water.

Mesmerised, I saw the six flickering lights return to Peter's hand, and form a perfect circle, as though they were all caught in a tiny whirlpool or eddy, one light following another, swirling round and round before him.

It was a strangely beautiful thing to see, caused no doubt by a one in a million current as the lazy river meandered past.

I smiled beneath my face veil at the sight, and then for no more than a heartbeat I could have sworn I saw another hand reflected in the water below Peter's, as well as the face of a woman reflected in the centre of those circling offerings.

This was accompanied for the briefest moment by a familiar chorus of distant drums travelling over the night air to mix with the singing and music of the people that surrounded us.

It was only then that I remembered what Peter had

told me about his dreams, and how, without looking for it, he'd fallen in love with one of those shimmering spirits in the dreamlands that stood forever in a circle around the raging column of fire into which Marlow had stepped.

I stood transfixed, until those six little boats of light broke out of their circling pattern and drifted one after the other out into the river.

Peter continued kneeling by the water with his hand just barely touching its surface for a moment more, watching the offerings he had made recede into the distance.

Eventually he stood up and walked back over to me, an unmistakable expression of sadness on his face after this briefest of contact with his love.

'I can't cope with any more delays in finding this temple,' he said, looking me squarely in the face with a determination I'd rarely seen in my otherwise easy-going friend. 'I need to find out how to reach that dream place more consistently, so that I can spend more time with her.'

'I understand,' I said, with genuine feeling.

We had to succeed in rounding up these charlatan holy men, so that we could get on with the business that we'd come to India to resolve: finding the first great temple of Ziusudra.

Those distant drums had sounded for the briefest of moments when Peter had placed his floating candles in the water, but I knew that the others, including Selene and Androus who hadn't been at the original ceremony beneath the Singing Stones, would have heard or sensed it also.

The one person in our group who had no idea about our real reason for coming to India was Abhra, of course, so when we returned to our apartment a couple of hours later, we had to play the same game of cat and mouse, in order to answer everyone's questions without letting Abhra know what we were talking about.

I knew Peter didn't want to tell the rest of the group about his relationships with Danu, the spirit of the rivers and streams from the dream-place, so I told the others that the drums had just come to us unexpectedly while we were making the fire sacrifice by the river, which they seemed to accept without suspicion, although our experience of apparently summoning the distant drums again was clearly stirring something in Marlow.

'I'm sure we're missing something when it comes to sensing or summoning the drums and reaching that place of dreams,' he began. 'We keep hearing them, even when we're not specifically trying to sense them, and yet I've tried to deliberately sense them countless times since we left Haridwar with absolutely no success.'

'You do not mean you have been experimenting with narcotic substances by yourself,' Jean asked, with concern in his voice. 'Just as we did in Corinth all those months ago?'

'No, my friend,' Marlow replied, genuinely. 'We clearly don't need anything like that to reach the dream-place, if my experience in Haridwar and now Peter's experience by the river is anything to go by. I've just been trying to evoke the right state of mind, which I'm convinced is the key.'

We talked further about the dreams and distant drums, and what little we knew about them, and the occasions when they'd come to us unbidden, but we only had so much time before Abhra returned, so it resulted in no new insights.

ENTRAPMENT

THE TRAP IS NOW LAID, and the local street urchins are enjoying some sweet pastries they have stolen from the baskets we have been carrying.

This is the second lot of pastries we have dosed with the sedative provided by the police doctor. A simple vanilla syrup that we have poured liberally over the pastries at the back of the long baskets. The baskets we then tuck under an arm in such a way as to leave the back end poking out behind us, and at just the right height for acquisitive little hands to delve into while we are looking the other way.

This is also the second lot of fake holy-men that we have visited today and it is still not yet lunch-time, the prime time for the crowds to stop and listen to the soft words of visiting holy men.

The street urchins we saw an hour ago will probably already be starting to feel drowsy, hidden away as they are in the nooks and crannies of the streets surrounding the first group of charlatans, while their brothers and sisters in this neighbourhood are still greedily eating their way through our sticky, syrup covered pastries, expertly licking their fingers and hands before the sedative infused sweetness can escape down their forearms in long sticky drips.

Peter was approaching from the other side of the market to where I am, strolling up and down the streets leading into the square, providing morsels of un-drugged food to the beggars as he goes, just as I have done, before finally moving into the square itself to offer up the remaining pastries to the fake holy man who has been preaching and meditating on this spot for the past two hours.

He is a striking figure. Tall and thin with a long flowing grey beard and unkempt darker hair that is wound into thick dreadlocks and knotted up on top of his head. His robes are similarly dishevelled, the sacred orange garments, now distinctly yellow in places, but none the less still draped stylishly across one shoulder, in order to better display his slender form.

It's time for us to leave this place and return to the site we visited an hour ago, collecting the two groups of policemen that will be waiting nearby as we go.

With luck, Marlow and Jean will be doing the same at the two sites they are covering, while Harry and Selene cover the locations occupied by the final two fake holy men.

There is no need for us to rush, because the sedative which we've applied to the pastries will put these children asleep in about half an hour, and will last for a least two hours.

Everything has so far gone as planned.

A quarter mile away, we find the dozen police officers assigned to us, waiting in the designated spot, and we split into two groups in order to approach our first target from two sides. Peter and I proceed a little ahead of the constables, who bring a cart with them to place the sleeping children into as they find them.

We advance on the charlatan and his helpers who are still in mid sermon, taking up our positions covering two different streets to those the police are approaching by, in case they should sense what's afoot and bolt. But as we draw closer they still have a good crowd around them and appear in no rush to bring their sermon to an end, preaching loud and confidently for all to see.

Then without warning the police have arrived, surging suddenly through the crowd to apprehend both the holy man and his helpers before they even realise what has happened.

This is the moment of danger, the point at which we hope the crowd will stand back in shock rather than surging forward to attack the police.

If he'd had a greater presence of mind, the supposed guru could have played up to the audience, inciting them to riot. But the mystical calmness and enlightened manner which he so perfectly emulated just a moment before, now dissolves before the audience's eyes, and in the moment the police lay hands upon him he becomes a snarling, shouting beast, even pulling a pistol from somewhere in his tattered robes to shoot at one of the policemen arresting him. Despite his struggles the constables know their job, and as the revolver appears, one of them forces the charlatan's arm up so that the gun is discharged harmlessly into the air, causing the crowd to take a few steps back.

While the fake guru continues to resist arrest, his helpers give in to the police more quickly, and a few minutes later as the dust begins to settle, all the enemy agents sit shackled on the floor while the police constables wait for a wagon to arrive to take them away.

In the scuffle the long wild hair of the resisting charlatan appears to have fallen off his head, revealing it to be nothing more than a carefully crafted wig, beneath which his skin is noticeably cleaner, and his own hair is neatly trimmed. The same seems to be true of his long tangled beard, which appears to have also become dislodged on one side, where the glue sticking it to his face has come unstuck in the heat of the struggle.

Realising that this holy-man is a fake, the mood of the crowd now finally turns ugly, and it is only because a police sergeant fluent in Hindi steps forward to address them and explain what has happened that they don't try to wreak their own vengeance upon the charlatan and his helpers.

Neither Peter or I have had to get directly involved in the arrest, so our disguises remain intact, and as the police lead the shackled men away, we begin to walk over to our second rendezvous point, where we will meet with another dozen officers before moving in on our second target.

By three o'clock in the afternoon all the fake holy-men have been taken into custody and we are finally able to head back to our apartments for a few hours to rest.

Abhra and Androus have prepared some refreshments for us on our return, which I barely have the energy to consume.

Harry is the only one injured, after one of the holy-men, a very short and rotund figure, sees the police coming at the very last minute, and surprises everyone by leaping through the crowd with unexpected agility, straight at Harry who in his shock, completely fails to move and is knocked over by the fleeing guru, before the rotund figure is brought down by Studgeon with his truncheon.

The operation has stretched the police force in Allahabad far more than they had anticipated, and left them to deal with dozens of sedated street children, fake holy men and their helpers, as well as confiscated equipment, weapons and correspondence which some of these enemy agents were carrying with them.

But their work doesn't end there. While we relax out of the sun back at our apartment, Butterworth's men will be searching the residences where the holy men were staying, some of which still remained to be located, some of which they'd already found details of in the possessions of those arrested.

The following morning Peter, Marlow and I make our way to the police headquarters, for what we hope will be our final meeting with Butterworth and Studgeon.

'Gentlemen, do please come in and take a seat,' Butterworth welcomes us, after we have once again been conducted through to his office.

'I probably don't need to tell you that the operation yesterday was a resounding success,' he continued. 'We have already obtained strong evidence that the men arrested yesterday were in the employ of the Chinese government, and several of those that we detained seem willing to tell us even more in exchange for being treated leniently when it comes to the courts.

'To the best of our understanding we've swept up the entire ring of enemy agents in one swoop, though of course we won't know for sure until we've found and seized any material in their residences, which could take a few days yet.'

'Does that mean we've done enough to earn the twelve-month travel permits that we requested?' Marlow asked, very matter-of-factly.

'Done enough man!' Butterworth declared. 'After

the success of this operation I think Jenkins will give you whatever you want in spades!

'To begin with though, when I telephoned him yesterday evening to give him my initial appraisal of how the operation had gone, he informed me he would have your travel permits waiting for you in Varanasi, if you still wish to travel down-river to that glorious city. And as an additional token of his thanks he would be happy to provide you with the continued services of your guide Mr Balakrishnan, should you want them.'

'That's a very kind offer,' Marlow replied, without hesitation. 'Thank you. We would indeed like to retain Abhra's services, as he has been an enormous help to us so far.'

It was obvious that Butterworth was delighted with how the operation had gone, but after Marlow replied I was sure I noticed a slight hesitation in this one-eyed giant of a man, as though he had something else to ask, but was unsure about how to broach the subject.

'Captain Butterworth, is there something else you wish to ask us,' I said, attempting to help the man out.

'Ah Mr Whitaker, you are very observant. As a matter-of-fact, there is one thing.

'While I was speaking to Commissioner Jenkins yesterday evening, I suggested to him that we try to retain your services, if there's any way in which we can do so.'

'We have some work of our own we need to get on with,' Peter quickly interjected.

'Of course, of course,' Butterworth responded, careful not to pressure us.

'In truth, we need your help, gentlemen, so we're simply asking you to do what you can without interfering with your own plans.'

The captain had been fair with us so far, as had Jenkins for that matter, so we agreed to listen to what they wanted us to help with.

Tea and sandwiches were once again ordered, and

while we waited for them Butterworth produced a large manila folder containing maps and documents about the north-east corner of India, the very place that we suspected the directions on the lapis lazuli tablets would lead us.

'As you may or may not know,' Butterworth began. 'The Arunachal Pradesh area of north east India, known to the locals as "the land of the dawn lit mountains" is a geographically remote, and in many ways, unique area.

'To the north and distant east, the area is surrounded by impassable and poorly mapped mountains which are the home to countless small tribes, many of which speak their own dialects or languages, and who the government has only managed to extract an uneasy peace with, on the condition that we leave them alone to live as they will.

'In exchange they leave the valuable tea plantations of the alpine foothills alone and allow us to move the shipments of the harvested tea down river to the port of Calcutta.'

We were aware that this area was tightly controlled, with travel permits being rarely granted and only for short durations of one or two months, but we had no idea this was because of the political situation with those living in the area.

'Unfortunately,' Butterworth continued, passing round a moderately detailed map of the region for us to scrutinise. 'Although the British government, and the East India Company before it, has held claim to this area for many years, our neighbour to the north and east beyond the mountains has also recently laid claim to it, stating that the peoples of the region are Chinese subjects who have a long cultural relationship with mother China.'

'And this is why they have been sending agents into northern India, in order to distract attention away from their real target in the north-east?'

'Exactly so,' Butterworth confirmed.

'Now, for obvious reasons the governments

presence in the region to the north-east is low profile, with minimal military and police presence, almost non-existent governmental function or non-tea business.

'There is a limited network of train-lines and a robust river boat infrastructure, but little else, so our intelligence in the area is limited.'

'So, you'd like us to spy for you?' Peter asked, rather bluntly.

'In a word. Yes,' Butterworth replied, equally bluntly. 'Your ability to move around the country without being recognised as British subjects is beyond price.

'If you should end up travelling around this north-eastern region in your disguises, you would have a much better chance than us of spotting any further Chinese influence.'

'And if we don't end up in the north-east?' Marlow asked.

'Then you've gone to a great deal of trouble to obtain travel permits which cover that area,' the police captain joked. 'But that aside, wherever you go, whether in disguise or not, all that we ask is for you to keep an eye out for anything unusual that might represent more interference from our friends in the east.'

That was it. In exchange there was little they could offer us, beyond the continued services of Abhra our guide, and a personal letter of introduction from Commissioner Jenkins. We were otherwise entirely free to do as we would, on the understanding that we had given our words that we would not act against the government in any way.

We were all fairly sure the rest of the group would be happy with the arrangement, and said as much to Butterworth, but explained we'd still have to run it by them before giving a final answer.

Butterworth was more than happy with this, and after suggesting we could send him our answer within the next week, we changed the subject to lighter topics, including more of the story of our journey to Samarkand on foot with a merchant caravan and in Bedouin clothing, which seemed to fascinate him.

VARANASI

THE GANGES WAS A LARGE RIVER before it reached Allahabad, but once joined by the equally massive Yamuna, it took on the aspect of something more akin to a slow-moving ocean rather than a river.

We traded in our horses for some cabins on a large diesel barge carrying pilgrims and trade goods up and down the river between Varanasi and Allahabad.

Jean and Peter had researched the route ahead and concluded that the description on the tablets and the path of the Ganges were one and the same for the foreseeable future. While nowhere near as fast as the trains, the barge was a definite step-up in terms of both speed and comfort in contrast to travelling on horseback.

There is however another advantage, and one which I can't seem to get enough of, and that's the river itself.

As we glide downstream with the imperceptible current the river is everywhere, the nearest bank is at least half a mile away for most of the journey, the barge only rarely drawing closer to the land, the constant chug, chug, chug of the big diesel engine the only sound, and one which is so familiar after the first hour that it goes almost unnoticed. In contrast the deck and compartments are being constantly bombarded by a medley of aromatic spices from the food which is always being prepared by the crew and passengers, occasionally intermixed with the harsh, almost acrid smell of the burning chillies which can leave the eyes of those unaccustomed to it streaming with tears.

We have discussed Butterworth's proposal between

us at length, and for the moment agreed to maintain our disguises, allowing me to at least pull the cloth from my turban across my eyes when the smell of cooking spices becomes too much.

What would have taken a week on foot, takes us just over three days on the barge, and we arrive in Varanasi a little after sunset, well rested and keen to stretch our legs. More importantly we are here to find out if one of the directions translated from the stone tablets could be describing this most ancient of cities, or whether we have gone astray.

But Varanasi has a dark side, which Abhra feels he must warn us about once we have checked into our hotel, another establishment commonly used by merchants visiting the city, and somewhere that our guide has stayed at before on many occasions.

'Lady, Gentlemen,' he begins, after asking us all to meet in the breakfast room which is currently not in use by any other residents of the hotel. 'During the time we have travelled together you have offered me the great compliment of trusting me to educate you in the ways of my country and my faith, and along the way you have learned to speak a little of the Hindi language, and come to understand many of the myths, legends and customs which serve as the foundation for the Hindu faith.

'However, despite what you now know and understand, there are certain aspects to our culture that I am sure you may still find troubling if you were to come across them unprepared, some of which you will surely encounter here, in this city of Lord Shiva, Varanasi.

'I know it may be confusing for you, during the time of the great festivals to understand how important the holy cities are to the people of India. So, let me begin by saying that Varanasi is possibly the most ancient and most sacred city there is in all India. This city and this alone is considered the home of Lord Shiva the greatest of the gods.

'For a Hindu to die in Varanasi is for that person to

escape the cycle of Moksha, of rebirth altogether, with no further births into this world or any other.

'Consequently, many of the faith will travel here when their life is drawing to an end specifically so that they may die in Varanasi and be cremated here.'

'I noticed there were several large fires burning along the water's edge when we arrived,' Peter observed. 'Are these the cremation sites for the city?'

'Sahib Machandru, you are most perceptive,' Abhra replied. 'But in this most sacred of cities you will discover that any place may be used to burn the bodies of the dead, for the whole city is sacred. Many will choose to build their pyres on the shores of the Ganga river, but not all.

'Furthermore, you should be prepared to see the bodies of those who have not yet been consumed by the flames, lying on the ground wrapped only in a white cloth, until their pyre is complete. This is normal here in Varanasi and should not be criticised, for this is our way.'

We'd all seen the occasional funeral pyre in the past, especially while we were in Haridwar or travelling along the banks of the river Ganges to Allahabad, but the prospect of an entire city being devoted to death and the cremation of bodies was something else, and something I found a little unsettling.

Surely so many dead bodies waiting to be buried must increase the chances of disease or infection, but when I put this question and others to Abhra, he calmly and politely answered them all without being offended.

After a deliberately light breakfast we head out to get our first look at the city in the morning light.

As was usual for us now, we split into smaller groups in order to perform the different tasks needing to be completed.

Marlow, Peter and I once again made our way to the Police headquarters to collect our transport permits, as well as to send a response to Butterworth and Jenkins informing them that we had discussed their request within our group and had agreed to help out in any way that we could.

Harry and Androus were off to try and match the directions contained on the stone tablets which included a reference to "a pure white settlement on the land where two rivers meet". What the pure white might refer to, they weren't sure, but they were hopeful that a study of the city's most ancient monuments might give them some kind of clue.

That left Jean and Selene, who would together check to see if there was any sign of the Icarii being present in the city, and then arrange passage further down the river toward Patna, another almost equally ancient city further downstream just past where the Changhara river joins the Ganges.

The antiquity of Varanasi was almost palpable as we stepped out into the bright sunlit street outside our hotel. To begin with I couldn't quite square Abhra's warnings about this city of death with the stately buildings that crowded in around the narrow streets and covered bazaars, the open-air market places and countless temples and shrines which seemed to dot our path.

The walk to the police headquarters wasn't a long one, as the city was certainly not as big or spread out as Allahabad, the architects here, albeit in former ages, clearly preferring to build up rather than out.

According to Abhra, this was because the sacred city area was considered to be only the land between the Ganges and the Varuna rivers, and unlike the other cities we'd visited on the Ganges which drew status from their proximity to the great Ganges, this was not the case for Varanasi which was sacred in its own right, irrespective of its proximity to the mother of all rivers.

The effect of these ever-present tall buildings that towered over the comparatively narrow streets was a constant oasis of shade and cool air, which in India was only usually available in the evening after the sun had set.

Here as we walked through the city, the temperature must have been at least five degrees cooler at street level, which felt like even more when we were obliged from time to time to walk in the bright strips of direct sunlight that pierced to street level through the lofty architecture.

But with the morning light the ever-present funeral pyres which Abhra had warned us about were lit again, and as we proceeded the first tendrils of smoke and the occasional odour of burning flesh came creeping up through the twisting streets from the river.

It was subtle for the most part, though there were areas, like the very narrow alleyways where the smoke seemed to linger.

I didn't put two and two together for several minutes, but as though drawn out of the buildings by smoke, the bodies wrapped in plain white cloth slowly started to appear on the pavements and in the doorways or entrances to courtyards.

I was glad that Abhra had prepared us at that point, for even as it was, there was something which felt unmistakably alien about these cloth wrapped forms and the way they were present on the streets and alleyways alongside living members of the family or friends while they sat or stood talking, even eating and drinking.

Without Abhra's warning I think my mind would have rebelled at the strangeness of it all, but instead I reminded myself that in India death was very much a part of life, and only the everlasting cycle of rebirth and reincarnation was something to strive against and reduce. Consequently, for those attending their loved ones here in this city, that cycle was now over, and would be celebrated.

My mind was still grappling with the cultural attitudes to death here in India when we reached the shelter of the police headquarters.

I wasn't quite sure what to expect when we showed up. But there was a part of me that knew it wouldn't be as straight-forward as just walking in the door and picking up the documents.

As usual, we queued with everyone else who had business with the police that day, and then when we reached the front, we presented our letter from commissioner Jenkins to the desk sergeant, who this time waved over one of his colleagues to take us through to a room at the back of the building.

To our surprise, we found both Butterworth and Jenkins waiting for us inside, with a pot of tea already prepared and waiting, and only some more cups being required to make us feel at home.

'Welcome, your time-keeping is excellent, gentlemen,' Jenkins began, indicating we should take a seat around the table where he was drinking tea with Butterworth.

Then before he did anything else, he walked over to the desk at the other end of the room and retrieved a folder, which he opened at the table and produced our signed and fully prepared travel documents, each of which was dated with a full twelve-months duration on it from that very day.

These he handed over as a bundle to Peter, who was sat nearest to him.

'I wanted to hand your documents over to you personally,' he continued. 'As an indication of my sincere thanks for the work you have done.

'We're still only beginning to work our way through the significant amount of evidence and intelligence that was gathered as part of that operation, which I'm sure Captain Butterworth here will be happy to update us on.'

'Of course, sir,' the police captain replied, looking at ease in his employer's presence.

'As you know, gentlemen,' he began. 'On the day we arrested the six fake holy-men, another fifteen assistants and helpers, and took nearly seventy young urchins into custody to sleep off the effects of the sedative they had self-medicated themselves with.

'These children, had very little in the way of information to offer us, but they also had very little in the way of loyalty to the conmen that had hired them, so within a matter of hours we had the details of how the urchins had been recruited, before the youngsters were all released with a caution.

'We used this first piece of evidence against the assistants, who then gave us information about where the charlatans had been staying, allowing us to raid those premises and discover a number of letters and other documents which implicated several senior members of society in the scam, and gave us the leverage we needed to talk to the six main culprits.

'Needless to say, they soon realised the game was up and started to cooperate in order to be treated with as much leniency as they could attract.

'Naturally, our primary aim has been to discover whether they're aware of any other operatives at work in the country, and while we're a long way from getting to the details, they have given us enough information to confirm that this is the case.

'Where these other agents are operating, and what they're engaged in doing, may take us a while to discover,' Butterworth continued. 'But we have enough evidence to monitor the movements of, and then arrest the individual who recruited this batch of charlatans, but we're not rushing the process.'

'The point we're trying to make, gentlemen,' Jenkins summarised. 'Is that we now have evidence that there are other agents of the Chinese government at work in India. We don't know what they're doing, or where they're operating, but if I were them, I would know exactly where I'd be concentrating my efforts.'

'The very place which we've recently been given travel permits to go and visit,' Marlow concluded for Jenkins.

'Precisely,' Jenkins replied.

'Gentlemen, we need your help,' he continued. 'We need your eyes and ears in that territory, we need your disguises, your understanding of the situation and your willingness to travel to what is the most dangerous territory within India.

'I can offer you practically anything you might want in return for helping us in this matter.'

After a quick glance between us, Marlow replied on our behalf.

'Commissioner Jenkins, Captain Butterworth, we appreciate you being open with us in this matter, and also the way you've treated us to date. Yes, of course you can rely on us to help, though with no further intelligence to work on, I would urge you to keep your expectations low.'

As for what they could offer us, there was of course nothing more that we needed. Abhra would continue to accompany us for as long as we needed him, and Jenkins offered to supply us with a fresh warrant to confirm we were acting in his name.

But I was more interested in Marlow and why he had agreed to Jenkins appeal for help. I knew Marlow didn't like travelling in disguise as we had been doing because of the vision he'd had, in which we were ambushed by the Icarii. Yet, he hadn't hesitated to give his approval when Jenkins had asked for help.

Hopefully, I'd get a chance to talk to him about it once we'd left the police headquarters.

For the moment though, we took our leave from Jenkins and Butterworth, and headed back out into the streets of Varanasi to catch up with the others.

FINDING THE PATH

E'D SPENT LESS THAN TWO HOURS in the police station with Jenkins and Butterworth, so it was only mid-morning when we left, but as we stepped back out onto the streets of Varanasi the change in atmosphere couldn't have been more stark.

There had been a handful of bodies out on the streets earlier on that morning, shrouded in simple cloth until their loved ones had finished preparing their funeral pyres, but judging by the increased levels of smoke drifting through the streets now, many more of those pyres had finished being built and had now been lit, complete with the mortal remains of the former loved ones on top.

Despite having increased, the smoke wasn't everywhere all of the time, and as we made our way through the city to the waterfront, there were some places where it collected and seemed to hang in the still air, and others where the light breeze dispersed it entirely.

Consequently, there were moments when it felt like my senses were being assaulted, and others when the comparative cool of the streets and the smoke free atmosphere made Varanasi seem like the loveliest of cities.

Hand in hand with the smoke though, there was an unmistakable mood of celebration in the city, with vendors selling not only a wide selection of food and drink, but also bells and whistles, brightly coloured ribbons and even brighter coloured spices and paints, which some of the visitors to the city seemed to enjoy throwing into the air, or even at one another, judging by the occasional individual we saw liberally doused in the stuff.

But it was the expressions, clothing and energy coming from the visitors to the city that really made me realise how differently the act of death and cremation were viewed in India than they were in the West.

Walking through the streets filled by brightly dressed people, with a constant background murmur of music and song, then down narrow alleys congested with the smoke and incense of the cremations, or witnessing the sudden eruption of bright vermillion or blue powder paint being thrown high into the air, we eventually reached the waterfront half intoxicated by the sights and sounds and sheer sensory overload of the place.

For the briefest moment as we surfaced from the narrow streets into the open air of the waterfront, I couldn't help but wonder how we would have fared if we'd come straight here from New Delhi, as we had been planning, without Abhra's advice and the gradual acclimatisation into Indian culture we'd had over the previous weeks.

But as was often the way in India, I didn't have long to reflect on what might have been, before I was once again confronted by something new that required all my attention to comprehend.

The waterfront in Varanasi wasn't quite the same as those we'd seen in Haridwar and Allahabad. There were still spaces along the water's edge where pilgrims could wash in the waters of the Ganges, the steeply stepped Ghats as they were called, but here in Varanasi the space devoted to them was quite small, while the space devoted to boats and shipping was enormous.

The reasons for this were also fairly clear, because the funeral pyres that we were expecting to see on the river front were actually constructed on an enormous sand bank in the middle of the river. It was easily a mile long and at its closest point two hundred yards away from the busy riverside fronting the city, along which countless small and medium sized boats lined up to ferry those who needed to visit the sandbank across the intervening water, including friends and family members, brahmins and other officials and of course the dead bodies of those about to be cremated.

Lumber was also being transported and built into the pyres, though this was generally being transported on larger skiffs, manned by several men who also did the loading and unloading.

The sandbar already had over a dozen funeral pyres burning, each surrounded by a small crowd of onlookers, but there were at least another dozen being built and still more skiffs of lumber being ferried over.

We walked the length of the waterfront for half an hour or so, but could see no trace of our friends, so we decided to take a boat over to the sand-bank to see if we could find them over there, while simultaneously having a closer look at the cremation ceremony as it happened.

Our disguises by now were second nature, and our command of Hindi sufficient to attract no additional attention, so while a few people still stopped and stared at the sight of three turbaned and veiled strangers, it was only for a moment before they returned back to what they were doing.

After quickly negotiating passage to the island, we hopped aboard a small boat and five minutes later we were stood upon the sandbar looking back at the city.

We'd first arrived in Varanasi on the river barge after dusk, so hadn't had a proper look at the place then, but now, in the morning light it was spectacular, and seemed to glow. So much so, that I instantly thought of what Androus had said earlier about looking for a 'pure white' settlement.

This must surely be the place we were looking for, especially if it were described as being pure and white at dawn, but after asking Marlow and Peter, none of us could remember whether a specific time of day had been mentioned.

Making a mental note to raise the idea with Harry and Androus when we saw them, we set out to explore the sandbar.

We started making our way back to the hotel later that afternoon, tired, but more at one with the city that was home to Lord Shiva. If our preconceptions had been challenged once, then they'd been challenged many times during that day alone. The funeral pyres on the sandbar had been grave and stately affairs, so carefully prepared and arranged for the deceased, and yet once all the ceremonies were complete and the fire was finally lit, they had been a strange mixture of sadness and joy for those assembled to witness it.

Whether my understanding of the situation was correct or not, I wasn't sure, but it seemed the Kumbh Mela celebrations we'd witnessed in both Haridwar and Allahabad, while they included some funeral pyres to cremate the dead, they were far more about the living, and the removal of sin and impurity from those able to travel there and bathe in the sacred waters. In contrast, Varanasi was almost wholly about the dead and escaping the cycle of reincarnation known as Samsara. And while the dead were cremated on a sandbar in the middle of the river so they could receive the blessings of both Lord Shiva, and later when the waters rose and washed the ashes from the sand in the spring, the blessings of the holy Goddess Ganga.

Later, when we returned to the city the smoke from the fires and the incense had lessened, and we contented ourselves with exploring the many bazaars and markets which seemed to exist around every other corner. We stopped to drink sweet tea and eat a light meal in a shaded courtyard café.

There were also more westerners here in Varanasi than any of us had noticed since leaving New Delhi, though none of them paid us even the slightest attention dressed as we were.

It was odd not having to stalk through the city streets on the lookout for fake holy-men or visiting a long list of shrines to find out if anyone were preaching dissent. Then it really struck me that we were finally moving forward with our own search again.

While we were strolling, we stumbled upon what appeared to be a university campus, the Central Hindu College, set in impressive grounds and with a number of prominent newly built faculties.

Here our disguises worked against us, and we were seriously tempted to dispense with them in order to better interrogate the English-speaking students, but instead, when we did manage to stop someone, we had to try and question them using our pidgin Hindi to try and find out whether they had a faculty of history.

It wasn't easy, with academic terminology not being part of our limited vocabulary, but thanks more to the patience of the two young students that we stopped, and to a lesser degree some random examples of Hindu myth, we finally managed to discover that there was indeed a department which taught the history and mythology of the sub-continent.

This was potentially a real bonus, as neither Harry nor Androus had made any mention of the city college, suggesting that neither of them knew it existed.

When we finally stepped back into our apartment, we discovered Selene and Jean were already back, and had brought mixed news with them.

Firstly, they'd discovered a team of Icarii agents in the city, who they'd identified by watching a Catholic Mission house, the location of which they discovered via an innocuous advert pinned to a noticeboard in the city library.

From the Mission House they'd followed the agents to the waterfront, and then to the university college, the police station, railway station and the bigger hotels.

'They're a young and inexperienced team,' Selene explained, neutrally. 'They're just performing their search by numbers, using the contacts they've established and expecting that if we do travel this way, we'll be making use of the same kind of hotels, academic research facilities and transport options as you have used before.'

'So, they're underestimating us,' Marlow asked.

'Perhaps,' Jean replied, less confidently. 'But it is perhaps more likely that they just have a very large area to cover, and believe they once again have the element of surprise.'

'Well, we've been travelling in disguise,' Peter observed. 'Will that be enough to keep them off our trail.'

'Not indefinitely,' Selene responded, looking at each of us.

'But I have taught you to understand what they will look for and what will eventually give us away.' she added, testing us.

'Group size is the obvious giveaway,' I suggested, after a few seconds, knowing that the seven of us, plus Abhra, was just an awkward number. Too few to be a trade caravan or squad of soldiers. Too many to be a typical group of friends.

'Good,' Selene replied. 'But what else?'

'Jenkins and the Police?' Peter asked.

'Correct,' Selene confirmed. 'Commissioner Jenkins may have issued our travel permits discreetly, but there's no disguising our numbers, and sooner or later the Icarii informants working within the Commissioner's Office, or other departments, will find a trace of those permits and report it.

'Either that,' she continued. 'Or one of the officials we meet on the way will contact the Commissioner's Office for confirmation that the permits are real.'

'Of course,' Peter replied. 'And the very fact that we've been issued with travel permits for twelve months is unusual and therefore bound to make some officials curious.'

'The reality is what it is, mes amies,' Jean chipped in. 'We cannot travel without the permits and to attempt to find what we seek in a mere two or three months across such vast distances as India, would be to accept defeat before we have even started.

'Therefore, our question to Ms Autieri must surely be,' he continued, though the mirthful glint in his eye that usually accompanied such questions was noticeably absent on this occasion. 'What can we do to disguise our presence or our movements?

'Would you suggest we split into smaller groups again, as we did when we travelled from Tunis to Turkey.'

'An excellent question,' Selene replied, with the faint trace of a smile on her face.

'Smaller groups would work well if we were travelling as Europeans amongst countless other Europeans,' she explained, giving us another lesson in subterfuge and spy-craft. 'Or if we could convincingly pass ourselves off as natives of the sub-continent, but our disguises simply don't work that way.'

'What about half of us going in disguise while the rest travel as Europeans?' Peter asked.

'It's unlikely to be of benefit,' she replied. 'To those searching for us, a group of four Turkomen travelling the same route as three Europeans will still obviously add up to seven.

'No, in this case, I think we need to dramatically increase the size of our group if we want to go unobserved.'

'You mean, hiring a few people to travel with us?' I asked, wondering what she might mean by dramatically.

'Yes, exactly,' she replied. 'Ten or fifteen people should do it, and we'll arrange turbans and robes for them, and then adapt our desert robes to match, tie our turbans in the Indian style so that we seem part of the group.

'If we ensure they're all Indian citizens,' she continued. 'They won't be subject to any of the travel restrictions or permits that we need to have, and consequently there's a good chance that anyone looking for us would completely ignore a group of that size.

'We could even ask Abhra to make the arrangements and do the hiring, so that even the people we hire don't know who we are.'

It was a simple enough idea, which we could put into practice at any time once we had an idea of where we would be heading next. With luck Androus and Harry would be returning soon with confirmation that they'd managed to match Varanasi with the directions described on the tablets.

PIECES OF THE PUZZLE

I F OUR TRAVELS THROUGH AFRICA, the Mediterranean and the Near East had taught us anything, it was that the journey we were on was far from predictable. All kinds of barriers could be encountered at any time which would stymie our plans for weeks or months on end, only for a way around them to suddenly present itself, or the barrier itself to unexpectedly weaken.

As we waited in our apartment in Varanasi for Androus and Harry to return we had no idea that we were on the brink of one such change in our fortunes.

With no specific plans for the evening Abhra had requested an evening off so that he could catch up with some business acquaintances who were visiting in the city, so we had the apartments to ourselves. After preparing a pleasant meal, most of us had slipped out of our disguises in order to relax with a pipe and some English newspapers.

We hadn't agreed on a particular time for everyone to be back at the apartments for dinner, but by seven o'clock we were becoming a little concerned for our friends, when they finally returned, tired, hungry and thirsty.

Despite their obvious weariness though, there was something in their manner which made me think they had good news.

'We've got it,' Harry blurted out, as soon they'd been handed a drink and given the chance to sit down.

'You've confirmed that Varanasi is one of the

places mentioned on the tablets?' Marlow asked, suddenly very focused.

'More than that, Rob,' Harry replied. 'We've confirmed that both Allahabad and Varanasi are places described on the tablets, and that the directions then go on to describe the rest of the route along the Ganges across India and down through Bengal. They then also describe the meeting place of that great river with the equally powerful Brahmaputra and its course northwards up into Arunachal Pradesh, and the land between Darjeeling and Assam, or possibly even beyond.'

'Incroyable!' Jean exclaimed, clearly as surprised as the rest of us. 'But how... where did you manage to find this information?'

'Would you believe, it all stemmed from the smallest of mistakes,' Androus replied, smiling gently as he unwound the cloth of his turban.

'We had examined some of the older buildings on the edge of the city to see if we could establish a link to the description in the tablets, and as we were working away along the river front, there appeared to be nobody around so we slipped back into English to discuss some of the technical points we were observing.

'Unknown to us, there was an elderly gentleman,' Androus continued. 'A fellow academic, sitting at the stern of one of the boats waiting to be ferried to one of the sandbanks for a funeral service and cremation. Anyway, this Professor Naranjan, as he later introduced himself had not only heard us, but happened to have made a special study of the ancient history of Varanasi and the other early civilisations of the subcontinent.

'Well, the cat was out of the bag as far as our disguises were concerned, so we decided to come clean and tell him who we really were, in the hope that he might be able to shed some light on our question about Varanasi being the white city.'

'It was a gamble,' Harry conceded. 'But we

managed to persuade him that we were tracing the route described in an ancient text written in Sanskrit, and still had a great many doubts about its authenticity, so we were travelling incognito to prevent potential embarrassment to our respective institutions.'

'Precisely,' Androus continued.

'Anyway, our little subterfuge must have intrigued the good professor, because no sooner had he heard of this unusual script and taken a quick look at my notebook in which I rendered the various different forms of the translation from the tablets, than he begged us to follow him onto the sandbar so that he could continue our conversation further.

'Well, what he then proceeded to tell us during the short boat-ride, was that although the great Ganges flows generally from west to east and north to south, there are a couple of places along its route where the river twists quite dramatically back on itself to flow south to north, and Varanasi is just one of these location, not only that, but because the city is located on the west bank of the river, when the sun rises, as it recently had done, the city is bathed not only in the bright morning light of the rising sun, it is also bathed in the reflected light from the river, which results in the city appearing to be the most brilliant of any city on the Ganges, and it is for this reason that it is considered to be the home of Lord Shiva.

'He concluded this story as we disembarked onto the sandbank, and there it was, the city bathed in the dawn light was absolutely dazzling.'

'The entire city practically glows for the first hour and a half after dawn,' Harry informed us. 'It was spectacular.'

'Naturally, having helped us once,' Androus went on. 'Our new-found colleague was eager to help us with the rest of our text, if we wouldn't mind waiting for a couple of hours until the funeral service for a former colleague of his was completed.

'After that, he took us to the college campus and what they hope will become the city's first university, where he proceeded to show us around both his own department of ancient history and the adjacent Geography department.

'Anyway, the man was a veritable font of knowledge,' Androus enthused. 'His department library was immaculately organised and the breadth and depth of his personal knowledge, unsurpassable.

'With my notes from the translation, we went through the various descriptions contained on the tablets and one after another he was able to identify the location on the Ganges and then subsequently the sites that were described along the course of the Brahmaputra.

'There were a handful he couldn't be sure about, but the rest he could identify with comparative ease.'

'His knowledge was less comprehensive when it came to the Arunachal Pradesh area, but he had visited the place a few years before, so was at least able to help us narrow our search area to the eastern Himalaya beyond Bhutan, and what they call the 'Dawn Lit' mountains, rather than the Meghalaya range and eastern Nagaland to the south.'

'He also pointed out,' Harry added. 'That the seasons in this Arunachal Pradesh region were very varied, especially in the summer where the land became very damp and humid, and was overrun with insects, spiders and snakes, while the waterways teemed with leaches, so if we were intent on going there we would only have about four months at the most before the conditions would become unbearable and we'd have to retreat beck to the Ganges plateau or the foothills of the Himalaya where the weather was more temperate, until the season changed again.'

This is both good news and bad. If we were reckless and travelled with all haste, using the trains we could probably reach Siliguri, just south of Darjeeling at the mouth of the north-east region in a couple of days. Whereas if we were careful and travelled predominantly by foot in order to keep a low profile, the same journey would take us at least a month and half.

That would leave us with only two and half months to navigate another five-hundred miles in the valley itself, not including the countless diversions up into the mountains that we would doubtless need to make.

It was a difficult decision, and as I looked around the apartment in which we were all sat, I could see the same realisation on everyone's face.

'This will clearly require some careful consideration,' Jean finally declared. 'And unless I am seriously mistaken, we are all tired out from the day's exertions.

'Consequently, I suggest we put this issue from our minds for the moment, while we all enjoy a good meal and something to drink.'

He was right of course. So, after putting away the maps and notebooks which we'd all just started to produce, we focused instead on clearing the dining table and settling down for a hearty meal.

Varanasi had affected and impressed all of us in the short time we'd been there, and during the course of our meal we discussed the various things we'd witnessed, so much so, that when as we finished our meal and cleaned up afterward, Marlow suggested we take the rest of the evening off as well in order to see what the city was like at night.

This idea seemed to chime with everyone, so we all donned our disguises once more and as a group ventured out, through the city, to the waterfront.

It was cooler now, almost fresh beneath the cloudless starry sky, but the tell-tale drift of smoke and incense on the gentle breeze told us that the funeral pyres were still burning on the sandbank well before they came into sight.

There was a relaxed atmosphere to the city after dark, with much of the crowd and bustle from the day no longer present, and everywhere there were tiny shrines to Shiva, each illuminated with an oil lamp or ghee candle, which together gave the streets a serene almost magical air.

We chatted as we walked, slipping effortlessly back into the hybrid Turkic tongue which we'd all mastered on our long journey to Samarkand along the ancient silk roads, pointing out different sights and scenes to one another as we went.

The river-front after dark, was the domain of the Aarti fire ceremonies, and again while not as large as the equivalent ceremonies in Haridwar or Allahabad it was still an impressive sight.

Here in Varanasi, there was a small area just down-stream from the dock where all the boats operated, where Aarti devotees sang and played music while offering their small flames to the river, mirrored on the sand bar where similar offerings were also being made, in front of the numerous funeral pyres which were still burning brightly and casting their reflected light into the waters of the river.

We decided to take a boat over to the sand-bar again, in order to see what this jewel of a city looked like in the fire-light with the stars above it.

So beautiful was the scene from the boat that a part of me was almost tempted to ask our boatman to sail us down the river a short distance, into the path of the little flaming offerings, or at least nearer to that stream of flickering lights as they made their way down the river.

It was a mesmerising sight, and while nobody asked him to do so, I'm sure our boatman hesitated a little to allow us to enjoy the scene for a few moments, before finally delivering us to the sandbank.

Fortunately, the view from the island was equally enchanting, with the tall buildings of the city no longer illuminated by the bright morning sun, but instead by the flickering light of the funeral pyres and countless tiny floating offerings.

This was a different view of the city, still so calm

and reposed, but now half-dreaming of the day ahead, a city in autumn, warmed by firelight and serenaded by the Aarti musicians on its shores.

I could have gazed at that scene until dawn had there not been so many other sights to behold.

The funeral pyres were a good case in point. Any semblance of the bodies which once lay atop them were thankfully long gone, consumed by the flame, or at least collapsed into the pyres fiery heart.

Like everyone I couldn't help but look into those still fiercely burning embers at the strange shaped coals and charred pieces of wood, wondering if I were looking at something that might once have been a human being, but the fire revealed nothing.

Leaving the funeral pyres behind, we walked over to the shore to make our own votive offerings to the river. Each of us, including Selene, who I thought might hesitate to engage in the practices of another faith, took part. Buying the kit from one of the many vendors and a light from one of the many other people taking part.

I watched Peter as he placed his small boat of fire into the water, just in case anything should happen again, but all seemed normal this time, though still hauntingly beautiful.

Fire and darkness were a heady combination, so after making our offerings we retreated to a smaller camp-fire which someone had lit with smaller pieces of wood than those used on the pyres.

It wasn't really cool enough to merit an extra fire, so the camp-fire had perhaps been made purely for the light it created, or as somewhere from which a burning brand could be obtained to light the funeral pyres. Either way, we now quietly gathered around it while we decided what to do next, and then when nobody suggested anything we simply sit and enjoy the spectacle.

Sitting around this small fire as a group reminded me of the countless similar fires we'd kindled on our long walk from Ankara in Turkey to Samarkand. Often, like this evening, the fire wasn't needed for the heat as much as the light and as a general focal point between us.

We enjoyed the fire in silence for a while, listening to the constant crackle and hiss of the surrounding funeral pyres, as well as the song and music from the Aarti devotees.

Eventually Jean broke the silence and brought our attention back to our current dilemma.

'Please forgive me for breaking the mood my friends,' he began, with a sad smile. 'But I believe I may just have had an idea about how we should move forward.

'Androus, Harrison, you have highlighted after talking to your professor Naranjan that we need to travel over to Arunachal Pradesh quickly if we are to stand any chance of finding the first temple before the changing seasons make travelling there practically impossible.

'And you Ms Autieri have highlighted that we cannot continue to travel as a group of seven people plus Abhra if we wish to avoid the attentions of your former colleagues. Suggesting instead that recruiting a dozen or more people to bolster our numbers would help to throw anyone off our sent.

'Well, the thought occurs to me that we could do both, and not only that but we could perhaps use the exercise to help a friend of ours out in the process.'

'Are you talking about Luke?' Harry asked.

'Precisely,' Jean replied. 'His mission is located in Sikkim to the north of Darjeeling. We know he's there to help with several engineering projects. Why don't we send him a couple of dozen men via train to help with this endeavour?'

'Of course,' Harry responded, thoughtfully. 'You're suggesting we advertise for men with construction and building experience, then send Luke the money to cover their wage and living costs for six months, and then we simply accompany them on the train.'

'It is perfect, is it not?' Jean asked, looking around

the fire.

'Many of those we recruit will not know one another, so we could easily join their number without them being any the wiser, we could even offer to equip each man with suitable clothing for the journey and the conditions in Sikkim.'

To my mind the idea was an elegant one, but it was Selene who had the necessary understanding to gauge whether it would be likely to throw her former colleagues off our scent, so it was to her that we all naturally looked for the final verdict.

'Yes, it could be made to work,' she finally agreed, with an uncharacteristic hesitation.

'But there are details to work out of course,' she continued, still sounding a little distracted. 'But, yes, yes it could work.'

It was clear everyone else had noticed the change in Selene's manner, but nobody chose to say anything, assuming she would explain in her own time if she wanted to.

SILIGURI

ABHRA WAS A NATURAL LEADER OF MEN, and while he clearly enjoyed the experience of having nearly thirty men in his employ, he didn't even attempt to abuse his position beyond using it to show off to his countrymen.

It had taken a whole week to find the men, interview them and make the necessary travel arrangements, but it had all gone without a hitch, and we had even received a telegram from a surprised Luke, thanking us for the assistance and informing us he would personally travel to the railway station at Siliguri Town to welcome the people we were sending him.

Selene didn't think it was likely that anyone from the Icarii would be watching Luke, but it was impossible for her to say for sure, which is how we now found ourselves on the platform in Siliguri looking our old friend straight in the face, but unable to even say hello.

It had been over two years now since we'd last seen him in Rome, while we were making our fateful preparations to break into the Icarii catacombs to steal back our possessions. Shortly after which we had gone on the run from the Icarii to Nice and then Tunis, before making our way to Ankara in Turkey, where we'd stayed hidden for a while, before commencing the journey we were now on.

Meanwhile, Luke would have finished his own preparations before travelling to the humanitarian mission in the highlands above Darjeeling, where he'd now been working for eighteen months.

Now here he was, a dozen feet away, looking tanned and strong and at peace with himself.

He was trying his best not to keep looking at us, though clearly recognising us through our disguises, while Abhra, unaware of our previous acquaintance wittered on about one thing or another to him, after explaining that the seven of us were being sent to another mission further to the east.

It was a strange new kind of torture to be so close to such a beloved friend without being able to even say hello to him, and I could tell from the body language of my friends that they felt it also.

Finally, unable to delay any longer, Luke turned to Abhra to say goodbye and wish him well for wherever we were heading.

'Thank you again, Mr Balakrishnan,' he began, looking over Abhra's shoulder at the rest of us as he spoke. 'I cannot begin to explain how much the mission appreciates this donation, and should you or your employees wish to call into the mission to see the good work which these men will be helping with, then I implore you to do exactly that. There may not be a train from here in Siliguri to Namchi, but there is a connecting bus service from Darjeeling which takes only half a day, that will bring you within a short cart ride of the mission.'

The message was clearly intended for us and couldn't have been clearer. But we simply didn't have time to take another detour now without risking running out of time for our search.

It felt so wrong to be separating from Luke after seeing him again, that I resolved to write him a short letter by way of an explanation before we travelled too much further on our journey.

From Siliguri Town we caught another train to Guwahati in the heart of Assam itself, and what on the maps looked like the very end of the railway network in India.

As we rattled along in our comparatively comfortable second-class compartment, which was only just large enough for all of us, the scene through the window seemed to suggest that the closer we came to the end of the line, the closer we also came to the end of civilisation as we knew it. Even the endless blue skies that we'd become accustomed to on the Gangetic plain were now obscured by increasingly thick and grey cloud.

The towns and villages here in this north-eastern annex to the sub-continent were also noticeably more industrialised the further we went, designed and constructed around the tea trade, with processing plants and warehouses dominating every stop on the journey, and even signs for hotels or guest houses becoming less prevalent.

As if dominating the towns and villages weren't enough, the tea industry also seemed to have taken over the entire natural landscape of the foothills, which had been transformed by the endless acres of tea plantation into an almost homogenous single shade of brilliant green.

Tea bushes covered the land in every direction from the lowest slopes just above the towns and villages, up steeper and steeper inclines, until they reached the low clouds, where it seemed the tea pickers would surely need some kind of rope or ladder system to pick the tea.

If the cloud had been thicker, it would have been easy to think the plantations continued right up to the top of the mountains, but every now and again the towering mountain peaks came into view through the cloud, the dark stone and wild vegetation creating a stark contrast with the uniform green of the plantations.

The foothills and rugged mountains were not the only contrast with the never-ending horizon of the Ganges plain, for we were also back in the country of rushing and gushing rivers, which seemed to flow in such abundance down the mountainsides, it was a wonder the distant Brahmaputra river wasn't even greater than it already appeared.

Beyond the Brahmaputra the land opened out into a softly undulating landscape, flat and level in places, but never for very long. Then beyond, and always drawing closer to the opposite bank of the great river there was the unmistakable presence of yet more mountains, the Meghalaya.

The entire area, as Peter had shown us on the few maps of the region he'd been able to find, consisted of a long strip of land surrounded on three sides by mountains. But rather than running simply west to east, this large mountain valley turned northward half-way along its length, and became Arunachal Pradesh, or what we now knew was more colloquially known as the Land of the Dawn Lit Mountains.

This knowledge had been the final gift which Professor Naranjan had shared with Androus and Harry before we'd left Varanasi, which allowed us to confidently take the shortcut to Assam by train.

We'd all gone over the directions contained on the lapis lazuli tablets countless times since leaving Turkey, including the section which described the area where the first great temple was supposedly located. Described from the perspective of a traveller who had descended from the temple in the mountains, those same mountains were described 'shining red and gold in the morning light' when they were viewed from the river below.

'It had become clear to me some time ago,' Androus explained, when he finally figured out the last piece of the puzzle.

'The directions on the tablets are for the journey from the first great temple to the second temple in Africa, and they describe a route across the Gangetic plain, with the traveller journeying largely by boat up-river instead of trying to find a route through the tropical forest.

'What hadn't occurred to me before now,' he continued. 'Was that if Varanasi was surrounded by forest, and located in an area that is completely flat, the only direction that would allow the sun to hit the city first thing in the day, and the only direction from which that sight could be viewed, was across the broad expanse of the Ganges river itself.'

'That seems like a very subtle point to pick up on,' Harry observed, stating what I was sure we had all been thinking.

'Perhaps, Harrison, perhaps. But subtle or not it is of singular importance for anyone attempting to follow the directions carved into those tablets. Both because it helps us to identify Varanasi definitively as one of the locations mentioned on the tablets, but also because it points clearly to Arunachal Pradesh as the location of the last leg of the journey.

'You see, for Varanasi to be visible in the dawn light, it must be viewed from the east, where the sun rises, and the land, or water, in that direction must also be clear of tall obstructions, like mature forest, for at least a mile, preferably more, all of which means the city must be on the west bank of either a north or south flowing river.

'Now there are places where the Ganges flows directly south or north, but there are very few settlements located in these spots and none with the age or significance of ancient Varanasi, making it actually the only city where you could stand between the rising sun and the city without being surrounded by the massive trees of the forest which covered the Gangetic Plain at that time.'

He looked at us hopefully for a moment or two, before realising we still didn't get the significance of what he was explaining.

'Likewise,' he continued, patiently. 'When it comes to the Himalayan mountains, for the most part they exist in a roughly west to south-east configuration, leaving nowhere where anyone can stand between the rising sun and the mountains without being surrounded by mountains.

'That is with the exception of Arunachal Pradesh at the eastern end of the long valley which contains Assam.

'Because half-way along its length that valley turns due north.'

'Just like the Ganges river at Varanasi,' Jean observed with the first hint of a smile.

'Precisely,' Androus agreed.

'And in the same way,' Jean picked up. 'That it is only possible to stand between the rising sun and glowing city of Shiva at this point because the river provides a nice open space to the east of the city… it would only be possible to view mountains in the dawn light from a point where the valley turns north, creating the space to the east where the dawn rays could penetrate and bathe the receiving mountain sides in their light.'

'Incroyable!' Jean concluded, overwhelmed by the purity of Androus's logic.

Once Androus had put the pieces together for us with the description of the 'Dawn lit mountains' it was obvious. Not all the directions on the tablets pointed to such a unique place, but with one such place clearly identified it became so much easier to find sites that matched the less distinctive features nearby.

When we had two solid points, like we did with Varanasi and the Dawn Lit mountains of Arunachal Pradesh, it was almost too easy to follow the trail between them. From Arunachal Pradesh along the course of the Brahmaputra past Guwahati, where the foothills of the Meghalaya encroach upon the course of the mighty river. Then further downstream to where the river broadens to become a 'slow moving sea', over fifteen miles wide, before it is finally able to turn southwards around the western end of the Meghalaya.

Finally, there is the point where the confluence of the Brahmaputra and Ganges, where the combined water flows through and between dozens of massive islands, and 'the river becomes a hundred rivers'.

As the train steamed along toward Guwahati and we sat in our compartment chatting, I found my attention more and more drawn to the spectacular scenery across the valley, where the mighty Brahmaputra flowed, and in my mind's eye I could almost spot the different places described on the tablets.

THE SCHOLAR

GUWAHATI COULD NOT BE DESCRIBED as an attractive city, but it bustled with a level of life and energy it was impossible not to admire.

For us it was also just a stopping point, but it was a significant one because this was the point where we went from searching maps and documents, to exploring the miles of wide-open landscape which lay before us.

Guwahati was also where the plantations ended, and where the land was farmed, or left wild, by the local hill-tribes. The population here was also of a noticeably different ethnic stock to mainland India, appearing much more oriental in appearance, rather like a mixture of Chinese and Indian ethnicity.

The clothing and general manner of dress was also different, with the locals wearing more tailored garments bearing more intricate designs, made from wool as well as cotton, and with beads and bright needlework for the patterns, this despite the fact that, to me at least, the increased humidity made the heat feel less comfortable than the drier heat of the Gangetic Plain.

The languages spoken here were also much more varied, and for the most part wholly unintelligible to me, though thankfully everyone still seemed to understand Hindi.

Not that there weren't also a large number of people from other parts of India. Like the other cities we'd visited across the north of India, Guwahati was a melting pot of races and cultures, but it was just markedly more Assamese in nature.

After finding a tidy little coaching house that was prepared to give us rooms, we divided up into pairs or threes and disappeared into the city to carry out our tasks.

Androus, Abhra and Harry wanted to visit one of the local temples which was dedicated to Shiva, because according to their research, there was also a possible link to Dhanvantari, the God of Ayurvedic Medicine which we suspected might also have a link to Ziusudra the creator of the first great temple, which we sought. If that was the case they were hoping there might also be some local legends about why there was a shrine at this location.

Abhra was accompanying them principally as a translator, but also as a way to make him feel useful. The further we had travelled into this north-east territory the less comfortable our guide had become. Warning us not only of the dangers that this region was reputed to harbour, but also of the fact that he would be of less value to us the further we travelled, both because he had fewer business contacts to assist him, and also because he didn't have any command of the tribal languages commonly spoken in this region.

It was clear that we'd reach a point before too much longer where he'd ask to be allowed to turn back, but for the moment we continued to value Abhra's presence and never-ending willingness to teach and explain things to us.

While they were off to the temple, Peter and Jean would attempt to find a boat to take us upriver. Ideally we wanted a vessel that was big enough to act as both our accommodation and base of operations while we travelled up into Arunachal Pradesh.

We hoped this would provide more flexibility and be quicker than buying or hiring more horses, but it would be a gamble, and we'd just have to find out how useful it was in reality.

That left Selene, Marlow and me to pick up some supplies. Provisions of course, as well as some of the excavation equipment we might need to get into an ancient temple, including shovels, picks and digging bars as well as a small amount of explosives and detonators, a camera and film, some hand torches and various medical supplies, including quinine to help us avoid malaria, anti-venom treatments, iodine, insect repellent, and a dozen other things which Jean had suggested might make life a little more bearable in the damp and heat of the rainforest.

On the plus side, if we could find a boat, all the weight and bulk of these items wouldn't matter as much.

With the exception of the explosives there was nothing too specialised, so we just divided the list up into three so that we could cover the ground more quickly.

I also took the opportunity to write a letter to Luke, apologising for our last meeting and explaining what our itinerary was going to be as we headed into the Arunachal Pradesh valley, and our hopes that we might be able to catch-up with him once we'd found the temple.

I didn't bother to explain why we were all in disguise when we met at Silguri station, but I did tell him how we all wished we could have taken the time to catch up properly.

Finding the supplies we wanted in Guwahati proved incredibly easy, the medicines in particular which I thought we might struggle with were obviously a staple of everyday life for those who found themselves living or working here, but who didn't have the natural immunities that the natives had.

So, with time on my hands, I decided to head over to the small island where the temple of Shiva was, to see if I could catch up with the others and perhaps learn a little more about what had interested them so much about this particular temple and representation of Shiva.

I knew the temple was located on a small island in the middle of the Brahmaputra, and after finding my way down the river to the bathing ghats I spotted a small boat returning from one of the islands which seemed to have structures on it, so I walked over to where that boat was landing, and for a few rupees managed to buy passage to what appeared to be called Peacock Island, along with a handful of other people who had been waiting for the boat to return.

The boatman delayed setting off for a few minutes to see if anyone else would turn up, and then quickly ferried us over the choppy water to the island.

I'd noticed that the island appeared to be heavily wooded before we cast off, but as we drew closer I could see it also rose quite high above the water, with a rocky shoreline, above which the grass, undergrowth and trees quickly colonised the banks, so densely that the ground could barely be seen between the greenery.

Cutting up through the trees was a single set of carved stone steps, which led on to a twisting path, a ceremonial archway and more paths until we reached the top of the island, where an assortment of both newer and increasingly ancient looking buildings had been constructed, several of which while possessed of tall spires, seemed to have entrances that descended into the earth.

Being out in the middle of the river there was also a light breeze blowing over the island, and this in combination with the abundant shade from the trees reduced the temperature to a balmy warmth rather than the sticky heat of the city.

The entire island was only a hundred and fifty yards across, so I was fairly confident I'd find the others quickly, but at the same time I was reluctant to start sticking my head into the various buildings and disturbing anyone within. So to begin with I thought I'd enjoy the cool of the island by having a stroll, just to get the lay of the land.

The place was made up of what appeared to be various shrines and a small temple, presumably all dedicated to Shiva, as well as several utility buildings, including a small kitchen offering anyone who was hungry some simple food, and a low wall which circled the place.

I'd already had something to eat and drink from one of the vendors in the centre of Guwahati, so I bowed but declined to visit the kitchen and eating area when one of the temple staff motioned me towards it.

Then, as I was walking around the perimeter of the walled area at the top of the hill, I heard voices a little way off to one side down a small path.

Following it through some dense bushes, I soon came to another smaller clearing bathed in dappled sunlight with a view out over the Brahmaputra, where, seated in a small circle I found my friends talking to an ancient looking holy-man.

Seeing me as I entered the clearing, the holy-man waved me over to join the rest of the group.

'Ah these ancient tales of Lord Shiva are of such slight interest even to his followers,' he was explaining in perfect English, 'I do not think a single person has come to ask me about them in over ten years, and yet now so many of you come at once, it gives me hope that they will not be forgotten.'

'You are kind to spare us your time, O Panditje,' Harry replied, after nodding a welcome to me.

'You were telling us of the other names by which Shiva was once known…'

'Yes, yes of course,' the priest responded, as he turned his attention back to what he'd been talking about.

'The earliest name by which Shiva was known is Rudra, who was thought to be the god of all things, but who later became known as simply the Fierce One.

'This is of course inaccurate and the result of poor scholarship. Originally Rudra was known as the Shining One, who taught great wisdom and healing knowledge to the people, instead of just being a fierce god of destruction and renewal.

'It is for this reason that Lord Shiva is often confused with Dhanvantari, the healer of the gods who is more commonly considered to be an incarnation of Lord Vishnu.'

'This is most interesting,' Androus chipped in. 'Are there any specific tales or descriptions that date back to when Lord Shiva was called by this other name of Rudra?'

'Of course, of course,' the holy man replied, clearly eager to explain as much about the subject as we were to listen to it. 'Sri Rudram is one of the most common prayers which occurs in the fourth Kanda of the Taittirya Samhita in the Yajur Veda, which is chanted daily in Shiva temples across India, including our own small temple here on this island.'

I saw both Harry and Androus glance at one another, but the holy man didn't appear to notice so he just continued on with his explanation.

'However, if it is the early tales of Rudra that you are interested in, then surely you have come to the right place, for we have some of the oldest known examples of pre-Vedic literature in all of India located within the temple shrine.'

'Pre-Vedic documents?' Androus asked. 'To have survived to the modern age, they must now be very fragile.'

'The writings are unusual in that they are inscribed onto clay tablets which have subsequently been baked in the sun to harden them,' the holy man, explained. 'Although, to the best of our knowledge the original tablets were copied onto new tablets around two thousand years ago, when they were also translated into modern Sanskrit, which was written on the back of each new tablet.

'Fascinating, and how many stories are contained on these tablets,' Harry asked, becoming noticeably more animated as he did so.

'The tablets contain but a single story,' the old scholar explained. 'Would you care to hear some of it?'

Indicating that we would, the polite holy-man closed his eyes and took a deep breath before beginning his story.

'In the beginning the story tells us Sri-Rudra dwelt at the source of the waters, high-up in the mountains to the east, where his temple was constructed as much from snow and ice as it was from pale stone.

'But one day while gazing into the eternal flame which warmed his temple, he saw the faces of others like himself who sought for the eternal and he knew he must leave his home to find and befriend them.

'Before leaving his palace in the high mountains he first thought upon what he should take with him, for he did not wish to spoil the solitude of his mountain abode, so he must take with him all that would be needed to build a second home, as good as the first, where he could welcome strangers and befriend them.

'To this end he resolved to take the eggs of the sacred serpent whose bite was deadly poison, but whose skin exuded the nectar of immortality.

'These eggs, he took from the waters running through his home, and sealed them, along with the water and the plant on which the snakes fed inside a metal jar.

'Next he took his bow, with a handful of long arrows, with which he hunted the beasts of the high mountains for their sport and their meat.

'And finally, he took his bag of healing potions, salves and powders, by which he could cure all the ills known to man, as well as the wounds great or small that a person could receive while hunting or in battle, for it was by his healing arts that he hoped to persuade those he would meet of his friendship.

'So prepared, Lord Rudra descended from his mountain abode, planting the seed of a golden pear tree in the soil outside the entrance to his home, which he then sprinkled with the sacred water which ran through his home, so that the thorny branches of a pear tree grew up instantly to hide the entrance from any people and animals that might pass by, while the golden pears in the autumn would clearly mark the location for Lord Rudra whenever he should return.

'With his home thus protected, Lord Rudra travelled down from his mountain abode, through dense forests full of serpents, spiders and tigers, to the mighty river which flowed through the valley of the dawn.

'But the fellow hunters and searchers which Lord Rudra had beheld within the sacred fire of his home were nowhere to be seen. Far and wide did he travel, and while he encountered many of the folk from the valleys, they drew away when he approached, greatly afraid of his strange and wild appearance, even though he had done nothing to harm them, none of them offered him shelter for the night, and being a creature of the high mountains, he felt no loss from the lack of shelter, beyond the opportunity to meet and come to know the people that dwelled in the valleys.

'Then, one day, after he had travelled down the river for several days, he came upon a village greatly beset by a strange illness of which their holy men knew no cure. To stop the sick from infecting the healthy, the village had begun taking the sick out to a nearby island in the river, where the air was sweeter, in the hope that this would help the sick to recover more quickly.

'When Lord Rudra saw what was happening, he summoned the holy men of the village to him, and while they were greatly afraid of his visage, he proceeded to teach them some of his healing ways, so that the sick could be cured, which they were.

'The people of the village gave much praise to the wild stranger that had appeared from the river and helped them, and in gratitude they constructed a home for Lord Rudra on the very island where they had taken their sick, which the strange lord accepted, for he found the island to possess both great beauty as well as some of the solitude of his home, which he had missed since descending into the valleys.

'Thus, accepted by the people of the nearby village, Lord Rudra chose to make the island his home for many years while he taught the people of the village how to hunt with a bow, and trap wild animals and make them work for the people of the village, how to make fruit trees grow where you wished and make bread from the wild grains that could be collected.

'The villagers became strong with this knowledge and prospered. Their village growing to many times its original size because of the things they had learned. But still Lord Rudra waited for those people he had seen in the fire to appear, and still he did not see them.

'Eventually, and with much sadness from the villagers the strange lord took his leave in order to travel further down the river in search of those he had seen, but with him also travelled one of the holy-men from the village, by the name of Jawanarth, who offered to speak to other people on the lord's behalf, for still the lord appeared strange to the people of the valleys and wild in his visage and his ways.

'Jawanarth was a young man when he left with the lord, and did not return to the village until he was an old man.

'Along his many travels he had learned to draw the words which people spoke, and so after returning to the village he showed the other holy-men, few of whom remembered him, how to read the words which he drew, and how to draw them also.

'He then proceeded to write an account of his travels with Sri Rudra across the entire lands which we now know as India and even beyond. These are the writings of the clay tablets which are still held at the temple to Lord Shiva, here on this island, even to this day.'

'Thank you, O Panditje,' Androus said, evidently thinking about something in the story. 'What you have told us is but the first part of this story, I assume?'

'Indeed it is,' replied the holy man. 'But the first small part.'

'And may I ask approximately how much more still remains to be told.'

'It is perhaps easier if I were to show you the tablets for yourselves,' smiled the ancient holy-man.

With this he rose effortlessly and lead us out of the clearing and over to the main temple, which was walled only on three sides, the forth being completely open to the refreshing breeze which blew through it.

While quite small compared to many of the other temples we'd seen, it was easily large enough to accommodate two hundred or so people beneath its roof, without overcrowding.

In design it was a simple construction that looked as though it was only a few hundred years old. Stout wooden columns held up a squat pyramid shaped roof made of equally stout timbers which extended out past the columns to provide a substantial rain shadow.

Atop the wooden beams the roof had been laid with large curved clay tiles of a type quite common in northern India.

As we stepped inside the structure I noticed for the

first time that the three walls were just that, they didn't connect at the corners and didn't extend quite to the roof. This allowed both light and air to penetrate above and around them, giving the shrine to Lord Shiva which sat at the back of the structure a surprisingly fresh and open feel, despite the smoky fire pit laid out in front of it.

The shrine held one of the golden images of Shiva we had seen countless times before, sat cross-legged in contemplation, but where other statues usually depicted the god with a trident sat on animal skins, this statue depicted him with one hand held up in peace, with a bow across his back and handful of arrows grasped in his other hand, where it lay across his knee.

Giving us a moment to look around, the holy man spoke to one of the other temple attendants who fetched a set of ladders, which he propped up against the left-hand wall.

Thanking him, the ancient holy-man moved the ladders along about three feet from one end, and then effortlessly climbed to where he could reach the top of the wall.

'The story of Lord Rudra which I have shared with you,' the holy-man informed us. 'Is covered on the tablets contained on this top row to this point.'

With that he removed a small six inch by four-inch clay tablet from the centre of what I had assumed was just an ornate clay brick.

It took a moment to grasp what the holy-man had shown us, at which point I saw Harry step forward to stand beside the ladder which the holy-man was now descending.

Harry touched the wall tentatively for a moment, then moved his finger to a slot in which another tablet was secluded, side on, like an upright book in a library.

'There are ten rows on each of these walls,' he observed. 'And… twenty tablets on each row?'

'Precisely,' confirmed the holy man.

'So, there are six hundred tablets in total,' Harry

continued, looking flushed. 'And the story you have shared with us so far, is covered in the first… six tablets!'

'That is correct,' the holy man affirmed. 'And you are the first people to have shown any interest in these tablets in years.'

In the couple of hours that we'd listened to the holy man, we'd heard only about one percent of the total story.

It was an absolute treasure trove of information, older than the earliest Vedic texts and containing a first-hand account of the travels of Lord Rudra, the very figure we suspected of building the first great temple that we sought.

TIME

I T TOOK A WHILE for us to fully grasp the reality of what we'd found, hiding in plain sight, there on the tiny Peacock island in the temple of Shiva. However it was something of very little interest for Abhra, who excused himself as soon as he was able in order to return to the mainland.

The rest of us, except the holy Panditje, followed him shortly afterward in order to catch up with the others and discuss what we should do next.

Back at our lodgings, where we had space to relax, Androus started us off.

'I do not quite understand how we have gotten to this point,' he began. 'But it seems to me that the coincidences are now too many for this Sri Rudra, or Lord Rudra, not to be one and the same individual as the Ziusudra whose home we have been searching for these past two years.'

'The similarity in the names did strike me as soon as the scholar mentioned this Sri Rudra,' Jean responded.

'Are you saying it is more than a coincidence?'

'What I'm saying, Jean,' Androus replied, without a heartbeat's hesitation. 'Is that Ziusudra from Sri Rudra is exactly the kind of name morphology that I would expect to see as that name moved from one country and culture to another, or as habits and fashions for pronunciation change over the centuries.'

'I would agree entirely,' Harry chipped in. 'It's like the famous example of Zeus from the classical Greek pantheon becoming Romanised over time. Zeus the father of the gods becomes Zeus Pater, then Zeupater, Iupater and then finally Jupiter.

'Sri Rudra is much the same, Sri Rudra becomes Srirudra, which gets shortened to Sirudra, its then mispronounced or written using a letter with multiple phonemes to make Xisrudra, which leads to Zisudra and finally Ziusudra. It's practically a textbook morphology.'

'That presents us with a problem then,' Marlow interjected. 'Because the sheer volume of writing contained on those tablets would take us months to translate and document.'

'Absolutely,' Harry agreed. 'But we can't just ignore it either.

'The fact that those tablets have survived for so long is a miracle in its own right,' he continued. 'If we don't manage to find the temple while we're here this time, then those tablets might be our only hope of narrowing the search down.'

'Not to mention the other historic treasures that they might reveal,' Androus added.

'Well, what about copying them and sending the copies to somewhere safe?' Peter asked. 'We brought everything we'd need to do the job with us, to document the temple when we finally find it.'

'That's a possibility,' Harry conceded. 'We could photograph and document the tablets in situ in a day or two, for later translation.'

'Yes, but where would you send them?' Selene asked, cautiously. 'Anything sent to your library in Jerusalem or your friends and family would be easily spotted and intercepted by the Icarii. Either by operatives working in the postal service here in India before it left, or in the receiving country, if it was addressed to a flagged address.

'I'd even advise you against sending this material to your cousin in Turkey, if you want to avoid compromising his address.' she continued.

'Well that makes things difficult,' Peter replied. 'Because we don't want to be adding more bulk to everything we're already travelling with.'

'What if we don't send this material out of the country?' I asked Selene in particular.

'In country post would be almost impossible for the Icarii to trace,' Selene responded. 'But who could you trust with such information?'

'Well, what about Professor Naranjan, back in Varanasi?' I asked.

'We needn't tell him the full context or potential value of these tablets to us, but he might well be interested in them from a purely historic perspective.'

'That could work, George,' Androus conceded. 'He might even be able to dispatch an archaeological team to come and investigate the tablets in detail, and begin the mammoth task of formally translating them.'

'That would take months to organise though, surely!' Harry asked.

'Absolutely,' Androus confirmed, without hesitation. 'But its directly relevant to his field of study and it would be a real coup for the college in its bid to become a recognised centre of research and learning. And I don't think Professor Naranjan would forget who had given him the lead if we contacted him next year and asked to travel with his team.'

Everyone liked the sound of this plan, so we agreed to delay our departure for a couple of days in order to document the tablets on Peacock island, before sending the lot to Professor Narajan who had helped us out so much in Varanasi.

This delay, it turned out, would also work well with the boat which Jean had arranged to take us up river, that was just being refitted after spending several years hauling coal, before more efficient craft had arrived to take over the job.

All the supplies were ready to go, and Selene had found no obvious trace of her former colleagues operating in the area, so with the holy scholar's consent we descended on the temple over the next two days with our cameras and sketch-pads, our rubbing paper, rulers and notebooks, and with a will we set to work documenting every detail of the temple and the walls of tablets found therein.

It felt like an age since we'd last settled down to complete this kind of work, but it felt good to be preserving something for history and exercising our skills.

The work was reasonably familiar to Selene, as in her former line of work, while they'd been keen not to allow anyone outside the church to find the artefacts they retrieved, they still did their best to capture the details of where and how they'd found something, so that the scholars that worked for the church could see the proper context of the find.

In stark contrast, Abhra had never done anything even remotely similar to this before, and moreover had absolutely no interest in it. For him the future and the progress of his nation were where his burning interests lay, followed by his business activities as a close second.

Accordingly, after a few hours work on the tablets, Abhra came up with some excuse to return to the city, and we didn't see him again for the rest of the day.

The old scholar or Panditje was delighted to see someone taking such a keen interest in these lost tales of Sri Rudra. Both because they described a hitherto unknown and ignored chapter of Indian history, but also because the stories had been captured and described by a holy man from the village that had subsequently developed into Guwahati.

He was also keen to encourage Professor Naranjan to come and study the tablets in more detail, so after we'd finished photographing and documenting the tablets, we sat with the venerable Panditje to transcribe a letter of introduction and welcome from the temple staff there on Peacock Island to Professor Naranjan at the college in Varanasi.

By the end of the second day on the island we'd documented all six hundred of the mostly well preserved clay tablets. There were a handful that had been damaged slightly due to mishandling or some long forgotten accident, but none of them were beyond reading, though they were written in the pre-Sanskrit script, which the Panditje assured us was still a recognisable form of the Hindu language, albeit rather old fashioned and lacking in metaphor.

When our work was complete, the documents and film filled a whole tea chest, everything scrupulously catalogued and organised by Androus, who insisted on packing the box personally so that 'everything would be found in its proper place' and make sense to the scholarly mind of Professor Naranjan.

Finally, with a certain sadness we took our leave of Peacock Island and the holy Panditje, who had been our host for the previous few days.

The following morning we saw the consignment of paperwork dispatched to the university college in Varanasi, and then we returned to our apartment to pick up our belongings and transport them over to the boat which Jean had hired for us.

The Uma Parvati was a sizeable vessel captained by one Manash Raubingha, a fellow Bengali like Abhra, who had been plying his trade on the Brahmaputra for the previous twenty years, as both the captain of his own vessel, and in various roles aboard other boats while he learned his craft.

We'd looked at the Uma Parvati the previous evening after returning to the city, during which Abhra had spent a good deal of time with the supremely confident boat captain, so it was of no great surprise the following morning, once we'd loaded up the boat with our things, Abhra finally asked if he could have a word with all of us.

'Gentlemen, Lady,' he began. 'I feel the time has come when I must return to New Delhi and the life there which I have left behind.

'I know I have promised to travel as far with you as you wished, but I find I am increasingly of less and less value to you as you travel further from the lands I know.

'To this end I beg you to release me from my promise, and travel forward with Captain Manash in my place, who I have spoken with and found to be as knowledgeable in this area of India, as I myself could ever hope to be in the territories with which I am familiar.'

It had been coming for a while now, as we headed further and further into what most Indians considered to be their wild north-eastern frontier. So, with our genuine appreciation we naturally agreed to allow him to turn back, on the promise that we would meet with him again if we travelled through New Delhi on our return.

This seemed to please him considerably, and so on the day we loaded our possessions aboard the boat, Abhra sent his few belongings on to the railway station, so that he could see us off before he too departed.

The first leg of our journey by boat upstream along the Brahmaputra was about three hundred miles to Dibrugarh, which acted as the state capital for Assam, its key trading point and the last line of defence against the apparently quarrelsome hill-tribes which occupied the region.

More importantly, Dibrugarh was also the last point before the Brahmaputra was joined by several large tributaries, all of which filtered down from the mountains we wanted to explore to the west.

There were half a dozen of these tributaries, which would each be considered sizeable rivers in any other part of the world, but which here in India had to take their place as mere feeders of the gargantuan water-courses which dwarfed them.

Overland, even in the modern age where much of the tropical rain forest had been cleared from the lowlands for cultivation, it would have taken several days and a robust truck to make the journey, but aboard the Uma Parvati under Manash's knowledgeable control we made the journey in both comfort and style in just under three days, pulling up at the port outside the garrisoned fort town about two hours before sunset.

Of necessity we'd been a little more open about our plans with Manash than we had with Abhra, telling him not only that we were Europeans in disguise, but that the reason for our disguises was that we were covertly searching for ancient archaeological ruins which our research had indicated might exist in this area.

He took this very much in his stride, telling us that a group such as ours was exactly what he'd had the Uma Parvarti refitted for.

'As you will realise after a few days aboard,' he explained. 'The Uma is now fitted out with the transport of explorers and adventurers, academic researchers, hunting parties and military surveyors in mind.

'Many times over the past few years have I seen that businessmen, academics or government officials needed to travel up into the distant back-country, and time and again I have been able to offer them only the most basic accommodation, with almost no space where they could work while aboard.'

Good to his word, as we sailed up river to Dibrugarh, we found the bedrooms to be comfortable, and the communal spaces well laid out and provisioned.

In addition, every tool we could have wanted was available, from gun oil, brushes and cloths, to a good sized map table, chalk board. Even a wild game processing room, that contained everything needed to skin and butcher whatever beasts or wildfowl a hunting party might return with.

There was also a sizeable gun closet, ammunition and explosives magazine, which we dutifully took advantage of for our more volatile supplies.

Finally, there was a large safe aboard for the storage of personal valuables.

The service that went with the vessel didn't end there though. Each evening when we moored up for the night Manash would arrange for fresh food to be prepared by the local people and brought aboard. Most of the time this would be arranged and ready in advance if we could tell our boat captain which way we wanted to head each day.

While we were heading up the river to Dibrugarh, we'd sat down with Manash and showed him on the map all the different tributaries of the great Brahmaputra that we wanted to explore over the next few weeks.

He was familiar enough with each one to be able to tell us exactly how far upstream he could take the Uma Parvati, and which local guides he would recommend that worked in that area, and which of course he would not.

HEADWATERS

D IBRUGARH IS WHERE ALL OUR PLANS tried to come unstuck, or more accurately where they would've come unstuck if it hadn't been for Commissioner Jenkins.

We'd had things so easy while we travelled this far, that we'd almost forgotten about the fact that access to the place was restricted because of the local political sensitivities. A fact which the commanding officer of the

Assam Rifles stationed in Dibrugarh took very seriously.

Manash had of course seen our paperwork before we left Guwahati, so we had thought nothing more of it, and he hadn't mentioned that the garrison in Dibrugarh was likely to check up on us. As such after docking at the river port near the fort, we'd all started to relax before dinner in our regular western clothes, and while we'd all elected to retain our beards and moustaches for the sake of our disguises later on, a bit of judicious trimming and grooming had taken place during our two day boat ride.

So, relaxed as we were, the first thing we knew of any problem was when a Nepalese sergeant from the military garrison was shown into our onboard lounge by Manash.

'I'm afraid there seems to be an issue with your travel papers,' our boat captain explained.

'According to Sergeant Rana here, the duration of the permitted stay on your papers appears to be non-standard.'

'Yes, that's correct,' Marlow replied, standing up and walking over to Manash and the Sergeant. 'The term on our papers was agreed by Commissioner Jenkins personally.'

'Unfortunately, this is not something Sergeant Rana is authorised to deal with,' Manash interpreted for us. 'So, he asks that you present yourselves to Lieutenant Colonel Beaumont in the morning to resolve the issue.'

'Of course, if that's what is required.'

With that the sergeant saluted, and we, hopeful that the delay would only be a short one the following morning, went back to relaxing for the evening.

The following morning Marlow, Peter and I entered the fort and made our way to the commander's office, only to discover that Lieutenant-Colonel Beaumont was already engaged in his weekly staff officers meeting, from which he wasn't due to emerge for another three hours at eleven o'clock.

With no need to look around the markets or stop in Dibrugarh for any other reason, we walked back to the boat to inform the others of the delay, before strolling back over again at half-past ten.

Finally, just after eleven o'clock, when all the staff officers had dutifully left, we were ushered in to see Beaumont, a slightly built but immaculately dressed man in his early forties, with a pencil line of a moustache, round-eyed tortoiseshell spectacles and thin brown hair brushed straight back from his brow.

'Gentlemen, please take a seat,' he greeted us from his desk rather formally. 'I'm rather busy today, so let's see if we can deal with this quickly shall we?'

'So, according to the note I have here, your papers appear to have been issued for a period of twelve months rather than the standard two, and upon being challenged you informed the sergeant that your papers were issued by Commissioner Jenkins personally.

'Well, how very grand. I suppose if you're going to lie you may as well go with a big lie,' he said with all semblance of cordiality, before settling his gaze directly upon us. 'If memory serves me correctly, the regional commissioner for the north of India is Commissioner Arbuthnot, not Jenkins as you would have my man believe, so your counterfeiter hasn't done a very good job I'm afraid.'

'I'm sure Commissioner Jenkins will be upset to hear that,' Marlow replied, completely unruffled by Beaumont's attempt to dupe us. 'Perhaps you should mention it to him the next time you go riding, George?'

'Well,' I almost flustered, trying to think of a witty response. 'I can't imagine he'll be too happy to hear it, especially after I bought that grey mare out from under him before we left New Delhi.'

'So, you are in actuality acquainted with our good commissioner then,' Beaumont replied, more good naturedly. 'Please forgive me for testing you. You'd be surprised how many hunting parties we catch trying to sneak through with fake papers.

'I will still have to wire through to his office and confirm you haven't just done a little more research than most.'

'Naturally,' Marlow replied, handing over the letter which Jenkins had given us. 'And I appreciate you're busy, but if you wouldn't mind making that a personal phone call to the commissioner.'

'I see, yes, of course,' the Lieutenant-Colonel responded, handing back the letter but still reserving our other papers. 'I'll ask for the call to be laid in straight-away, and will return your papers to you once I've spoken with Commissioner Jenkins.

'In the meantime, irrespective of what the good commissioner has to say, I'm afraid I'm going to have to ask you for at least a basic itinerary for your stay in Assam and Arunachal Pradesh.

'The political and religious sensitivities here are very delicately balanced most of the time, and I won't willingly jeopardise that balance or put the people of this region at risk by allowing it to be disturbed unknowingly.'

He seemed in earnest as he said this, and the prospect of doing anything that might lead to a widespread conflict was as far from our plans as was imaginable.

The others clearly thought the same, so a moment later Peter asked if there was a map of the region he could use to explain our plans.

'Our maps of this region aren't brilliant,' Beaumont conceded as he led us over to a wall cabinet which he opened to reveal several layers of maps of different scales and locations. 'But the maps we do have are the best there is.'

After selecting a large-scale map which showed the entire area, Peter then proceeded to explain our anticipated route.

'We intend to use Captain Raubingha's boat to sail up this first tributary of the Brahmaputra to a place called Pangin. From there we expect a further three to four days trek into the mountains, before returning to the boat and repeating the exercise moving west to KongKul, Dambuk, Bomjir, Asali and Maselo.'

'That's incredibly difficult and hostile terrain,' Beaumont observed. 'We don't normally have much trouble with the tribes from the sunny-side of the valley, but I'll be blunt with you gentlemen, I don't like the idea of a group of inexperienced westerners traipsing around the place for reasons unspecified.'

It was the closest he'd come so far to asking us why we were there, and I suspected this was perhaps another test to see how cooperative we were prepared to be, before he simply demanded the information if we didn't play ball.

After looking at both me and Peter, it was Marlow who replied.

'Alright,' he began. 'Though it's imperative that you keep everything we tell you in the strictest confidence. We haven't even shared much of this detail with Commissioner Jenkins, though he surely guessed most of it.'

'As you wish,' Beaumont agreed.

'What may not be immediately obvious to you from our papers, is that we are travelling with two eminent archaeologists, who both specialise in pre-classical age sites and writing. Dr Adroushan Chukjadarian from the Armenian Library in Jerusalem, and Dr Harrison Sutherland of Harvard University in Massachusetts.'

'No, you're right, I didn't realise,' Beaumont conceded, taking a second look at our papers in front of him.

'Well, almost three years ago now, Dr Sutherland discovered an archaeological site containing some very unusual artefacts, which seemed to suggest a previously unsuspected link with either the middle east or India. He took the artefacts to a friend and former colleague in

Jerusalem, Dr Chukjadarian, and together they deciphered a series of directions which described a route across Asia which had existed in antiquity. An ancient silk-route if you will, but a silk route which they couldn't pinpoint without travelling it.

'Preparations were made, and the group you now see set off from the starting point in Turkey on foot, almost ten months ago.'

'You set off on foot… from Turkey!' Beaumont interrupted, incredulous.

'We did, as there was no other way to be sure we were following the directions correctly to begin with,' Marlow explained.

'Six months later and we arrived in Uzbekistan with one of the trade caravans, and after confirming the route must lay south of the Himalayas, we entered India via the Khyber Pass.

'As I'm sure you can imagine, the journey to this point was a rather arduous one, but along the way we'd learned to travel as the local traders' did, that is, in the style of the Bedouin, using the desert clothing which protects against both heat and cold.

'Naturally, we also became fluent in the Turkic language spoken almost universally in that part of the world, which as it turns out has a certain amount in common with Hindi, another language we have also now developed a good command of as a consequence of the assistance we agreed to give Commissioner Jenkins in a delicate matter.'

'You worked for the Commissioner then?' Beaumont interrupted again.

'We did, and we are still helping to identify the presence of foreign agents working in country against the interests of the Crown and the government here in India.'

'I see,' Beaumont replied after a moment.

'Naturally, I'll have to confirm these details with the Commissioner when I speak to him. But I have some awareness of the issues that you've mentioned, and while occasionally a little unorthodox at times, I know our Commissioner well enough to know he doesn't act arbitrarily, so if he chose to trust you in these matters then I shall do the same.

'I would like to know a little more about this archaeological prize that you are going to such pains to find, but for now I have enough information to be going on with. I'll speak to Commissioner Jenkins at the earliest opportunity and return your stamped papers after that.

'And as you're working in the government's interests, I'll also have one of my people prepare an intelligence briefing for you.'

With that the good Lieutenant-Colonel thanked us for our time and our candour, and promised to get everything finalised before the end of the day.

As we took our leave from the fort commander and made our way back to the boat, I couldn't help but wonder at Marlow's account of what we were doing here in India. On the one hand he had been absolutely truthful, painting a high-level picture of what had happened and why we were in India, but without any mention of the other, less rational elements of our search, or the fact that we had tangled with a murderous religious order, who were still intent on stopping us.

Four hours later, and we were visited by Sergeant Rana again, this time to return our stamped and approved travel documents, along with the folder of additional briefing information and a private letter from the Lieutenant-Colonel wishing us luck in our undertaking.

With that, and only a hint of surprise from our boat captain, we set off to the first of the tributaries we were intent on exploring.

We were all quite comfortable aboard the boat by now, and as we chugged steadily northward, I retired to a comfortable spot on the foredeck where Manash had placed a couple of deck-chairs to update my ever-present journal while I watched the world go by.

I'd been adding updates to my journal for several weeks now, but I hadn't actually stopped to read through and review what I'd written since we'd left Ankara almost a year ago, so I sat down now with a tall glass of fruit juice to do exactly that.

Reading back through my entries was a strange experience. It already seemed like we'd been in India for the longest time, but flicking through the pages back to when we'd just left Ankara, when we were trying to figure out how much walking we needed to do to be sure we were still following the directions laid down in the tablets, and then later how quickly the subsequent entries went from describing aching legs and feet, to the miles and miles of country we covered each day with ease.

Rounding the southern end of the Caspian Sea, finding a trade caravan to take us north to Samarkand, the heat and dust storms, and camaraderie of the traders when we started to hunt and bring back meat for the caravan, and their subsequent offer of the desert robes and the polite awkwardness the men of the caravan exhibited around Selene, which eventually transformed into respect and even protectiveness.

I read also of the first, almost tentative attempt by Selene to understand why we were on this journey, and her surprise at learning of the drums, the dreams and the visions.

How long ago it all seemed now, and how far away. And that was just the most recent leg in what had become a strange and twisting journey, the final outcome of which was still completely unknown to us.

And now, in just one more day the boat will have taken us as far upstream as it's able to go, and we will finally begin our search of the mountains which hopefully still hold the remains of the first great temple, and within it the secret of physical immortality.

Later that day, while Manash busied himself in his quarters and our cook for the evening was at work in the galley, the rest of us gathered in the main prep room aboard the Uma Pavarti to review what we knew and plan for the journey into the mountains.

'Let's begin with what the directions on the tablets tell us,' Harry suggested, looking at Androus.

'As you all know by now, in the directions contained on the tablets, irrespective of which set they belong to, there is always a section which describes Ziusudra travelling down from his first great temple into the valley of the dawn, above which his own red mountain can be seen.

'This has led us to this region of the Himalaya where the curve of the mountains turns north and dawn light strikes the eastern face of the mountain, clearly visible from the valley below.

'What the red mountain refers to, we have, as yet, no idea. We do know from subsequent references that the time of year is likely to be in the Autumn or Fall, so the colour red could refer to the autumn leaves, or some other aspect of the mountain which is only visible once the leaves have fallen.

'And that's all we have as far as the physical description in the tablets is concerned,' Harry added. 'But there are other details which we can perhaps add to that, both from the African temple we found, and from the various visions and dreams which we've had.'

With this he looked around the room, inviting the rest of us to pitch in.

'Well, running water seems to be significant,' Peter stated, before going on to explain. 'The first temple had a stream running all the way through it from that deep pool at the heart of the complex where we found the scroll.'

'Yes, and each of the locations where we found the tablets seems to have been located next to a stream,' Jean reminded us. 'Even if only a seasonal one in Nelion's case.'

'The stream in the temple flowed with warm water,' added Marlow. 'Either a thermal spring or because it flowed over the surface somewhere, and we found no other surface water anywhere nearby.'

'That's an interesting point,' Harry observed. 'I'd forgotten about that.

'And didn't you say something about seeing Ziusudra testing the water, in that vision you had while we were in Haridwar?' he asked.

'That's what it looked like, though it was only a fleeting glimpse on that one occasion,' Marlow confirmed.

'This is good,' Androus summarised. 'If the first temple also lies upon a thermal spring then it would be a simple matter to test the water-courses we come to, to find out if the water is cold or warm.'

'It may also taste different,' Peter added. 'Both the hot springs that I know of in England, Bath and Matlock have a distinctly sulphuric taste and smell.'

'I believe that is a common feature,' Jean confirmed. 'Certainly, the thermal spa in Monetier has a sulphur taste, as did the water at the temple we discovered in Africa'

'Then we must taste the water also,' Androus confirmed.

'As for the rest,' he continued. 'There seems little point in searching the mountains above the permanent snow line. Even with the benefit of a thermal spring for heat, the practicalities of living in an area permanently covered in ice and snow would be difficult.'

'Anything else?' Harry asked, carefully noting down everything anyone mentioned.

'Well,' Peter added, almost hesitantly. 'By the look of it, the entrance to the first temple had been deliberately collapsed. What if the same is true of this one?'

'If that is the case then we will have to proceed much as we did in Africa,' Harry added. 'We'll excavate to see if we can find any trace of human workmanship, and if so, dig our way in.'

As had become our routine, we went over the questions again to make sure we hadn't missed anything, during which I noticed that Selene once again seemed to have very little interest in what was being said.

Not that she'd ever promised to help us find our goal, all she'd ever offered was to help us avoid the attentions of her former colleagues, and that she had done with numerous pieces of advice, and by keeping a constant watch for any sign that the Order were actively seeking us in any of the places we passed.

But it felt like we were drawing very close to our goal now, and the closer we got, the more difficult a position we would be putting her in. On the one hand she'd promised to help us avoid the Icarii, but on the other she'd taken a solemn vow to find and remove this kind of forbidden knowledge from the hands of humanity, until we were ready for it.

Perhaps, like Abhra, it wouldn't be long before she too decided she could go no further.

FORBIDDEN FRUIT

THE DAWN-LIT MOUNTAINS of Arunachal Pradesh were simply beautiful. Here, unlike their sister peaks further west they had not been blanketed in the endless uniform growth of tea bushes, and the lower slopes were instead still covered in the majestic and varied growth of natural rain-forest.

What this terrain would be like in another hundred years if the demand for tea continued to grow, I couldn't imagine, but for now, the sheer otherworldly splendour of the forest was breath-taking.

The route through the forest, below the massive

trunks and between the twisted branches of the endemic rhododendron was surprisingly easy going. The canopy of the trees high above was so dense, there simply wasn't enough light on the ground to allow anything to grow.

The humidity though was another matter, so while we gave our Bedouin robes a try, it wasn't long before we'd dispensed with the multiple layers in favour of light, flappy shirts and trousers. Anything which allowed the air to pass more readily over our skin, that didn't trap the dampness.

We'd left Manash and the boat early that morning in a medium sized town called Pasighat, where the tributary was still the best part of a mile wide and the waters flowed at no more than walking pace, and by early afternoon we had already reached Pangin, the last village of any note contained on Peter's maps.

Unfortunately, it had been a while since Manash had travelled this way, so the guides and bearers he was hoping to arrange for us were no longer around, and we'd just had to accept the recommendation of the tribal elder in Pasighat.

There was also a marked caution toward us in the faces of the people there. They weren't hostile, but they definitely weren't worried about being unfriendly either, a feeling which our pistols and hunting rifles probably didn't do much to alleviate, but which we simply couldn't risk entering the forest without.

We were still in the foothills when we left Pangin, and the paths which criss-crossed the hillsides through the forest were numerous, but the autumn was also thankfully the dry season, so while there were still numerous small streams and rivulets of water running down the hillsides to join the main tributary, it was easy enough to dip a hand into each as we passed to see if the water was warmer than expected or tasted noticeably of sulphur.

We'd asked the guides of course, whether they knew of any thermal springs in the area, but if they did, they were keeping it to themselves for the moment, not wanting to do anything to jeopardise their work as paid guides.

The main difficulty of course was the river tributary which we followed. This was still far too wide and too deep for us to be able to cross, so we just had to pick one side to walk along on our way out, with the intention of crossing to the other side to check that out once we climbed higher up into the mountains proper, where the tributaries would get smaller.

By the end of the first day, we'd climbed almost all the way out of the rain forest. Those towering giants with their lofty canopies which shaded the ground so effectively, had gradually been replaced by more and more rhododendrons, bamboo and other tough shrubs, interspersed with the occasional taller tree.

This had meant having to cut our way through the undergrowth blocking certain sections of the path, a task our guides performed at the front of the line with the effortless efficiency that comes with having to do something for your entire life.

On the plus side, when it came to making camp there had been no shortage of firewood to create a cheery blaze for us to sleep around and keep any potentially dangerous animals, like the much-feared native tigers at bay.

We still took it in turns to keep guard, along with our guides and bearers, who seemed genuinely surprised and appreciative of the fact that we were prepared to pull our own weight when it came to keeping a watch.

Over the next two days we climbed higher and higher up into the mountains, testing the waters of practically every stream we passed along the way, even tasting the water in the main tributary every now and again, all to no avail.

We were out of the forest now, and up into the mountains proper, crossing the smaller tributaries feeding the main river, so that we could gradually make our way around to the other side of the valley and the other side of the river proper.

This appeared no more promising than the side we'd ascended on, but as we worked our way around, we did find one large rivulet which did have a distinctly sulphur taste to it.

That got everyone's heart beating a little quicker, and despite our guides insistence that there was nothing worth climbing the steep slope for, we did it anyway, finding a zigzagging game trail to lead us up through the low and often prickly shrubs that grew on this part of the mountain.

An hour's climb and we crested a ridge into a small hanging valley, the upper slopes of which still had a light covering of snow and ice, and the bottom of which held a series of different sized pools along the course of a lazy stream, the largest of which was perhaps fifty yards across.

Each of the pools and the stream which disappeared around a bend in the valley, carried a light mist, which occasionally spilled over onto the surrounding land, suggesting the water in these pools was warmer than the other streams we'd been walking along, and that the difference in temperature with the cool mountain air was what caused the mist to form.

The day was getting on toward evening, and the string of stepped pools were a lovely natural feature, almost like watery stepping stones along the slowly climbing valley floor. We therefore suggested to our guides that this would make a good place to make camp for the evening. This they only reluctantly agreed to, because the water to them not only tasted bad, but also often attracted the big leopards which hunted along these high slopes, rather than the tigers further below.

There was something about this unusual little valley which really made me think we might not be far from what we sought, but if we were going to make camp, we'd agreed to not only gather a large store of good firewood to keep a couple of fires burning brightly all night, but also to construct a thorn fence, similar to the boma we'd all built countless times back in Africa.

It took a couple of hours to make a good job of both tasks. Our guides once again clearly surprised that we were both willing and knew how to do these things, even showing them the African way of building the thorny barrier.

With less than an hour of twilight left to us, we improved everyone's mood further by bagging a good-sized mountain goat to eat, while Marlow, Jean and I also had our first reconnoitre of the twisting valley.

It was difficult going through the dense underbrush which seemed to grow everywhere, much of which looked like an azalea type shrub, though the odd evergreen dwarf rhododendron still managed to maintain a foothold in the shelter provided by the valley.

The valley itself twisted after about a hundred yards, around the corner where we'd managed to shoot the wild goat while it was drinking. Beyond that it kinked again after another hundred yards, climbing more steeply, before continuing on, but even following the game trails was difficult through the dense brush, which at times grew well over waist height, providing a little too much shelter for the leopards which prowled these upper slopes.

'With a thermal spring for heat, and these pools of water to attract game to the area, hunting would be possible all year round here,' Marlow suggested, as he surveyed the place.

'My thoughts exactly, Mon ami,' Jean added. 'And who knows, these pools may also contain fish large enough to eat. Elsewhere on these high mountain slopes we have seen hazels and numerous species of berries growing, so subsistence would be far from meagre, even if it wouldn't include wheat, bread or rice.'

The particulars which we'd discussed with Androus for identifying potential sites where Ziusudra's temple might be hidden, were still exactly as we'd agreed, but as we'd climbed, Jean suggested we refine the limitations we'd initially set.

It would still be completely impractical for any human being to live much above the permanent snow line, but even lower down, there were areas of the mountain where the slopes were almost barren, where even the small mammals which often inhabited the cracks and crevices between rocks didn't live.

In consequence, finding a valley that provided shelter and a good supply of water for wildlife was a good sign that the place could actually be inhabited by a person.

Dusk however, was not the time to explore any further, because even though our eyes would adapt to the growing gloom, we just wouldn't be able to see the small details which might help in our search.

So, turning around, we made our way back to the camp where by now the fires were burning bright and the meat beginning to roast.

The following day saw us refreshed and raring to go, but with no idea how long it was going to take us to explore the valley we decided to leave most of the heavier equipment and food behind, so that we could move more easily through the brush.

This meant we could also give the guides and the two men who we'd paid to carry the food and cooking equipment an easy day looking after the camp, for as long as it took us to properly explore.

We'd been lucky with the weather since we'd climbed above the rain-forest, and while the skies still looked clear, giving the men time to gather more dry firewood and erect a shelter from the tarpaulins we carried would make for a much more comfortable camp if the weather did suddenly deteriorate.

With that we headed off once again up the valley.

In the bright light of morning, the place was even more attractive than it had appeared the previous evening, with the lofty snow-capped peaks visible above the valley walls tinged with the golden light of dawn.

As the valley was only a small one, no more than

four or five hundred yards wide at its top, we decided to split into two groups so that we could explore both sides of the vibrant little rivulet as it splashed its way down through the series of pools that dotted its course.

I headed up the right hand, more easterly side with Jean, Harry and Selene, while Marlow walked up the westerly side with Androus and Peter.

As we walked, we often split up to follow side paths in the game trails through the shrubs and grasses, looking for any evidence of human workmanship.

We checked both sides of the pools as we passed them to see if their edges had been deliberately cut rather than worn away, as well as the rocks and outcroppings for symbols, up past the first and second turn in the valley. Hacking a wider path where we needed it, we checked in with the team on the other bank whenever we drew close enough to one another to be easily heard.

Along the way we found more goat tracks, as well as those of a small deer and some kind of rabbit or squirrel like mammal, and of course the unmistakable prints of the elusive snow-leopards.

But we found nothing even suggesting people had been here before, barring the brass casing from a hunting rifle round, left behind in modern times by one of the more adventurous hunting parties that Beaumont mentioned, which must have come this way during the last fifty years.

On we pressed, past the second and third turn in the valley, where we found a small lake occupying most of the valley floor, again with edges which showed no signs of being deliberately created or shaped.

Still further onward we ventured.

Just after lunch-time we found a narrow point, where the warm water from the stream had cut its way through some harder stone, and we managed to easily jump across to join up with the others to discuss how to proceed.

'We have some time yet,' Marlow said. 'If we're not searching as we go, we can probably make our way back to camp in no more than two hours.'

'That's true,' Peter conceded. 'But this valley could go on for another twenty miles.'

'No, it cannot continue to climb much further,' Jean observed. 'At this inclination it will surely reach the permanent line of snow and ice well before then.'

'Well, if we turn back now, we won't have time to move the camp very far before nightfall,' Harry very reasonably observed. 'Whereas, if we press on for another two or three hours, we should still have time to get back to the camp before dark, if we walk at a march.'

'That makes sense,' Marlow conceded. 'If we haven't found the end of the valley in another three hours, then we'll need most of tomorrow just to move the camp up to this point, before we can explore any further anyway.'

Two hours later, and the question became academic, when the thermal watercourse we'd been following suddenly came to an end in a large steaming pool at the head of the valley.

I couldn't quite believe we hadn't found anything for all the work we'd put in. But there it was, a pool with no stream feeding into it.

'It must be an underground spring,' Peter observed, looking down into the water.

'Yes, there it is,' he pointed. 'There's an opening just there, ten feet or so from the edge, you can see the plant-life being whipped around by the current of water that must be coming out of that opening.'

'That looks like quite a large opening,' I observed, squinting past the reflections on the pool's surface. 'It must be at least as big as a dustbin lid.

'Do you think it's natural,' I asked, wondering whether this could possibly be the entrance we were looking for.

'Well there's only one way to tell for sure,' he indicated.

'A few moments later, while we built a small fire to

help him get dry afterward, Peter stripped down to his underclothes and then jumped into the warm water with a splash.

'Well, it's not quite bath temperature, but it will do,' he joked, as he waded out into the deep water where the thermal spring seemed to enter the pool.

Then ducking down beneath the surface of the water, we could see him go down into the mouth of the spring, before coming back up and resurfacing with a splutter.

'Yes, completely natural from what I can see,' he indicated as he swam back to the shore.

It had probably been foolish of me to think we might find the first great temple so easily, but this valley seemed so unusual and so promising.

There were still a few game paths leading through the brush, so while Peter dried himself in front of the fire before getting dressed, I decided to follow one of them which led up to the top of the valley wall.

It was an easy climb, which only took a minute or two, and brought me out on a wide shelf which we hadn't noticed from below. The ground was stonier here, so the brush grew a little shorter for the most part, although the back of the shelf seemed to be completely overgrown by a rather twisted and gnarly tree covered in small green fruit.

From a distance I thought they might be the greengage style of plums that were so common back in England, and thinking it might be a nice surprise for the others, I strolled over to pick a few and see if they were ripe enough to eat.

Fortunately, I spotted the huge spike-like thorns hidden amongst the leaves and branches so I focused my efforts on the more exposed fruit around the outside of the bush, carefully inserting my hand before twisting and tugging at a couple of the largest and ripest looking ones.

My caution was not rewarded though, as the fruit stubbornly refused to come away at first. So, careful as I was, I still succeeded in pulling the self-same thorns straight into the exposed skin of my hand an wrist.

It was only when I'd received several deep scratches to my hand for the sake of two rock-hard and unpleasantly sticky fruit that bore no relation to the sweet plums I'd been expecting, that I finally recognised the sound of a low growl coming from somewhere deep within the thicket of trees.

I couldn't place the source of the sound precisely, but now as I slowly stepped back from the thorny trees, I noticed a distinctive game trail leading beneath the thorny barrier of branches, some of which even had the tell-tale pale tufty fur of a snow leopard caught on them.

Like an idiot I'd walked straight up to these trees, without even thinking that they could be the lair of one of these ferocious big cats. Not only that, but in the process, I'd slung my rifle over my shoulder and then grabbed these two worthless lumps of fruit with my right hand, so I couldn't even draw my revolver which was holstered on my right hip.

If the creature attacked, I wouldn't stand a chance.

With a cold sweat on my brow, I backed away from the leopard's lair, slowly placing the thorny fruit in my other hand so that I could draw my revolver.

I walked half a dozen steps backwards, away from the trees with my revolver now pointed straight at the narrow tunnel through the thorns, when I heard a sound behind me also.

'Keep walking, George,' Selene calmly said to me. 'Don't turn around, the path is straight behind you, and I've got you covered with my rifle.'

'I believe I've just found the snow leopard's lair,' I replied, doing exactly as she'd instructed.

'I guessed as much,' she answered, as we both now saw the face of the leopard slowly emerging from the darkness beneath the trees.

There was something not quite right about the shape of the creature's head as it moved forward into the light, and then I recognised that it had one of its young in its mouth, and was probably as keen to be away from us, as we were to be away from it.

Slowly, so as not to spook the creature we both backed away to the lip of the valley wall, where we found Jean and Marlow both waiting with their rifles trained on the hollow beneath the trees.

Only when we reached the edge and crouched down beneath the low brush, did the mother finally fully appear, cub in mouth, to slink away to one of her other hideaways.

She moved effortlessly beneath the thorny trees then up an area of steep cliff which was over-grown with more of the spikey Azealia like shrubs and away.

We watched for another half-hour as the mother returned twice more to rescue another two cubs from her old den, which I'd practically walked into.

REGROUPING

AFTER THE DISAPPOINTMENT of not finding the temple and the excitement with the leopard, I would have been more than happy to call it quits with this first tributary of the Brahmaputra, but we had struggled like this before, only then to make some kind of breakthrough. So, after staying another night in our camp at the foot of the secluded valley, we continued our search of the river valley on the way down.

It took another four days to reach Pangin, and then one more day after that to reach Pasighat during which our luck with the weather finally changed and rain started to fall in sheets. It wasn't as heavy as the African monsoon, but it was more than enough for us all to get thoroughly soaked, before finally re-boarding the Uma Parvati and heading back to Dibrugarh.

We'd contemplated asking Manash to take us straight to Sadya at the mouth of the next tributary we wanted to search, but we'd learned from long experience when to rest and when to keep pushing on, and now, after a major disappointment, it was time to relax for a few days and regain our perspective.

The down-time would not only give us the chance to recuperate and enjoy the luxury of a decent bed and hot bath, it would also give us time to dry, clean and service our sodden equipment, as well as to get our clothes laundered before heading back into the wilderness once more.

Manash's boat could produce almost unlimited amounts of hot water for bathing, so we didn't even have to wait to get back to Dibrugarh before we could all bathe and freshen up, though sadly he couldn't get the laundry done while we were on the move, which left us with a limited supply of fresh clothes to get changed into.

It was only for a couple of days though, as Manash knew of a good laundry service in Dibrugarh that would be able to quickly wash and press our things while the boat was refuelled and restocked.

This would give us six days down-time before we'd be leaving the boat again, two days back to Dibrugarh, two days stay at the fort and then two more days back upriver to Sadya.

As a courtesy, once we arrived back in Dibrugarh we decided to stop by Beaumont's offices in the fort, to update him personally on our return, and as the rest of our clothing was being laundered, we decided to put the cat amongst the pigeons by doing so while disguised in our Bedouin travelling robes.

The scratches on my hand still itched from my encounter with the thorn bush, but worse still, our day of walking in the rain on our way back to Pasighat had given me a head cold, so by the time we moored-up outside the fort my head felt like it was full of cotton-wool. As such, I left all the arrangements for our search of the next tributary to the others and concentrated on resting and recuperating.

The rain had stopped by the time we reached the fort town, so to stay out of everyone's way, I took myself off to the upper deck, which had some folding chairs I had used before, with the intention of doing some more work on my journals, only to promptly fall asleep for the better part of the day.

Manash, ever thoughtful, arranged for the cooks who had come aboard to ply me with tea and lemonade regularly, as well as a few spicy pastries at lunch time, which I somehow managed to find an appetite for, despite not feeling hungry beforehand.

The spot I was in was perfect for this kind of leisurely recuperation. It was shady for most of the day, but warm, and with pleasant views along the river past the town and fort, which I admired in those moments when I found myself awake.

I was oblivious to the comings and goings during this time, but by the early evening I was feeling a little better, so I decided to go below decks to see if anyone had returned from the town yet.

On the way I stepped into my cabin to return my unopened journal, and noticed the laundry service had already cleaned, pressed and returned my clothes, which were now laid out in neat piles on my bed.

With nothing better to do I set about putting everything away, and in the process, found that the laundry service had also placed the loose items that I'd left in my various pockets, in a small linen bag. Amongst the contents of which I found a few odd coins, train ticket stubs, a small pocket knife which I think belonged to Jean, a battered old pencil which I didn't recognise, and those two yellowy-green fruits from the spiny plant which had scratched my hand.

I didn't even remember pocketing them, but in

fairness to myself, my attention had been focused on the cornered leopard at the time, so it was hardly surprising I didn't remember what I'd done with them.

Shaking my head at my own stupidity for approaching that thicket of trees so carelessly, I almost threw the hard-green fruit into my waste basket, but as I retrieved them from the bag their stickiness once again drew my attention.

For all the world, now that I looked at them more closely, they looked like some kind of lumpy lemon or lime, but without the citrus pattern on the skin.

With nothing better to do, I picked up the small pocket knife of Jean's, which I'd also found in the bag, then after placing the empty cotton bag on my closed journal, I cut one of the fruit in half horizontally to see what it was like on the inside.

To my surprise, when I separated the halves, I realised it must be a relative of an apple or pear. The flesh was dense and quite fragrant with the all too familiar seeds in the centre that were just beginning to turn brown, just like an apple or pear seed.

In fact, as I continued to look at it, it suddenly occurred to me that this must be a relative of the quince trees I'd seen growing all over Turkey. The fruit had been larger in Turkey, but had a very similar lumpiness and a slight stickiness to the skin when they were green and immature, before they turned a deep golden yellow at the point of ripeness.

'Now what is a quince tree from Turkey doing all the way over here in east India?' I asked myself aloud, 'And in that strange little valley of all places.'

Curious for its own sake, I moved to the waste basket in my cabin and was just about to tip the dismembered fruit into it, when a memory from our visit to the temple of Shiva in Guwahati suddenly came back to me. Wasn't there some mention of Shiva in his guise as Lord Rudra planting a pear tree outside the entrance to his home in the dawn-lit mountains?

Placing the remains of the quince carefully on top of my chest of drawers, I extracted my journal from beneath the cotton bag and flicked through the pages to find the entry about the temple and the story which the old priest had told us.

And there it was, as clear as day on the page before me:

'And finally, he took his bag of healing potions, salves and powders, by which he could cure all the ills known to man, as well as the wounds great or small that one might receive while hunting or in battle, for it was by his healing arts that he hoped to persuade those he would meet of his friendship.

'So prepared, Lord Rudra descended from his mountain abode, planting the seed of a golden pear tree in the soil outside the entrance to his home, which he then sprinkled with the sacred water running through his home, so that the thorny branches of the pear tree grew up instantly to hide the entrance from the people and animals that might pass by, while the golden pears in the autumn would clearly mark the location for Lord Rudra when he returned.

'With his home thus protected, Lord Rudra travelled down from his mountain abode, through dense forests full of serpents, spiders and tigers, to the mighty river which flowed through the valley of the dawn.

Sri Rudra planted a golden pear tree with thorny branches outside the entrance to mark its location for his return and protect it against unwanted guests.

I had to sit down on the bed. I looked at the entry in my journal and then at the green lumps of immature quince sat on top of my set of drawers.

For several minutes I just looked from one to the other, my head-cold completely forgotten, and replaced by simple shock, until I heard the unmistakable sound of my friends returning to the boat.

In a daze I walked through the lounge with my journal in one hand and the cut-up quince in the other.

'Hullo, George,' I heard Peter say, rather jovially from across the room as he started to unwind his turban. 'Feeling any better?'

'I… I think I've just figured out where Ziusudra's temple is.' I heard myself say, in a rather detached voice.

I was still reeling with my own shock as they all crowded round to hear what I'd got to say and show them. Then it was my turn to watch them as they too looked at the strange knobbly fruit and the entry in my journal.

Harry and Androus still had their own rough notes from our meeting with the scholar on Peacock Island, and they confirmed what I'd written down was accurate.

'Of course, it all begins to make sense,' Androus confirmed, looking at a piece of the quince I'd cut in half with a small smile. 'We are simply too early. How could I have overlooked this fact.

'We began this trip on foot in order to follow the directions contained on the tablets when they were intended to be followed, starting when they said to start so that we would see the land corresponding to the directions in their proper season. But ever since Commissioner Jenkins diverted us to Haridwar we have been trying to make up time, and now after taking the trains to get here we have arrived perhaps two months too early.'

'You mean that mention of the red mountain is a reference to what… autumnal foliage which hasn't started to turn yet?' Harry asked.

'That is exactly what I mean,' Androus replied, with a gentle chuckle. 'It is only early autumn here in Arunachal Pradesh now, in another month or six weeks this quince would be fully ripe, delicious and golden. Who knows this particular variety may also have bright red foliage, but certainly all those other shrubs that we had to cut our way through in that hidden valley, I'd wager their foliage will begin to turn in the next few weeks.'

As my wits returned, I cast my gaze around to see how the others were taking the news.

Peter was stood next to Jean smiling happily, while Jean as ever appeared thoughtful and observant, and noticed me watching him almost immediately.

Likewise, Selene was stood with a glass of lemonade in her hand watching Marlow, with just the faintest trace of a frown on her face, as she too noticed my observation and returned it.

Marlow was sat in a lounge chair, a forgotten glass of lemonade on the coffee table in front of him and his gaze fixed on an unseen far horizon, lost in thought.

It had been his vision which had started this impossible search, and his need to find the truth which had propelled us forward in those moments of doubt and low morale, and now finally his goal was almost in sight.

Over the next few hours we discussed the implications, and in particular, how we should go about returning to the valley and searching the hillside behind the quince trees. What tools and equipment we'd need if we didn't want to get scratched to ribbons in the process of clearing away that thorny barrier.

Saws and axes would obviously be required, as would thick leather gloves and maybe a butcher's or metalworker's apron for whoever ended up at the front, but the fort closed and barred its gates at nightfall whether you were inside or out. Now, with the sun sinking behind the mountains that we would soon be heading back into, there was no hope of getting in, finding the supplies we needed and getting out again before the gates were locked, so there was nothing more we could do until the morning.

As usual Marlow disappeared up on deck to watch the setting of the sun, as he had done on so many other occasions before now, and head-cold or not, I went up with everyone else to join him.

Soon, we would set off on the journey back toward

Pasighat and the land of the dawn-lit mountains.

PASIGHAT

IT ONLY TOOK HALF A DAY of foraging to find all the equipment we'd need to deal with the thorny quince trees in the hidden valley, but the trip back to Pasighat would still take us two full days, and there just weren't that many options for the overnight stop on the first night, so we took the rest of the day to get our cameras and notebooks, labels, stencils and other excavation and recording equipment ready to be carried up the mountain.

This would save us important time when it came to arranging our bearers and guides in Pasighat, who quite reasonably charged by the weight and size of the bags they were being asked to carry. But even with a head-cold the extra waiting around was still irritating, especially when it seemed so many other vessels were coming and going.

Our plans though, were very nearly brought to nothing by Manash, who had a run-in with some thugs while he was making his way back to the boat on the evening before we were due to set off.

It was after the fort had closed its gates for the evening, so the garrison who patrolled the docks had finished for the day, but fortunately another boat owner and his sons had come to his aid and driven his attackers off.

He'd clearly been shaken up quite badly by the experience, and had been given a split lip and a black-eye as a memento, so he'd asked if we could spare his services for a few days after we reached Pasighat so that he could go and visit his family, which we naturally agreed to.

This meant putting the rest of our belongings in storage while he was away, and hence even more packing.

Finally, after reporting the incident to the fort

authorities, we left Dibrugarh a couple of hours later than we had hoped on the third day.

While cruising up the river might have seemed a much slower exercise this time, the journey aboard the Uma Parvati was still an undeniably comfortable and beautiful one, which gave me all the time I needed to get over my head-cold and feel back to my usual self.

Rested and relaxed, but eager to get on, we landed in Pasighat two days later.

As a town it hadn't been a particularly memorable or friendly place on our first visit, and now as we pulled back into the harbour we had to dodge a large pontoon full of felled tree trunks making its final trip down-river, where these once mighty trees would doubtless be processed into expensive timber, generating an income for the local Pasighar tribe, with whom we would also soon be arranging guides and bearers.

If anything, as we unloaded our possessions onto the quayside this time, the place felt even more like a hostile, edge of the wilderness town than it had before. People seemed to scuttle back and forth wanting to conclude their business before the sun sank behind the overarching mountains.

Stowing the cases we wouldn't need for the journey at a small guest-house overlooking the docks, we emerged into the quickly darkening evening, and gathered our bags together before setting off for the tribal leader's home, where we were hoping to arrange for the services of the same bearers we'd used before.

There was a good walk ahead of us with the heavy and cumbersome bags, but nothing we couldn't manage after our months of walking to Samarkand, so we hefted our respective burdens and set off along the now quiet quayside, through the streets connecting several warehouses and storage buildings and then up through the market to the centre of the town where the tribal leader's residence was located.

The first shots to ring out in the still twilight air caught us almost by surprise, but Marlow's shout of warning and our heavy backpacks saved our lives.

This was the ambush which Marlow had dreamed of, and it was his cry of warning a second before the bullets started to fly that caused us to turn and then duck behind the nearest cover.

It was still touch and go, and I felt at least three bullets thump into my backpack, which contained the bulk of the camping gear we carried, just as I turned around to look at Marlow when he shouted.

Needless to say, I didn't need telling twice, and I dived behind a pile of lumber, as more bullets whizzed past my head, wrestling out of my pack and freeing my rifle as I did so.

There were at least a dozen people shooting at us, careless of their own safety in their eagerness to fire, but not all of them were taking the time to be accurate.

The pile of logs in front of me provided the perfect cover, and my first shot clearly caught them by surprise as it downed one of the shooters with a bullet straight through his chest.

My second bullet missed the shoulder of the man I was aiming for, but hit his rifle just as he was about to fire, sending his shot wide and his gun clattering into the open.

Foolishly his instinct was to go after it, and a shot from somewhere to my left hit him.

With two of their number down, the others started to be more careful, so I took a moment to look around to see if anyone was hurt on our side, but thankfully everyone seemed to have found cover.

I wasn't sure who our attackers were until Selene fired, she managed to wing another shooter I hadn't seen, whose cry revealed her to be female and therefore probably one of the Icarii agents.

Having lost their element of surprise, and all of us now behind cover it became a sniping game, with odd shots being taken every now and again at real or imagined targets, followed by return shots at the shooters muzzle flash.

But it was far from a stalemate. We were cornered and unable to get off the quayside, with big gaps in the cover available to us, and while there were also significant gaps in the cover available to the Icarii, making it difficult for them to storm us, they could easily retreat if they wanted to, in order to either outflank us, or merely find another spot from where to target us.

That was until someone started to fire at the Icarii from behind. It sounded like whoever it was, was firing a revolver, just the occasional pot shot into their rear. The first took another one of the female agents out, followed by a second shot which clearly missed its mark, but it must have been close enough to make the target jump up and try to run for better cover, only to be taken down by a much more accurate shot from Jean.

Now it was a game of cat and mouse, with our ambushers being the mouse. The revolver continued to fire at them from the rear, forcing them to move or abandon their hiding places, which gave us the chance to nibble away at them from the front.

Five minutes later and our ambushers knew the game was up. Without warning, one of the female agents shouted a command to retreat, which they did with surprising composure, laying down covering fire as they went, both fore and aft, so that we struggled to even get a shot off as they went.

We still waited for a few minutes, before tentatively breaking our own cover and advancing.

It was only then we discovered, that just like in his dream, Selene had been hit in the initial volley of shots, but unlike in his dream she'd taken a bullet to the thigh, as she limped over to join us.

The other surprise was seeing Studgeon come walking out of the shadows behind where the Icarii had been holed up, reloading his Webley as he came.

'Gentlemen, Lady,' he said, by way of a greeting. 'I had ma suspicions that following them peculiar women might lead me to you, but I did'na ken they would be so friendly.'

'Well, Sergeant Studgeon, it's a long story,' Peter replied, still scanning the darkness for any sign that the Icarii might be returning. 'One we'll be more than happy to share with you, but this is perhaps not the place.'

'Yes, we need to get to the tribal leader's residence,' Harry added. 'To make him aware of what's taken place here, and ask him to support us.'

'Well now, you may do as you will,' Studgeon replied, holstering his now reloaded revolver. 'But I tell ye now, I've been followin' this group for two weeks since Commissioner Jenkins caught one O' his junior clerks issuin travel papers to them, an that includes trailing them to yer head man's house here in the town.'

'Of course,' Jean observed. 'They would not dare strike at us so openly if they did not have the local officials in their pockets.

'I cannot help but wonder if they are perhaps not also responsible for assaulting Manash back in Dibrugarh, and his sudden need to go and visit his family.'

'Well, we cannot stay on this quayside,' Marlow added. 'And nor can we stay in the town by the sound of it.

'Can you walk, Selene?'

'Yes, if I bandage my leg, but this bullet needs to come out,' she replied with a grimace.

'We should start walking down the river bank,' I suggested. 'It's comparatively flat, and as soon as we get into the darkness we can find somewhere to make camp and treat Selene's injury.'

'No, that's what they'd expect,' Marlow added, 'And they can use the river to easily get ahead of us and lay another ambush.'

'Well, Rob,' I replied, concerned that he still wanted to push on to the secret valley. 'Going uphill will be harder, and keeping a wound clean in that jungle…'

'I regret, we do not have a choice, George,' Jean added, simply. 'They could cut us down from a distance with their rifles in the open country between here and Dibrugarh. The rain-forest will at least give us cover.'

With that we transferred Selene's pack to Studgeon, who volunteered to take it, then found her a makeshift walking stick to help her keep the weight off her injured leg, before setting of north along the banks of the river, skirting around the town until we reached the same narrow road we'd used the last time we travelled into the mountains.

Selene's limp didn't seem too bad for the moment, but she had already warned us that she might not be able to maintain our normal pace for the whole fifteen miles or so through the jungle.

But before we could take a proper look at her injury, we needed to put some distance between us and the Icarii.

A couple of miles further on, when we reached the rainforest proper, we spotted a small ferry with a solitary oil lamp burning over its prow as it made its way across the river toward the bank we were on.

Descending quickly and quietly to the side of the river, we hid until we could see who was coming across, before we asked about passage to the other side.

Fortunately, the foreshore here was lush and plentiful, so we had no difficulty keeping out of sight, and a good thing we did too, for as the ferry drew closer, we spotted the tell-tale shock of red hair passing back and forth in the pool of light from the lamp. That could only indicate the presence of Miriam.

She was stamping back and forth across the ferry impatiently while the owner of the ferry laboured to bring her and several other people across the wide river.

'She always was impatient,' Selene observed, from where she crouched down beside me. 'Despite the number of times it cost her the advantage, and the opportunity to lead her own cell. But the more it cost her, the more rash she became.'

That flash of red hair was visible as she paced back and forth past the lantern all the way to the shore, when she was finally able to stamp off the ferry, leading her horse behind her.

With her were the two guides that had taken us up the mountain the last time, a couple of those strangely docile men, and another young blonde woman who I could almost have mistaken for Thea, had I not known her to be dead, slain in her prison cell by Miriam.

Forcing the guides to run after them, all those with horses including Miriam, her new sister and the two docile men, all saddled up and raced off as fast as they could in the now fairly complete darkness.

They'd obviously forced the ferryman to bring them over much faster than he would normally, and he slumped into a chair now to get his breath back, and didn't notice us approach, but he took the surprise in his stride, especially once he realised we weren't in the same rush as the last group he'd carried.

After paying his price, he was ready to set off again, this time helped along by both Peter and Marlow on the rope, much to his obvious gratitude.

The journey across gave Jean a chance to have a quick look at Selene's leg.

The bullet had caught her in the lower thigh, six inches above the knee, and while bloody, didn't seem to be bleeding very much anymore, even with the walking she had done.

'You are fortunate, my dear,' Jean commented, as he examined the wound.

'The bullet appears to have entered from the front and travelled straight toward your femur,' he added, with a slight frown. 'But it clearly has not damaged the bone.'

'I came to the same conclusion,' Selene replied. 'It must have passed through something else before hitting me, to take the force out of the bullet.'

'It could have passed through my pack,' I confirmed. 'I felt three solid impacts as I turned back toward Rob, when he shouted his warning.'

'Oui, his alarm saved me also,' Jean confirmed. 'Though I counted only two bullets hitting my own backpack.'

'However much this bullet was slowed, it was regrettably not enough to prevent your injury altogether,' Jean added. 'I am afraid we will need a fire, some time and some space to remove it.'

'Have ye any experience o' removin' a round, M'sieur?' Studgeon asked.

'A little,' Jean replied. 'And you, sergeant?'

'Ay, a little also.'

'Good.

'And you Ms Autieri,' Jean asked. 'Has your unique training included any battlefield medicine?'

'Yes, it has,' she confirmed. 'But I am no surgeon, and I have never had to use my training in this way.'

'Well, the bullet is buried deep enough to be awkward,' Jean explained, as he carefully re-wrapped Selene's leg with a fresh bandage. 'And it is lodged either directly in front of, or perhaps a little to the side of the bone. Fortunately, it is nowhere near your arteries, and from the lack of bleeding appears to have missed the larger veins also.'

Surgery would still be dangerous, but by crossing the river as we had in the dead of night, we might just have evaded anyone pursuing us, which, if Miriam had anything to say in the matter, would be sooner rather than later.

Our more immediate problem was travelling in the dark. We had to push on for a while to get away from the ferry and deep into the trees, but the local tigers made it a dangerous place to venture after dark, even in a group.

The night sky was clear of clouds so we could just about follow the path by the starlight until we reached the canopy of the big trees, when the inky darkness made travelling completely impossible, and we had to dig out the hand lanterns we had brought to explore the temple.

These lanterns were only small, but burned for a good long time, and they were easy to conceal with a hand or behind a coat. The drawback with them was that their light just didn't reach as far. They made enough light to follow the path with, which twisted along the river bank, but they were useless for seeing into the forest when we thought we heard something.

Selene was still managing a good pace, so if we could just find somewhere to hole-up, we could try removing the bullet out of her leg. Unfortunately, while we passed the odd track leading off the main path, deeper into the forest, we found nothing that we could use as an overnight shelter, or where we could try and build a shelter for the night. which meant we just had to push on.

Despite stopping for a few minutes every hour we kept a good pace for most of the night, though by the early hours of the morning, Selene's wound had become quite inflamed and Jean was concerned that if the bullet wasn't removed soon, then the chance of her wound becoming infected would increase dramatically.

'Ms Autieri is healthy and fit,' he explained from a little distance away from where she was resting. 'But if we do not stop soon, her chances of survival will be very poor.'

'What if we divided the group in two,' I suggested, thinking as I spoke. 'One group could press on ahead until we come across one of those side tracks that lead further into the forest, they could check it out for somewhere that's concealed enough to pitch camp for a while. Make a small fire to prepare some food, clear a space for you to remove the bullet, and create a shelter where Selene could rest for a while afterward.'

'Yes, this idea may work,' Jean conceded. 'If you can make a fire big enough to boil some water, we could sterilise the medical equipment and ensure she stays warm.'

'Aye, an' we could maybe build a stretcher while we're at it,' Studgeon added. 'To carry the lassie for a while?'

'An excellent idea,' Jean conceded. 'But we must put this proposal to Ms Autieri, and ensure she is willing.'

It was the longest time I'd seen Selene hesitate over a decision, but after considering for a few moments, she finally nodded her agreement, and we split the group into two halves.

I went ahead with Studgeon, Peter and Harry. While Marlow, Jean and Androus followed with Selene, as quickly as they were able in the second group.

We found the next side track, and quickly traced our way along it, opening up our lanterns to their fullest as we moved further away from the river.

A few hundred yards in Peter spotted some tall rocks and boulders among the trees, which, when we investigated turned out to be grouped into a rough semi-circle, with the gap facing away from both the path and the river. A good defensive position, should we need it.

Better still there were also some flattish boulders inside the half circle, including two that would make a good operating table, one slightly higher than the other, which were the right height to allow Selene to sit.

We'd have to cushion them out with our packs to make them more comfortable and raise the height slightly so that Jean could operate, but she'd be off the ground, and if we built the fire to one side, she would also be plenty warm enough.

Fortunately, there was also plenty of wood around for a fire, and enough leafy rhododendron shrubs to allow us to quickly fill in any of the gaps between the rocks to prevent any light from leaking out.

We'd just managed to get the fire going properly, and set a pot of water over it when we saw the others making their way along the side track toward us.

We must have done a reasonable job of hiding the fire, as they hadn't spotted it when we went out to meet them, but it would only be dark for another few hours anyway, after which the light from the fire would be less of an issue.

Jean was pleased with the setup for Selene, and after a few minutes of adding more packs and padding to the rocks to make her comfortable, he examined the wound again by the light of the lanterns, and then gave us our instructions.

We had a couple of scalpels and some tweezers in our medical kit, which were boiled and then laid out on a clean handkerchief. Jean washed his hands as best he could with soap and hot water, then sterilised his hands and the scalpels again with some whisky which Peter was carrying.

With all the preparation done, it was now or never. Jean began by carefully removing the old bandage and dressing, which Studgeon took from him to wash and sterilise. The rest of us crowded around with our lanterns to provide Jean with as much light as possible.

I was the next one to wash and sterilise my hands, as well as several pieces of cutlery which we carried.

After cleaning the wound with boiled water which had cooled, Jean then tentatively used the back end of the tweezers to open the now inflamed wound so that he could locate the bullet.

This must have been agony for Selene, but she never once complained or asked him to stop, only biting down on a folded leather belt when he removed the bullet itself, while he used the sterilised cutlery to hold the wound open.

It was a slow process, made all the worse by the fact that once the bullet was out, Jean had to re-open the wound to remove a small piece of fabric which had been dragged deep inside by the bullet itself. Only then, once he was satisfied the wound was clean, did he stitch it closed with cotton thread which had been soaked in whisky.

Just watching Selene endure the removal of the bullet was exhausting, so what it must have been like for her

I could hardly imagine.

Unfortunately, with none of us having any formal medical training, the only pain-relieving medication we had with us were some headache tablets, which we gave to Selene in the highest dose we dared.

With the wound dressed, all that remained was to keep her warm while she rested, and then to take it in turns to get some sleep before the sun rose.

RETURN

THE CANOPY OF THE RAINFOREST grew thicker further away from the river, so we all managed to get some rest in our camp among the boulders, despite the bright sunrise above the trees. Selene in particular slept until well after dawn, when, after testing her leg, she declared it to still be painfully sore, but perhaps a little less than it had been with the bullet in it.

The bleeding, which had naturally started again during the surgery, had also stopped, and while the wound still seemed quite inflamed, that too was apparently no worse than it had been the night before, when Jean once more examined the wound.

Having said all that, we clearly wouldn't be able to travel far until Selene could have some more time to heal and recover, so after a basic breakfast, we cleaned up the camp and set off once more, with no expectations of how much ground we might be able to cover.

Studgeon and Peter had constructed a stretcher, just in case it should be needed, and Harry had also made a better crutch.

Selene opted to walk with the crutch to begin with, but asked us to take the stretcher poles with us, just in case her leg failed her.

After taking it very slow to begin with, once we got moving again we made steady progress, stopping for a break after every hour of walking, reaching Pangin only a little after midday.

This presented us with our first dilemma.

The people of Pangin were of a different, albeit affiliated tribe to the people of Pasighat, so we didn't know whether it would be safe to stop and pick up some supplies including some medicine for Selene.

But we couldn't afford to take any risks, not while Selene was injured, so we decided to bypass the main road on our side of the river where the ferry crossing was located, in the hope of finding a decent vantage point from which to observe the town, to see if there was any sign of the Icarii being present.

Our caution was rewarded almost immediately though, for as we crept through the undergrowth twenty yards behind the ferryman's hut, we saw three horses tethered nearby, where they'd be out of sight to anyone approaching the hut along the path, or crossing the river on the ferry.

'It is as I feared,' Jean whispered as we crept through the forest. 'Pangin is as far north as it is possible to travel on horseback, before the trail becomes too rugged and steep for them.'

'So, this is where you think Miriam was returning from last night,' I asked.

'Precisely, my friend,' he replied. 'This will have been her backup plan, in the event of us evading the ambush.'

'Of course,' I replied, suddenly grasping what must have happened. 'That would explain why she wasn't present for the ambush. Which I'm sure she would have intended to be back for. This is a second ambush, designed to catch us as we crossed on the ferry, while we were completely exposed.

'Setting the trap here must have taken a little longer

than she had anticipated, and the growing darkness combined with the rougher path on this side of the river then slowed her down further.'

'That appears plausible,' Jean concurred.

With no option of stopping off in Pangin, there would be no opportunity to pick up any medication for Selene, or to buy any fresh food to go with the limited supply of rice and lentils we had in our packs.

For the moment though, we moved past Pangin and then a mile or so further on, started to emerge from the rain-forest also, which grew thinner as the terrain became steeper and rockier.

There was still plenty of cover around for the moment amongst the shrubs, rocks and patches of smaller trees, which we tried to use as much as possible to hide our presence.

We continued to stop regularly, both to give Selene a rest, and to more thoroughly scan the hillsides on both sides of the river for any kind of movement, or sign of lookouts, but time and again we found nothing.

'Perhaps they think we've gone the other way, down the river,' suggested Peter, after we'd once again stopped and found no trace of our adversaries.

'Possibly,' Jean conceded. 'But I think it more likely they are perhaps spread a little thinly. They do not know which side of the river we are on, or whether we have gone upstream or down. Hence they have placed lookouts in Pangin, in case we should go upstream, and possibly also a day's walk down the river, in case we should go that way. Which then leaves nobody to search the areas in between or beyond.'

Whatever the reason, it was good news, and we continued to climb steadily, taking breaks and scanning the mountainsides for anything out of the ordinary.

Of course, this time there was no need to do the methodical searching of every gully and stream as we'd done before, so we progressed quickly, climbing at least a third of the way to our destination before nightfall.

The next two days were by turns easier and then more difficult. We maintained our pace, thanks mostly to Selene's leg beginning to heal, but we then climbed into the steeper and craggier parts of the mountain, which just took longer to traverse because the paths were more difficult.

Each night we sheltered where we could, hoping that the weather wouldn't deteriorate, and lighting a small fire to cook some food, when we could be sure it wouldn't be visible for miles. But even then, the comparative lack of wood at these altitudes meant we only really had the stretcher poles for fuel, so we could only keep the fire going for as long as it took to cook our rice and lentils.

Finally, three days after leaving Pangin, we made it back over the mouth of the hidden valley. Nowhere had we seen any sign of our adversaries or of anyone looking out for us, but there had been half-sightings. Unexpected glints or flashes from the sunlit slopes on the other side of the valley, or small movements which may have been a person or may have been an animal, and which had disappeared by the time we got the binoculars trained on the right spot.

This valley, where we'd previously spent a day and a half, was surely the place the Icarii would have someone waiting for us, if they were going to be anywhere. Hence, we took our time and scouted the approach to the valley carefully.

After an hour of slowly creeping up on the place though, it became evident that nobody was sat waiting for us, so with relief we made our way into the comparative shelter of the hanging valley with the thermal spring running through its centre.

The place was exactly as we'd left it, the thorn fence, spent fire pits, even the spare wood we'd collected was all still there, and better still, we had enough daylight left to get cleaned up and try to catch some game.

On Jean's advice, Selene also took herself off to one

of the pools to bathe her injured leg in the sulphur rich water, to see how it was healing and judge whether it was time to remove the stitches which he'd put in to keep the wound closed.

We still wanted to be as careful as we could when it came to attracting attention, so we tried to muffle the sound that our guns would make by wrapping some cloth around the muzzles. This would reduce our accuracy a little as it obscured the forward sights, but only partially.

As we'd arrived at a similar time the last time we visited the valley, we made a beeline for the spot where Peter had bagged the mountain goat, just around the first bend in the valley, crawling the last few dozen yards through the dense foliage, to be rewarded by the sight of several animals drinking around the edge of a pool. Including several mountain goats, countless birds and small mammals and a dozen rugged looking antelope.

This time, I was at the fore, so I selected one of the antelope, as they were most numerous, and almost without a sound brought it down with a clean shot just behind the shoulder blade. So quietly in fact that the rest of the animals continued to drink, until we stood up from our hiding place and walked over to claim our prize, which would give us a welcome break from the rice and lentils, but more importantly, enough food by itself to last us for three or four days.

With a decent meal inside us and protected by the thorn fence and a fire, which we had enough wood to keep burning all night, we found ourselves for the first time since leaving Manash's boat with the leisure and the energy to simply sit and talk.

As always, it was Jean, our resident philosopher who poked the fire to create a bit more light and then start us off.

'Well, I don't mind admitting to any of you,' he began, enigmatically. 'That as I sit here by the fire, on this mountain in the eastern Himalaya, on the brink of uncovering what is likely to be one the most ancient archaeological sites known to man, that I was not sure we would ever find this goal which we have so long sought.'

'You astonish me,' Harry replied with a cough of gentle laughter, and a small shower of sparks from his pipe.

'In truth, I find myself more than a little astonished also,' Jean replied, oddly candid for once.

'I think we all feel the same,' added Marlow, extracting himself from whatever deep thoughts seemed to pre-occupy him these days. 'Do you think we should go on?'

'What!' Harry exclaimed, sending another eruption of embers into the night air, from his only just re-tamped pipe.

'Robert, there are times when your sense of humour is really... not very amusing.'

'Sorry, Harry,' Marlow replied with a rare smile. 'I know we must press on and hopefully find the temple tomorrow. But I think back to those early days in Kenya, when we first spoke of needing to find a purpose for our lives, and I barely recognise myself now.'

'And you are perhaps wondering,' Jean asked, with a familiar gleam back in his dark eyes. 'What you will do with your life if our long quest should happen to come to an end tomorrow.'

'Yes, my ever-insightful friend, I do wonder just that,' Marlow replied.

'And what answer have you come up with in response to that most difficult of questions?' Jean asked, pushing a little further than I thought he might.

'Well, we will continue to be hunted by the Icarii, I assume,' Marlow replied, building up to his real answer. 'But that is of no great consequence to me, nor to any of us, I think.

'No, I think I must continue the search, irrespective of what we find tomorrow. Perhaps we will continue to experience those strange dreams which accompany the distant drums, and through those I will be able to seek out other artefacts that have been lost to humanity.'

'And you alone will decide which of these lost secrets it is safe for the world to become aware of?' Selene asked, with more emotion in her voice than I had heard before.'

'No,' Marlow replied, seeming to focus upon her wholly for a moment, with that timeless gaze of his. 'Not I alone, but I would trust my friends, men and women of integrity and honesty, including people of faith and those with none, to help me with such decisions.'

'Including the secret which perhaps lies less than a day's walk from where we now sit?' Selene pushed, for the first time since we'd known her. 'Could you abandon your search for a secret that could extend your life so far beyond that of your friends, a secret which was so powerful that the individual who discovered it is now thought of as a god amongst the people of this continent?'

'If that is indeed the secret which this place holds,' Marlow replied, that familiar look of dark and brooding thoughtfulness now back on his firelit face. 'Then yes, if the thought of sharing such a secret with the world was of such profound concern to my friends around this fire, then I would agree to hold that secret back from the world at large.'

'And from yourself also?' Selene asked without hesitation.

'That must be a personal decision,' Marlow replied equally quickly. 'For each of us.'

Even Studgeon, to whom we'd explained what we were doing only at a high level, seemed to pick up on the significance of the words which were passing between Selene and Marlow. After all, this was the first time since we had begun the search that Marlow had conceded he might not share that secret with the world, if we, his friends advised against it.

'And what of you, Ms Autieri,' Studgeon unexpectedly asked, fearlessly stepping into the conversation. 'From what I ken of your former colleagues, these daughters of Icarus. They hold that all these ancient secrets should remain buried indefinitely, but could you agree to be one of those who decides the whither and the when of it all?'

'I…' she began to respond, before hesitating for a moment. 'With the people gathered around this fire, who I have come to trust and respect, I could make that decision.'

Again, I was shocked by what I was hearing. Granted, Selene had travelled with us for nearly two years now, through all the dangers of our flight across the Mediterranean as we tried to get away from her former colleagues, our stay in Ankara while we learned to speak Turkish and the Turkic language of the old silk roads, and of course the long walk to India followed by our journey to where we were now.

'In fact, as I think about it now,' she continued, thoughtfully staring into the fire. 'The mission you're describing is, in many ways, closer to that which the Order of Icarus was founded upon, than that which the modern Order pretends to follow.'

'Well said, Ms Autieri, well said,' Jean added.

'Ah but there are times when I wonder if I have become a little too sanguine over the years,' Jean continued, before pausing momentarily at the sight of yet another cloud of sparks from Harry's pipe. 'But there are times, when I am gathered like this with my friends, and the thoughts they share are so very noble, that I feel a great swelling of pride in my already great Gascon heart, and I think I might never feel jaded again.'

We did of course still need to uncover and enter the temple of Ziusudra, and discover its secrets, all before we could find our way down from the mountain past our enemies. So, while we continued to talk, the topic gradually changed until all those who were not on watch slept.

ENTRANCE

AFTER TAKING SOME CARE to make our camp look as though it hadn't been used since our previous visit, we began the final approach to Ziusudra's first great temple.

It was an odd feeling to be walking so confidently towards our goal, but not being quite certain that what we sought would be found there.

The situation was comically reversed when it came to the thicket of spikey quince trees, not knowing whether the maternal leopard which I'd encountered last time, might have since returned with her cubs.

But after approaching without any sign of the creature, and then giving a few of the branches a good shake with a stick, it became clear we had the place to ourselves, and it was time to get to work.

There wasn't space for us all to work on the thorns, so Marlow, Peter, Jean and I set about removing the trees, cutting and sawing at the tangled mess of branches, then passing the material we removed over to Androus, Harry, Selene and Studgeon, who took it and started to create another thorn fence around the entrance where we planned to pitch our camp that evening.

It was steady going, but with the benefit of the axes and saws the spike filled barrier soon started to give way, and within a couple of hours we'd cleared a path twenty feet wide and a little more deep, right back to the stone cliff which had been mostly hidden behind the trees.

Removing the trees was of course only the first stage, because it had revealed a significant bank of earth against the cliff, which must have accumulated over the centuries or however long it had been since anyone had last visited the temple.

Now was the time to use the folding spades and heavy digging bars we'd also brought with us, and which I for one had often lamented the weight of on the climb up the mountain. But this is what they were for, and now the earth too started to give way beneath our efforts.

We began at the cliff face, Marlow and I working a few feet apart with the shovels after Jean and Peter had first loosened the packed earth with the bars. Steadily and slowly working our way down, so that we could at least be sure we were in the right place before we started work on the mound of earth behind, which we'd also have to remove as we dug deeper.

It was heavy work, but the anticipation washed away any thoughts of fatigue, and then as the hole got down to about four feet deep, I removed a shovel full of earth, and just before the surrounding soil filled the hole back in, I saw it. A straight carved line in the stone.

'I think I've got something,' I exclaimed, excitement gripping me as I pulled another shovel full of earth out of the way, momentarily revealing another glimpse of the carved line.

The others stopped to watch as I removed several more shovels of earth, until the soil falling back into the bottom of the hole didn't hide it anymore. It was the top and one side of a cleanly worked piece of stone that had been set back into the surface of the natural cliff face.

This had to be the top of the doorway, so now, on Androus's suggestion, I resumed work, focusing on the earth to the right of my hole to reveal more of the line. The results came quickly. Jean loosened the earth into the hole, and I shovelled it out, gradually revealing a few more inches of the carved line as we moved to the right.

First we saw some more of the clean horizontal line in the stone, then a vertical line of the same depth and width joined it, forming a corner and suggesting this was an inlaid block of stone. Next to this another block and another, until finally the horizontal line continued no further, revealing what must be the corner of the doorway.

Meanwhile, as Jean and I moved to the right, Marlow and Peter excavated to the left. There was just enough space for us to work side by side without getting in one another's way.

Finding the top corner gave us all a burst of energy, but as Marlow worked his way along, he followed the top but found no end to the doorway where we were expecting it, so had to keep going, which meant moving some of the earth he'd already cleared for a second time.

On my side, about fifteen inches from what we were hoping was the top of the doorway, I uncovered another neatly carved line, confirming that what we'd revealed was a row of stone blocks.

Even more interesting, just below this top row of blocks the stone was recessed slightly, and a little more coarse in its finish.

I'd also discovered that the right hand edge of the doorway appeared to be sloping further to the right, so wasn't quite square. By this point though I was getting tired, so after giving Harry and Androus a few minutes to look at what I'd revealed, I swapped places with Jean, taking the bar from him to break up and loosen the earth while he shovelled.

By lunch-time, Marlow and Peter had discovered the left side of the doorway, revealing the door to be a few feet wider than its modern equivalent. In the process they'd also dug out another few feet of earth from their side of the doorway, much the same as Jean and I had done on our side.

At noon we took a break while Studgeon, Harry and Androus documented the scene so far, and then set to work themselves shifting the ramp of earth that led up to the cliff face. This would need doing before too much longer as the hole down to the doorway was getting quite steep, making it difficult to work. But it was also full of roots from the quince trees, so the three of them had to half excavate the roots before they could properly remove the earth below them.

A couple of hours later and we had a clear trench leading to the doorway, five feet wide and already a little below the bottom of the hole that was showing the top of the doorway.

'It appears to be the same shaped doorway as the ones we saw at the African temple,' Harry observed, resting on his shovel.

'And also constructed with a very similar command of stonemasonry,' Peter added.

'Of course, there's no knowing whether this style of architecture and the stone working originated at this temple,' Harry replied. 'Or whether it's a later addition by those who were returning to… renew their breath, I think they called it.'

Whenever it was constructed, it was impressive. The doorway was about six feet wide at the top, with a lintel and frame of smooth, precisely carved limestone, exactly the same type of stone as the cliff face itself. Whether these were simply carved into the rock-face or pieces of stone from elsewhere which had been set into it we couldn't yet tell.

Inside the frame, the doorway itself appeared to have been walled up with largish blocks of slightly more roughly cut stone, approximately ten inches tall and twenty inches wide.

There was no obvious sign of mortar between these stones, but they resisted our initial attempts at pushing them inwards.

After lunch, and with a clearer path to the doorway, we set about shovelling the rest of the earth away from the stonework, swapping roles as we got tired and taking regular breaks from this strenuous work.

Another couple of feet down and we discovered a stone with a bronze ring set flush into its surface, which when we pulled and pushed on it came easily out of its stone recess.

Not only that, but once the ring was free of the stone it revealed the slot it fitted into was much deeper on one side than the other.

'It is almost as though the ring were intended to be pushed in on one side.' Androus stated after examining the indentation more closely.

'Could it be a key of some variety?' Selene asked. 'Or perhaps a handle?'

'Yes, a handle perhaps,' replied Androus, as he tentatively inserted the ring of bronze back into the carved recess, and then pushed the right-hand side of the circle into the stone, which caused the left-hand side to be levered out, until the back of the ring was buried in the stone block and the front was left sticking out, just like a handle.

With a raised eyebrow, he stepped back so that Harry, the larger man, could step forward to get a good grip on the ring and give it a pull.

And pull it he did, though it clearly came out a lot easier than he was expecting, as he very nearly threw the stone block and the metal ring which was inserted into it over his shoulder and at the rest of us as we watched.

'A little easier than I was expecting,' he apologised, putting the stone and ring down on the ground beside him.

'These other stones seem to be a little bit thicker,' he said, after peering into the hole left by the first block.

'Try pushing on them again,' suggested Peter, over his shoulder.

'No, I don't think so,' Harry replied, as he scrutinised the hole, and then suddenly stuck his left hand into the it.

'Ah yes, as I expected,' he said, his body hiding the hole, as he stepped backward to pick up the bronze ring which had formed the handle in the central stone.

Without another word, he inserted the heavy ring into the hole left by the first stone, and then with an audible thud, we heard him knock the ring against the back of the next block.

One, two, three thumps with the heavy ring and then the block next to the hole shifted just a fraction.

Removing his hand and the ring, he then reinserted his hand and pulled the loosened stone block out with comparative ease.

'Ingenious,' he declared, holding the heavy stone out for all of us to see.

'Each block is ever so slightly tapered,' he explained. 'Like the keystone in an archway. You could push on this side all day and with all your might and get nowhere, but put a hand into the hole and pull, and they come out easily.'

Looking through the hole we could see there was a regular carved corridor on the other side, and all we needed to do to get to it was remove the rest of the blocks from the upper half of the doorway which we'd cleared.

Each block was a good weight, but by forming a line we quickly extracted them one after another, and stacked them in the order they were removed, so it would be easier to put each block back in its proper place when we needed to.

A few of the blocks needed a tap with the bronze ring just to loosen them, but within half an hour, and with at least two hours of daylight still left, we had removed the top half of the doorway, an opening four feet high and six feet wide.

Nobody was going to be staying behind when we went in, so we closed the thorn fence to prevent any wild animals, especially the leopard from following us, and then, thoughtful of the fact that the Icarii were still out there, we lit our lanterns, picked up our packs and followed Androus and Harry through the excavated doorway.

Sliding in over the remaining stones we found the floor was about four feet lower, but it was clean and free of both soil and debris, with a small entrance room about twenty feet wide by fifteen feet deep and ten feet tall.

As soon as I set foot inside I was reminded of the African temple, with its floor of perfectly carved and squared paving stones, and the walls of smoothly worked stone.

The ceiling was different, a large overhanging slab of rock which had been carved to be geometrically flat, but a little more course in finish.

This was a perfect reflection of the African temple, and the giant slab which we guessed had been deliberately demolished to block the entrance to the complex.

The only differences here were the scale and the lack of water. This temple was definitely smaller, judging by this first room, and there was no stream running down the centre of the corridor, covered in stepping stone slabs.

With all of us standing inside the entrance way, Androus set off down the corridor, commenting on the construction as he went.

'The stonework is like the doorway, exquisitely crafted,' we all heard him say, as he proceeded. 'The corridor is broadly rectangular with a slight but noticeable bowing of the side walls, and seems to extend some distance into the cliff face.

'I can see a chamber ahead. Yes, the corridor is perhaps fifteen yards long, straight and plain, and is now opening out into a second chamber which has three other exits…

'Oh, my goodness, Harrison, the walls are covered with carvings, with language and pictures.'

'I see it, Chuck, it is very similar to the place we found in Southern Rhodesia.'

'How incredible,' continued Androus. 'The room is seven, eight, no nine sided and each wall contains writing in a different language or alphabet, I see Egyptian Hieroglyphs, Classical Greek, Cuneiform, Sanskrit, another alphabet that I don't recognise at all, the block script of the Jews… what looks like ancient Greek.'

'Yes, that's right,' Harry confirmed. 'As I live and breathe, that's an entire wall of Linea A, the oldest Greek script that has ever been discovered.'

'Another script I don't recognise at all,' Androus continued, 'And finally Arabic or Farsi, I'm not sure which.'

'Do you think this could be the equivalent of the Rosetta Stone, but with nine languages?' Harry asked.

'I am sure of it,' Androus replied, breathlessly. 'Here, at the top of the Cuneiform inscription, it clearly reads 'welcome traveller to the home of Ziusudra'.

'And here, at the top of the classical Greek inscription, does it not say the same?'

'Yes, it's identical,' Harry confirmed. 'The Sanskrit also, I cannot read more than the first couple of words, but it starts with a welcome.'

'What of the exits,' I heard Marlow ask, from further up the corridor.

'Two more chambers, one to each side,' Harry replied, moving through into one, then the other.

'I'm not quite sure of their purpose, though there are wooden tables and benches in each.'

As the two archaeologists moved through into the adjoining rooms, it created space enough for the rest of us to move up to the second chamber.

This chamber with the writings on the wall, was again reminiscent of the second chamber in the African temple, minus the nine-sided pool of water and the black carved stelae, but one thing that was familiar was the sight of Marlow disappearing off ahead down the central corridor.

'Rob,' I called, seeing him almost out of sight down the steps, but it didn't stop him.

Realising that he'd again gone on ahead, Jean went to follow him, with me coming directly after.

The stairs were quite broad, perhaps five feet wide, and over seven feet tall like the other corridors, but where the first corridor had been quite straight, the stairs twisted and turned as though they had been carved on the course of some natural tunnel.

We descended perhaps twenty feet before the corridor levelled off, turned again and descended another fifteen feet into a huge open cavern, that appeared to be a natural formation for the most part.

It was at least thirty yards across, with a glowing pool of steaming water in its centre that illuminated the majority of the cavern in a weak blue-green light.

But while the water rolled and twisted with a lively current, it didn't overflow into the rest of the room, though it did warm the place to a pleasant temperature.

Around the pool in a perfect circle, nine waist-high, black stone stelae had been set into the smooth and level floor of the cave.

Above the pool, the cavern stretched upward by about sixty feet, with a few thin stalactites hanging down from the ceiling, probably created by the condensing water from the steaming pool as it cooled on the stone, slowly dissolving and then redepositing some of the minerals it contained.

On all sides I could see tunnels leading through to other caverns, though the natural watery light that illuminated this central cavern didn't stretch far enough to reveal their contents.

Marlow was already by the side of the pool when we reached it, and had knelt down to take a handful of the water to his lips.

'Robert,' Jean called, as we walked over to him. 'We really should stay together, at least to start with.'

'I know, Jean,' he replied, drinking the water from his hands. 'But after all this time I just don't have the patience to sit and catalogue everything before we even have a look around.

'It tastes the same as the water flowing through those pools in the valley,' he observed. 'Though a touch warmer in here.

'All right,' Marlow continued, looking around. 'Where shall we begin?'

Just then the others arrived down the stairs.

We split into two groups now, and recognising our natural desire to just see the place, Androus suggested that Harry join Jean, Marlow, and I, who would search clockwise from the stairs, while he went with everyone else to search anti-clockwise.

Selene also reminded us, that we should return to the surface before too much longer anyway, just to make sure her former colleagues weren't drawing any closer to the valley.

'We may have been lucky enough to get past them, and up into these mountains,' she cautioned. 'But make no mistake, sooner or later they will come, and if the doorway and tunnel are still visible when they arrive, they won't hesitate to destroy it and trap us in here.'

'Are you suggesting we should re-seal the entrance after looking around down here, and re-bury it before they should arrive?' Peter asked.

'That's exactly what I'm suggesting,' Selene confirmed. 'Right now, they have no clue where this temple is hidden, and probably aren't even sure we're on the mountain rather than hiding out on the plains.'

'It is a point well made,' Jean conceded. 'We have enough food now to simply lay low for a few days. If we were to rebury the entrance and disguise where we've been digging with the branches and boughs of the quince trees, they would probably stay green and look as though they haven't been disturbed for at least a week or two.'

'No, no, we can't just leave this now that we've finally found it,' Marlow protested, the disappointment and resignation palpable in every line of his frame.

'I'm sorry, Robert,' Selene replied, earnestly. 'With no other way out, it would be suicide to corner ourselves so perfectly.'

I felt for Marlow in that moment. This search had

clearly consumed more of him than he'd allowed us to see, and the prospect of walking away from the prize so soon after finding it, was a crushing blow, but at the same time, he knew what Selene was saying was right.

'It will be fully dark in a couple of hours,' I heard myself say, by way of a compromise. 'At which point we won't be able to see if Miriam and her agents are getting any closer. So how about I head back up now with someone else to see if they've reached the mouth of the hanging valley?

'If they haven't, we'll make our way back to the doorway and start putting some of the stones back in place to narrow the entrance.

'We can check the main valley again at dawn, and if there's still no sight of them, we can use the time to start hiding the entrance, so that when they do appear it will only be a small job to finish it off and lay a false trail up and over the head of the valley?'

'That sounds reasonable,' Selene replied, 'If you're happy to do that George.

'And I would be happy to go along wi' the lad,' Studgeon added.

'Thank you, George, Alasdair,' Marlow said simply, before we picked up our things and started to make our way back up to the surface.

THE ENEMY

WHY HAD I VOLUNTEERED to go back up to the surface and keep a lookout for the Icarii? As I walked back through the corridors and up the steps with Studgeon, I couldn't help but ask myself that question, again and again.

After all this time, I was just as eager to take a look around this mysterious place as anyone else, barring Marlow perhaps, who seemed to have invested his entire sense of self into the search.

Now, I would probably have to wait until tomorrow morning, when it would be someone else's turn to walk down to the mouth of the valley to see if our enemy yet approached.

On the plus side though, at least Harry and Androus would be able to fill some of the blanks in by the time we got back. They might even have time to make a tentative stab at deciphering some the writings located in different parts of the site.

'Well I have ta concede, laddie,' Studgeon said unexpectedly, as we made our way outside. 'When you said you were seeking an ancient ruin, I wasne expecting it to be quite so intact.'

'You're right to be surprised,' I replied, thankful for the distraction. 'Most of the sites we've uncovered previously haven't been so well preserved, but the first one we discovered was very similar to this, only the entrance was damaged.'

He was fascinated by the subject, so as we walked back along the twilit valley, I explained a little more about how we'd all gotten started on the path we now followed, and the shamanic ritual we'd taken part in that had given Marlow the strange dreams which had led us to the first site in southern Rhodesia.

It whiled away the time, and in response Studgeon talked about some of the strange ruins and temples he'd encountered since he'd been serving here in India, including places that he'd stumbled across in the deep pockets of forest that still existed further south, which were so overgrown that some of the trees covering the ruins had roots as thick as a man's waist.

Just before we rounded the corner to the first thorn fence that we'd constructed at the mouth of the valley, Studgeon excused himself to go and answer a call of nature, so I wandered on alone to the mouth of the valley, where I expected to see no sign yet of our pursuers.

'Mr Whittaker, how very nice to see you again,' I heard Miriam say, as she stood up out of the bushes where she'd been hiding, cocking the bolt back on her rifle as she did so, a sound I heard echo from several other rifles all around me.

There was nothing I could do but try to warn Studgeon, so he didn't walk straight into the same trap.

Dropping my own rifle, which I'd been carelessly carrying over my shoulder, I backed up slightly and raised my arms over my head, in the hope that Studgeon might see me before he got too close.

'Sister Miriam, how very unpleasant to see you again,' I replied, as loudly as I thought I could get away with.

'Oh, now don't be like that,' she replied, walking over to me, her wild red hair floating on the gentle breeze.

'Especially when it was your letter that brought us here,' she said, just before she brought the butt of her rifle round to slam into my stomach, winding me, and sending me crumpling to the floor.

'What letter?' I just about managed to ask, as her underlings cut the straps on my backpack, and stripped me of my revolver.

'Why your letter to your friend Luke Cassanelli in Sikkim of course. We'd had an incredibly difficult time even confirming you were here in India, until you very kindly wrote to your friend telling him not only where you were, but also where you were headed.

'Oh, it was like the most generous of presents all in one little white envelope. I'm surprised that traitorous coward Selene Autieri allowed you do such a thing,' she practically snarled, as she grabbed a handful of my hair and pulled my head back savagely.

'Unfortunately, she had to leave us in order to go and sort out… what was the phrase she used now? Oh yes, the 'self-serving incompetent fools' that had taken over the Order,' I growled back at her, hoping to mislead them about

Selene's presence at least for a little while.

'Oh really, and yet she was seen travelling with you at the docks in Pasighat,' Miriam replied smugly. 'One of my sisters even thought she'd managed to put a bullet in her.'

'Ah yes, the ambush which we all walked away from without a scratch, and yet several of your people had to be dragged away from, that certainly fits the "incompetent" and the "fools" part of Selene's description.'

'How dare you,' Miriam snarled, letting go of my hair with a savage twist, just so she could then punch me in the face with all her might.

I was seeing stars for a second afterward, but as she turned away from me, I couldn't help but try to goad her further, in the hope it would give Studgeon more time to escape.

'Now I come to think of it,' I continued, wiping blood from the corner of my mouth. 'The way you led us to your headquarters in Rome, hidden beneath that little bookshop, and the way you brought that ferry across the river for us, just to the north of Pasighat, that is sort of leading by example isn't it Miriam? One incompetent example after another.'

That hit home. I saw her freeze in outrage at my words, and slowly and deliberately she turned back to me and raised her rifle.

The shot when it came was almost silent, and took Miriam just below the shoulder against which she had raised her rifle.

From the look on her face, she barely even realised what had happened as Studgeon's bullet ripped through her lungs and heart, killing her almost instantly.

I saw confusion, then fear and outrage flash across her handsome features, as she first dropped the rifle and then sank to her knees in front of me, before finally toppling, lifeless, onto her front.

I was forgotten for a moment, as shots peppered the valley side where Studgeon was running between the gorse, as he tried to escape after saving my life.

Lunging at the figures that had been holding me, I tried to distract them from their shooting, but all I succeeded in doing was being knocked unconscious by the female operative that I was closest to, as she expertly reversed her weapon just long enough to hit me on the side of the head with the butt of it.

That I woke up at all was a surprise to me. That I had been carried or dragged up to the area beside the last big pool at the top of the valley, just below the flat area which had contained the quince trees and the entrance to the temple was all too predictable.

I was tied firmly to a piece of wood which had been passed across my shoulders and behind my neck, and from the acute pain in my shoulders and neck, I'd been tied this way for some time, and had perhaps even been dragged up the valley this way with a man on either end of the pole.

As I looked around, I counted well over a dozen of the capable young women that served as operatives for the Order, along with a similar number of those lumbering subservient men that served them, and one older woman, Agostine, who was ordering them all about.

Someone eventually realised I was awake, and informed Agostine, pointing over to me as they did so.

Even from a distance I could tell she was seething with fury.

A few moments later she walked over to me with two other operatives, perhaps even her second and third, as the members of this order named themselves.

'Mr Whitaker, I would like you to tell me what the layout of this underground… temple is like.'

'Mother Agostine, you'll forgive me if I don't jump at the opportunity to help you.'

'Need I remind you, that one of my best operatives is already dead because of your… associates, so I am already more than a little inclined to simply put a bullet through your brain,' she said, raising a polished silver revolver to my face. 'So, if you are hoping for any show of mercy you will tell me exactly what I want to know.'

'Madame, I have already seen what your idea of mercy looks like, in those catacombs beneath Rome that you call your home. So, to be frank, a bullet would be preferable.'

'You amateurs, playing at this adventure like it is some kind of game,' She seethed at me. 'You have neither the wit nor the imagination to know what I am capable of.'

'Gag him, and drag him to where they can see him.'

With that they forced a knotted rope into my mouth and tied it tightly behind my head, so that I almost choked, then two of the docile men dragged me breathless up to the top of the valley wall, and the flat area in front of the doorway to the temple.

Forcing me to my knees they then looped another rope around my feet to tie them together, and tied the other end to the cross bar that lay across my shoulders.

One of the men then stepped forward to loudly read out a message which had been written down for him.

'By the command of Reverend Mother Agostine and the Order of Icarus, you will throw down your weapons and step forth from this heretic site, or your collaborator George Whittaker will be shot.

'You have until noon tomorrow to comply!'

With that the man stepped back and took up his position just behind me with his colleague.

It was dark by this time, and there was no light coming from inside the doorway, but the Order had lit fires twenty yards to either side of the entrance to give enough light for all those with rifles to be able to see their target.

This allowed me to see the doorway itself, but there wasn't enough light to see inside, not that I would be left waiting for long to find out whether anyone had heard me.

'Agostine of Padua,' came Selene's clear and commanding voice. 'Release Mr Whittaker immediately and leave this place, or the next time we meet you will wish I had granted you the mercy of the Tiber when last we met.'

I was surprised to hear that it was Selene who was responding, but as I knelt there, powerless to even move, my brain working overtime, I realised that Selene was perhaps the only one who would have any idea how to negotiate with these people.

'We will not speak with the oath-breaker, Selene Autieri,' came the almost instant response of Mother Agostine as she crept up behind me and placed her polished silver revolver against the side of my head. 'If you do not wish to see your friend die in front of you, you will surrender yourselves to our mercy now.'

'We will not tell you again Agostine,' came Selene's response. 'Release Mr…

And then, just as I felt Agostine's arm tense beside me, a shot rang out from the doorway, the muzzle flash faintly illuminating Marlow's features behind the gun, before his bullet ripped through the left-hand side of my chest, just above my heart.

The pain was excruciating and seemed to flood my entire being until there was nothing else.

And I fell backwards, the branch that had been tied across my back and shoulders suddenly flexible in the middle where the same bullet had exited my body and then punched straight through the wood.

Somewhere behind me I heard Agostine gasp in surprise.

How I remained conscious I don't know, but the men who had been guarding me, somehow dragged the reverend mother out from beneath me, leaving me lying half propped up against one of the large heather bushes that covered the area.

'My arm, look what they've done to my arm, those savages,' I now heard the enraged reverend mother bellow.

'Bring it down, bury them in that place. Do it now!' she shouted.

As though on cue, I saw the movement atop the cliff above the doorway then. There were several people with lanterns and ropes by the look of it. But they weren't using the ropes to descend, their plan was far more cold-blooded than that.

They attached explosives to the end of the ropes, lit the fuses and then one after another threw the explosives out over the cliff, the ropes catching it before it went too far and bringing the burning explosives back toward the cliff face and the open doorway.

Marlow and Selene managed to catch one lot as it swung straight into the doorway, throwing it back out again. But the explosives were accompanied by a terrible rain of bullets, and a second and third charge fell straight into the doorway.

It was a terrible way to destroy the place, but destroy it those explosives most certainly did.

In the confines of the doorway, which at least two charges had fallen into, the explosive force of the detonations was amplified and brought half the cliff face down on the entrance, sending lumps of stone and earth flying for hundreds of yards in every direction.

What few quince trees survived were set alight by the explosion, and I was left, wounded and unable to move, to watch as the slowly clearing dust and smoke revealed the complete collapse of the cliff face above what had once been the temple entrance.

Hundreds of tons of rock littered the area, burying the temple beneath a mountain of debris.

I simply lay there and watched, unable to believe what my eyes were showing me.

LOSS

A T SOME POINT, content that they'd destroyed the temple and everyone inside it, Agostine and the Icarii operatives remembered that I still existed, and for reasons they never explained, they bandaged my wound, and then dragged me behind them as they descended the mountain.

I can't remember the details of how they transported me back to Siliguri, but at some point they must have thought my time was up, as I found myself abandoned outside the city station with my backpack, and a fever raging through my body from the wound in my chest, which refused to stay closed.

Somehow, I managed to produce Luke's address and with the help of strangers get a train north to Darjeeling, from where, with the last of my strength, I somehow got myself delivered on a cart to the humanitarian mission where Luke was working.

I was unconscious for three days and delirious with a malarial fever for another two weeks after that, during which time the hole in my chest was cleaned and treated and began to heal properly.

How the wound hadn't become infected was a minor miracle, but slowly and steadily I began to get my strength back.

By this time though, there was no hope for the others. If they'd been lucky the explosion would have brought the roof down on them and they'd have died quickly, but if not, the idea that they might survive for a whole month trapped underground was impossible.

Water wouldn't have been a problem, but the air

couldn't have lasted for more than a couple of days, and the food no more than a week.

And then there was my gunshot. I re-lived that moment time and again while I was ill, the ghostly outline of Marlow's grinning face as he pulled the trigger and shot me. No doubt convinced he was a good enough shot to hit Agostine without harming me, too late realising he wasn't.

Luke was mortified to hear how our friends had ended their days, and to begin with he became determined to take the engineers we'd sent to work on the mission, to go and affect some kind of escape or at least to retrieve their bodies, but we both knew it was pointless, and that excavating the complex would take years.

It was just his grief making him want to do something, even if it was pointless, but eventually, when we stopped to think about it, we both realised there could be no better grave than the one they were already in.

I stayed at the Mission for over a year after I was healed, helping Luke out and slowly healing my soul with the honest charitable work that we were doing there.

Eventually though, as the work there drew to an end, I travelled back to England and my old home in the Shropshire countryside, the home that had never really felt like home before, and still didn't after I returned.

And there I stayed for the next sixty years, trying my level best not to even think of friends I'd lost and the great adventure we'd almost had.

Epilogue

RESSURECTION

IT HAS BEEN NEARLY SEVENTY YEARS since I last opened my journals. So bitter was I about that period in my life that I more than once considered burning them, but instead I have allowed them to languish. Only now have I finally re-read and re-lived the events which took place so long ago.

A whole lifetime of loss and regret which I did not think it possible to forget or to move past. Of dear friendships and friends lost beneath the cold heavy stone of those far-away mountains, where nobody could ever properly mourn for them.

I realise now, that in that time, I have allowed my own bitterness about how it all ended to warp and change my fever-tinged memories until I hated my friend, Robert Marlow and everything which his quest to find that ancient temple and the secret of immortality had cost me.

But I see now how wrong I was.

I have remembered my friend unfairly, unjustly, and only my own words written down in a former age could remove the scales from my eyes to correct that injustice.

It has been three years since Marlow appeared on my doorstep, when I welcomed him into my home looking barely ten years older than he had all those years ago. Three years ago, when in my bitterness, all I hoped for was enough life to expose him and his plans to the world.

But in the three years since that visit I have not only had the opportunity to reflect and re-consider, I have also, through some unknown means which I can only attribute to Marlow's visit, begun to grow young again. Not just in my mind from re-living the events which changed the course of my life, but also unmistakably, in body.

Though I am now nearly one hundred years old, my body is growing younger, my hair which so long ago turned white and thinned, now has traces of colour returning to it and is growing thicker. My skin which had become so thin and papery, now has elasticity again, and my limbs are once more filling with strength and vitality.

I know this is Marlow's doing, and that I am but the first person to feel the effects of his decision to share the secret of immortality, which we discovered in the land of the dawn-lit mountains.

More importantly, I have also begun to hear the drums again, though I now realise they have always been sounding and always been there for me to hear. It is only my own bitterness and resentment that has covered their sound.

But now, not only have I heard their twisting, sinuous rhythm again, I have also once more stepped into the dream world from whence they sound, where my friends have all been waiting, so that they could take me to that fire at the centre of everything and show me the truth of what happened all those years ago.

—

I see myself as a young man, crucified by my captors outside the entrance to the temple, the threats of Agostine to shoot me, still vibrant and hanging in the air.

'She means it,' Selene is saying, from behind the stones that block the lower half of the doorway to the temple. 'She has always been a petty-minded creature, so after Studgeon killed Miriam, she will want nothing more than to kill George to make things even.'

'Then surely our only course is surrender,' Jean replies. 'Irrespective of the cost, we cannot allow her to harm him.'

'If our surrender would stop her,' Selene replies, with a small shake of her head. 'Then I would willingly suggest it to you, even though I would be the first person that she would execute in front of you, but I fear that time is passed, and now, irrespective she will kill us all.'

'Then we must kill George for her,' Marlow informs them, emotion rasping his voice. 'Or come so close that she believes he lives only by chance.'

'Robert, you cannot,' Jean implores, as Marlow aims his rifle at my chest. 'The margin for error is minute.'

'I know, Jean,' he replies, a tear falling from his normally so still and calm eyes. 'Forgive me, George.'

The shot rings out in the shadowy entrance chamber, and they watch as my body falls backward onto the injured form of Mother Agostine, whose right arm has been badly damaged by the same bullet that has opened up my chest.'

'They will not stop now until this place is destroyed with us inside it,' Selene explains.

Marlow appears not to hear, he simply stares at my injured form over the top of his rifle.

'It is not much,' Jean confirms, as he studies my injured form through his binoculars. 'But he is still moving, mon ami. You have done all you can to save him.'

'How will they come?' Marlow asks, his voice still hoarse with emotion.

'Explosives from the cliff above,' Selene explains, without hesitation. 'Attached to a rope so that they swing into the entrance.'

'Then we should retreat to the lower chambers and hope the detonation does not reach us there,' Jean suggests.

'You two get moving,' Marlow responds. 'I'll guard the entrance until the charges start to drop.'

'Be quick, Robert,' Selene replies. 'The charges will not have a long fuse.'

The rest unfolds as I saw it the first time. The first set of charges appear while Jean and Selene are still in the corridor, so Marlow catches them and throws them back out of the opening, then sprints down the corridor after the others, and just makes it to the stairs leading down to the main chamber, before the second charge drops straight into the doorway where he had been standing.

The next corridor is longer and twisting, Selene and Jean just make it to the main chamber where Peter, Androus, Harry and an injured Studgeon are anxiously waiting, when the detonation happens, shaking the stone fabric of the place noticeably, and filling the corridor they have just appeared from with dust and debris.

A second later and Marlow emerges, unharmed from the dust cloud.

There are subsequent smaller detonations which I don't remember seeing at the time, but my friends are all safe, albeit trapped in the temple beneath the ground.

I see the place now in all its wonder, as they explore their cage in the hope of finding another way out.

One cavern after another reveals its treasures, including a library with texts from antiquity undreamed of by even the most wishful scholar. Sumerian and Babylonian cuneiform tablets, Egyptian hieroglyphs painted on papyrus, as well as demotic and hieratic script covered vellum, early Sanskrit clay tablets and Hebrew scrolls. Arabic and ancient Greek sit side by side categorised apparently by subject, much to Androus's approval.

There are tools and a workshop with stores of many semi-precious and precious stones, including large pieces of lapis, identical to that from which the tablets were formed.

In another cavern there are stores of powders and medicines, many sealed in small jars to keep them airtight, others kept at the end of a long corridor which is sealed off periodically by a series of large heavy wooden doors, behind each set of which the temperature steadily drops until in the final storage room it is well below freezing. Here there are row upon row of cold stone jars with tightly fitting lids that contain seeds, leaves and roots of every imaginable variety.

Another smaller and entirely man-made cavern contains only steps which spiral down into the earth, past a natural crack in the rock through which cool fresh air flows into the rest of the complex. But the steps do not end there, leading on to where the thermal spring emerges as a waterfall, dropping through a ragged hole in the ceiling into a deep dark pool with a wide ledge carved next to it.

Back up in the main chamber, I see my friends split off into one of the other caverns and discover living spaces with simple furniture and decorations, and an area where food can be cooked and eaten, complete with more cracks in the rock which seem to let the warm humid air of the caverns pass out of the complex via some natural vent in the stones and earth above.

Strangest of all though, there is a room with a curtain of barely visible flame that burns constantly but without heat, apparently just erupting from cracks in the floor, and disappearing through cracks in the ceiling above.

Beyond this barrier are sat a series of statue like figures, or so they appear. For they are clad in clothes of many different places and times, and very few appear to be of the same ethnic origin, but their clothing and everything about them is as though carved from pure white alabaster, which is just touched every now and again by the glow from the flames.

There are seventeen of these figures, with space for several dozen more, and among them my friends can see Nelion, exactly as we last saw him at the Singing Stones just a few short years ago.

Around the curtain of fire, I also watch my friends find a series of glass orbs, that glow with a bright natural light, rendering their lanterns redundant.

Harry fishes one of these out of the flame with one of the folding shovels which we used to dig our way into the temple, the metal of which is slowly turned the same alabaster white as the figures when it enters the flame.

The orb he retrieves continues to glow once it is out of the flame, and is strangely no more than body temperature. Yet when Harry places his hand close to the flame the pain is clearly considerable.

Examining the whitened shovel, my friends find the white alabaster coating simply crumbles away leaving the metal looking clean and polished.

'Could this be what the tablets are referring to when they describe individuals returning here to… renew their breath?' Harry asks, clearly wonder-struck.

'If it is,' Marlow replies, also pulling his hand back quickly from the flame after placing it too close. 'Then it must surely be something that is only possible once they have prepared or changed themselves in some way.'

Search though they might, I see my friends thwarted time after time in finding another way out of the complex, although they at least have water to drink and air to breathe.

They even investigate the demolished entrance by which they entered the complex, which is filled with rubble and large blocks of stone right the way up to the second chamber, in which the many translations of the same text are carved into the nine walls. But while some of these surfaces now show alarming cracks, the room itself and the two other entrance rooms are still intact, though again they reveal no other signs of an exit.

Even more frustrating for my friends is the knowledge that Nelion must have found his way into the complex without excavating the main entrance by which the rest of us entered, but still they cannot find it.

In hope that it might shed some light on an exit, I watch as Androus and Harry turn their attention to the stelae surrounding the large pool, the water of which rolls with an unseen current in the centre of the main chamber.

This they discover is the source of Ziusudra's longevity. Though dark in its depths the pool at the surface glows slightly with some luminous substance excreted by a plant which grows in the water thirty or forty yards down, which when ingested bestows upon the eater the gift of life everlasting.

But the water is deep, too deep for anyone to dive and live, so to survive the seeker must sink to the depths, gather the plant and eat it while they are down there, in the knowledge that they will surely drown on the way back to the surface.

As my friends gather to hear this news, I recognise the glint in Jean's eyes which indicates his approval.

'Ah but the final challenge is sublime, is it not my friends?' He observes, philosophically. 'Only those whose quest to find everlasting life is more important to them than life itself may taste of the plant that will grant their desire.

'Those who seek to live longer merely out of fear can never pass this test.'

'Of course. I should have guessed it would be something like this,' Marlow replies, resigned. 'Do not all the accounts described in the tablets begin with the seeker forsaking all that life offers and even risking their lives by fighting wild beasts or crossing oceans and deserts to find the elusive secret of immortality.'

'Well, if we could find a way out, a decent set of bellows and some rubber tubing would probably relieve us of having to make that choice,' Peter suggested.

'No, I don't think so,' replied Marlow. 'If I were to guess, whatever substance is contained in the plant which grows at the bottom of this pool, will only take its full effect on a body which has gone through the subtle changes that follow death.'

'Tres bien, mon ami,' Jean agrees, smiling. 'I will make a true philosopher out of you yet. We should not even try to avoid the cost of what we have sought for so long, as that would I think… cheapen its final achievement.

'Though perhaps it would be best not to attempt this thing until we have discovered a way out?'

'Of course,' Marlow agrees, without even

attempting to hide his intentions from his friends.

It takes four days before they finally find the way out, and it is Peter who discovers it.

With the hope of finding an exit fading, he walks off by himself with one of the glowing glass orbs to be alone for a while, down the spiral staircase to that place where it is possible to sit beside the waterfall and pool of thermal water.

He is I suspect, hoping to see Danu, the spirit of all rivers and streams that he has fallen in love with.

As I have seen him do once before beside the river Ganges, he first removes his jacket and rolls up the sleeves of his shirt, then kneels beside the water and places his open hand just in contact with the surface, wishing only to see her face, and after a few minutes of waiting patiently she appears.

The water in front of him that had been full of ripples, calms suddenly and in the now still water a reflection of her hand reaches out to mirror his, but from the darkness beneath the water, closely followed by the appearance of her face and shoulders.

I feel as though I am spying upon them when the dream shows me this, but I am glad they have found one another, even if it seems Peter's time on this earth is now limited.

For an age they seem to just gaze at one another with no need for words, before she finally breaks the silence by asking him to cover the light globe with his jacket.

Unsure why she is suggesting this, he trusts her and does as he is instructed, so all is darkness, but as his eyes adjust, he can still see her in the water, because there appears to be a light coming from the submerged channel into which the warm water runs.

'Come,' she says. 'Join me.'

Without hesitation he leans forward to embrace his lover, falling into the water, fully clothed, where the watery form of his beloved embraces him and then guides him down, into the submerged tunnel, which has several air pockets along its length, before leading out into the final pool at the top of the valley, where the sun has just risen and the entire mountain is flooded in the bright dawn sunlight.

He embraces his beloved one more time before swimming to the edge of the pool to pick a sprig of heather, which he then carries back into the tunnel with him, swimming effortlessly up the darkening stream of water until the rock gives way and he can climb back out onto the ledge where he entered.

Sopping wet, he uncovers the globe and makes his way back up to the main chamber to share his news with the others.

The dream shows me the relief on my friends faces as they slowly transport all of their belongings back to the surface, and the world they weren't sure they'd ever see again. But with that relief is a tinge of concern about what will come next.

Nevertheless, they prepare as best they can by building a fresh camp, well away from the thermal pools and the now blocked main entrance to the temple. They stealthily creep down the valley to find out if there is still any trace of Agostine or the Order, and they search also for any sign of my remains, only to find that there are none and I have been taken by the Icarii.

Reassured that they have taken all the precautions they are able to, they return to the temple and what will surely be the biggest decision that any of them will ever make.

Marlow of course has the fewest doubts, so he is the first to descend into the pool of water, a rope around his waist so that his friends can help him return to the surface, a heavy weight on another rope with a loop for him to grip onto to assist the descent against the rolling current of water which wants to carry him back to the surface, and one of the glowing orbs to provide him with light.

Even with the weight, the descent takes far longer than anyone has anticipated, nearly a whole minute, as the pool is much deeper than it appears, and the ropes which are attached to his waist and the weight which carry him down are only just long enough when he finally hits the bottom.

Five seconds, ten seconds while he gathers and consumes the rare plant which will supposedly grant him the gift of everlasting life, and then a frantic tug on the second rope and his friends are pulling him to the surface as fast as they can.

Marlow attempts to help himself by pulling on the second rope arm over arm, but there is something wrong with his movements, they seem laboured and slow even to begin with, and then with well over half the depth of the pool still to go we see the last of his breath escape from his lungs and he convulses violently, painfully as he drowns.

Together his friends haul him back to the surface, and calmly they set about emptying his lungs of the water he has inhaled, but something else is wrong. There is blood on the stones around him, dilute and pink against the bare pale stone.

Jean finds the source of the wounds, in the form of countless pairs of pinprick holes in his skin. Bite marks of a small venomous snake, one of whom is unlucky enough to have been hauled back to the surface clutched in Marlow's hand.

It is a pale, almost eyeless thing, which is also dead now, crushed by the convulsions Marlow suffered on his return to the surface.

His lungs have been drained of water, and Harry is breathing one large lung full of air after another into Marlow's mouth, while Peter pushes down on his chest to expel the air afterwards and simulate the breathing process, but as the seconds slip by, their fear grows.

One by one they stop trying to revive him, and look at the prone form of their dead friend.

'Perhaps the pain from the curtain of flame?' Peter suggests.

But before he can go on, they all hear the faint but distinct rhythm of the distant drums, and a few seconds later as the sound swells and fills the chamber, Marlow's eyes flicker open and he draws a great lungful of air.

They leap to his side, but he seems momentarily unaware of them, and then his eyes find their focus and he sees them again.

'I feel it,' he murmurs quietly, looking down at his bare forearms and the numerous little bite marks, once he has coughed the last of the water from his lungs.

'It is the venom in combination with the plant that is the secret. The viper nests amongst the weeds, so bites to protect its young.'

'I feel the two compounds combining and flowing through my veins.'

He's obviously still very weak, so together they carry him through to one of the side rooms and place him on his bedroll.

Scarcely an hour later he wakes and re-joins them in the central chamber, now apparently fully recovered and hungry, the small wounds which covered his forearms completely healed and no longer visible.

'How do you feel, Robert?' Jean asks, though he can see his friend is looking more rested and refreshed than he has done in months.

'Better, Jean,' Marlow replies with a genuine smile. 'I feel stronger yet more relaxed, my thoughts seem to be clearer and all my senses are... more than they were.

'I feel exceptionally well,' he finally adds.

'Well enough to swim back to the surface?'

'A hundred times over,' Marlow replies. 'But first...'

He walks back over to the pool and after picking

up the glowing globe, he draws a deep breath and before anyone can stop him, he dives straight back into the water without either of the ropes.

Strength seems to flow through every sinew of his body as he swims effortlessly down through the swirling current to the bottom of the pool.

Two minutes, three minutes, four, and he finally returns to the surface barely even breathing hard, two living vipers in one hand and a handful of the plant which grows in the depths of the pool in the other.

'Who would join me?' he asks simply. 'The venom from these snakes will still bring on your death, but there is no need to experience the agony of drowning.'

Almost without hesitation Peter and Harry step forward to eat some of the plant and receive the fatal bites from the vipers.

They both attempt to put a brave face on the experience, but as their hearts slow and then stop it is still clearly very painful.

Androus steps forward next, clearly less sure.

'The contents of the library here, let alone the other inscriptions which fill the place...' he explains, knowing his friends already appreciate his passion for knowledge.

After Androus receives the leaf and the venom, Marlow returns the vipers to the pool, as there is no more leaf left, and then he helps Androus, who is by far the oldest amongst us, to lie down on the floor as his heart fails.

A few moments later and first Harry and then Peter begin to stir, their hearts pumping once more to drive the strange compound created by the venom as it combines with the plant extract, into the farthest corners of their bodies.

Like Marlow, both are disoriented to begin with, so their friends help them through to a separate room where they can sleep.

This leaves Jean and Selene as well as the injured Studgeon, who have yet to accept Marlow's offer.

I feel my heart ache at the thought that they might refuse, but the dream shows me them talking amongst themselves for a while, Marlow reaffirming his view that such a gift must eventually be shared with the whole world, but concedes that much work would be required first to work out how this could be done properly and fairly.

'It is a convincing argument, Mon Ami,' Jean responds. 'But if this choice can never be undone, unless perhaps through the most violent of deaths, then to offer this option to all, including those who would choose it merely out of fear, that is surely wrong?'

'I agree,' Marlow replies, rather surprisingly. 'But it must be possible to divine some test other than this pool to provide a proper check.'

'Oui, I agree,' Jean concedes.

'I understand your reasoning,' Selene adds, but I find myself tempted for far more selfish reasons.

'Like Androus you need more time to complete the work you have set your mind to?' Jean suggests. 'The reclamation of the Order, from the hands of those who have led it astray.'

'Precisely,' she replies.

'You'll forgive me I hope, Lady, Gentlemen,' Studgeon adds, appearing relaxed and at ease with himself. 'If I did'na make a decision just yet. I ken the why's and the wherefores of your own choices, but this is a wee bit too new for me. I need a while to allow the idea to sink in, before I could decide such a thing.'

'Of course, mon ami,' Jean reassures him. 'If you wish to return one day, I for one will be only too happy to return with you.'

They wait then for Harry, Androus and Peter to recover and re-join them. Which they do a few minutes later, all pleased to hear that both Jean and Selene have decided to accept the gift of life eternal.

With nothing more to wait for, Marlow again picks up one of the glowing orbs and prepares to descend back down into the depths of the pool, but as he does so, Jean steps forward and begins to tie on the rope that was used to haul Marlow back to the surface the first time.

'Jean, there is no need...' he begins to explain, before seeing the expression on his friend's face.

Nothing more is said; his friends just take up the rope and prepare for his descent.

After taking several deep breaths and picking up the heavy weight which will carry him to the bottom, Jean takes one last look at his friends and steps calmly over the edge of the pool.

He sinks quickly through the turbulent water for a moment and then Marlow dives in after him, swimming once more unassisted against the current that tries to keep him on the surface.

Seconds pass, until eventually Jean reaches the bottom a little ahead of Marlow, where he calmly selects some leaves from the plants which grow all about, and then hesitates.

We all know the vipers will be biting into his flesh while he does this, sinking their venom into his veins, but still he waits. Finally, after what seems an age, he moves the leaves to his mouth, chews and swallows them, before pushing off the bottom just as Marlow gets there, passing his friend on the way.

Now the rope is being gathered with tremendous speed by Harry, Androus and Peter who move with a strength and speed I can barely believe, and Jean rockets back to the surface so quickly he is still just conscious when he gets there, and is able to cough the water up from his lungs before the venom overpowers him.

Marlow appears a moment later, once again holding a living snake in one hand and the leaves of the plant in the other, which he offers to Selene over the now lifeless form of Jean.

She too hesitates for a moment before taking first the leaf and then the viper from him, and while the snake immediately buries its fangs in her wrist, all she does is regard its efforts to free itself for a moment before she too swallows the leaves that will save her life.

As the venom begins to take its effect, she walks over to the pool and releases the snake back into the water. Then with a little difficulty because of her injured leg she lies down next to Jean on the hard-stone floor to die, stretching out her hand to Jean's just before she loses consciousness.

Thankfully, the dream persists not just until they both awake, but until they have both fully recovered and have all made their way out of the complex and back into the sunlight.

As a consequence of the transformation Selene's injured leg completely finishes healing without even a scar, though the deep scar which Marlow still carries on his right forearm from that fight with the rogue lion back in Kenya is unchanged.

I hear the drums returning now, and know that the vision I have shared is almost at an end, but there is something, a nagging question which rises in my mind as the vision of my friends in the hidden valley begins to fade.

Epilogue Two

THE BURNING TRUTH

A...g...o...s...t...i...n...e...' I hear a familiar voice calling as I approach the fire once again, with its circle of bright and exotic figures standing around it. '

'A...g...o...s...t...i...n...e...' I hear Selene's voice call again, much closer this time.

Turning toward the sound, I see the bemused figure

of the reverend mother approaching out of the shadows on one side of the fire, while Selene, practically radiant with life approaches from the other.

'You!' The reverend mother practically spits. 'What trickery is this, Autieri?'

'Oh, it's not trickery, Agostine,' Selene replies with a voice of pure ice. 'This is a warning, a demand, an ultimatum.

'In the waking world you still hold a friend of mine against his will,' she explains, reaching out a hand to grasp the reverend mother by the arm with a grip powerful enough to cause her some pain.

'You will release George Whittaker unharmed and with all his belongings before you leave Siliguri.'

'Let go of my arm you traitor,' Agostine replies, struggling in vain against Selene's grip. 'This is just a dream, I don't need to listen to a word you say.'

'Well, if this is just a dream, then you have nothing to fear,' the ex-Icarii operative replies, as she turns and leads the reverend mother forcibly towards the fire.'

'What pagan trickery is this,' Agostine demands, shielding her eyes from the heat and light of the fire, as they approach the circle of spirits which stand around it.

'No, stop, it's too bright, I'll burn!' she insists, as Selene takes her closer and closer still.

The figures around the fire part as the two women come within a few yards of them, and now nothing stands between Agostine and the flames.

She collapses to the ground, as she tries to shield her face with her free hand, her skin visibly reddening and forming large red welts.

'No, stop,' she now pleads. 'I'm burning, I'm burning.'

'Oh, but we can go much closer than this, Agostine,' Selene explains calmly, apparently unaffected by the heat and light as the fire steadily increases in intensity, forcing the circle of spirits back.

The welts on the older woman's skin are splitting and cracking now, her clothes smoking and darkening.

'You will release George Whittaker unharmed and with all his belongings when you reach Siliguri,' Selene explains again. 'Or I will bring you to this place every night for the rest of your life!'

With that she thrusts the older woman even closer to the fire, which rages ever higher in response, turning the woman's clothing and skin black in places, before Selene allows her to retreat a few steps.

'Do you understand, Agostine?'

The terrified woman cowers at Selene's feet and can only nod her head, sobbing openly as she tries to pull away from her iron grasp.

'And when you return to Rome, tell the others I will be coming for them soon!'

With that, Selene finally relinquishes her iron hold on Agostine's arm, and the older woman crawls and then stumbles away from the fire, back into the darkness.

The dream fades and then brightens to become the scene at Siliguri train station.

I see Agostine, but almost don't recognise her, she has changed so much.

Not only is her hand and forearm bandaged from Marlow's bullet, but her entire demeanour, even her posture seems to have shrunken in on itself, and she appears a broken remnant of the hateful figure she once was.

Her agents do not understand, but do not need to, so they simply carry out her wishes and set me free along with all of my belongings, the malarial fever burning bright in my eyes as I slowly make my way north to Luke.

The End

This is the third and final part of the Flames of Time trilogy, but it's only the first of several adventures involving Jean, Marlow, Selene, Peter and Androus, so if you'd like find out what they got up after leaving the temple of Ziusudra, then do please let me know.

I hope you enjoyed reading this book, if so, please visit my website and sign up for my newsletter so I can let you know about other titles when I publish them.

You can find my site at
www.knytewrytng.com

All comments and feedback are welcome and all polite emails, even critical ones will be replied to in person.

Thank you for reading this book.

Peter Knyte

And finally:

In the next few pages you'll find a taster from my The Ghosts of Winter novel.

Here's the back-page blurb, followed by a sample of the first few chapters.

'It is a commonly held view in this, our modern age, that there are few places on earth which we have yet to explore.

The photograph of a wintry mountain landscape fascinates a young novelist when he finds it printed in a book of poetry.

A fascination which eventually compels him to seek out the place pictured and travel there.

But this snowy valley, hidden deep in the backcountry of the southern French Alps also hides a secret which may turn his fascination into a complete obsession.'

THE GHOSTS OF WINTER
PART THE FIRST
Peter Knyte

THE SMALL HOURS

I DREAMED OF THE MOUNTAIN again last night, and that hidden alpine valley which so enthralled me even before I'd visited the place. With its perpetually snow-covered slopes that summer never touched.

I had come to the mountains a little later in life, having been a rather bookish youth, content to pass my time absorbed in almost any type of book. From novels, poetry and short stories, to travel guides, histories and biographies. Virtually every subject fired my interest or imagination, leading me indirectly to my second great passion in life, a love of nature and walking.

I'd picked up a charming pocket-sized volume entitled 'The Lays of Ancient Britain – a walker's guide to the countryside and how it was shaped by our ancestors.'

It was generously illustrated with sketches, but I found it impossible to read more than a paragraph without wanting to pull on a pair of boots and get out into the countryside it described.

Spring, summer, autumn or winter would find me striding the field boundaries and moors, tracing the ancient drover's trails or simply walking the old forgotten roads and pathways which had once been the only connection between quiet hamlets.

In no-time the idea of choosing between reading and walking had become as unthinkable as choosing between breathing and having a pulse. For years, they were all that mattered to me. Simple pleasures, but the things I enjoyed most in life.

It was of course my love of books and walking which led me to the valley and my undoing.

A more adventurous friend had stumbled upon a quaint leather-bound volume of poetry which she thought might appeal to me, because every poem contained therein was dedicated in one fashion or another to nature and the wonders of the natural world.

The poems within were simple yet elegant and heartfelt, and they described nature in a way I appreciated. But the real joy were a dozen or so photographic plates scattered unevenly throughout the work, including one of an isolated alpine valley, half shrouded in mist, which represented what was possibly my idea of perfection.

The scene it depicted was framed by mature but twisted trees in the foreground, which parted to reveal a snow covered alpine meadow with a long wooden building, a barn and some smaller sheds.

These buildings, and the meadow, were surrounded by a dense looking forest, which covered a steep and craggy mountain slope that climbed right to the top of the picture and beyond.

Over a few weeks I read the poems and admired the photographic plates, but as the weeks became months, while my other books and my walking continued to sustain me, I found my mind often returning to that one picture of the valley. Time and again I found myself bringing the slender leather book of poetry down from its spot on my overcrowded shelves just to enjoy that impossibly idyllic scene. Before long I simply stopped putting the book back on the shelf altogether, instead giving it a permanent place amongst my stack of current reading.

The picture in the book was infuriatingly vague in its attribution, described simply as 'A secluded valley in the French Alps in late spring – taken by the author.' But where in the French Alps, and how long ago it had been taken were not stated.

The publisher's details though, I did have, and one evening toward the end of the summer I finally cracked and wrote to them, explaining how much I admired the little book, and in particular the print of the 'Secluded valley'. So much so that I would dearly like to know where it was.

I wasn't especially optimistic that the details would be immediately forthcoming, but I did hope the publisher might forward on my letter to the author, and from him I might eventually receive the details I sought.

A couple of weeks later and the response I'd hoped for arrived in the form of a letter from the author, who it turned out, lived not so very far away from my home in Huntingdon. Not only did he provide me with the details of where the 'Secluded valley' was located, and how to reach it, but he explained, if I were in earnest about travelling there, he would be happy to meet me before I left, to show me a few more photographs and discuss how the journey could be most easily made.

Now, I'd said nothing in my letter about actually travelling to where the photograph had been taken, and my instinctive response was to write back to this unusually named Mr Wendig, and correct his assumption. To explain how my enquiry had stemmed purely from an intellectual curiosity, and much lesser desire to obtain a better-quality print of the photograph in question.

But just as I was thinking this, the absurdity of my response suddenly struck me. Here I was, comparatively fit and healthy, with both the means and the leisure to be able to engage in an excursion to the continent. Not only that, but if the picture was anything to go by it was surely somewhere that I would enjoy visiting for myself, and yet now, with someone practically on my doorstep offering to provide all the directions and assistance I might want in order to get there, I was thinking of turning him down.

'Algy,' I said out loud to myself. 'I think you might be in a bit of a rut here. A comfortable and familiar rut, but a rut all the same.'

Half wondering what I was letting myself in for, I wrote back to Wendig, thanking him for his kind offer of assistance, and explaining I would very much like to visit him to discuss how the trip could be made, and enquiring as to a convenient time for me to call.

Thinking nothing further of it I proceeded about my business expecting it would probably take a day or two to receive a response.

POSSESSION

ONE OF MY FAVOURITE HAUNTS in Huntingdon at the weekend was an attractive old pile of a place at one end of the town, called the Old Bridge Hotel. It was a sturdy Georgian place with ivy covered walls, some nice big airy rooms, as well as a sheltered veranda at the back overlooking the river, which remained lovely and cool in the summer. Toward the front it also had a couple of smaller, lower ceilinged snugs with big fireplaces, which made for a cosy retreat in the colder months.

There was plenty of good walking around Huntingdon, especially along the river, which naturally wound its way directly past the old bridge from which the hotel drew its name.

Wanting to test my 'stuck in a rut' hypothesis, I decided to sound-out a few of my closer acquaintances who also happened to frequent the Bridge Hotel, so after stretching my legs along the river for a few miles I popped in for a late bite of lunch to find out who was still around.

It had been a distinctly chilly morning for November, one of the first properly cold days we'd had, following a distinctly mellow and dry September and October, but there had been no mistaking the frosted grass verges and ice edged streams and culverts which fed into the river as I'd walked along.

True to form the veranda and big summer rooms were all but abandoned as I approached the rear of the hotel from the river, so after ensuring my boots were clean, I made my way through to one of the snugs, where I found several small groups of the regulars clustered around the warmly glowing fireplace.

The comfortable armchairs to one side of the fireplace were the most hotly contested seats on days like this, tucked away as they were beside the steps which led down into the snug, but with the high wing-backed chairs to protect the occupant against any chance of a draught from the rear, and the blazing fire to the fore, these were colloquially known as the 'basking' chairs.

On stepping down into the snug I noticed with a smile that the Williamsons had once again laid claim to the basking chairs, and that Mrs Williamson, was practically reclining in her chair before the fire, her half-lidded hazel eyes staring languidly into the depths of the embers, while her husband was stood over by the bar retrieving some drinks.

'Hello, Algy,' Natasha, Mrs Williamson purred from her cat like repose. 'We were just wondering whether we might see you today.

'Hello, Tash,' I replied, pleased to see them both. 'Mind if I join you for a bit?'

The Williamsons were exactly the folks I'd hoped I might run into. She was an émigré from South Africa, who'd moved to England after meeting and marrying Jonathan her husband, who was something or other in the Civil Service.

Despite being well settled in Huntingdon, they both travelled extensively, and while they were often to be found in The Bridge, it was unusual for a year to go by without them popping off to visit some far flung and exotic corner of the world.

With John returned from the bar we settled into the usual banter, during which I broached the topic of my possible visit to the French alps.

'You, Algy?' John voiced, a little more surprised than I would've liked. 'I thought you preferred pastures a little closer to home.'

'Well, I must admit, until I received this reply from Wendig, I'd have agreed with you. But for some reason, it made me stop and wonder whether I've allowed myself to settle into a rut,' I explained. 'I mean, it's not like some of the high adventures which you two disappear off to enjoy, it's only over the channel to France.'

'There's nothing wrong with being a home bird,' offered Tasha, exchanging an all too knowing glance with her husband as she said this. 'The real question is why do you suddenly feel like changing your routine?'

I'd explained about the book of poetry and how I quite liked some of the photographs it contained, but I hadn't been entirely honest with them about the fact that it was one particular plate that had entranced me.

'Well…' I began.

As soon as I hesitated they both knew I'd been holding back.

'Come on, Algy, you may as well come clean now the Memsahib has you under her paw,' John commented, with a twinkle in his eye as he referred to his wife using one of his favourite pet names.

'Alright,' I conceded. 'But you must promise not to laugh at my foolishness!

'What I told you about the book of poetry was true, but while all the pictures are well framed and interesting, there's one in particular that absolutely fascinates me.

'I can't explain it. I've had the book off the shelf dozens of times just to look at that one picture, and for the life of me I'm not sure why.'

'Oh, Algy,' Tasha purred sympathetically. 'I'm afraid you've got a touch of the fever.'

'Yes, Tasha is right I'm afraid, old chap,' John agreed. 'Something in that picture has clearly infected you.'

I didn't understand what they were talking about to begin with, so tried to re-assure them that I was feeling fine, but after humouring me for a minute or two they eventually explained.

'We're not talking about a cold or a bout of the flu, Algy,' John continued. 'Let me get you another drink and I'll try to explain.'

I strolled over to the bar with him at the other end of the snug, while his wife continued to bask in the heat from the fire, and as we ordered our drinks he began.

'It's almost impossible to explain the fever, as we call it, to someone who's never experienced it, though it's fairly obvious to anyone who has,' he began, in unusually sombre terms for Jon, whose eyes always glinted with a trace of humour, even on the worst of days.

'Now I don't know whether it's a good thing or bad, but the vast majority of people will never experience it, and their lives will often be all the happier as a consequence.

'I know you're probably thinking I must've already had a few too many drinks, to be talking like this, but bear with me a while before you make your mind up.

'I don't know why this picture has affected you as it has, but what I can tell you, is that whatever the reason, that picture will stay with you for the rest of your life. You're still in control for the most part now, but if you try to ignore it or deny its attraction then it will just get stronger and stronger, until you can think of nothing else.

'It sounds ridiculous, I know, and it's difficult because the fever takes many different forms, so there's no knowing what will set it off in someone, or even if anything will at all. I've known sailing, rock climbing, hillwalking, the open desert to do it, as well as painting, poetry, music, and even the growing of delphiniums!

'I can't say for sure, but I suspect a lot of the creative types are more susceptible to it than most. An obsession which inspires and drives them to practice their art even when they've got barely two coins to rub together.

'For us it's sleeping under the stars, no roof, no canvas, just a bedroll and the heavens. If I can just sit and watch the stars or the passing clouds for a few hours a week, with nothing between me and them but open air, then I feel content.

'Of course, if I'm cooped up indoors for too long because of the weather or some such, then the opposite is true, and I start to get a bit irritable.

'I don't suppose the book I see in your jacket pocket is the same one you were talking about, the one with the picture in that you admire?'

I indicated it was, and as the barman gave us our drinks I took it out of my pocket and showed him the picture.

'It's certainly an attractive scene,' he commented. 'But what is it that interests you so much about it?'

I'd never looked at it with someone else before, or tried to describe its appeal in words, but as I turned the book back to me so that I could look at it properly, I found the words coming naturally.

'It just fascinates me,' I heard myself say. 'Not for any one thing…

'It's clearly winter, the snow on the ground and on the boughs of the trees in the foreground are a dead giveaway, but there's something about it that makes me think that winter has only recently arrived. The snow is deep but there's no sign of the harshness that often comes at the end of winter, when everything has been covered in snow or ice for weeks and weeks. Here winter seems to lie only gently on the land, there are even a few leaves still clinging to the deciduous trees.

'Then there are the mountains, I've never been to the high mountains, but something tells me this valley is very high up, where the summers are short and the mild weather passes quickly, but the cold lingers on for months.

'Having said that, the woods are deep and dense, broken only by the occasional craggy outcrop, or the course of some stream or gulley, and there's no trace of roads or man-made fences.

'I can see hints of a dozen or more trail lines just visible beneath the covering of snow, paths which just look so… inviting, all the more so because it's clear nobody has walked them yet.'

I droned on for a while longer, almost forgetting that I was stood talking at the bar, until John broke in to gently stop me.

'The thing is, Algy, I don't see half of what you do in this picture,' he explained, kindly. 'To me this looks like a lovely stop over on the way to somewhere, there's some pasture beneath that snow, a barn by the look of it, and an interesting trail down into the valley, but the snow is hiding too much of the detail for this to be a picture I could fall in love with. What I'd like more than anything is to see this valley in the summer or Autumn, when the trees are full of leaf and the sky is that clearest of blues you only get in the high mountains.

'But I can see from your expression as I say this, that you can't imagine it as anything other than snow-covered winter.

'I'm getting away from the point though.

'The fever…

'The fever is something beyond sense, beyond reason, it's more than just liking something, its finding a thing you can live for. You could call it an all-consuming passion in the very literal sense of those words, but even that doesn't do it justice. Right now, the fever will drive you and it will make no sense to you at all, until you fulfil that passion for the first time, and then the world as you know it will become the thing that lacks sense until you satisfy the fever again.'

'I don't think I understand,' I admitted, though I was sure he was trying his best to explain the idea to me. 'I mean to say, it's just a picture in a book. Even if I do try to find this place I might get there and discover it's just a good photograph of an otherwise mediocre little place.'

'Yes, it's all possible,' John conceded. 'But unless I miss my guess, you've already spent so long looking at that picture that you know that isn't true. You feel you know the place, you've studied the paths and openings in the woodland so well, you almost feel like you've been there, that your footprints could appear in the snow the next time you look at the picture and you wouldn't be surprised.'

He was right of course, and deep down inside me I knew there was something unusual about the way this picture seemed to fascinate me.

I don't know why I asked, as even without knowing the details, I was sure his own story must be very personal in nature to say the least.

'I'm still not sure I properly understand,' I replied, although there was definitely something in his words which had rung true. 'Do you mind me asking how it happened to you?'

'Ah, well now, that's a bit of a tale to tell, but… the Memsahib looks comfortable enough for the moment, so let's see how far we get.'

STARLIGHT

THERE WAS A SMALL SHADOWY TABLE with a couple of stools in the corner next to the bar, which was rarely used in the colder months on account of its lack of proximity to the fire, and before he began John motioned me over to it, to take a seat with him.

'I was in my twenties when I went out there, twenty-six, twenty-seven, something like that,' he began, looking off toward the distant fire as he spoke. 'I'd been feeling restless for a year or two, as though I was supposed to be somewhere, or had forgotten something, but couldn't quite put my finger on where or what.

'Anyway, a friend of a friend was looking for an energetic youth such as myself to pop out to South Africa and do a bit of survey work. Someone was thinking of planting vineyards out there where the land was cheap and the sun plentiful, but the maps weren't good enough, so they needed a handful of people to go out and take some soil samples, and if the soil looked good, do some mapping.

'I was one of the first to be trained up and sent out, and when the results I returned looked promising they would send a more specialist team out to verify and double check my findings, while I went on to another area.

'It was technical but undemanding work, and if I wanted it, it was mine for a couple of years at least.

'Well, I started with the areas near to established settlements, driving out each morning before the sun came up in an old single horse wagon, in order to make as much of the light as possible before heading back again once the light started to fade.

'It wasn't the kind of work which would appeal to everyone, but it suited me nicely, and I got into a routine that I enjoyed.

'As the locations became more remote I purchased a tent and started spending the odd night out at the site, in order to save myself the long journey there and back.

'It was wild country, with more than a few dangers to be aware of, but I'd put my time in by this point, and knew my way around most of the hazards. I'd also become accustomed to the way of life, picking up some of the native words and ways of doing things. Before long the tent was staying in the wagon most of the time and it was just the fire and the night skies for company. I still had a few near scrapes mind, as is normal in that part of the world.

'Anyway, the initial two years came and went, and without realising it, the fever had infected me. I still had to make the odd trip into the nearest town every now and again to drop off the samples I'd collected and to pick up a few supplies, but now the shoe was on the other foot and without realising I'd started to plan my visits so that I could get in and out without having to stay overnight.

'I hadn't realised how feral I'd become until one evening, the weather had been wet for a couple of days so I'd had to put the tent up. I was feeling all sorts of grumpy because of it, but finally as I was making camp on the third day the cloud had broken and the stars had returned, and I'd immediately begun to feel more at ease.'

As he continued to speak I could see John had slipped into a half-daze, with a far-away look in his eyes as he spoke, as if the memories were too powerful to recall without reliving them.

'It was then that she walked into my camp, accompanied only by her two wolf-like dogs. She appeared through the flames of my fire like some spirit of the veldt, her amber eyes glowing in the firelight as she approached.

'But I was feeling so at one with myself again with the stars overhead that I'd not heard her calling into the camp as she approached.

'Of course, she recognised the fever in me immediately, so without another word she simply laid her bedroll down on the ground on the opposite side of the fire to me and went to sleep.

'In the morning. . .'

'John, are you boring Algy with the tale of ancient histories?' Tasha said, having walked over in her stocking feet while we were talking. 'Perhaps you should both come back to the fire, before the circling predators make a move on our seats.'

'Oh, goodness me yes, I was getting quite lost in my own thoughts there for a bit,' John responded, gathering his wits by downing his drink. 'You really should've stopped me Algy, rather than letting me prattle on like that.'

I joined them back over by the fire, and continued to chat about one thing and another for an hour or so, but the moment had now passed, and all talk of 'the fever' or their early life together was forgotten in favour of lighter and more sensible subjects.

As the evening approached I made noises about moving on, and the Williamson's decided it was time they did the same, so we all stood up and left the hotel together, the very picture of quiet weekend civilisation. But as we reached the point on the street where our paths parted, Tasha turned back to me when we'd each gone just a few steps.

'Do come and tell us how your trip went, when you get back, Algy.'

I promised I would, almost automatically, before I realised that for some reason she was expecting me to be travelling so soon that I wouldn't have time to see them both again before I left.

I couldn't help but smile at the idea that I could be travelling overseas in just a few days, but just as I was about to dismiss the thought out of hand, I remembered that this time last week I hadn't even been considering a trip, so who knew what could happen in another week?

The story continues in:
The Ghosts of Winter

For more information visit:

www.knytewrytng.com